THE LAST DAYS OF ATLANTIS
MOTHER INK

NICHOLAS BRUNER

Other Books by Nicholas Bruner

The Last Days of Atlantis series
Mother Ink (Book 1)
Brother Flute (Book 2)
Daughter Cloud (Book 3)

The Heroes of Atlantis series
Sister Honey (Book 4) (coming Fall 2024)

Hard Santa Case Files
O Trolly Night (Book 1)

Other Books
The Ballad of Dani and Eli
A Far Ocean's Tale and Other Stories
Jesus Bugs
The Love Machine
Roll dem Bones

All books available at Amazon
(amazon.com/author/nicholasbruner)

Sign up for my mailing list and receive *Orphan Stone*, the free prequel to the Last Days of Atlantis trilogy!
subscribepage.io/s8d7d6

THE LAST DAYS OF ATLANTIS

MOTHER INK

NICHOLAS BRUNER

Mother Ink
© 2022 Nicholas Bruner

ALL RIGHTS RESERVED. No part of this work may be reproduced or transmitted in any form or by any means, electronic or mechanical, including photocopying and recording, or by any information storage or retrieval system without the proper written permission of the appropriate copyright holder listed below, unless such copying is expressly permitted by federal and international copyright law.

ISBN 978-1-7354892-6-1

Cover design by Moorbooks Design

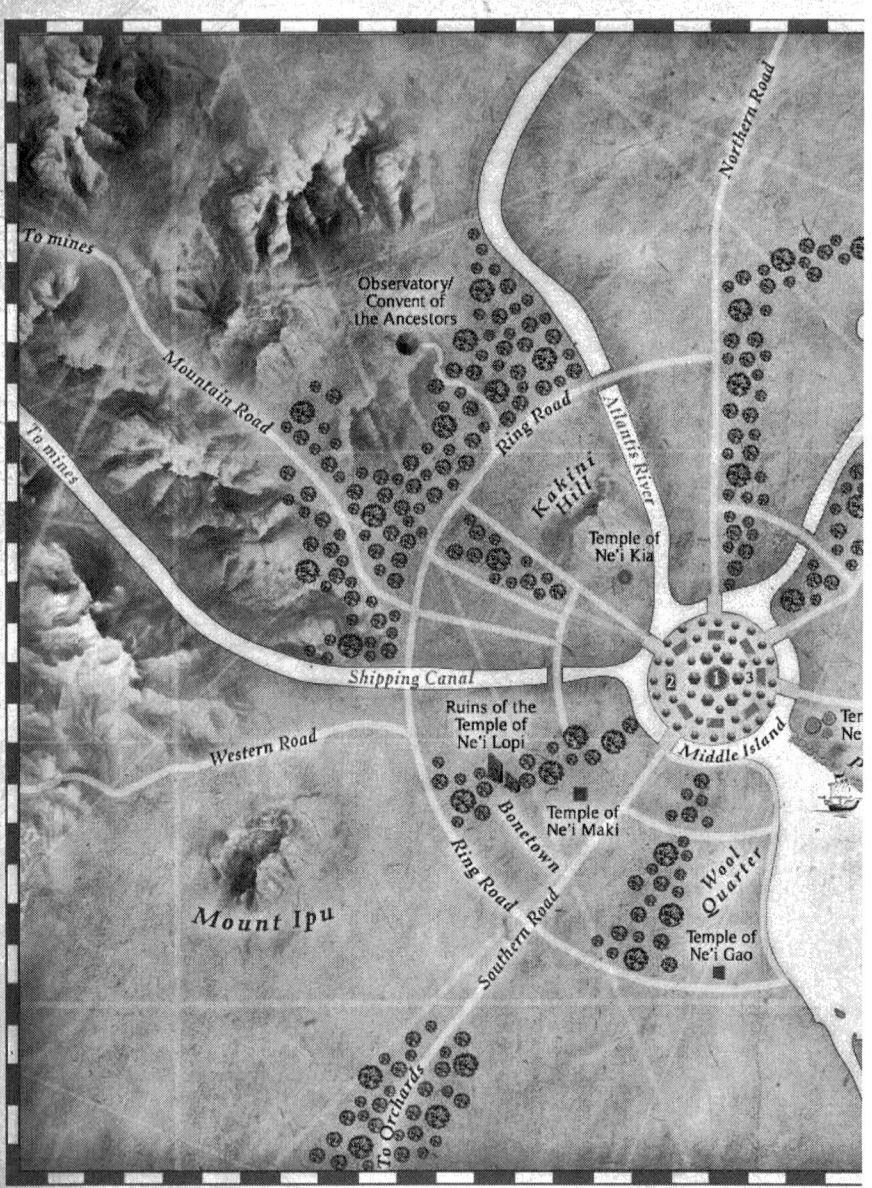

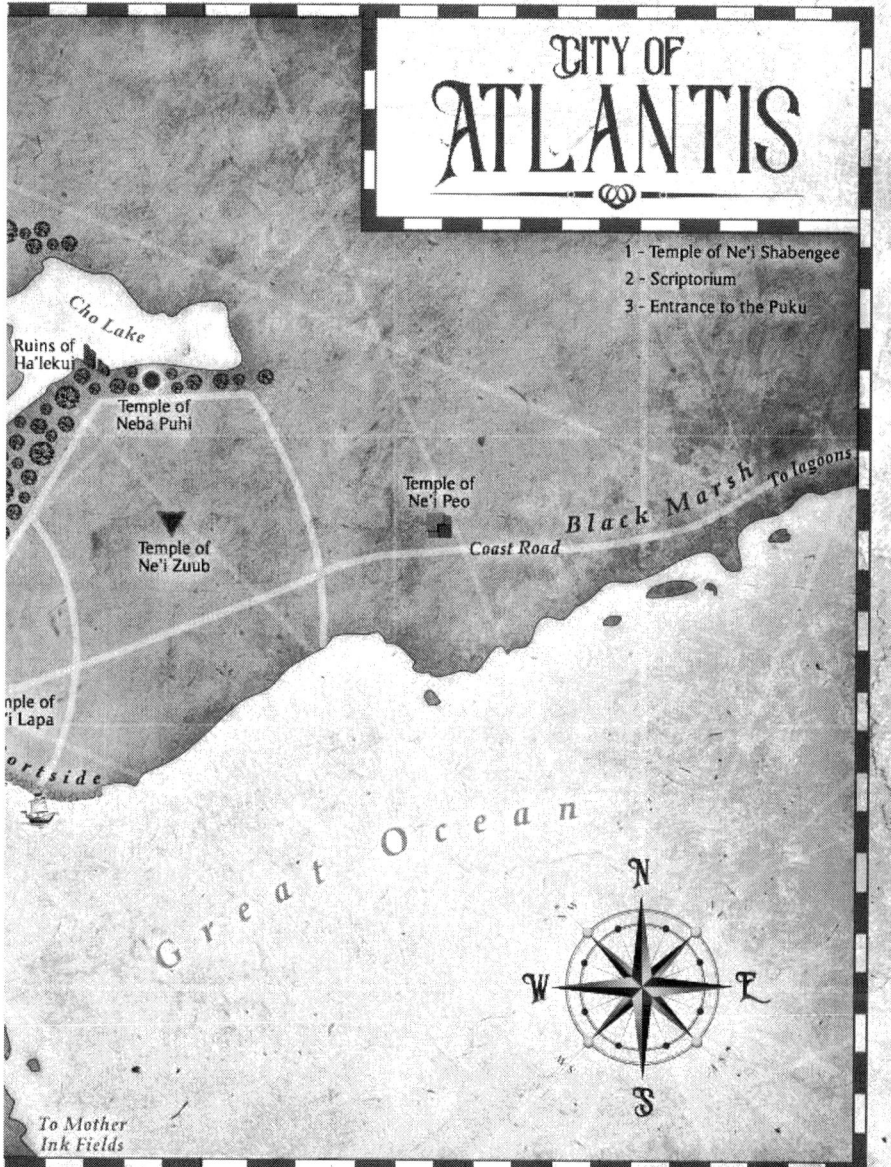

LIST OF CHARACTERS

Aku an 11-year old street urchin
Godi Aku's adult partner and a member of the Ho'oule
Lono a 17-year old acolyte at the Convent of the Ancestors
Hulu master of the scribes at the Scriptorium
Captain Ino head of the Shabengee contingent at the Scriptorium
Opio a high-ranking scribe at the Scriptorium
Prioress Wa'e head of the Convent of the Ancestors
Keki a friendly crow
Iwali Lono's best friend
Alani Hulu's late wife
Tua a tattoo artist and member of the Ho'oule
Malu a prisoner in the Puku, secretly head of the Ho'oule
Kaneke, Wi'he some of Malu's men
Kai a Kaiman trying to find his way back home
Pepehi an imprisoned Kaiman
Ka'le scribe in charge of the infirmary
Akahi, Maki, Oleli scribes at the Scriptorium
Iule a Ho'oule contact of Tua's
Conger, Moray Puhi hunters
He'u chief priest at the Temple of the Owls
Keola chief priestess at the Temple of the Eels
Okoa a prisoner at the Temple of the Eels
Imi Au'o head of the mother ink laboratory
Anahua, Kikima, 'E'epa Imi's monstrous assistants

PART ONE

Now when Ne Wa'e, the queen of the gods, allotted the realms, she assigned to each God his or her place to rule, as she saw fit. To Nema Oa she assigned the moon and to Neba Sha she assigned the oceans and the waters, and so on to all the gods, each given his or her proper place. For herself, she took the stars, and to her consort Neba H'aa Shee, she gave the sun.

But when she came to the last god, Neba Puhi, the eel, she found she had already given all the realms away. Now Neba Puhi coveted the oceans that had been given to Neba Sha. So Neba Puhi got his scent and hunted him in the deeps, and wrapped himself around Neba Sha to choke him and kill him, and to take his place. But Ne Wa'e saw this and came to Neba Puhi and took him up and prepared to cast him away.

But Neba Puhi begged for his life, saying, "Have mercy on me, for you have given me no place to dwell, and I sought only a realm of my own, as you have given to my brothers and sisters."

Ne Wa'e felt the justice of his complaint and said to him, "Neba Puhi, you shall dwell in the oceans as you wished. But you shall not rule them. Your home will be the holes in the sea floor, the chasms and crevices, and you will always be on the watch, for when you are in the open all the creatures of the deep shall see you and chase you back whence you came."

"Very well," Neba Puhi said. But he had got her scent, and he bided his time, nursing the resentment in his heart in the knowledge that someday, Ne Wa'e would have a careless moment, and he would have his chance for revenge.

--from *The Book of Awa*

ONE

"More wine, my lord?" Aku asked as he approached a grotesquely obese man reclining, dressed only in the fur loincloth and shawl indicating he was a priest of Ne'i Kia, the deer god. With his huge brown belly overspilling his clothes he hardly cut the lissome figure one would hope for from a servant of that temple.

"Yes, of course, you little fool," the man said, grabbing the golden goblet away. "You waste my time with your inane questions!"

Drink it up, you fat bloated toad, Aku thought. He carried six cups of moonplum wine on a salver, his measured steps not only avoiding spills, but also providing time to overhear the conversation as he advanced around the lanai. A half dozen great men sat or sprawled on sofas in the mild air and fresh breezes, gathered to celebrate something or other. He could hear the falsity in their tones—deep and jesting on the surface, but anxious underneath.

"Have you heard?" Fat Toad said. "Earthquake in the mountains yesterday. Reports just came in this morning. And there's a place now they say the sea boils, off the southeastern coast."

"Yes, yes," said another lord, this one in a cobalt loincloth and shawl, though much leaner, sitting cross-legged on his sofa. He took a fresh cup from Aku and handed him his emptied one in exchange. He fluttered his hand in the air as if to dismiss the news. "And the summer is hot and the winter is cold! Earthquakes are nothing new to Atlantis. It's the buzz of the hysterical crowd you hear, that's all."

"Think you so?" replied Fat Toad. "The people say it's a bad omen. They say Regent's latest changes have upset the gods. They say his creations are unnatural, and that the gods have turned from us." After a moment's thought, he added, "I'ke Regent."

"I'ke Regent," the others murmured in unison.

"Of course the people say that," said Cobalt. "But it's only the mutterings of those with short memories. Fix your thoughts on your own estates, that's what I say! Tend to your lands and your ships, beat your slaves when they're lazy, and leave the gods' affairs to the gods."

It seemed to Aku that Cobalt's words, or at least his conviction, had swayed the others. But as he continued around the lanai, perhaps he should have paid more attention to his own task, for he tripped with the last cup, splashing its contents across the long white shawl of a stern-looking, well-built man. The strong peppery aroma wafted into his nostrils, its very smell almost intoxicating. "Oh, I'm sorry, my lord!"

"You cur!" The white-shawled eminence sprang up and cuffed Aku with a swing of his hand. Aku flew to the ground, salver and empty cups dropping and bouncing across the wooden floor. "You vile pig shit!" His clipped words indicated he was a foreigner, a visitor from a western province. The others looked on, amused, while White Shawl continued to rage with oaths at Aku's clumsiness.

As he retrieved the spilled goblets, Aku stole a glance at Fat Toad, who had already slumped across his sofa in a deep sleep. The powdered me'lau herbs certainly worked quickly. *Careful now, Godi. Don't break character yet,* he thought.

"Get out of here, you malignant growth! Tell the steward to send another serving boy who's not inept, if he has one!" The rant continued, and now Cobalt drooped and slid off the couch onto the floor. By the time Aku had fished the last goblet out from where it had rolled under a serving table, laden with pale green sea pears, thin slices of smoked venison, and more food than most people in the city would see in a month, the others had succumbed as well. Only the white-shawled man still stood.

Aku rose, grinning. "Your accent was perfect, Godi! You had all these moneybags eating out of your hand!"

"Yes, it was rather brilliant, wasn't it?" Godi said, dropping the foreign accent in favor of his familiar, rapid-fire but clear Atlantean cadence. He reached under the chin of one of the sleeping men, a bejeweled, dark-skinned man dressed in a saffron robe, and gave his necklace a quick yank, breaking the cord. "Come over here, would you, Aku?"

Godi fastened the broken cord around Aku's neck. From it hung a heavy bronze cylinder, about eight inches long and hollow, etched with irregular notches across its surface. "What is this?" Aku asked. "Some sort of key?"

"Something like that." Godi tied the knot extra tight and tucked the cylinder under Aku's barkcloth shift. He put his hand on his shoulder. "You know Tua's tattoo parlor near the Temple of the Monkey, don't you?"

"Of course. I've met Tua plenty of times."

"Good. Take it to him. He'll know what to do with it. And don't let anyone see you with it. Only Tua. Do you understand? Hurry now, no dawdling. Lives could depend on it."

"What about you, Godi? Aren't you coming?"

"My work's not done here." He pulled a dagger out from a hidden place in his wine-stained shawl. "I'll see you soon."

"Are you going to kill one of them?" Aku asked, eyes widening.

"Better if you don't know. Get going, no time to waste." Godi gave him a little push toward the door.

Aku made his way down the stairs carved through the multiple trunks of the kimunu tree and skipped through the kitchen, where a dozen men cut herbs with knives or pulled pastries from racks in fireplaces, baking the finest delicacies in the city. Aku had worked here for weeks, accepting abuse from Atlantis's richest citizens, and he wasn't sorry for it to be his last day on the job. Before he could slip out the rear door, a hand grabbed him by the shoulder. He looked back in fear and relaxed when he saw it was only the steward.

"So? How did it go with my lords?" the curly-haired man asked. "Do they need anything else?"

"It went well," Aku said. "Nothing else. In fact, they said under no circumstances were they to be disturbed for an hour."

The steward's face tightened. "An hour, you say? Well, I suppose their graces have important matters to discuss."

"May I go into the back garden?" Aku asked. "I need to pass water."

"Yes, of course. But be back quickly. Another large party has just arrived."

Aku went into the walled garden and through the delivery gate out onto the street. He took a quick look to get his bearings. Good, things were busy with shouting hawkers pressing their wares into the hands of passersby and shoppers going into the buildings along the road, some made of stone, others hollowed out of the massive kimunus whose massive girth, numerous column-like trunks, and trainable branches made them the desired location for finer establishments. *And best of all, no sign of whisper birds*, he thought.

Aku wondered which of the drugged men was Godi's target, or why he deserved to die. Not that it worried him. His nearly twelve years on earth had already convinced him the rich were slavers and exploiters, the lot of them. He hoped the target was Fat Toad. *Nothing worse than priests and temples, demanding their sacrifices from those who can least afford it.* Anyway, the Ho'oule had its reasons, and when they succeeded in overthrowing Regent, the men who had killed his older brother would get what they deserved. A day like today provided a bit of justice on the way to that later goal.

Just as he was about to blend into the crowd, he noticed two hooded figures in a stone alcove in the building across the way, and froze. Had they seen him leave? Yes, one was already pushing his way through the multitude towards him, the other headed toward the winehouse.

What to do? Warn Godi? No, the man was almost to him already. And best not to visit the tattoo parlor, either, at least until he lost the hooded fellow, whoever he was. Aku took off at a run, headed for the usual route he took to throw followers off his trail.

The air in the underground chamber was damp and chilly against Lono's back, and the basalt stone was cold against her knees and bare feet where she knelt with the other acolytes in a circle. But the brazier stood upright in the middle of the ceremony chamber and the radiating heat from its flames coaxed a trickle of sweat down Lono's cheek underneath her hooded barkcloth robe. Her heart beat far faster than the ritual drum accompanying the ceremony, in nervous expectation of what was to come.

She adjusted her breathing as she'd been taught in her exercises, drawing the smoky, aromatic air in through her nose and out through her mouth, slowing and deepening her breaths. *Ne Wa'e, be with me,* she repeated in her mind. *Be with me and help me be brave.* It worked, sort of, as now her heart was only beating worrisomely fast, rather than insanely fast. She kept her head down, neither willing to look at the brazier nor the two Sisters stirring its red hot coals with long irons.

In came Prioress Wa'e, the head of the convent. She strode through the circle of girls and clapped, the signal for them all to look up. She gave a small smile and spoke soothingly. "A big day for you, girls. Do not be anxious. You have each been selected specially for this ceremony because you have proved you have the necessary gifts and have excelled in your studies." She turned to the Sisters. "Is all in readiness? Is it hot enough?"

"Yes, Prioress," one of the Sisters replied.

"Then let us begin." She unclasped her long owl-feather cape and tossed it aside, revealing her naked body, tall and lean, tattoos inscribed on every surface from neck to ankle. She raised her head, letting her long silver hair fall behind her, and folded her hands together. The Sister on the drum in the corner switched to a faster, more complex rhythm.

Had she been calmer, Lono would have been able to identify the constellations mapped precisely across Prioress Wa'e's skin—the Serpent and the Bee on her back, the Monkey and the Owl on each thigh, and all the other important star signs on various limbs and other parts. As it was, Lono's eyes could only fix on one tattoo, on the Prioress's inner right forearm: the telescope, the symbol of the Convent of the Ancestors, and the way it truly seemed to glint and focus in the wavering light of the flames.

"Join with me in prayer," said Prioress Wa'e, and the Sisters and acolytes repeated the words they'd known since girlhood.

Ancestors, lead us, guide us, inform us of your ways.
Ne Wa'e, Goddess of Stars, light of the old spirits,
be with us now, and keep our feet forever on your path.

At a nod from Prioress Wa'e, the Sisters disrobed as well, revealing their less extensively tattooed bodies, each with their own unique combinations of constellations and heavenly objects. All three began to sing in unison in time with the drum, a chant of concentration that the acolytes had never heard before.

At another nod from Prioress Wa'e, the acolytes too rose to their feet and shed their robes, the shifting orange light from the brazier playing across the faces of a dozen seventeen year-old young women. Their skin was unmarked and clean from the sacramental bath they had taken earlier in the day.

Lono, shivering, leaned over to the girl next to her and whispered, "Are you ready, Iwali?"

"I hope so," Iwali whispered back. "This is what we've been working for all this time, isn't it?"

Lono thought back to all the hours and days spent in study, struggling through the math and astronomy scrolls written in ancient Atlantean dialects, the tedious memorization of the epic poems, the endless practice of mind-focusing stretches and exercises. It hardly seemed real that the day of the Twin Ceremonies had finally arrived.

One of the Sisters went to the dais at the far end of the room, empty except for a broad stone bowl. She put her hand in the bowl and removed a cloth dripping with a viscous black liquid. The other Sister pulled an iron from the fire and raised it, the telescope shape at its end glowing with heat.

"Iwali, step forward," Prioress Wa'e commanded. Iwali took Lono's left hand in hers and gave it a quick squeeze before approaching the Prioress. "Hold out your arm."

The Sister at the brazier took Iwali's wrist with one firm hand and pressed the end of the iron against her forearm with the other. Steam rose from Iwali's skin with a searing sound. She bit her lip until blood ran down her chin, though she did not make a noise. A sickly sweet burning smell spread through the chamber. Then the first Sister drew back the iron and the other Sister immediately applied the cloth to the fresh wound, saturating the brand's pattern in the thick liquid: mother ink, the rare substance that gave the Sisters the power to hear the ancestors.

When the Sister removed the cloth, Iwali returned to her place in the circle. Lono studied her face, the sweat pouring out of her skin, her expression contorted with the pain she was trying so hard to keep inside. Iwali reached with her left hand to trace the new picture on her right arm.

"Don't touch it now, child," the Prioress warned. "It needs to be left alone to heal."

The Sister with the iron had returned it to the brazier. After a couple minutes, the Prioress asked, "Is it hot enough now?"

"Yes, Prioress," the Sister answered.

"Good. Lono, step forward please."

No time to think! Aku leapt the five foot gap between two tile-shingled roofs, scrambling up the far side of the other building and scanning ahead desperately for his next move. He was out of roofs to jump to. This building backed up to a wall of green—trees as far as the eye could see. Sweat dripped from his hair and his muscles ached, but he coulnt't stop now. He stole a quick look back. The man in the hooded cloak completed the leap only a few steps behind him.

Where to now?

It seemed like he'd been running across half the city the whole afternoon, repeatedly believing he'd gotten free, only for the hooded man to reappear from around a corner or emerge from a crowd.

Not the first time he'd been tailed, but this pursuer was tenacious. Aku's usual rush through the labyrinthine alleyways of Bonetown hadn't shaken him, and neither had the chase across the rooftops. The tattoo parlor, Godi had said, but Aku couldn't very well walk up to the rendezvous point while his tracker had him in hot pursuit. He had to get rid of his unwanted shadow, and only after that could he let Tua know they'd been found out, that the mission that had seemed like such a success at first might now be compromised.

Perhaps Godi was even dead.

No time to dwell on that, though. No more roofs, and it was a fifteen-foot drop to the street. He'd break a leg or a foot for sure.

Wait, there. The branches of that kimunu tree hanging down. He'll never be able to follow.

At a jog, Aku took one wide branch that hung onto the roof like a ramp, keeping his arms out to maintain his balance, the bronze cylinder bouncing on his chest as he ran. A reckless jump and he grabbed another branch with his hands, swinging to a mass of boughs that formed a sort of small platform where he could catch his breath. He glanced back, expecting to see the man still on the edge of the roof.

No way. It can't be possible.

The man hadn't stopped at all, and was making his way along

the wide branch. "Give it up, boy," the man called. "You can't escape."

But Aku smiled to himself. *Give up? Never!* He realized where he was now: Lopi Park, with its temple ruins and wild, overgrown kimunu trees. Their intersecting branches and multiple trunks created archways, tunnels, chimneys—lots of places a small body could wiggle through where a larger body would become hopelessly entangled.

For a moment he flashed back to playing here with his older brother, Kuana, back when he'd been a small boy. He must have come here instinctively, his feet knowing the way his brain hadn't had time to consider. Even here at the park's edge, Aku's practiced eye could discern a pattern of thick, crisscrossing branches spreading before him, and begin to map woody paths through the air.

He picked a likely route and walk-climbed across, hands gripping branches overhead while his feet bounded nimbly on boughs underneath. He brushed through a curtain of vines, clambered around a trunk with radiating branches. This was perfect. He could climb higher or lower, hide in thick foliage, and change directions at any time. A glance back showed he was already gaining distance on the hooded man, who was much taller and heavier and had to make his way along sturdier branches to hold his weight.

Fifteen minutes in here should be enough. Half an hour if the man was really stubborn. Bonetown and the rooftops hadn't done it, but in Lopi Park Aku would lose him for sure. He touched a hand to the bronze cylinder, still safe under his shift. *And then the tattoo parlor.*

TWO

The sun had long since gone down but still Lono sat by her friend's side, applying a fresh, damp cloth to her head. The fever had come on soon after the branding ceremony. It was probably a reaction to the mother ink. Not everybody could handle it, and Iwali had always been delicate.

She lay now on a cot under a textured barkcloth blanket impressed with black and green striped serpents, a powerful healing symbol. Only her newly-tattooed arm hung out, the area around the brand red and inflamed. Her eyes fluttered and she murmured something unintelligible. Lono stroked strands of damp hair from her cheek.

"Shh, quiet. You'll be fine. I'm here with you. I'm not going anywhere."

Iwali turned towards Lono with a whimper and closed her eyes. She seemed to drift into sleep and Lono let herself relax for the first time in an hour. She leaned back on her arms and stretched out with a deep exhalation. She ignored the sharp pain of her own tattoo; didn't even look at it. *Keep it out of mind. No time for that, I have to be here for Iwali.*

Iwali, slight and gentle, was the brainiest of all of them, a natural scholar, picking up the archaic vocabulary and grammatical forms of classical literature like the latest playground chants. But when it came time for the focusing exercises, the afternoon sessions of lowering the body with one leg until the rear touched the ankle, of lying supine and raising the abdomen into a bridge, of pressing the torso up with one hand while reaching around one's back with the other, Iwali was hopeless, out of breath and exhausted while the other girls daily reached new levels of strength and agility.

Iwali cried out in her sleep and Lono took her hand. "It's okay. Only a nightmare. Go back to sleep."

Lono and Iwali had become fast friends from the time they arrived at the convent as young girls on the same day, a time so long ago Lono could barely remember her life before, with only vague recollections of a large house somewhere near a lake, with her parents and fine furnishing and servants. Studious Iwali and athletic Lono may have appeared to be opposites, but they recognized right away something they had in common: a shared diligence, an assiduity in purpose, a commitment to strive for excellence at what they each loved, and a peace with being just passable at what they didn't. Even when others fell away in the scroll room or the exercise field, Iwali and Lono remained, encouraging and helping each other until they were the last ones left.

But over the past few months, something had happened. They had drifted apart, somehow. Lono had begun to feel a wildness in herself, something that rebelled against the discipline and the routine, a force she couldn't name that shook awake her need for something beyond the walls of the convent. Iwali, not knowing about her friend's new feelings but sensing Lono was different, had subconsciously distanced herself, retreating deeper into her studies.

Lonely, Lono had taken to walking the convent's inner gardens by herself, or to gazing out of high windows to the city in the distance, thinking about her friend and the changes in herself. What was out there that could be drawing her away from Iwali and the convent, all she had ever known? What caused her heart to ache so acutely she pressed her hands against her breasts at night to still it?

"Lono, you should get some sleep," a voice came from over her shoulder.

Lono jumped. "Prioress! I didn't hear you come in."

"I'm sorry, I didn't mean to frighten you." She held out a steaming cup to Lono. "I've brought you some pala tea."

Pala tea? But that's for the ill. "You mean for me to serve to Iwali, when she wakes?"

"No dear, for you." She held a hand against Lono's forehead. "You're a bit warm yourself. No surprise after the ceremony, and staying up with your friend."

Lono took a sip. She'd never drunk it before, having never missed a day of class from illness. It wasn't bitter, as she'd expected. A bit tangy, actually, and quite good. She took another sip, longer. It felt soothing going down her throat. "She would do the same for me."

The Prioress sat on the floor beside Lono with crossed legs. "Yes, I have no doubt she would. But nevertheless, you have to get up in only a couple hours, remember?"

Lono nodded. Yes, the second of the Twin Ceremonies. The Ceremony of Fire and the Ceremony of Sky.

"You need your sleep. You go and lie down, and I'll stay with Iwali." When Lono hesitated, the Prioress's voice sharpened. "That's an order, Lono."

"Yes, Prioress." Lono rose and left the sick room.

Night had fallen in the thick of the kimunu trees, but still Aku barely kept ahead of his pursuer. His plan had not worked out like he'd thought. Oh, he could temporarily shake the hooded man now and then, even hide for a while in a thicket of leaves or a niche in a trunk and catch his breath. But as soon as he started moving again, the fellow was right behind him once more.

Aku was exhausted, his stomach growled, his mouth was dry. He'd ripped his barkcloth shift at one point—a jutting branch tearing the lower half right off—and his bare skin burned and ached from the thousand places he'd scratched, scraped, or bumped himself. And now he couldn't even see. No help for it. He'd have to go higher, where there was less foliage and more starlight. Aku started to climb.

Actually, maybe this isn't a bad idea. Now that he thought about, maybe if he got high enough, the branches would get too thin for the weight of his larger pursuer. *Now why didn't that occur to me before?* Because he hadn't had enough time to consider his options, of course.

The climb was going well. *Grab hold and pull with one hand, feel with the toes until they find a footing, then push off and grab hold with the other hand.* He must've gotten twenty feet up by now. He looked down to see if he'd made any headway.

Aku didn't hear anybody coming up after him. He poked his head out to see if he could make anything out, and in that moment the branch he was holding broke off. For a sickening moment, Aku dangled in free air, long enough for the idea to pop in his head that he might not actually fall, just remain suspended like a hawk, but then he did drop, smashing through branches and leaves until he landed on cold stone, on his right side, and rolled into a painful heap. He heard something hit the stone a few moments after him, heard footsteps pace around. It wouldn't be long until the man figured out where he'd dropped.

Aku grit his teeth against the pain. He dared not move, but he used his senses to assess his situation.

First, his body. Wet and warm under his right side. Blood, no doubt. Right arm hurt like hell, too. Possibly broken. Other than that, deep aches, but nothing he couldn't ignore.

As for his surroundings, there was just enough light to make out heaps of stone around him. The ruins of Ne'i Lopi's temple, most likely, which would put him right in the center of the park, far from any help. His left foot and lower calf dangled over an empty place. A crevice, a narrow opening, though Aku couldn't see how far down it went from where he lay.

A dark silhouette loomed over his head. A foot nudged his

body, pushed him onto his back. Aku groaned. Everything hurt.

The hooded man breathed hard through his nostrils. "At last," he growled. "Nowhere to run now, Ho'oule filth."

The man shed his cloak and Aku gasped. Huge tattoos of pike conger eels with blue-gray scales entwined his legs, torso, arms, and neck. The tattoos glowed with power, so real the eels seemed to slither around the man's body.

"First I'll take back what don't belong to you. Second, I'll gut you chin to groin for the trouble."

No wonder, Aku thought. *No wonder I couldn't get away.* A Puhi hunter. Not one of the usual slow and brutish Shabengee guardsmen that had swarmed the city at Regent's command. The Puhi were spies, assassins, fugitive trackers, living shadow men who relied on stealth and silence to go where others could not go, to see what others could not see. Aku hadn't actually been sure they were real. He'd thought they were just stories the older men told to scare kids like him, to keep them from bragging in the neighborhood about their Ho'oule connections.

In his hand the man held something, long and so black it seemed to suck in all the light around them. That would be his maka, the dreaded Puhi obsidian dagger. Sharp enough to cut bone, and unbreakable.

Aku's insides churned with panic, but damned if he would let it show. "Regent must be awful scared if he's sending Puhis after the likes of me."

"Regent grows weary of a thorn in his foot, that's all." The man squatted down and blew his stinking breath in Aku's face. "He gave me permission to pluck it out."

"Regent *lets* you clean his feet? That's nice. Do you use a cloth, or do you prefer to lick his heels?"

The man laughed. "You got spirit, boy. Almost a shame to kill you." He pointed the dagger's tip at Aku's eye. "Tell you what, though. I'll make it fast."

At that moment, a bird flew in, from where Aku had no idea, its claws outstretched towards the Puhi's face. The Puhi slashed the air with his maka, but the bird danced out of reach.

Aku wasted no time. Pushing himself with his good arm into the crevice, he squeezed himself into the opening in the rock and slid down, probably twenty feet or more. He hit the ground with another painful thud.

"You down there, boy?" came the Puhi's voice. "I don't suppose you care to toss up that trinket around your neck?"

Aku couldn't have answered if he'd wanted to, his body hurt so much. He checked for the bronze cylinder. Still there. Maybe he should toss it up, end this chase. What did the cylinder matter to him, anyway?

No. Then Godi would've died for nothing. And Kuana too. Aku steeled himself. He would never give in.

From above came the sound of something scrambling or scratching on the rock and the thin line of gray light above him vanished. The scratching went on for a minute but it didn't seem to be coming any closer. The Puhi was trying to come down after him, but it wasn't working. The crevice opening must be too narrow for him to fit.

Finally, some luck, Aku thought. *If you can call it that.*

"Damn it," the Puhi muttered. "And I got to meet the others in Bonetown soon." The line of light reappeared and the man's mocking voice came calling down. "Don't go anywhere. I'll be back later. With a skinny friend." A pebble came tumbling down the incline and landed on Aku's face. He was unable to move even to brush it off. The Puhi laughed.

…the plaza was strangely empty of people, though it was full of stalls, ready for the day. The stalls held bronze cages of every size and shape, smaller ones hanging on wires from poles, larger ones set on the ground. Lono strolled along, inspecting cages as she liked, finding them full of birds. A tiny filigreed cage held a little green Mele bird with a delicate and beautiful song. She bent over to see two green and red parrots in a large cage who touched the tips of their wings, as if holding hands, until they saw Lono and hopped onto their perches. She wandered for a long time, enjoying the birds but feeling lonely for another person to visit them with.

Lono came to a pergola in the plaza's center, grape vines growing along the trellis overhead, dappling the sunlight, cages suspended at regular intervals. She noticed a man in a feather cape some ways ahead of her, tall with shoulder-length dark hair, but he stepped behind a stone pillar before she could get a good look.

Lono, scared but curious, felt herself compelled somehow to follow him. The birdsong grew louder and as she passed by the cages she felt the birds eyeing her. She reached the pillar but the man was no longer behind it, though he had dropped his cape there.

Lono picked up the man's cape, made from black crow feathers and still warm from his body. She rubbed it against her face, taking in its softness and smell. It smelled like…him, though she could not identify or describe the scent any further.

Two arms grabbed her from behind and Lono tried to scream but a hand covered her mouth. She turned her head and saw dark curls—she knew it was him and relaxed.

Isn't this what she had wanted? To have his arms around her?

In a cage dangling nearby, two little blue birds nuzzled each other, stroking their tiny golden beaks into one another's feathers, cooing and whistling softly.

Lono leaned back into the dark-haired man's body, feeling the same warmth that had imbued his cape, breathing in his scent. His large hands rubbed her shoulders, brushed her arms. One reached down to her hip, another caressed her breast and she moaned. His breath was on her neck and in her ear. She wondered what his voice sounded like but could not think of what to say. His hands continued to roam, finding parts of her she hadn't known were there. Lono wanted to give herself to him fully.

Caw!

Lono looked up. Seeing nothing, she let her attention return to the man's hands, still on her body, still moving everywhere she wanted.

Caw!

The man's hands were gone, she knew not where. Irritated, her attention broken, Lono scanned the cages nearby. The birds in them eyed her warily. They did not seem as friendly now, their black eyes somehow angry.

Caw!

There it was, on a bush to her right, a huge crow, so black it almost shone. Why wasn't it in a cage like the other birds? Had it escaped, or had it always been free? Lono strode towards it, indignant that it had interrupted her and the man, determined to grab it and put it in a cage where it belonged. It hopped along ahead of her, forcing Lono to chaise it through the pergola and out into the stands.

The birds there were different, their colors garish and their songs loud and harsh. Something was off about them. One bird had wings in the wrong places, as if sewn on by a child. Another stared at her with hard red eyes. A third grinned at her with a beak lined with teeth. These were larger birds, too, specimens who had outgrown their cages, and they rattled their bars as if to break out, menacing Lono with their glares. Lono feared one would succeed, and come after her.

What about her dark-haired man? Maybe they could fight these birds together.

Lono turned and saw him duck into a stall. She still held his cape in her hands, surely she could give it to him and he would help protect her from the birds. She ran towards the stall. But when she reached it and looked in, she saw only an old man with matted white hair, squatting amidst the cages. He stared up at her and one of his eyes was milky white. She backed away from the old man into the open.

Behind her Lono heard the fluttering of wings, lots of wings. Somehow some of the birds must have freed themselves. She whirled around. A monstrous, muscular bird in a big cage squeezed its head out from the bars and pushed them apart with a flick of its powerful wings. Another bit down on a bar with its beak, snapping it apart. Birds formed around her in a circle. There was no way she could break through.

Caw!

Where was her dark-haired man? There!—in the distance. She tried to call to him, she tried to scream, but no sound escaped her throat.

Not hearing her, the man turned his back. It was covered with long, bloody wounds.

THREE

Caw!

Hulu lifted his head from the writing table. The candle was out and the room was completely dark. *Such a strange dream. Why would I be at the bird market?* And the oddest part was, he never saw the woman's face. Still, she'd certainly been beautiful from the back.

Hulu grinned and shook his head to clear it. Obviously it'd been too long since he'd been with a woman. *Not since the last time Alani had...* Well, not for a long time.

Caw!

"Okay, okay!" Hulu threw open the room's shutters. "Somebody wants me awake. Who's out there?"

New moon, no light. A rustling of something flying away. Obviously not a whisper bird, not with that call. Just a damn crow.

Hulu felt his way back to the table and picked up the scroll he'd been examining before he fell asleep, rolled it up and tucked it under his arm. Another of the odd scrolls Regent's advisor had brought to the scribes for copying. Legends of early Atlantis, stories of the ancestral line of kings from the ancient past to nearly the present day...but altered. Names changed, dates shifted, the winners and losers of battles reversed. All obviously part of a propaganda effort to justify Regent's reign. But who did they think would fall for it? There were thousands of scrolls with the real stories and correct information in public temples and schools, or in the private collections of wealthy men.

Regent's men even supplied the ink for their sham histories as well, an inferior, brownish kind of ink. Why? Of course, in one way it made sense, for one could not write falsehood with the mother ink. For five hundred years, the Scriptorium had provided Atlantis with copies of all the important texts it needed, the power of the mother ink making their words and figures come alive in a reader's mind and providing abundant proof of their truth and accuracy. So, if one wished to relate an untrue history, an alternative ink mixture would be necessary. But if Regent hoped to give his own version of history, how could he hope for any other ink to convince those who read them? Mysteries upon mysteries.

A shout from somewhere in the Scriptorium drew Hulu's attention. An argument at this hour? He wrapped his crow-feather cape tight and exited the study chamber. He knew the place well enough that even in the dark, his steps were quick down the stairs and through the passages.

The yelling and sounds of a scuffle grew louder as he approached, coming from the direction of the locked vault where they kept the mother ink. No doubt the disturbance involved one of Regent's guards, then. They had been a constant nuisance since their arrival the previous year. Seems Regent's Council had decided the Scriptorium wasn't being run as efficiently as it might be, and deployed a small contingent of Shabengee guardsmen to supervise the learned scribes. *As if a home for history and knowledge needs military discipline*, Hulu thought.

He rounded the corner. In the illumination from the ever-lit torches in their sconces, a pair of guards held somebody between them in a rough grip. The guards wore Shabengee black breeches and dark gray, red-trimmed sharkskin capes, their muscled arms and torsos tattooed with sharks and other symbols of battle. Hulu recognized beefy, thick-lipped Captain Ino, head of the unit assigned to the Scriptorium, holding one of Hulu's scribes in place by his shoulders. The other guard, Ino's subordinate, had a fist raised, preparing a blow. Blood already ran from the scribe's nose and his lip was swollen.

"What in Honua's name is going on here, Captain?" Hulu said, striding quickly and with authority, but taking care to address the guard by his title.

"Master Scribe," Captain Ino said, surprised. He brought his fist to eye level. "I'ke Regent!"

"I'ke Regent," Hulu repeated, suppressing an eye roll. "Please explain to me what is happening here."

Captain Ino signaled to his guard to take a step back. He sneered at Hulu. "Yer damned clumsy little fool, here, is the problem. Stealing mother ink, he was. And now look, he spilt it. I got to take him out for three lashings, I do. Regent's law."

Hulu glanced where the Captain gestured. Earthenware shards lay on the floor around a small blotch spreading across the basalt. Hulu sighed to see even a few drops of the liquid wasted.

"Kindly unhand him," Hulu said. "He's not going anywhere."

Captain Ino shoved the scribe, who stumbled a couple steps before righting himself. He looked up to Hulu with a pleading expression. "It w-wasn't me, sir."

"Who was it then, you sniveling little—"

Hulu held his hand up to silence the soldier. "Tell me what happened, Akahi."

Akahi straightened a bit and wiped blood from under his nose. "I needed to fetch a cruse of ink and the guard wasn't here. But we need it for the tax estimates, we ran out. And you know how late we have to work now to finish them all, so I was in a hurry, and why should I wait for a guard to check me out? We never used to have to do that."

"To keep you little cheats from stealing ink in the middle of the night, that's why!" Captain Ino bellowed. "This place is already over its quota for the year and it's not even late summer yet!"

Hulu eyed the Captain coolly. "Go on, Akahi."

"So I guess the guard heard me in the vault and as I was coming out the door, he came charging around the corner and knocked me aside. Of course I dropped the cruse and of course it broke."

"So it was just an accident," Hulu said.

"No, it was—" But here Akahi noticed the glares he was receiving from the guard and Captain Ino and stopped himself. "Yes, it was an accident. Nobody's fault."

"I see." Hulu stroked his chin. He had to choose his words carefully here, to make his point without causing offense. "Sounds like your guard wasn't on duty, Captain Ino. My understanding was that you would always have a guard posted at this door. We are very busy here, Captain. Contracts, property assessments, even marriage certificates depend on us working quickly. We don't have time to wait around for your men when we need more ink."

Captain Ino didn't answer right away. He made a fist and flexed his bicep, the hammerhead tattooed there in mother ink undulating as if really swimming in water. "Ink been spilled, Master Scribe. The law's the law. Three lashings. And it weren't my man had the ink in his hand."

Hulu did not speak for several moments. *Damn the law. Damn Regent. And damn these buffoons.* But, out loud, "I told this man to get mother ink whenever he needed, and not to tarry. It's my fault. I'll take the lashings."

Captain Ino raised an eyebrow. "You'll take the lashings?"

"Of course I will." Hulu stood up straight.

"Very well." Captain Ino gave an evil little smile. "In that case, I'll give you the honor of having me administer the lashings myself, I will. Wouldn't do for a common soldier to whip the master of the Scriptorium. What time today would be most convenient for you, Master Scribe?"

"At the first tolling of the morning bells," Hulu said. "I would hate to see justice be delayed a single moment."

Lono woke with a start. It was still dark, but something was stirring around her. It took her a moment to realize she wasn't still in the dream with the birds, but back in the same dormitory room where she had slept every night for years. At the door, two candles entered, the faces of Sisters flickering above them, and Lono sat up on edge of her bed, rubbing sleep from her eyes. It was time for the Ceremony of Sky.

Despite the cool of her room, sweat beaded on her forehead and she felt the heat of her flushed skin. Was it the expectation of the coming ritual? Or residual embarrassment from the nature of her dream? A tinge of worry entered her mind, for only acolytes untouched by a man could receive a message from the ancestors. But she hadn't actually been touched, of course, even if it had seemed so real. And then another twinge, guilt this time, for having such indulgent, unchaste dreams when her own best friend was ill, possibly even close to death.

Who was he? she wondered on her way to wash up. The man had seemed familiar, somehow. Older than she, she thought, but it was hard to tell without glimpsing his face. She did not see many men here at the convent. Only the Shabengee guardsmen who had appeared a year or so before, who lived in temporary quarters outside the gates because the Prioress had forbade them entrance to the priory.

"Rise, young ones, rise," one Sister called. "Wash your faces and prepare your minds."

The Prioress soon arrived, along with more Sisters, and together they led the yawning acolytes through the halls of the priory and up the long winding stairs to the Equatorial Room. The Prioress fell back to walk beside Lono. She spoke softly in her ear. "Iwali sleeps deeply now, and I think seems in more comfort than earlier. The swelling of her wound has gone down as well."

"So the danger is passed?" Lono asked.

"I cannot say that," the Prioress said. "But I can say the danger is lessened. Let your mind be easier." She squeezed Lono's shoulder and returned to her place.

Lono resisted the urge to touch the throbbing telescope inscribed on her own forearm. She contented herself with a glance at the black outline under her raised red skin. It really wasn't too painful, if she didn't think about it.

The Equatorial Room's high dome atop a tower was the most visible feature of the temple compound, but it was a place she and the other acolytes had never been. Before dawn this morning, and for the first time, they would finally be allowed to view the goddess Ne Wa'e through the great telescope as she returned from her journey across the sky. And, perhaps, one or two lucky acolytes would hear messages from the ancestors during their first meditation after the tattooing ceremony.

At the landing of the stairwell, the Prioress took the key from around her neck and opened the towering bronze door. The Sisters and acolytes filed in. The Equatorial Room was huge, its floor made of large wooden planks, sanded smooth, with a great bronze mechanism mounted in the center, a massive machine of gears and levers topped with the polished ebony gleam of the telescope shaft itself. Intricate murals depicting the cycle of the great Atlantean myths graced the walls and interior of the dome, though Lono could hardly make them out in the pre-dawn torchlight.

"Open the dome," the Prioress murmured. Four Sisters gripped a thick looped chain hanging down from the top of the dome. The chain was so heavy that it lifted their feet off the ground when they pulled it, and only when all four of their bodies were in the air did the chain advance, each link giving a deep groaning clang as their combined weight levered the dome open a crack. The Sisters pulled again and again, inching the dome's halves further apart until it was fully open to the glory of the firmament, stars shining down like lamps.

Overhead the constellations Ne'i Zuub, the bee, and Ne'i Shabengee, the shark, shone brilliantly. Soon, on the southeast horizon, the star Ne Wa'e would appear, the first time in more than a month she would arrive before her consort, Neba H'aa, the sun, to mark the height of summer.

Now another group of Sisters spun a series of bronze wheels attached to the mechanism to maneuver the telescope into place, rods and cogs and gears turning as they steered it along guidelines drawn onto the floor generations before to assure all was positioned precisely. As they did so, the Prioress and the remaining Sisters seated themselves along still another guideline that spiraled out from the telescope, the acolytes finding places along the spiral and following their elders' lead in assuming the cross-legged, straight-backed posture of meditation.

Lono closed her eyes. For those who were to hear a message, now was the time. Cool air wafted down and felt refreshing against her skin. She wondered absently which of the ancestors might speak to her. She knew better than to expect a literal voice, but she wondered what it felt like to "hear" those words in your head. Of course, there was the possibility that the man in her dream had ruined her for hearing prophesy… Lono shook her head to clear her thoughts. She would find out soon enough, perhaps, if she kept her mind empty.

She let her sensations wash over her, as she had been taught—the smooth wood against her buttocks and the edges of her feet, the even sound of her neighbors breathing, the slight salt tang in her nose from the gentle breeze off the ocean. She did not try to prevent thoughts from entering her mind. She simply noticed them as they arose and let them go as they passed. Soon she was in a relaxed, receptive state.

Lono, came a whisper in her ear. *Stand up*. She squinted her eyes, irritated at whichever acolyte was interrupting her peace. But no one else stirred. All sat in the posture with their eyes closed, telescope tattoos glowing faintly on their arms. She resumed her own meditation.

Lono, came the whisper again after a few minutes. This time she did not open her eyes. Was this her message from the ancestors? *Stand up and walk out of the Equatorial Room. Continue down the stairs, through the meeting hall, and out the front gate. A sign will be waiting for you.*

Lono swallowed. This wasn't right. Ancestral messages weren't like this. They were supposed to be vague words or phrases that required the recipient and the Prioress and the wisest Sisters in the convent to mull over possible interpretations for hours. Sometimes a visitor would ask for specific guidance and receive it, but even then it would be in the form of an epigram or a poetic line, not step-by-step instructions. Lono opened her eyes and turned her head to the left and the right. Surely somebody was playing a trick on her.

"Is anything the matter, Lono?" the Prioress asked. "Have you received a message?"

"No, Prioress," Lono said.

"Then please resume."

Lono closed her eyes. The whisper wasted no time. *Stand up, Lono.*

No, she responded in her head. *I have to stay here. I have to see to Iwali. I can't just leave.*

Lono, why do you wait? Do not tarry, for the sign will not remain at the gate for long.

There was no use for it. Her stomach tight with misgiving, not knowing what else to do, Lono stood and quietly walked out of the Equatorial Room.

FOUR

"Master?" The under-scribe knocked for the second time on the door to Hulu's apartment. "Are you there?"

The heavy oaken door opened slowly inward, and Hulu stood there in his usual crow-feather cape, a dozen swan quills in one hand. "Ah, Opio, there you are. Please bring it in."

Opio carried the heavy wooden basin of warm water. He looked around, curious to be in the private quarters of the head of the Scriptorium. The front room was large but sparsely furnished. A simple writing desk with some parchments on it stood near the open window, a trunk rested in a corner, and a couple wooden chairs waited for visitors. Several yellowed scrolls written in elaborate script hung from the walls. Opio stared, trying to make sense of the unfamiliar language. He thought he could make out a word here and there, but even those were spelled differently than in than the familiar Atlantean tongue. Many letters were unrecognizable altogether.

"Go ahead and set it down in the middle, if you please." Hulu placed the swan quills on the desk next to a sharpening stone and turned to see what was taking so long. "Do you have an interest in the classic texts, Opio?"

"Yes, sir. I mean, I've never seen any that old before."

Hulu pointed at one near the window. "That's the oldest there. From the second dynasty. It tells the story of Prince Kanai and his wooing of the queen in the orchard. You are familiar with the story, I think?"

"Yes, sir. I know it. But the second dynasty? That was...well, it was almost..."

"Four hundred years ago." Hulu smiled. "A long time, no?"

"Yes, sir. A long time." Opio hesitated. "Sir?"

"Yes, Opio?"

"I...I mean we, we all heard what happened this morning. All the scribes I mean, and how you took the punishment due one of us. And none of us think it's right what happened, the whipping and all. But we're all on your side."

Hulu nodded. "Thank you, Opio. I appreciate it."

"You're welcome, sir." Opio backed towards the door. "Is there anything else?"

"See that I'm not disturbed the rest of the morning, if possible."

Opio nodded and closed the door behind him.

Left in peace at last, Hulu discarded his cape and took a sponge from the basin of water. He applied it gently to his wounds, as far across his back as he could reach. He could have one of the novices come and help him, perhaps, but it did not seem a fit duty for him to assign to another. He winced with each dab against his skin, but it was important to keep them clean. They would heal eventually.

When he was done, Hulu pushed the basin to a corner and checked the door, bolting it and double-checking the latch. He went through his chambers closing all his windows as well, although the birdsong in the tree below made him hesitate for a moment at the last sill. Mele birds twittered, robins called back and forth, and a pale yellow pala bird warbled a melody. Beyond the tree spread the elegant gardens and courtyards of the Scriptorium, and past that the monumental Middle Island of Atlantis, its spired palaces and temples and official buildings all built of the ubiquitous blue-gray basalt, connected to the mainland with a series of handsome stone bridges. From there, broad avenues lined with kimunu trees unrolled through wealthy neighborhoods and slums, the districts interspersed with extensive public parks, and in the distance far to the northwest, amidst its lush green grounds, he could even make out the hill on which rose the Observatory and the attached Convent of the Ancestors, that isolated home of enigmatic oracles. And of course, looming to the northwest, Mount Ipu, dark green at its base and rising to the two brown peaks of its caldera.

He closed the shutters of the final window and took a candle, lighting it with a spark from a flintbox. In the front room, he removed one of the antique hanging scrolls and set it gently on the ground. Behind where it hung, he pulled out a loose stone, revealing a small niche from which he withdrew a vial. Hulu took the vial to the desk and held it carefully over the inkwell.

One drop. Mother ink, thick and black, spread its earthy aroma. Two drops. A trace of sea salt. Three. Enough.

Hulu stirred the mixture with the nub of a swan quill, mixing the mother ink with the regular ink made from lampblack. Then he took up a well-scribbled sheet of parchment and placed it on one side of the desk and spread a scroll out on the other side. In fact, it was the same suspect scroll he had wondered at earlier in the day, before the unpleasantness with Captain Ino.

Finally, from a chest in a corner he took a clay pipe and a bag of aromatic herbs—cinnamon and appleweed and the crushed roots of the tiko plant. Hulu slowly let drip three more drops of mother ink into the little nest of herbs in the pipe's bowl. He replaced the vial in the wall and slid the stone back in place, carefully returning the hanging scroll. He pulled a chair up to the desk and lit his pipe from the candle.

The hot sweet smoke gusted down the back of Hulu's throat as he inhaled. He held his breath, the heady vapor warm in his mouth and lungs like steam, but living, even sentient, its tendrils threading their way into every alveolus and up to his brain, traveling along the nerve endings. He blew the smoke back out through his nose, slowly, all the pain from his back and anxiety from his mind flowing out with it in a plume that dissipated into the air. Gone.

A shame truth-smoking must be such a risk, Hulu thought, taking in another puff. If he were ever caught, it would get him expelled from the Scriptorium, at the least. Possibly he would even be executed. Regent had taken total control of the mother ink trade and declared truth-smoking to be *kupu*—not only a crime, but an offense against the natural order. Whether it was simply an expedient way to guarantee a steady supply for official uses, or a suspicion of its ability to unveil lies, Hulu wasn't sure. *Or maybe Regent just hates for people to have a good time.*

Still, here in his private apartment, six floors above the ground, the chance of being discovered seemed low. In any case, Hulu could hardly get through a day without it.

He took the quill delicately between his thumb and forefinger, tapping the nub in the little inkpot to saturate the chewed nub-end. He returned the quill to the parchment page and picked a blank space, skritch-skratching characters while keeping his eyes on the vellum of the scroll, writing slowly to allow his thin lines to spread as they soaked into the paper fibers. He spoke each word aloud as he copied it from the master text, following the teaching of scribe lore. And as he wrote and spoke, the figures in the text danced in his mind.

"King Hree'u," Hulu recited, "in the eighth year of his reign, led a band of one hundred hand-picked men into the mountains of the giants, for they had kidnapped his daughter, Nihea. At a ford in the river Us Wpu, they met Ukua, the giant king, while he bathed, and when he rose from the water, forty hands tall he was, and he slew the king and his men with his fists, brushing aside their arrows and spears as a cow brushing away flies. He slew ninety-nine of them, all but one. As for the final man, he did not die, but cut off a hand of the giant and escaped, the hero Hano—"

It was here that the writing faltered, that the dance took a bad step, and Hulu could push the quill no farther. His brow lowered with concern. As Hulu remembered it, indeed, as every schoolboy in Atlantis remembered it, it was Prince Hrea, not this Hano fellow, who cut off the giant's hand. This act was one of Prince Hrea's many famous feats of strength. As Hulu had suspected earlier, the text in the scroll was false.

Why? Why this deception? He took another long draw from the pipe. Perhaps because Hrea was the forefather of the royal lineage, so this change of history could be a subtle way to cast doubt on the legitimacy of the royal line. Prince Ka'moe was thought to be still alive, but had not seen since the Exile, ten years before. He would be nearly twelve years of age now. Did Regent think this was the time to could take control in his own name, before Ka'moe might show up again when he reached the age of majority? But the effort was so amateurish. Who would believe this false history, since it was not, indeed could not, be written with mother ink?

The apartment suddenly shook, breaking Hulu's thoughts, and then stopped as quickly as it began. *Another earthquake. Just a small one this time.* They'd become more frequent lately in Atlantis. *Hopefully not a foreshock.*

Hulu rose and replaced his fallen writing tools on the desk, straightened the scrolls on the walls. He hesitated in front of one in particular, its flowing script penned by none other than the Scriptorium's founder. *What would Old Master Makule have done in my position? Would he have let the soldiers into our sacred halls? Would he have allowed Captain Ino and his men to dictate our schedules, control our use of ink, misuse the scribes? And if not, by what cleverness would he have prevented it?*

He stopped a moment, knelt in front of the scroll, and closed his eyes. "Makule, give me wisdom."

A wish, maybe a prayer? Hulu wasn't sure. He felt a bit silly. Who knew if the ancestors really listened? Still, he went on. "I'm too young, Master Makule. I have not even reached my twenty-seventh year. Who ever heard of such a young master? Maybe in better times it would be an honor. But now it is a burden. Help me, if you can. Teach me how to lead these men in troubled times."

Hulu returned to his chair and relit his pipe. If Master Makule had any ideas, he kept them to himself. Hulu didn't notice when the candle went out and he fell into slumber, or the round black eye observing him through a knot in the shutter. Nor did he hear, a few minutes later, the soft hissing and muted flutter of wings away from his windowsill.

Lono stood before the convent gate, the bright stars vaulted overhead, the dewy grass of the Great Meadow spreading away below her to the treeline in the distance that marked the edge of the convent grounds. The only things to mar the beauty of the scene were the crude wooden shacks where the Shabengee guardsmen slept at the meadow's far end.

Lono scanned the area but saw no "sign" waiting for her. Not that she had any idea what she was seeking. Was somebody supposed to meet her? Or maybe a star in the sky she would recognize, somehow?

"I'm here," she called out softly. "What now?"

She had been silent enough in leaving that nobody had followed or seemed to notice her absence. Probably because they were concentrating on their own meditations. *As I should be doing.* An irritated feeling sprouted in her that the whisper had been a lie. Maybe it was an idea cooked up by her own subconscious. Perhaps this is what happened to those who couldn't keep their hearts pure. *That stupid dream. How could I let a man touch me, the very night of the Ceremony of the Sky?*

She decided to go back. She could tell the Prioress she had felt ill but was better now. Maybe it would not be too late. Maybe the Prioress hadn't noticed her absence at all. She turned on her heel only to come face to face with a great black crow standing on a low branch in the cherry tree next to the entrance.

Lono jumped back. "Oh!"

The bird eyed her unnervingly. An ugly scar around its right eye made it seem to bulge out. A line of stitches ran up from the base of a wing to its nape, and its feathers were ruffled and unkempt. "Is…is it you? Are you the sign?"

A low caw, almost a purr, and the crow flew from the branch and alighted a bit ahead of her on the path. It hopped around a couple times and rotated its head back to gaze at her with that bulging black eye.

"You definitely want me to follow, don't you?" Lono stepped after the bird, and every time she neared it would fly a short distance until she caught up again. Her heart beat faster as she followed the bird along the path deeper into the trees. She had not been this far from the convent since she was a little girl of only seven, the day her mother had brought her, her eyes nervous and voice anxious in the city streets teeming with soldiers. Her mother and the Prioress had dedicated her to the faith in a brief ceremony and then her mother had left. She had never seen her mother or father again.

Through the woods Lono and the bird went, flying and walking, until they came out on the other side where the path widened into a road. Buildings grew more plentiful as they approached the city. Lono had seen the city often enough, from the top of her dormitory building, When she had a free hour on a holy day, she and Iwali would lie on their stomachs together and gaze out with a small telescope to see the people, carts, houses, boats. The city had always struck her as a wonderful confusion, and a thrill ran through her to be in it now. Fear as well. There were only a few people about in the pre-dawn hours, but they were strangers. Lono pulled the hood of her barkcloth cape over her head to keep their eyes off her.

She studied the bird as she walked. It flew in sort of a lopsided fashion, as if the surgery that had caused the stitches had not healed yet, or not healed properly. *And who would operate on a bird, anyway?* As they continued through broad commercial streets and down narrow alleyways, around twisting lanes of small houses or across plazas, even crossing a bridge over a river at one point, Lono wondered if they had a destination or if the bird was simply leading her around. They must have been traveling for an hour by this point. The sun was coming up. *Am I foolish for following this creature? What if it was outside the convent by coincidence?*

"Tell me, Mr. Crow, are we going somewhere? Does this journey have a goal?" She felt ridiculous asking a bird a question, but it did give a click in response, like the *clop* of a child playing horse, that she took for an affirmation.

They crossed another bridge that led to the neat paths and ornamental trees of one of the city parks. Soon the path gave way to dirt and the trees grew thicker and wilder. Just when Lono was sure the bird had no idea where it was going, they came to a place where a huge tumble of stones lay overgrown in vines and kimunus. Trunks poked up through gaps in the ruins, branches weaving a leafy canopy twenty feet or more overhead.

The bird stopped and peered up at her, hopping from foot to foot and nodding his head as if to say, "This is it."

"Okay, I see," Lono said. "But where are we? And what am I supposed to do here?"

She glanced around. Trees, ruins, nothing obvious to do. She sat on a stone and realized she was exhausted. She'd stayed up so late with Iwali, had only a couple hours' sleep before the ceremony, then exerted herself on the long walk here, not to mention the aching wound on her arm around the fresh tattoo. Maybe she could curl up on the rock under her cape, just for a few minutes. The bird could wait.

Caw!

"Shut up, bird!"

Caw!

And then the ground shook and Lono leapt up. The earth wobbled, the trees vibrated enough to send a cascade of leaves drifting down. Somewhere in the pile a rock shifted and pebbles tumbled. And from within the pile a voice cried out.

FIVE

Boom boom boom!

Hulu woke to the pounding on his door.

In his delirium, he had slumped out of the chair all the way to the floor, but at least he'd had the sense to ball up his cloak under his head as a pillow. His mouth was dry and foul from the pipe smoke and the skin on his back was oozing and itchy from the lashes.

How long have I been out? Judging from the light leaking through the shutters, it must be somewhere past midday. A hole in the louvers spotlighted a place on the floor, dust motes floating in and out of a sunbeam. Hulu waved a hand through it, feeling its concentrated warmth.

Boom boom boom! Louder and more insistent this time.

"Alright, alright, let me get some clothes on!" He stumbled across the room, knocking over the chair in the process, groping in the dimness for something to slip into. He felt something like his breeches and pulled them up his legs.

BOOM BOOM and the door flew in, crashing to the floor to reveal three guards outside his apartment, two men armed with cudgels on either side and Captain Ino in the middle, holding a small scroll. Mother ink sharks swam up and down their burly arms.

"Hey, you can't just barge in here!" Hulu said.

Captain Ino stepped into the room and pumped his right fist. "I'ke Regent!"

"Yes, i'ke Regent. Captain Ino, how pleasant to see you again so soon," Hulu said, trying to pull the breeches over his buttocks. "If you'd given me some warning I'd have made lunch for you."

"Pathetic as ever." Captain Ino hocked and spat on the ground. "Stand up, so I can arrest you."

Hulu gave his breeches a last tug and rose. "Arrest me? Whatever for?"

Captain Ino unfurled the scroll and cleared his throat. "Hulu Scribemaster is hereby placed under arrest on suspicion of grand theft, unlicensed prophesy, and defying lawful authority. His quarters and personal effects are authorized for immediate and thorough inspection."

Unlicensed prophesy? Hulu thought, his stomach turning queasy. *Do they know about the stash of ink? How?*

Captain Ino nodded to his guards, who fanned out through the rooms opening trunks and drawers and dumping their contents on the ground. "Now, if you'll come with me?"

Hulu ignored him and followed the guards, Captain Ino on his heels. "I don't know who you found to sign your warrant, but whatever you think you're looking for, you won't find it. And I'll have your commission if this disgrace continues any longer."

"Is that so?" Captain Ino remarked, sounding utterly unconcerned.

One guard had reached the wardrobe in his bedroom and was pulling out loincloths and undershirts. When he grabbed a delicate rose-colored gown, Hulu slapped it out of his hand. "Don't touch that, you swine!"

The guard swiveled and caught him in the ribs with his cudgel, the force sending Hulu stumbling backwards, knocking him against the wall. He pushed himself back up to his feet. "My scribe spilled the ink by accident, you maniacs!"

Captain Ino growled back. "This weren't about last night's incident and you know it. Now will you come along calm and dignified-like, or does we have to beat you? I know which I'd prefer." The hammerhead on his bicep seemed to be grinning.

"Fine. Tell your ape to stop pawing my late wife's clothes and I'll go with you."

Captain Ino turned to the guard, who still held the gown in his hand. "Sergeant, put the gown back where it came from. Seems it be a sentimental item for the Master Scribe." He gave a mean grin to Hulu. "Alani, I believe her name was?"

Hulu only glared while the guard replaced the gown.

"Very well, then. Shall we go?"

Hulu nodded and grabbed his crow-feather cape.

Captain Ino issued orders. "Sergeant, stay here and continue with the search. You know what you're looking for. Private, come along with us."

They marched into the corridor, the Captain in front of Hulu and the private behind, while the sergeant continued ransacking his home. *Really, it's just a matter of time until they find the ink. Might even know where it is already, and just looking for an excuse to make a mess.*

Scribes stopped to stare, sensing something was going on, as two guards escorted their master through the halls of the Scriptorium. Hulu waved and spoke to them with a business-like calm he did not feel inside. "It's alright. How are things coming along with those receipts? Back to work. Did you finish with that chart of the Eastern Ocean?"

As they reached the gate of the Scriptorium, Hulu ventured a question. "Where are we headed, anyway, Captain?"

Captain Ino chortled. "First class accommodations, Master Scribe. We're headed to the Puku, we are."

Hulu's stomach clenched. The Puku, the notorious hole where Regent stashed enemies of the regime. Those who went down didn't come back up. As awful as that was, an even worse thought came to Hulu. *So, the real question is, if I die, who will protect these scribes after I'm gone?*

Lono stood on the lip of the crevice in the stone, peering down into the darkness but unable to make out what might be at the bottom. The voice had not called out again, though she was certain she had heard it, and it had come from roughly this spot. A broken branch lay nearby, and several tufts of leaves. Lono thought the rust-colored patch on the flat stone a few feet away might even be dried blood. Could somebody have fallen from the tree branches overhead? It would have been quite a drop.

"Hello? Anybody down there?" Lono called. No answer. She turned to the crow, still perched on an outcropping nearby. "Well, what do you think? Is this it or what?"

The crow looked back at her.

"Big help you are. Somebody might be hurt, you know." The crow cocked its head a bit. "It would be an awful waste of time if this isn't where I'm supposed to be."

Lono got on her hands and knees and gave her eyes a moment to adjust to the blackness below. It seemed she could sharpen her vision through sheer force of will. The details of the shaft slowly resolved themselves. Her elbow itched around the tattoo, but she ignored it. The rock face was almost vertical, but not quite—tilted perhaps fifteen degrees. Lono thought she might be able to climb down, if she had something to hold onto.

Farther down the rock face she focused on another smear of rust color, and then concentrated on a heap of something at the bottom. A body? Yes, she could identify limbs bent around a torso. Black hair. About the size of an older child. It wasn't moving, though.

Lono stood up and brushed herself off. "There's definitely somebody down there," she said to the crow. "Now we just have to figure out how to get them out."

SIX

Watery light struggled through the grates far overhead, barely penetrating into the recesses and winding passageways leading off the cavernous main chamber, but providing enough light for Hulu to make out his surroundings. Ragged, blank-faced men sat on the ground or wandered aimlessly, while younger, thuggish-looking men with heavily-tattooed torsos huddled in clumps, talking in low tones and eyeing other clumps warily. From time to time, two inmates who had found some offense worth struggling over, or perhaps simply grown bored, would interrupt the routine with a bit of yelling or a fight.

Hulu sat slumped against a wall, water dripping from an outcropping overhead to a puddle near his feet. The lashings on his back had already started to itch as the analgesic effect of the truth-smoking wore off. He shrugged to loosen his cape so it wouldn't chafe the wounds. Soon the itching would become real pain, and by the evening his back would be on fire. Yet Hulu's worst fear, by far, was what would happen the next morning when he didn't smoke his usual three-drop dose of mother ink. Already he was feeling listless, the bare beginnings of cramps forming in his guts. It would only get worse. The sickening agony that would wrack his body later would make the sting from his wounds seem a welcome distraction.

Better get used to it, he thought. Hulu felt sure he would spend the rest of the regrettably few days he had left here in the Puku. Captain Ino had read out some pro forma document with a promise of a trial before handing him over to the warden, but Hulu knew better: a trial date was as far away for anyone in the Puku as there were ways for Regent to delay, appeal, and otherwise cancel justice. The real trick would be surviving until the trial date. He'd been dumped in the Puku, and everyone knew no one who went in came back out.

Won't be long until I'm just another one of these lost souls.

Almost as if he'd heard his thoughts, an old man with matted white hair emerged from some tunnel or other and shuffled towards Hulu. He wore only a thin shift and loincloth, though he didn't seem to feel cold in the dank air. He stepped around the puddle and squatted in front of Hulu, sticking his face so close to Hulu's their noses nearly touched.

"Can I help you, *'ele?*" Hulu said, recoiling from the man's strong unwashed odor.

"Give me your hand," the man rasped.

Hulu kept his arms folded across his chest, unwilling to take part in whatever scam or hazing awaited obedience.

"I said, give me your hand."

"No, thank you." Hulu tensed his muscles and stared into the old man's face. One of his eyes was milky, the other clear blue. Liver spots speckled his temples and coarse hair grew bushy from his ears. Faded tattoos furrowed and folded under the wrinkled skin of his body. Hulu had no doubt he could easily overpower the old man if he had to, but he had little desire to physically confront this wretched senile elder.

"You smoke the grease, yeah?" the man asked.

Hulu was about to brush him off but hesitated. He recognized the term grease, street slang for mother ink. It hadn't occurred to him it might be available down here, although of course some of the prisoners must have been arrested for dealing in the black market. Would they still have access to their supply, even while locked up? It would save him so much misery if he could find a source, though he feared what he might be asked to do in exchange.

"Why do you ask?"

"Give me your hand," the man repeated. Slowly Hulu extended his hand. The old man took it between both of his bony ones and ran his fingers along Hulu's palms and the pads of his fingers. "Soft palms, tough fingers. It's true what they say, then. You're a scribe."

"Yes, that's true."

Hulu wasn't sure how word of his position had spread so quickly, but belatedly realized it must be his crow-feather cape. It struck him that wearing such a luxurious item could prove to be a liability in the Puku.

"You and I, we have something in common," the man rasped. He pointed at himself. "Ho'oule."

Did the man think he was one of those terrorists? Was that the rumor going around among the prisoners? Or was he just confused? Hulu shook his head. "We have nothing in common."

"Yeah." The man gripped his hand tightly between his two hands now. "The same. You have seen it, when you smoke the grease. What they do to the animals, the birds. The changes. The cages. Just like me. You know."

Birds in cages? Like his dream? Surely a coincidence. "I'm sorry, I don't understand."

"You're a scribe?" The man seemed impatient now, his voice rising in tone and volume.

"Yes, I'm a scribe. What does that have to with anything?"

"I'll tell you what I've seen." The man let go with one hand and pointed it at Hulu's chest. "You in your dreams. Me in mine. You can write it. People will know. People have to know what they're doing to the birds."

Two younger men emerged from a shadowed alcove, listening in while Hulu and the old man talked. Now they approached and one put a hand on the old man's shoulder. "Come, 'ele. You're bothering the fellow. Let's go wait in the food line, eh?"

The old man shook him off. "No, I'm telling him. He can help us."

Now both young men had the elder, each taking an arm and

hauling him off. In raising him, one of them had caught the old man's shift, lifting it partway up his back. Hulu stared. Underneath was a tattoo of an octopus, not with flat ink like most of the men down here, but a true mother ink tattoo, octopus arms writhing. We Honua, a symbol of dreams and prophesy. "The birds, scribe! I will tell you what they do to the birds!"

One of the young men looked back and forced a smile at Hulu. "Crazy old man, eh?"

"Yeah, crazy." Of course he was. Probably been down here decades, going slowly insane. *But the tattoo. Aren't all the priests of We Honua supposed to be dead? In any case, he must have real power.* Also, there was something about what he had said. Cages. The birds. *Like in my dream.*

Hulu had to know. He pushed himself up and followed down the dank, stinking tunnel he'd seen them go down.

At the bottom of the crevice, Lono examined the boy in the cramped space. He looked to be about ten or eleven. Awfully beat up, bruises and blood on his face. She bent over and put a hand to his cheek. Warm, though. Breathing.

"Hey, wake up." She gently shook his shoulder.

The boy groaned and his eyes fluttered. When he saw there was somebody above him, he jerked, weakly flailing at her with his balled-up fist. She put a hand on his arm and pushed it down. "Calm down. I'm a friend. I'm not here to hurt you."

The boy's body relaxed and he croaked out a response from a parched throat. "Oh. Thought…you were…somebody else." He closed his eyes and opened them again wide half a second later. "Got to…go…. Right now…. He's…coming back."

"I'd love to go," Lono said. "But I don't know if you're in any shape to move."

"Have to…. He'll kill me. And you… when he finds us."

Lono's stomach clenched. *What sort of trouble is this boy in?* "Who'll kill you? Were you in a fight?"

"No time...have to move."

Lono didn't know if she believed him about the killing, but somebody had sure beat him up. She looked up at the thin line of light above, the dangling vines she'd tied around the outcropping at the top. Could she make it back up carrying him? She could give it a try. "Okay. Do you think you can stand?"

He held out his hand and she helped pull him to his feet. He swayed and almost fell again before catching himself. "You got it?" she asked.

"I think so."

"Good. Now, try to put your arms over my shoulder. Like I'm going you to give a piggy-back ride."

"One arm," the boy said. "Other... might be broken."

"Well, okay. One arm. Can you do it?" Lono bent over and he somehow managed to grab ahold with his good arm, the right one, his legs wrapped around her waist.

Lono gripped the tough hihi vine and started the ascent, hand by hand, with feet walking up the rock. Not so different from climbing in the attic in the convent, where somebody in a generation past had left an old knotted rope suspended through an open roof panel. She had often climbed that rope with Iwali on her back, unwilling to leave behind her friend, who could not go more than twice her height before dizzying and falling to the dusty floor. This boy weighed about the same as Iwali, though the distance upward was much farther.

Halfway there and she was already tiring, but she could see the crow hopping around at the top. At three-quarters' distance, her muscles were aflame, but she could feel rays of sun on her skin. *Can't quit now.* She kept going, pulling with one arm and then the next.

Finally, she reached the top, but her work wasn't done yet. She and the boy couldn't both fit through the opening at the same time. The boy grabbed the lip of the crevice and held on with one hand while she pulled herself over the top, then heaved him up after her. They both lay gasping for breath on the flat surface.

It was the boy who recovered first, or at least by sheer will forced himself to rise, to get moving. "Come on. No time."

"Okay, fine. I passed a stream coming into the park, not too far from here. We can clean your wounds up a bit there."

The boy didn't object, and when they reached the place, Lono cupped her hands and brought the water to his lips so he wouldn't have to use his bad arm to bend over. When his thirst was satisfied, she took his bad arm, pressing her fingers along it. He winced but did not cry out.

"Good news," she told him. "I don't think it's broken. Some bad bruising, that's all. Maybe a pulled muscle. Did you fall from one of the trees?"

"Yeah."

She pulled a strip off her cloak and wetted it, dabbing away the blood from his face and neck. "What's your name, anyway?" she asked as she wiped a dirt smudge on his cheek.

"You seem okay." After slaking his thirst, his voice had returned to normal and his breathing had calmed. "I suppose it's safe to tell you. Aku."

"Safe to tell me! Are you this suspicious of everyone?" Lonoe reached out to wipe a fleck of blood from Aku's forehead.

"Yes. And you should be too, if you want to stay alive." He brushed her hand away. "Enough with the nursing."

She stepped back and looked him over. "Well, I guess you're feeling better, although what you really need is a thorough bathing. I'm Lono, by the way."

Aku grunted in reply. He seemed to be paying more attention to their surroundings than to her, his eyes flitting from the foliage above to the undergrowth, down the stream then up, scanning the trees as if somebody might jump out at any moment. Lono tore off another strip from her cloak and tied off the ends, looping it around his neck.

He tried to shrug it off. "What's that for? Leave me alone

now."

Lono frowned at his stubbornness. "We need to fit your arm in there."

"What? Why? You said it wasn't broken."

"To keep it from moving. A pulled muscle is still serious, and it'll heal faster if it's not jiggling all over the place. Doesn't it hurt?"

Aku looked at the older girl like she'd said the most moronic thing possible. "Of course it hurts. But that's not important right now."

"You don't talk like any kid I ever knew," Lono said. "How old are you, anyway?"

"And you don't talk like any grown-up I know. Don't you know any curse words?"

She sighed and took his arm, carefully fitting the sling snugly around it. Aku set his jaw until she was done. The odd crow stood on a stump nearby, observing the operation with its bulging eye.

No sooner had Lono finished than Aku squatted down and picked up a round river rock, drawing his left arm back.

"What are you doing?" she asked.

"*Shhh!* Whisper bird. Been watching us."

"No! That's a friend!"

Lono reached out but too late. Aku launched the rock and she screamed, and something dropped from a branch about thirty feet away. A rustling from a tree on the opposite bank of the stream and an abnormally large blackbird flew off into the sky with a soft hissing.

And all the time, Lono's crow remained calmly perched on its stump.

"*Caw!*" it let out, after it was over.

"Damn it," Aku said. "There was another one. They'll know we're here soon, if they don't already. We've got to move."

He strode off into the trees without waiting to see if she'd follow. Lono chased after. "Who is *they*? And where are we going?"

"Later. Don't know who'll overhear." Aku glanced back at her. "Or if you can keep a secret."

Lono caught up with him and grabbed his shoulder. "Well, I'm not going with you, then. I've done what the voice told me to and I'm going back to the convent."

"Voices in your head. Great." Aku shrugged his shoulders. "Do what you want. But they've seen you with me. You're not safe anymore, not alone. They'll come after you and kill you."

"Just for helping you?"

"Just for helping me."

Aku turned to go again, but when he didn't sense Lono following, he stopped. "Eleven," he said. "Almost twelve."

"What?"

"I'm eleven years old, I said. Now will you come with me?"

Lono considered this. "I will if you tell me how you knew my crow wasn't a threat."

Aku laughed. "Have you seen that thing? As soon as I saw its wonky eye and those feathers sticking up all over the place, I knew something that crazy had to be yours."

The crow emitted a low rattle from where it'd settled on a nearby branch ahead of them.

"You're not very grateful for someone who just had his life saved."

Aku pushed a branch out of the way as he walked and let it recoil back at her. "What am I supposed to do? Bow down before you and grovel about how obliged I am?"

"Of course not," Lono said. "But a simple thank you would be nice."

The boy hesitated a bit before speaking. "Less talk. It's slowing us down."

PART TWO

Atlantis is the jewel of the Great Sea, and at the sea's bottom dwells We Honua, the ever-sleeping Mother Octopus, whose eight arms hold all the parts of the world: the sun and the stars, the moon and the waters, the forests and fields, the earth and the dark places underneath the earth.

In her never-ending sleep, We Honua dreams the history of the world, and as she dreams she releases the clouds of ink that hold the power of life and death, of being and unbeing. The tides carry the ink to every corner of creation, and where they wash up, her dreams become reality.

-- from *The Book of Awa*

SEVEN

Kai woke to the blunt end of a spear jabbing his side. He groaned and tried to push away the offending instrument, only for it to return with a blow to his ribs and accompanied by a snarled instruction.

"Wake yer lazy ass, prisoner. There's work to be done."

Kai opened his eyes and his situation returned to him. Pale morning light glimmered into the undersea grotto from the opening above. He and the dozen other kai-men prisoners floated in the chill water, with only coarsely woven mangrove-root tunics to protect their crocodilian bodies. Worst of all was the heavy bronze chain tying him to the next prisoner, the shackle tight around his ankle. He was last in the line, newly attached only the day before. New Meat, as the other prisoners called him.

The guard with the spear swam back to the entrance and the other guard now entered, pulling half-rotted hunks of tarpon out of a sack and dropping it to the prisoners. As the chunks filtered down through the water, Kai extended his head and snapped his portion before anybody else could. Even fresh, tarpon meat was gamy, but he'd hardly been fed on the journey here so he gulped it down quickly, if not with relish.

Another prisoner noticed Kai's quickness. "You're eager for breakfast, ain't you, New Meat? Just the way your mate prepared it, eh?"

"Not likely," another said. "He'd be lucky to get fish this tasty back in his home lagoon."

There was a bit of general chuckling among the prisoners at

the low-grade humor, but before the conversation could continue the first guard was back, urging the line out of the cave with a bronze-tipped spear, and the prisoners emerged into a rock-strewn ocean floor landscape. First a quick trip to the surface, two hundred feet above, for a gulp of air, and then a swim to the location of the day's labor.

"Where to today, boss?" one prisoner asked.

"East Conch Field," came the answer. Kai didn't know what difference it made. So far as he could tell every part of the ocean floor was more or less the same here. All equally rocky and equally buffeted by never-ending currents of cold waters rolling in from the deep.

He stole a glance at the other prisoners. A mean-looking bunch of kai-men, their hides lined with scars, whether from the violence of their previous criminal lives or the rough handling from the guards, he couldn't say. A few had raw-looking wounds in the shape of bite marks. He guessed fights among them weren't uncommon.

They cruised about a league, the occasional flick of their powerful tails propelling them, called out in a regular beat by a guard so the prisoners wouldn't get tangled in their chains. Upon their arrival they descended and a guard handed each prisoner a rough burlap sack and set them to their task of scouring the ocean floor. The line advanced slowly, Kai and the others brushing away mud and overturning rocks to expose holes and crevices, small pebbles and shells. The work was boring but for the most part not too laborious, and Kai's mind drifted to the events of the past weeks, still almost inconceivable to him. His capture by a rival clan, the hasty trial on false charges of trespassing, the handing over to the work gangers and the forced, week-long trip from the warm shallow mangroves of his home, so unlike the barren gray muddy waste and wan light here in the depths of the open ocean.

"Hah, got one," one of the other prisoners said, interrupting Kai's reverie. He glanced over and sure enough, the prisoner had a dark blue globule in his webbed claw.

Kai flipped a flat rock and released another that had been

squeezed underneath. "Me, too," he said.

"Hah, not bad, New Meat," the prisoner next to Kai said. "Might be a good day. If our sacks are bulging before evening, the guards might even let us off early."

Kai eyed the globule for just a moment more. It was about the size and consistency of a frog egg, jelly-like and oily. Mother ink, the surface men called it. He slipped the globule into his sack. Hard to believe it was the most precious substance on earth.

"Are you sure this is the place?" Lono asked, looking skeptically at the half-rotted old kimunu tree with peeling bark and brown leaves. Her crow settled in one of the upper branches and cawed lightly, then seemed to fall asleep.

Aku had taken her through a dizzying tour of the neighborhood's alleys and small passages, doubling back on their own footsteps repeatedly to ensure no one was after them. She didn't know what a tattoo parlor was supposed to look like but found it hard to believe this decaying old tree could hold a viable business.

"Of course I'm sure." Aku knocked on the front door, a windowless round portal carved into the side of one of the trunks. Nobody answered.

"Maybe nobody's home?" Lono said.

Aku knocked again. A couple little urchins across the street stopped their ballgame to watch them curiously. They seemed almost painfully skinny in their barkcloth loincloths. Actually, everybody they'd seen in the neighborhood struck Lono as having hungry expressions and wary attitudes.

"We'll just go on in," Aku said. "They're probably pretty busy in there." He tested the door handle and found it locked. "Give me that pin in your hair."

"Why? What for?" Lono said.

Aku gave her a derisive look. "Just give it to me. I only need it for a second."

Lono pulled the pin out and handed it Aku, who poked around in the keyhole with it.

"Should you be doing that?" Lono said. "We can come back later."

Already, though, there was a click and the door swung open. Aku handed the pin back. "Best lockpick in Bonetown."

Inside, a bit of light filtered through the tree branches, but no torches or candles were lit, and Aku and Lono picked their way carefully across the dim room. The way was littered with broken-up chairs and tables, scattered bronze pots and urns. Lono stepped around a barrel, leaking a clear liquid with a strong alcoholic odor where it was crushed on one side, and let out a shriek.

"What is it?" Aku asked. Lono just pointed with one hand, covering her mouth with the other. Crumpled behind the barrel lay a man with his skull caved in, revealing glistening brain matter covered with a mass of crawling ants. Aku's voice came out small. "That's old Mohelo. He'd worked here since before I was born. Never hurt anyone in his life."

"I'm so sorry," Lono said. She put a hand on Aku's shoulder but he shook it off. "What do you think happened here?"

"Regent got here before we did, that's what."

"Should we go? What if they come back?"

"Let's just look around for a minute." Aku stepped carefully over a spilled rack of tattooing needles. "Maybe somebody's still alive."

At the back they took a set of twisting stairs that split repeatedly into walkways or more stairs as they led up to various rooms in the upper stories of the tree. Lono could look down into the main room at some points while other areas were completely private. Everywhere there was evidence of violent struggle; smashed furniture and kicked-in doorways, sprays of blood on walls. She didn't think the signs looked good for finding any survivors.

As they passed one closed doorway in a shadowed corridor, a door opened without warning and strong, calloused hands grabbed

Lono and Aku and dragged them inside before either could make a sound.

"He'll help us, you know." The old man's words echoed through the tunnel. Now the younger men who had pulled him away from the new prisoner walked behind him, as if in deference. "He just doesn't realize it yet."

"Yes, sir," one of the younger men said. "Shall I go ahead and light the fires?"

"Yes, why don't you do that?" the old man said. The younger man took off at a run.

Hulu hung back in the shadows, wondering at the changed deportment of the old man. He stayed well behind, advancing only when the others had moved far enough ahead not to notice him. The gradually descending tunnel was becoming wetter, with puddles growing more frequent and deep. At least the dripping water masked the sound of his footsteps. A drop plinked on his neck and rolled down his back. The cold felt good against his burning wounds.

Odd, this elaborate network, with frequent passages branching off. As far as he'd ever heard, the Puku was simply the flooding system for Middle Island, a place to drain off the drenching rains that came during the rainy season, which Regent had adapted for his own uses. But then, why so many tunnels, and why so deep? It was far more elaborate than needed simply to slough off excess water. It seemed almost like another city, beneath the one on the surface. Almost as if the city on top had been built on the ruins of some other place. But that couldn't be right at all. Hulu knew the histories, indeed, had copied them many times. The founders had built Atlantis five hundred years before, laying out the places for the temples, avenues, canals, and bridges, and yes, even the drainage system, as directed by the gods. There couldn't have been anything here earlier, could there?

Finally, the men turned into a small alcove and knocked rhythmically. Tap, ta-tap-tap, ta-tap-tap. A part of the wall opened with a quiet swish and admitted them, closing after they'd entered. Hulu felt the wall for seams, but found nothing. It was hard to see, as the nearest grating was far down the tunnel, but the wall appeared to be quite solid gray basalt. There was a crack here and there, but no more or fewer than any other part of the wall.

He cupped his hand and put his ear against it. Was it his imagination, or could he hear men's voices inside? Yes, there was the higher-pitched voice of the old man, the lower tones of the young men, and other voices too. A number of different voices, in fact, but no way to judge how many, let alone make out what they were saying.

Possibly a Ho'oule meeting place? Hulu had never given much consideration to how things in the Puku would work, assuming it was simply a non-stop violent orgy of all against all, insofar as he'd even thought of it. But it would make sense that the prisoners would form gangs to protect themselves and provide support, and if so, they would have their own spaces, as well.

He had no reason to doubt the men he'd followed were indeed Ho'oule, since of course Regent would toss them in here. Many Atlanteans had some sympathy for the Ho'oule and their fight against Regent. But as far as Hulu was concerned, they were simply making things worse, their campaign of poisonings and stabbings of high officials only feeding Regent's paranoia. And anyway, even if Regent's government did topple, however that might happen, what would the Ho'oule replace it with? Since nobody knew where Prince Ka'moe might be hiding, a restoration of the old monarchy seemed unlikely. An uprising would probably just replace one dictatorship with another, the only difference being it would be the Ho'oule on top.

Hulu found a recessed area across the tunnel and sat down. He could keep an eye on them from here. It was a better place than upstairs, with all the dubious characters hanging around. And maybe the old man would come out again later and he could ask him what he knew about his dreams.

EIGHT

The strong arms hauled Aku and Lono across the room and dumped them against a wall. A huge man, at least twenty hands tall and bald of head, loomed before them.

"I don't know who you two be, but you best start explaining your business," the man boomed.

Lono was so surprised and frightened she couldn't get a word out, but Aku exclaimed, "Tua! It's me! Aku!"

"Aku?" The man leaned over and peered into the boy's face in the dim light. "Why, so it be! I didn't hope to see you alive again. And I surely didn't expect you to come with a visitor."

Aku's words came spilling out in a mad rush. "I am alive! But I almost didn't make it. A Puhi hunter was chasing after me and I slipped down this hole and he couldn't come after me! And there were whisper birds, but I threw a rock and killed one, and then we ran here quick as we could—"

"Whoa! Start again, boy, and slower. You talk so fast I can hardly understand you." Tua clicked a flintbox and sparked a candle into life. With his other hand, he reached down and helped Lono to her feet. "To you, Miss, I must apologize for my rude behavior. You'll excuse me if I'm suspicious of company today."

Lono found herself dwarfed next to the man, who was as broad as he was tall and heavily muscled under his cloak. She couldn't quite place his slight accent, but thought it might be from the Eastern Islands. She noticed that despite his size he had sad, kind eyes.

"What happened here?" she asked.

"Hmph." Tua spat on the ground. "Shabengee guards. Seems they knew ahead of time about our little venture yesterday. Must have had Aku and Godi under surveillance for quite a while, and this place too, I'd wager. Word is, Godi's dead, and I assumed Aku here shared his fate."

Aku had a stunned look on his face and his voice came out hoarse. "Godi's dead?"

Tua put a hand on his shoulder. "I'm sorry you had to learn it like this, boy. I know how close you two was."

"First my brother, then Mohelo. And now Godi." Tears welled in Aku's eyes but he blinked them back.

"Aye." Tua sighed deeply. "The list of those we have to mourn for be long indeed."

Aku balled his hands into fists. "This isn't something to be sad about, Tua. This is something else to hate Regent for. To add to his list of things he'll be punished for."

"But is it safe here now?" Lono asked.

Tua considered a moment. "Oh, probably. For a while, at least. They killed two of our tattoo artists and their customers. Truth is, could've been worse. Tattoo parlors don't see much business during the day. The rest of the staff has scattered, gone underground already. I was just back here to pick up a few items."

Aku sniffled. Tua gave him a sympathetic glance. "I know it's hard, but tell me one thing, boy. This morning, at the winehouse, did Godi manage to give you an item? Something he took off one of the men there?"

"Oh, you mean this." Aku wiped his nose with the back of his hand and pulled the string with the bronze cylinder over his head. "Here, Tua. You have it."

"Good boy." Tua took it. "You wouldn't believe the trouble we gone through to procure this little item."

"What is it, anyway?" Aku asked. "Godi, before he... well, he said it was like a key."

"Sort of. More like a scroll, really."

"That's a scroll?" Lono asked.

"Aye, in a way. But it's in code, and you have to have a special way to read it." Tua inspected the cylinder, running his fingers over the etchings and round bumps on its side. "Supposed to tell us the place where Regent makes his whisper birds."

Yelling came from somewhere outside the building. Tua glanced about nervously.

"You know what? Might not be as safe as I thought." He hung the string back around Aku's neck and tucked it under the shift. "Here. If we have to split up, I try to make them follow me, and this cylinder stay with you. Now, we best be pushing off, lest Regent send a feather to check up on us. Or worse."

"Just as well," Lono said. "I have to get back. I've been gone long enough as it is."

"Get back?" Tua narrowed his eyes at Lono. "How come you to be trusting this girl, Aku?"

"Oh, Lono's all right. She saved my life. She and her freaky bird, pulled me up from where I'd slid down to get away from the Puhi."

"Please, I have to get back to the convent," Lono added. "My friend there is sick."

Tua laughed. "Back to the convent! I don't think that's a good idea. If Aku be right about the Puhi hunter, you won't make it fifteen minutes on your own."

"Of course I'm right!" Aku said. "He had the tattoos all over him, wiggling like an eel farm."

"Well, bring you with us it is, then," Tua said.

"But my friend, I have to see if she's okay—"

There was more yelling, closer this time, from the direction of the front door.

"You can return later, Lono." Tua kept his voice low. "A Puhi warrior catch you by yourself, he skin you alive and laugh while he do it. There be real danger about today and I think it best we move on together, and no dallying. First we cover our tracks, and then we disappear. And I knows just the place to hole up a good little while."

Kai lifted a weary head to survey the area. He had to blink his outer eyelid to clear the fogginess from his vision. The same rocky field they'd been in all day, but miles out from their starting point. How far had they gone anyway? He was sluggish from the cold currents, exhausted from the work and the heavy chains, and they hadn't eaten since breakfast. But he and the other prisoners had only collected half-full pouches of mother ink, so the guards weren't letting them head back yet. Kai stumbled over an uneven place and drifted to the ground.

"Get back up, New Meat," his neighbor growled low. "Before they see you."

Kai pushed himself up to his knees but couldn't do any more than that.

"Hey!" came the call from above. "Back to work!"

His neighbor tugged on the chain. "Look, you slow us down, we all pay. You want us all to get a beating or what?"

Another prisoner down the line added, "I promise you, New Meat, whatever the guards give us, the other boys and I will give you double tonight."

Kai struggled to get onto his two legs but could not find the energy. He could sense the guard swimming down from above and a spear jab into his lower back. "Back on your feet, prisoner! I said, back on your feet!"

The second guard was there now too. "If you are not back on your feet in three seconds, the whole line gets another hour!" The other prisoners groaned.

Strangely, Kai felt a vibration through his claws and his tail. Something in the ground, shaking. He lifted his head to see what was happening. The other prisoners had noticed too and were looking around. Though the guards were floating in the water above him, they also must have sensed it, for they glanced at each other uneasily. The vibration grew into a rumble and the whole seabed shook, and then it was over, fast as it'd started.

"Earthquake," some of the prisoners mumbled.

The guards conferred together for a minute, and then the

senior guard called out, "Okay that's enough for today. Time to head back."

Tua led Aku and Lono out the back of the tattoo parlor even as they heard the front door burst open. He held his finger to his lips to signal quiet.

He took them through a series of narrow alleys between endless rows of low rude shacks, made of little more than rotting wood boards and chunks of basalt, probably cast-offs from construction projects in finer parts of the city. They passed hanging laundry and painfully skinny children playing games, stepping over puddle-filled ruts in the packed dirt where flies buzzed in swarms. Lono found their trip through the mazelike warren to be dizzying, though Tua and Aku seemed comfortable enough. She'd never imagined when she and Iwali had looked out over the beautiful city that so much of it could be so miserably poor.

They spoke little and moved quickly. To Lono it seemed they must have redoubled or crossed their previous route half a dozen times. When Tua spotted a group of people on the path ahead, old women chatting in the sun, men drinking from gourds at a wooden table, they backtracked to find an alternate way.

After some time, they entered an area of more solid, stone dwellings. The dirt paths turned to paving stones, the children better fed, the clothes on the laundry lines less ragged. Just as the sun was setting, they stopped in front of their apparent destination, an unobtrusive gray building with a short stairway up to a wooden door.

Tua fished through the satchel he'd carried from the tattoo parlor, muttering something about a key. A caw and Lono's crow fluttered by, landing on the third step and hopping a bit in its awkward way.

Tua drew up short. "What deviltry be this?"

"Don't worry," Lono said. "He's a friend of mine. I was wondering if I'd see him again."

"This scruffy bird be your friend? The goings-on at your convent be stranger than I imagined."

"I didn't meet him at the convent!" Lono said in an indignant tone. "Well, I did, when I left early this morning. He was waiting by the door and he led me to Aku."

"So you've known him only for a day, then." Tua eyed the bird. "And he's followed us this whole way."

"I know he looks dumb," Aku said. "But I think he's the same bird who helped me against the Puhi warrior." When Tua looked skeptical, he added, "Flew in when he was about to slash me, distracted him just long enough for me to get away."

The crow hopped to the bottom step and let out a rough coo.

"Hm. He do seem uncommon sharp, for a bird," Tua said. "What be his name?"

"I don't know," Lono said. She considered a moment. "How about Keki?"

"Keki it is," Tua said. "And I hope he know how to keep quiet. He best come into the safehouse too, if he been seen with us. We'll find a crust of bread for him and something for our own bellies as well."

Keki emitted a low whoop, as if in agreement.

NINE

The light from the grating high above dimmed until Hulu was in complete darkness, his first night in the puku. The tunnel grew cold and he pulled his cape tight around him. At some point he began to shiver, whether from the cold or the mounting withdrawal pangs he did not know. Dull, aching pain throbbed across his back, while cramps fired unpredictably through his guts and limbs. He dozed when he could, but sudden excruciating convulsions of the muscles in his arms or thighs would jerk him awake. After some of these convulsive attacks, he would bend over on his hands and knees on the cold basalt floor and retch violently, though nothing but a few drops of stinging bile would spurt out.

After that, he could catch a short period of respite when he would squat, rocking back and forth on his heels, or sit if he felt too dizzy, his hair wet with sweat despite the chill, his member swollen with a painful erection that would not go away. *Alani, forgive me, but I'm glad you're not alive to see me in this state.*

There was a moaning in the tunnel and he shrank back in fear, until he realized the sound was coming from him. He kept going, though. Somehow the noise helped distract from the pain, if only a bit. He could concentrate on the low hum in his throat, let the vibration fill his head. And as the hours passed interminably the moaning turned to screaming, non-stop shrieks that kept awareness of the gut-boiling cramps from at least a part of his brain. He wondered if he was deep enough in the tunnels that the other prisoners couldn't hear him. He hoped so.

The light from the grating began to gray. Hulu heard men's voices speaking over him. He wasn't even sure when they had approached.

"Pathetic wretch, ain't he?"

"He knows where we are now. Better bring him into see Malu."

Hands grabbed him rudely and carried him through a large number of rooms. He couldn't count how many, or how they connected. The light from torches and candles stabbed shafts of intense pain through his eyes and into his head. It seemed to him he must be hallucinating, for many of the rooms were richly furnished with elegant furniture and hand-crafted tapestries. Finally, the hands dropped him in a heap on a woven rug and left.

It wasn't so bad in here. Dry and warm. A single candle flickered on a simple wooden table. A few other items on the table as well, but he felt too sick and delirious to have much curiosity about them. He returned to his moaning, crowding out the nausea with the sound in his head.

After a time a door opened and people entered. More than one, perhaps three. One of them leaned over him.

"Look at you now."

Hulu opened an eye. He was a bit confused. It looked like the old man from earlier, but he was different now. Dressed in a fine kihei shawl, white hair combed. He stood taller, without hunching, in control. Surely not the same person? But no, he had one blue eye and one cloudy one. There could hardly be more than one person with eyes like that. Was he the Malu the men in the corridor had talked about?

"Malu?" Hulu croaked from his parched throat.

"Yes, that's me. And you're Hulu, the scribemaster, no?"

Hulu gave a nod.

"Such a shame, Hulu," the old man said. "You've gotten sick on your beautiful long locks and your fine cape."

Hulu did not speak, but he was suddenly aware of how undignified he must look. And smelled, too, reeking of dried vomit, body odor, and stale sweat. He disgusted himself. He tried to concentrate, brushed caked hair out of his face, got himself together enough to notice there were two other men in the room, standing at attention. The same ones who'd accompanied the old man earlier, carrying him away upstairs? He couldn't tell, couldn't remember.

Malu picked up something on the table. A green leaf, broad and flat. He took pinches of something from several small bowls and sprinkled them on the leaf. Finally, he picked up a vial and dropped out three fat black drops onto his blend. "You know what this is, don't you?"

Hulu did. His attention was fixed.

Malu rolled the leaf carefully and lit the end with the candle. He brought it to his lips and drew the smoke in deeply, holding it in his lungs. When he exhaled, he blew in Hulu's direction, enveloping him in a sweet and spicy smoke. Hulu's brain went bright with the trace smell of mother ink. He forced himself to stay calm.

"Like I said earlier," Malu said. "We have something in common, you and I. Would you like some of this?"

Hulu did not answer.

"Well, maybe later then. Who was the girl in your dream?"

Hulu's words came out hoarse and guttural. "I don't know what dream you're talking about."

Malu laughed, but it was gentle. There was something oddly sympathetic in his manner for a Ho'oule terrorist. "Come, you of all people should know better than to lie to me now!" He took another drag, the end of the rolled leaf glowing red as he breathed in. "The young lady, she was quite pretty, no?"

"I don't know who the girl was."

"Ah, that's better. The truth. Unfortunate, though. I suppose the young lady must remain a mystery." He held out the cigar. "A bit of this? I know it will help you."

Hulu shook his head.

"Have it your way." At the table, he arranged the items,

covering the bowls, capping the vial. "What's it like for you, anyway? The ink truth, I mean?"

Silence.

"For me, it's like rain, dropping on a lake. Each drop hits with a little plink, a perfect pattern. But a lie, that's like a pebble. A pebble somebody threw from shore, and when it hits the surface, it's a ker-*plunk*. It disrupts the pattern, you know?"

No response.

Malu sighed. "I guess we won't be needing these things," he said to the other two. "Go ahead and put away everything on the table. Afterwards, take our friend here back to the tunnels. Somewhere deep, where he won't bother anybody while he screams."

Hulu felt a wave of cramping coming in his legs. *Not now. Not in front of these men.* But trying to stop it only made it worse, and he spasmed across the rug, lightning shooting from his feet through his thighs, straightening his body out, followed by a vortex of pain that doubled him over and left him gasping in the fetal position. When he recovered he looked up. The men were putting the things on the table into a sack. Malu was stepping out through the doorway.

"It's like a dance," Hulu called out.

Malu stopped and turned around.

"A dance, with everyone all in time, all the steps harmonious. Only a lie, it's somebody missing a step. It's that instant when the dance breaks down."

"Interesting," Malu said. "I wonder why a dance. Not exactly apropos for a scribe, is it?"

"My late wife and I...." Hulu stopped. Why was he talking to this man? Telling him about Alani? His own private memories, paraded before a terrorist.

Malu came back into the room and squatted beside him, put a hand on Hulu's arm. "Your late wife. I bet she was beautiful. You used to dance with her?" His cloudy eye was inscrutable, but his blue eye was kind. Hulu found he liked the old man despite himself.

"Yes."

"But she's gone now?"

Alani's face appeared in Hulu's mind as it'd appeared at the end, sunken and sallow with disease, her eyes haunted with pain. "Yes."

"How long?"

"Two years."

"Regent." Malu snarled the word.

"No." Hulu shook his head. "She was just sick. It was quick. Unexpected."

"I'm sorry, my friend," Malu said, and Hulu believed he really meant it. "We have things we need you to do for us. If you agree, we can end your suffering, this shameful state you're in. You'd like that, wouldn't you?"

"What would I have to do?"

"Nothing terrible. Something only you can do. Scribe for us. The truth, nothing else. Will you do it?"

The truth, that's all. Even as they talked, Hulu felt another cramp building inside, another nauseating wave. Hulu didn't know how he could stand another attack. Anything would be better than more pain.

He tried to fight it, push the cramp back down. But it grew and grew. This was going to be a big one. He could already feel it stiffening his legs, his back, his guts, up the nape of his neck and through his head. He could stop it, though. It would be so easy. Simply cooperate with this kindly old man.

"Okay!" Hulu whispered. "I'll... I'll do it."

"Very good. You've made the right decision." Malu rose and clapped his hands. "Put the things down, Wi'he. We'll be using them after all. Go make a cup of pala tea for our guest. And a hot towel, so he can clean up. And afterwards, we'll let him sleep."

...Hulu let the ink overtake him, and it was as if his waking life were the dream and his ink-dream the reality. He found himself strolling through a great manor, almost a palace, with dozens and dozens of rooms. Though dark, he could see perfectly well, and the cold stone floor felt as real to him as if it were under his own bare feet. More real, actually, for every crack, every small rise or rough place felt distinct to him in a way that he would never notice while awake.

Each room held a few simple pieces of furniture and a low bed, simple spreads of woven cloth looped at the corners to thick wooden stakes. In each bed slept a young lady, perhaps in their late teens, sleeping unclothed beneath rough white sheets.

But why had the mother ink delivered him here? Hulu continued on, quietly opening the doors to each room and closing them behind him, stopping at the beds to let his gaze pass over the girls. Some had clear skin, others freckled, some with curly hair, others straight. A few snored or stirred in their sleep as he watched, but most simply lay still, breathing quietly. Were these real women or mere constructs of the ink dream? Dreams could be for exploration, expressing or acting out one's truest feelings and desires, no matter how taboo in real life, could they not? He already felt heat rising up through his body, the threads of the robe against him as sensorily dense as the stone floor had been moments before.

Still, he sensed there was a purpose at work, that the mother ink had chosen this place for a reason. It would not be fit behavior for him to indulge himself, to pick any lovely young thing he chose and do just what he felt. Perhaps the ink was even testing him. Hulu walked on.

He arrived at still another bed, and halted immediately.

A face almost, but not quite, familiar. Features so similar to Alani's it almost made his heart break anew to see one so like her, so young, as in the *happy days after he and Alani had first been wed.*

Something tickled his foot. He glanced down. A little spider made its way across his skin. He bent and scooped it into his hand, let it walk on its jittery spider legs across his palm. Two yellow crescents on a broad abdomen: a lunar spider. A good sign, a symbol of romantic ardor. Yes, this is where the ink wanted him to be. The spider reached the edge of his hand and anchored a web from its spinneret, lowering itself slowly to the floor and scurrying under the bed.

Hulu brushed the web away and returned his attention to the girl. He studied her round face, her brown skin, her black curly hair spread across the pillow like a hand fan. She lay peaceful in repose, chest rising evenly under her sheet. One arm rested atop the covering, her right one. On her forearm, near the crook of the elbow, a raw, raised place, in the shape of a telescope. It reminded him of his own welted back. He took a finger and traced along her reddened skin. The girl shifted and moaned lightly, then opened her eyes, and smiled slightly at seeing him.

He wanted to draw the sheet back, see those pert breasts, discover if they were as beautiful as he remembered Alani's, if her bottom was as round, her thighs as soft. He knelt down and inhaled the clean scent of her hair and gently, gently placed his lips on hers. She kissed him back, then took his hand and slid it under the sheet, guiding it down her body and between her legs...

TEN

Shish! Shish!

Lono's eyelids snapped open and it took her a moment to realize where she was and remember how she'd gotten here. The rush through the alleyways to the safehouse, the dinner of hardtack and warm water, the settling into rough blankets on the floor. Her heart was still racing and her breathing heavy from the dream. Another of *those* dreams. She repeated the familiar exercise to settle her breathing and racing heart. *Ne Wa'e, be with me. Please help me. Please help me control the dreams.*

Why was she having them? How could she be so brazen, so forward with a man she didn't even know, and in her own room in the dormitory, no less? Was it just a harmless nighttime reverie, or something more serious? Were these dreams a reflection of her true inner self, a shameless, sinful creature who forgot the teachings of the Sisters as soon as she closed her eyes?

No! That's not me! It's something else, something being sent to me.

Shish! Shish!

What was that noise? Without moving, Lono scanned the dim room, lit only by a bit of faint gray light from around the drawn curtains. She concentrated and found she could make out the details of her surroundings, ignoring the tingling that came from the area around her tattoo. There was Aku, mouth open with his head resting on his hands as he slept across from her. Keki perched on the top log in a woodpile, head tucked under a wing. Tua she did not spot anywhere. Maybe he was outside. If he hadn't abandoned them in the middle of the night.

Shish! Shish! There it was, emerging from the woodpile and undulating on hundreds of legs across the floor: a huge red centipede, at least two feet long. Lono choked back the scream in her throat, pushed down the urge to shrink away. Noise or movement would only attract its attention.

Ne Wa'e, be with me!

Now the centipede was between her and Aku, its head raised and antennae twisting as if trying to find something, its mandibles opening and closing. Lono spotted a loose piece of wood near her, a small log, only an arm's-length away.

Aku snorted and rolled over in his blankets. Even as the centipede turned its head and *shish-shished* toward his bedroll, Lono leapt up and grabbed the log in a smooth motion, bringing it down onto the centipede's spine, breaking through with a crack about halfway down its body. The log bounced off and rolled across the floor.

The centipede spun, Aku jerked awake, and Keki let out a caw of surprise. Lono backed away as the centipede, walking with a crooked step but still very much in motion, approached her with clicking mandibles. She searched for something she could use out of the corners of her eyes. Her log was on the other side of the bug and the woodpile was too far. Maybe a blanket from her bed, to cover the creature's head? She wouldn't have the element of surprise this time, though. She doubted she could be quick enough to move before it struck her.

Her back hit the wall and the centipede continued, liquid venom dripping from the serrated inner edges of its mandibles. Lono felt very exposed in only her long barkcloth blouse, nothing covering the skin of her lower legs or arms, not even shoes on her feet if she had to kick. The centipede advanced, nearly in striking range.

The door opened and Tua stepped in. The centipede froze in the sudden cascade of light and Lono snatched a blanket, jumping onto the centipede's head and holding the blanket over it. It thrashed powerfully in her arms but she held on tight.

"Quick! Do something!" she shouted.

Tua was across the room in an instant, stomping the centipede's writhing body over and over with his heavy boots while Lono held the blanket down as tightly as she could. Keki flew around the top of the room cawing. Finally, the centipede's body let out one final twitch and the legs went limp.

"Ne'i Maki in the heavens," Aku said from where he still sat wrapped up. "What the hells was that?"

Lono didn't even bother correcting Aku's blasphemy. "Thank you, Tua. I don't know what I would have done."

"You would've done your best, girl." Tua studied her eyes a moment. "And even against that monster, I think I'd still bet on you. Now everybody get up and get ready. We head out in five minutes. If they sent this thing, they know we're here."

"Are you sure?" Lono asked. "It came out of the woodpile. Maybe it just lived there."

""You ever seen a blood centipede this size? Or one that come after people, instead of scurrying into some dark hole?" Tua shook his head. "Ain't natural. This is one of Regent's servants."

"So where are we going now, Tua?" Aku asked.

"First, to the convent, to deliver Lono back where she belongs. Second, we've got to make contact, so we can hand off that cylinder of yours."

Kai laid back on the high promontory with the other dozen prisoners, basking in whatever filtered sunlight they could catch on their morning break. It wasn't warm, exactly, but Kai had learned to take whatever bit of heat he could get and hold it inside, storing it and meting it throughout the long day.

"Hey, New Meat," one of the prisoners called down the line.

"What you done to get stuck with us, anyway?"

"They said it was trespassing," Kai answered carefully, not sure how much to trust this superficially friendly question. "Our rival clan."

"Yeah, and was you trespassing?"

"I was in the neutral ground the whole time. Hunting a mudsucker to take back to my home lagoon for dinner. Not even near the line."

"Ha, so you's here for nothing!" the prisoner called. "I knowed it. We's all here for nothing. Take Pepehi, he here for nothing."

"Damn straight," Pepehi said.

"Yeah, that's right," the first prisoner said. "He hunted down a kai-man 'cause he din't like the looks of him, kilt him in his sleep, mated with his cow the whole night, and in the morning kilt the hatchlings for good measure."

Pepehi grinned with his gap-teeth. "And I did it like it was nothin'."

"See, New Meat, you here for nothing. Pepehi here for nothing. We all here for nothing!"

"I guess some nothings got a whole lot more nothing to 'em than others," another prisoner remarked to general laughter.

It got quiet then, with a bit of warm current making the water comfortable, the mother ink field they were searching that day spreading out gray below them, but the open ocean in the distance deep green and shading into blue near the surface.

"Man, wouldn't you like to just swim out there and leave all this?" the prisoner next to Kai said.

"Look pretty, don't it?" one down the line said. "But you ever get the chance to escape, you stick to the coast."

When nobody else said anything, Kai asked, "Why stick to the coast?"

"Don't you know, New Meat? Out there is the Pentapi Empire. No way, you don't want that. Stay close to shore. Don't matter how many rival clans' territories you got to go through, you wait until night and sneak through."

"Why?" Kai said. "What's wrong with the pentapi?"

"What? Ain't you never heard about the pentapi?"

Kai shook his head.

"Listen, New Meat, and listen good. They's worse'n you can imagine. I heard they captured one kai-man and peeled off his scutes while he was still alive. Pulled out his claws one by one and laughed when he screamed. Plucked out his eyeballs and played catch-the-marble with 'em. Sliced him open slow and dined on his organs while he was still watchin'."

"Basically, made a night with Pepehi seem like a party on the eve of High Summer's Feast!" someone called, and they all chuckled.

Kai had more questions. Who was this kai-man who'd been so abused? How did the report of what happened to him get back? Had any of the others ever actually seen a pentapus? He didn't get a chance to ask them, though, because the guards were already swimming towards them and hollering.

"Alright, break time's over. Back to work!"

ELEVEN

The tower of the Observatory peeked through breaks in the trees and Lono quickened her step, leading Tua and Aku along the route. They were almost there now and her adventure about to reach its end. Only a little while more and she would see the Great Meadow rising up to the convent's familiar dining halls and classrooms, its lush walled gardens, all the acolytes and Sisters... and Iwali.

Would Iwali be recovered, healthy, full of stories of what had happened since Lono had left? Or would she still be sick, perhaps even worse than before, wondering where her best friend had been when she needed her most?

Lono was all but running up the footpath when Keki swooped down and landed right in front of her. She nearly tripped over him but took a leap at the last moment, tumbling in the dirt and pushing herself up in an instant. "You stupid bird! What do you think you're doing?"

A large hand on her shoulder, and Tua's voice spoke low. "Hold your temper, girl, and your tongue. I think he knows more than we do."

"What do you mean?" Lono replied, catching Tua's sudden worry and lowering her volume to match his.

"Best we proceed with care, not abandon," Tua said. "And let's move off the path."

He gestured with his forefinger for Lono and Aku to follow him, striding into the trees, checking their surroundings as he went.

Keki stayed behind, making little clicks at them, but not moving from his spot. They hadn't gone more than thirty yards when there was a rustling and Aku held his palm out for them to halt. He pointed at a pine tree in the direction of the tower. A large blackbird sat on a high branch, bigger even than Keki, with the telltale bare patches along its back indicating Regent's tampering. Its gaze was intent on the footpath, and it seemed not to have spotted them yet.

Aku squatted and felt around on the ground. Lono knew he was searching for a stone to throw, but she doubted he could hit the bird from this distance. Anyway, he didn't seem to find one. Now a pair of other birds fluttered and settled on a branch near the blackbird, huge orange-ish vultures with gray heads and cruelly curved beaks. Even from this distance, it was evident there was something wrong with them as well, an abnormal bend in their posture, an unnatural rumpling in their feathers. The blackbird hissed as if greeting them.

"Bearded vultures," Tua breathed. "Bone eaters. Come on."

They retreated through the trees for several minutes, still avoiding the footpath. Finally, Tua stopped. "Okay, we're out of earshot. As you can see, girlie, we have a problem."

Lono's irritation at this delay to her homecoming crept into her voice. "I thought bearded vultures only lived in the mountains."

"So they do, but you saw 'em as clear as me," Tua said.

Aku put his hands on his hips. "Let's just find some good rocks, and I'll go back and pelt them."

Tua laughed. "I wouldn't try it, boy. I'd hate to mess with a normal bearded vulture. Add in whatever evil Regent's done to this lot and I'll pass altogether. You see those beaks? Rip you to shreds in a minute."

"I'd drop them before they could get me."

"I'm sure you'd get the first one," Tua said. "But what about the second? And they may not be alone either. I think it likely the woods near the convent be full of nasties."

"How do I get back then?" Lono asked. "Can we go around

them somehow? Approach from the back?"

"I don't think so," Tua said. "Even if we find a way to get you in, those birds be watching all the time. Put you in serious danger, and anyone you know if they see you together."

"What are you saying? That I can never go back?" Lono felt herself on the verge of tears. *What will Iwali think if I never return?*

"Not today, *'one.*" The corners of Tua's mouth turned downward in sympathy. "I'm sorry you get mixed up in this."

Lono tried to hold them back but it was no good. Hot tears fell down her cheeks. Aku muttered something about girls and turned away, but Tua put an arm around her.

"Hey, hey. No need to cry. We'll try another path another day. We'll get you home yet."

"How?" Lono sobbed.

"I don't know yet," Tua admitted. "But we'll think of something. For now, dry your eyes. We still got business this day, and I fear it's not safe to tarry here too long."

Hulu selected a swan feather quill, suitable for the large letters and broad strokes he would need for the poster. He spread the large parchment across the writing desk and dipped the tip into the inkwell. He'd prepared the mixture himself, one hundred parts standard ink, one part mother ink. A fairly weak preparation, but for a simple message it would be sufficient for any readers to sense the truth of what they read. In plain but neat letters, he spelled out the words:

Do not despair, O people
Prince Ka'moe is alive
His day is coming

The dance went smoothly as he wrote, each step in its place, each dancer keeping the beat perfectly, each letter in perfect attunement with reality. When he finished, he checked over his handiwork and set the poster aside to dry. He immediately started on the next one. Malu wanted twenty ready by midday to hang in strategic spots around the city.

His mind wandered as he worked. Prince Ka'moe would be nearly twelve years old by now, only a couple years until he reached the age of majority. Would he come and reclaim his throne at that time, and extract vengeance on Regent for his exile to boot? But with what army? If he was somewhere on the island of Atlantis, any attempts to raise men would be known instantly. Regent had spies everywhere. Perhaps the rumors were true and he had taken a ship overseas, to one of Atlantis's trading partners on the edges of the Great Ocean, hiding among the grain growers of E'kip to the east or the aromatic herb traders of Senakomaka to the west.

When he had finished his task, he rose, stretched his legs, and put on his crow feather cape. Malu's men had cleaned it for him and returned it, salved his wounds, provided him a small but excellent blend of herbs and mother ink to smoke every morning and evening. Nor could he object to any of his work so far—posters, mostly, conveying simple truths. No, he couldn't complain about any aspect of his treatment by the Ho'oule.

Hulu wandered through the elegant rooms, taking time to admire a third dynasty glazed vase and a polished obsidian statue of beautiful Nihea, who had been kidnapped by the giants and rescued by Prince Hrea. Malu didn't seem to mind Hulu exploring, so long as he didn't try to leave. Not that Hulu had any interest in returning to the dank prison above, anyway.

From what he could tell, this complex of rooms, deep within the puku, was the nerve center of the entire Ho'oule operation, with Malu constantly sending instructions or assigning men to perform errands in service of the various Ho'oule cells around the city. How these men made it to the outside world, Hulu had no idea. He still abhorred the Ho'oule's actions and their consequences—their robberies of royal storehouses and assassinations of high officials had only led to a greater crackdown by Regent, an ever-escalating cycle of reprisals and atrocities by both sides. Yet, in actually meeting Malu and some of his men, he had come to believe they were sincere in their desire to bring down Regent and restore the real ruling family, even if their methods were questionable.

After a few minutes of wandering he found Malu, dressed in a fine pale blue kihei shawl, dictating a message to a pair of attendants. Malu held a finger up when he saw Hulu, bidding him to stay.

This particular room was itself something of a mystery to Hulu, holding a strange mechanism in its center set on a stone dais at waist level. With its intricate bronze gears and rods, he puzzled over this apparatus every time he passed through. He supposed it was some sort of machine for determining the dates of festivals and feasts based on the position of the moon and stars, but he had never seen one this elaborate or large before, being about the size of a great dog. Nor did he see the dials where one would align the configuration of heavenly bodies, as would be necessary for the calculation. Instead, there was a panel of numbers and letters imprinted on miniature wheels, although they didn't spell anything recognizable.

Malu sent the attendants off on their duty and turned his attention to Hulu. "Done already?"

"In comparison to the deeds and tax documents I copy most often, I'm afraid your tasks are rather simple," Hulu said.

Malu smiled. "Oh, we'll have more work for you as time goes on, I assure you."

Hulu reached out and idly turned a small handle protruding from the machine's bronze casing, but stopped suddenly when the wheels shifted, changing the letters and numbers on the panel.

Malu raised an eyebrow. "I see you're interested in this. One of our finest acquisitions from Regent. Go ahead and continue turning the handle."

Hulu did and the wheels continue to rotate. They didn't spell anything intelligible, though, seeming to be just a random assemblage of characters.

"How does it work? I can't find any dials to put in the moon phases or star signs."

"You misunderstand its use." Malu stepped over to a shelf on the wall and picked up one of several small bronze cylinders. "But understandably so. This is rather odd, but I think you'll get the idea when I show you." He dropped the cylinder onto a spindle on the top of the mechanism and pressed it down, where with a click it slipped perfectly into a gap in the machine. Malu then turned the same handle Hulu had turned, causing the cylinder to rotate. As it did, the wheels on the panel spun as well, flipping around until the letters formed recognizable words.

Eleventh hour – shipment mother ink – The Skatefish – two barrels – divert to Imi Au'o

"It's a way to…read codes?" Hulu said.

"Exactly," Malu said. "I should've known a scribe would catch the principle right away. It's so Regent can send out his secret commands, and no one the wiser. Except us."

"But what's Imi Au'o? I've never heard of that place."

"Not a place, a person. A servant of Regent."

Hulu nodded. "I'm amazed at what you have down here. Really, I don't understand how it's even possible. The code reader. The artwork. The furniture. The food. The mother ink. Where does it all come from?"

"All liberated from Regent and his allies." Malu chuckled. "As for getting it down here, you'd be surprised what a guard can overlook when he's been properly, shall we say, reimbursed."

"I see," Hulu said. "Still, who would ever have thought a place like this could be located in the Puku?"

"Ah, but what better place to hide than in a prison?" Malu said. Giving Hulu a wink, he added, "And for that matter, what better way to disguise the head of the Ho'oule than as a doddering *'ele*?"

Hulu did not respond but glanced around the room at the ebony furniture, the gold-threaded tapestry hanging on the wall, the intricately-woven carpet under his feet, all demonstrating that the fight to topple Regent provided surprising material benefits.

"You're skeptical," Malu said. "You think we're no different than a criminal enterprise, that we spread terror across the island and justify ourselves with idle talk of resistance even as we enrich ourselves and live in luxury."

"I didn't say that." Hulu chose his words carefully. "But it does seem a bit like a game, doesn't it? Staying in here concocting your plans in peace while sending your pawns out to carry them out."

"Ha, I knew you were thinking it! It's all over your face every time we meet." Malu removed the cylinder from the spindle and put it back on the shelf. "Tonight I want to show you something. Something I think will explain a bit about why we do what we do. Then we'll see if you still think it's just a game."

TWELVE

The vast plaza around the Ne'i Zuub's temple teemed with stalls selling honey, herbs, medicines, and all sorts of flowers, fruits, and vegetables, one of the city's main markets and a busy scene befitting the religious house dedicated to the god of bees. The temple itself rose in eight tiers, each level covered with varieties of flowering trees and bushes, its walls draped with blossoming vines, a giant garden soaring into the sky. And of course, everywhere, the buzzing and erratic flights of fat, happy bees, never brushed off or cursed, but welcomed as a critical link in nature and a symbol of the gods' bounty to mankind.

Lono and Aku munched on honeycomb drenched in rose petal syrup, sitting next to each other in a dark alcove while Keki pecked at a dropped kui nut at their feet. Across from them a bronze fountain sprayed streams of water from a sculpture of a hive into a broad low basin where children gleefully splashed. The two hadn't seen Tua for half an hour, but he'd left them strict instructions not to move unless they felt themselves in danger, in which case they were to flee to a certain stall he had pointed out.

That was fine with Lono. Her feet ached from two days of non-stop walking and she enjoyed simply sitting here, although she did wish she could join the mothers and lovers sitting on the lip of the fountain, feeling the heat of the sun and the cool spray of the water. But they had to remain out of sight, lest one of Regent's agents spot them.

"What would an agent of Regent look like, anyway?" she

asked. "How will we know if we see one?"

Aku snorted. "You're so stupid. Don't you know anything?"

"I'm just wondering," Lono said. "I don't think you really know what an agent looks like, either."

"Oh, I know. And if you thought about if for one second, you do too. You saw the whisper birds, the vultures, the centipede."

Lono's forehead furrowed. "That's not what we're looking for here. Of course, if it's a giant centipede, we'll know it's bad. But what if it's just a person? It's not like they'd be wearing any special clothes, right?"

"Don't worry about it and eat your honeycomb," Aku said with an eyeroll.

Lono continued to watch the rush of people go by with fascination until Tua's boots clomped in front of their space. He squatted down and peeked in. When he spoke, his tone was brusque. "Good, you're both still here. Come on out, let's go."

"What about your contact?" Aku asked. "Did you meet him? Don't you need the cylinder?" He was on his feet and already reaching in his shift but Tua slapped his hand away.

"Don't bring that out here, in front of all these people! You know better than that."

"I...I'm sorry, Tua," Aku said, his expression hurt. "I just thought you'd need it."

"Well, I don't, at the moment. And I didn't meet the contact. He wasn't there." Tua frowned. "Three hours past midday at the Hornet's Nest pub, that was the agreement. I just hope Regent ain't got to him." He looked at Lono and Aku meaningfully. "And that's something we need to discuss."

"What do you mean?" Lono asked.

"I mean, the safehouse weren't safe, and the path to the convent weren't, either. And now Iule weren't there, when he never been late before, not by a single minute." Tua eyed Keki, who'd finished with the kui nut and had moved onto poking at a bit of honeycomb, oblivious to their conversation. "Somehow Regent know where we'll be before we get there. And how do you suppose that is?"

"Someone's been following us, without us knowing?" Lono said. She didn't like the way Tua was looking at Keki.

"We'd know," Tua said. "It ain't like we ain't been on the lookout."

Aku touched his finger to his chin. "Maybe they knew about the safehouse all along, and that centipede was just waiting for whoever showed up."

"Yeah, maybe." Tua reached down suddenly and grabbed the crow by the neck. "Or maybe your bird here's been tipping 'em off."

"Let him go!" Lono grabbed Tua's thickly muscled arm with her hands but couldn't make him drop Keki, whose eyes bulged out from the force of Tua's grip, his wings beating weakly. "It wasn't him!"

"How do you know, girlie?" Tua asked. "He showed up just after the Puhi when you never seen him before, and he's been there every time we've been found out since then. Every. Single. Time."

The crow let out a strangled gurgle and Lono beat on Tua's arm with her fist. "Stop it! It wasn't him, I tell you!"

A thin, slight man with a mustache stepped out from a passing knot of people and tapped Tua on his shoulder. Tua whirled around but instantly his expression changed from anger to surprise when he saw who it was. "Iule! There you are!"

"Sorry to be running late," the man said. He stank of cheap moonplum wine and his brown barkcloth cloak seemed dirty and disheveled. "Is that crow bothering you?"

"I...no, we're just having a discussion." Tua released his grip and Keki dropped to the ground. Lono picked the dazed crow up and held him in the crook of her arm, stroking his head.

"Quite a loud discussion," Iule said. "It's how I found you. And it seems I'm not the only one to notice." He gestured at the fountain, where the crowd of people had stopped their activities to watch the goings-on. "May I suggest we find a quieter location? Preferably someplace I can get a drink?"

"Ah, Hulu, there you are." Malu took the last bite from his plate and handed the dirty dish to an attendant, wiping his mouth. He rose from the sofa and gave a little bow. "Was your dinner to your satisfaction, I hope?"

"Yes," Hulu said. "I can't complain about your treatment."

"Well, I can't complain about your work. You've done a good job for us, everything on time and just as we asked."

Hulu nodded. He still wasn't sure what to say about praise from a man like Malu. For that matter, he still wasn't sure what to make of this refined, erudite, elderly head of a terrorist organization.

"I can't blame you for your skepticism of our methods, Hulu. If I were in your place, I would feel the same way. And I promised you an explanation earlier." He moved to a sideboard where several small bowls sat, and began mixing the herbs they held. "Would you join me in a smoke?"

Hulu really preferred truth-smoking by himself, finding his habit shameful. It was almost time, though, the lack of mother ink in his system already gnawing on the edges of consciousness. "I suppose."

"Good." Malu carefully spread the herb mixture on a long green leaf. For the final touch, he picked up a small crystal vial and dropped out ten fat beads of ink. The black liquid soaked into the little trail of crushed herbs on the leaf, leaving it glistening darkly. He expertly rolled the leaf together and lit it from a candle, handing it to Hulu.

Hulu drew in the smoke and held it in his lungs, handing the rolled leaf back to Malu. They took a seat next to each other on the sofa, passing the leaf back and forth. The dosage was higher than Hulu was accustomed to, and he settled back in the sofa in a state of total relaxation and mindfulness, his perceptions of his surroundings heightened. He became aware of the individual knots of the carpet's weave under his feet, the cool texture of the sofa pillow behind his head, the interlacing floral and spice aromas of the herbs in the smoke.

"It's time," Malu said, the slight rasp of age in his voice, with a bass undertone and higher pitched resonances.

"For what?" Hulu asked, his own voice sounding distant in his ears.

"For the explanation. Will you join me?" Without waiting for an answer, he took Hulu's hand in his, rubbing his fingers across Hulu's palm and fingerpads, as he had on that first day they'd met. "Close your eyes and let your body relax."

Hulu did, and when he breathed in, the faint sweet aroma of Malu's cologne mixed with the remnants of the smoke in the back of his throat. Malu's fingers felt good against his palm, and he could distinguish individual ridges on Malu's fingertips, the smooth edge of a fingernail. When their bare feet touched, neither drew back. Tension drained from Hulu's muscles.

"Good." Malu's mouth was close enough to Hulu's ear that he could feel his warm breath. "Quiet your mind and let it open. When you're ready, let your thoughts slip into the All-Dream."

...Hulu and Malu wandered hand in hand through the extensive rooms of an ancient kimunu tree. Filthy cages filled the rooms, full of birds of every type, including species Hulu had never seen before. The birds were frightened by their presence, backing away to the far side of the bars as they passed, some letting out pitiful peeps but most silent except for the ruffling of feathers.

From somewhere came a horrible warbled shrieking. It went on for long seconds and stopped again. Hulu glanced at Malu's face, but if Malu was disturbed by the shrieking, Hulu could not tell.

Some of the rooms they entered held huge glass tanks or large ponds raised from the floor in giant wooden tubs, emitting warm smells of algae. The fish in the tanks and ponds reacted much the same as the birds, swimming away as soon as they sensed the presence of the intruders, darting to the far sides of their enclosures.

As Hulu and Malu advanced through the rooms, climbing stairs and ladders to reach different levels of the tree, the birds and fish grew stranger and sicker. Some had extra parts grafted on, superfluous wings or fins or even second heads, drooping lifeless and dead-eyed. Others had been molded into abnormal shapes, weirdly elongated or twisted. Nearly all had long scars or raw wounds with stitches from recent surgeries, especially along the spine at the base of the head. Hulu's stomach churned to see the painful injuries. He wanted to turn back, to leave this place, but his feet propelled themselves without his input.

In the rooms near the top of the tree, the birds and fish were angry and aggressive, glowering with wild eyes at Hulu and Malu or rushing at them, banging against the bars of the cages or glass walls of the tanks that enclosed them. The birds began to make noises, not chirps or songs, but angry hisses. Their smells were rank mixtures of uncleaned cages and putrefying flesh.

The warbled shrieking continued to start and stop, mounting in volume as the two climbed higher.

In a room at the very crown of the tree, Malu pushed a door open. Inside was a large chamber lined with dozens more cages and tanks, filled with frightened animals. Hulu noticed a huge water tank on the back wall with a ray inside, its wings propelling it silently through the water. The ray's body was light gray with a darker gray patch around one eye, and when the ray saw Hulu, they locked gazes. Hulu felt a wellspring of sadness open inside him. He turned his head away, and the feeling waned.

On a silvery table in the middle of the room, under a skylight to provide illumination, a crow was mounted on its back with tiny bronze chains binding its feet, head, and wings, a huge wound opened in its chest. A tall, slender, bald man with a badly scarred face stood above the bird. He wore a closefitting barkcloth tunic imprinted with red and green spiders, influential symbols of control and dominance. He held a dropper from which he squeezed beads of mother ink into the bird's bloody gash, only the ink came out brown and thin. The earthy smell of the ink combined with the strong metallic odor of blood.

"Yes, yes, there you are, my darling," the man muttered while he worked. "That will help the pain, won't it now?" He set aside the dropper and a black-robed assistant handed him a small obsidian blade and a bronze hinged instrument. Somehow in the wavering torchlight his face was not visible but his hands seemed hyperdetailed as they worked, their pale blue veins and carpal bones playing underneath the mosaic of his skin.

With the hinged instrument he stretched the wound wider, and with the blade he slowly cut away strands of fat and muscle, then sliced through the rib bones underneath with a dull ticking noise. The crow's head pushed back as far as the chain allowed and it emitted another of the warbled shrieks they'd heard earlier, only this close it was ear-piercingly loud. Hulu felt his stomach sicken and his consciousness began to rise...

"Not yet!" Malu grabbed his hand. "You can't wake up now. One more room."

"No more!" Hulu said. "I've seen enough!"

By way of answer, Malu only pulled him out of the operating room, back down the stairs and ladders and past the cages and tanks and frightened animals, down to the very heart of the tree. There he pulled open a heavy trapdoor in the floor and they descended a final set of winding wooden stairs.

In a damp underground chamber lit by ensconced torches, with walls formed by the roots of the kimunu, a huge octopus stretched across one entire side, its eight arms bound to the walls and floor by hooks driven through its flesh. A system of tubes hanging from the ceiling bathed it in intermittent sprays of water that flowed down its deep blue body, mottled with white, dripping onto the floor where little rivulets glinted in the wavering torchlight and flowed into the valleys between root tendrils.

The octopus writhed continually, its head squeezed awkwardly to one side, so that one great blue eye regarded the arrivals. The center of the body was sliced and held open with bronze retractors, revealing the glistening organs inside. A tube attached to a sac in the body cavity wound out to a pan on the floor, where a brownish liquid dripped continually. Realization hit Hulu like a blow to his skull.

It was the brown ink the Shabengee supplied the scribes to write their sham histories. This was where it came from. They were trying to make their own mother ink.

THIRTEEN

Hulu gasped and his eyes shot open. He pushed himself to his feet, repulsed by what he'd just seen. Malu beside him opened his eyes as well and lay back on the couch, panting from the intensity of the dream.

"Do you see now?" Malu asked. "Do you see why we do this? Why no assassination can be too terrible, if it can be used to turn the people against Regent?"

"The brown ink." Hulu shuddered, thinking of all the times he and his scribes had written falsely with the brown ink given them by the Shabengee, never knowing where it came from. "And it's where they make the whisper birds."

"Yes, I believe so. Those angry creatures will be twisted and broken until they are loyal servants. And as you can see, the whisper birds are only a start. Regent has a whole menagerie of abominations he's waiting to unleash on us."

Hulu paced across the room without speaking for a minute and stopped. "But if you know about this place, why not destroy it? The Ho'oule have committed any number of atrocities. Why not burn this place to the ground?"

"Well. I'll argue your use of the term atrocity another day, and simply agree we would love to destroy this place." Malu shook his head. "We've been searching. We know it exists, but of the actual location we have no clues."

"No idea at all?" Hulu said.

"We thought we had one lead, but that operation has gone

terribly awry." Malu looked at the floor. "Multiple agents dead, some still missing. A cover business burned, with employees and customers inside. It's obvious Regent doesn't want us to succeed in this."

"But in the All-Dream, you could find out, you of all people." Hulu recalled Malu's tattoo, the one he'd seen inscribed on his back his first day in prison: Honua, the octopus, the emblem of dreams. No wonder Malu had so much control in the dream, able to share the vision with others, to go to the place of his choosing. "You could go outside the kimunu and see where it's located."

"You think I haven't tried?" Malu said. "I have power, yes. But you know how the All-Dream is. In some ways you have complete freedom to do as you will, but the All-Dream must be coaxed, like a skittish kitten. It can't be forced."

That did ring true. Hulu had made love to unknown women in his ink dreams, choked the life from Captain Ino with his bare hands, even flown in the sky, but it was unpredictable. The ink guided you, and you could guide the ink, but you couldn't push. You had to act without thinking, in a way, proceed intuitively and without guile. Strategizing was a sure way to get released back into the waking world.

Another question occurred to Hulu. "The man with the knife conducting the operation. That wasn't Regent himself, surely. Regent is said to be corpulent and fleshy. Who was it? Do you know that, at least?"

Malu smiled grimly. "That, my friend, was Imi Au'o."

"You should really watch yourselves, you know?" Iule said, taking a long sip from his wine glass. Sweat beaded on his forehead and his eyes darted around the small winehouse nervously, though its dim lighting and basement location in a worn-down building off an alleyway suggested it wasn't the kind of place where patrons stuck their noses in others' business. "Avoid drawing attention to yourselves in public."

"We can take care of ourselves, thank you," Tua said from the chair next to Iule's. He regarded the greasy, smudged water glass in front of him and pushed it to one side. Lono sat in her chair with her arms still cradling Keki, glaring at Tua, while Aku slurped his glass of bubbled sea lime juice.

"Oh, I know you can," Iule said, leaning forward. "All I'm saying is, the word is out. The sole survivor of the tattoo parlor massacre, the kid who showed up a Puhi hunter, and the missing girl from the convent? They're not going to forget that. It might pay to keep out of sight."

Tua gave Iule a cool look. "We wouldn't have been in that situation outside if you'd shown up on time."

Iule threw his hands in the air. "Sorry, friend. I had to make sure no one'd followed me. You got a lot of heat on you nowadays."

"Well, what do you propose then?" Tua asked.

Iule drained his glass. "You give me the cylinder, that takes a lot of the heat off. That's the main thing they're interested in, anyway. Once you get rid of that, the three of you can get out of the city real quiet and don't come back."

"Let's get it done, then," Tua said. He nodded at Aku. "Bring it out, boy."

Aku pulled the cord from around his neck and held it out. Iule snatched it up and rolled it back and forth in his hand, ran his fingers over the bumps and indentions. "Don't look like much, does it? I wonder what you're supposed to do with it, anyway?"

"Maybe this," Tua said. He had quietly sidled his chair closer to Iule's, and now swiftly thrust a knife into the side of his throat. He grabbed Iule's hair with one hand and held his head down on the table as blood burbled out Iule's mouth, while bringing a finger to his lips with his other hand to shush Lono and Aku, who both stared with wide eyes.

When Iule stopped struggling, Tua withdrew the knife, wiped it on Iule's cloak, and replaced it in his tunic. He took the cylinder and handed it back to Aku. "Come on, time to go."

"I'm not going anywhere with you," Lono said, trying to keep her voice from shaking.

"Hurry now," Tua said impatiently. "I'll explain it all on the way."

"No." Lono wiped her eyes and found they were wet. "You choked Keki and you just murdered this man in cold blood. You go alone."

Tua remained calm. "I know you're shocked and angry, 'one, and I promise you later I will make a personal apology to your feathered friend. As far as Iule, ask yourself this: Why was he late? He's never been late before. And when he showed up, how did he know you were missing from the convent? Outside of the convent walls and the present company, who could even know who you are? Only the Puhi, or one in contact with them. Iule is the one who betrayed us, and I'm sorry I ever suspected it was Keki."

The corner of Lono's frown twitched. She had to admit it did make sense. Didn't it?

Tua continued. "Iule was right about one thing, though. We are in great danger, all three of us, and I suspect Regent's men are even now on their way. So I plead with you, save your tears for later and get on your feet, because we have to go."

Lono rose, reluctantly, still mulling over his words in her mind. Aku followed suit. On their way to the door, Tua dropped a couple copper coins on the counter.

"Your friend okay?" the barkeep asked, nodding his head towards the slumped Iule.

"Too much wine, that's all." Tua pulled out another coin, a silver one. "Here, this is for you if you leave him be. Just let him sleep it off."

"Aye, boss." The barkeep took the coin and slipped it in his pocket. "He look comfortable enough, don't he?"

"That he does," Tua said, herding Lono and Aku toward the exit and into the alleyway outside.

The light gray ray with the dark patch around one eye swam slowly from one end of her enclosure to the other. Her tank was big enough, she supposed, but nothing like the wide-ranging ocean she had once swum in so freely. She kept a wary eye on the wicked man, who had restlessly paced his lab for hours. She could sense the waves of worry and paranoia coming off his mind as easily as she could tell a cold current from a warm one. He hadn't performed any of his foul experiments all day, at least, but that might only mean he was planning something more depraved than ever. Gray-Patch wondered idly what evil designs he was concocting in his agitated state.

Not that she would ever mind-tap him to see his thoughts. Apart from the distaste of making contact with such an abhorrent creature, there was the practical matter of not wanting to reveal to him the intelligence and abilities of her species. Best to continue playing the part of the dumb beast. She would be a victim of his surgical tools soon enough, no need to draw his attention and rush the process.

Unless…there was a way out? The two visitors who had abruptly walked in the lab earlier, the elder one, and the younger, gentle one with the long hair she had mind-tapped. Even in their brief connection she had perceived his sympathy for her situation. Perhaps they could help? True, it had been only their dream-selves, not their physical selves. The wicked man had not seen them, of course, though it was their opening the door that had set off his current frenzy, giving him reason to believe there were intruders about. But now that the visitors knew of this place, the profane operations the evil man conducted, altering creatures, using the ink to prolong lives and suffering long past their natural limits….

Gray-Patch prayed that the two would be back.

PART THREE

When King Kanai set out on his journey, he stopped at a certain orchard, for the fruit there was good. And while he tarried, the daughter of the owner came out to prune the branches of the trees. When she saw him, she was frightened, but he took the pruning shears and pruned the branches for her.

"What is your name?" Kanai asked the daughter. She was doe-eyed and beautiful, and she answered, "Who are you that you should ask me such a question?"

Kanai laughed to hear her answer. But when he kissed her, she did not refuse him. And afterwards they both had tears in their eyes.

She ran to tell her father and her father came out to meet the man who had kissed his daughter. And he embraced Kanai and brought him to his house and asked him to dwell there as a guest. And when Kanai asked for her name, he told him, "Abakalia, for she is beloved by her father."

Kanai abode about a month there, and at the end of that time, he and Abakalia were married with her father's blessing.

--from the *Chronicle of the Dynasties*

FOURTEEN

As exhausted as he was, but still Kai had not been able to fall asleep. Perhaps the story of Pepehi's crimes had troubled him, or perhaps it was the sliver of moon shining into the prisoners' grotto, but all night Kai's thoughts chased each other in circles. He longed for his home lagoon. His hatchlings would be stronger in their swimming, almost big enough now for their first long swims, and he was not there for it. And did beautiful Kaipo, with her long, graceful tail, the elegant green scutes along her back with their double rows of creamy bone spikes, and the low sexy growl of her voice, wait for him still? He missed the days of swimming and hunting at leisure in the warmth of the mangrove waters, the nights putting the little ones to sleep with stories of their ancestors, the great battles and hunts, and afterwards mating in the balmy moonlit waters. And everything growing and lush, light filtered verdant through the abundant mangrove growth, everywhere greens and yellows and blues, not the dead gray that seemed to cover everything here.

A tremor disturbed his reverie, slight at first, so that Kai thought it was one of the other prisoners snoring. But it grew into a rumbling that could be felt in the rock. That was no snore. Kai glanced around. The other prisoners had felt it and were awake now, too.

"Ground not too stable here," Kai said.

"It happens," another remarked. "Go back to sleep."

"Shaddup, both a you," came a voice from down the line. "'Less you want a tail lashing."

Kai closed his eyes and tried to calm his mind. But he'd barely done so when the tremor returned, tenfold, a great rumbling that shook the grotto and everything in it. Now all the prisoners were up and active in the roiling water, shouting and roaring and pulling each other with chains in every direction.

A fissure cracked open beneath them and water flushed away in a powerful flow, sucking the prisoners down. They caught onto the nearly vertical cliff face that had suddenly formed in their grotto, Kai at the top with the others strung out below him, the water rushing around them. Kai clung to the side with all his strength. He could see the grotto opening above him, ripped open to several times its original size, and the graying sky beyond that. He tried crawling towards it, digging his claws into the rock face and heaving forward, but the bronze chains held him back.

"Break the chains!" somebody yelled, their voice barely audible above the roar of the current. "It's our only chance!"

Kai looked frantically around. Break the chains with what? A glance down, and he saw the prisoners below, some like him clinging to the rock, but at the bottom of the line, three or four prisoners twirled helplessly in the swirling water. His next neighbor down somehow managed to claw out a protruding rock and held it with both hands, smashing against the chain that held him to Kai. Once, twice, and finally on the third time the chain broke.

Kai had been the critical anchoring link, for only seconds after his freeing, there was another great rumbling and a powerful rush of water pulled the rest of the line of prisoners from the wall. They disappeared, spinning into the blackness.

Kai carefully climbed his way against the current and over the top of the opening. The whole landscape outside the cave was a mass of churning, turbid water and sediment that Kai could hardly see through, and as he swam to the surface for a gulp of air, all the debris of the ocean seemed to stream around him. He descended again and found a perch that felt solid enough. He clung there he knew not how long. An hour? Two? Or merely minutes, and it only seemed longer?

At last, ground and ocean calmed themselves and silt began filtering out, allowing the sun to dawn into the hazy water. Kai rose and considered things. He swam down the fissure until the light had nearly faded in the depths, but saw no sign anybody was alive. It seemed hopeless to go farther in search of the other prisoners. Surely they were dead, pounded to pieces at the bottom or covered in rubble, or perhaps still being pulled down to the center of the earth in that mighty suck of water. He could not truly say he felt sorrow at their deaths, but even Pepehi deserved a better death than that. He floated slowly back up to the ocean floor.

Under a nearby rock he saw something curious. A bit of loose cloth, flapping in the water. Maybe one of the other prisoners had also escaped, only to be crushed? Kai hurriedly swam over and planted his legs against the ground, heaving the rock up. Underneath, a burlap sack floated up. He grabbed it and untied the drawstring. It was full of the oily globules of mother ink, hundreds of them. This must be where the guards stored it overnight.

Kai took the sack and swam around a bit more. No signs of life anywhere, neither guards nor prisoners. He glanced out to sea. That would be the easiest way. But what about the Pentapi Empire? *If there even is such a thing*, he thought. Still, best not to take chances. He started swimming northwest, towards shore and home.

With the first tremor Hulu looked up from his table where he was copying out some Ho'oule financial records. The shaking passed and he returned to his task. "Nema 'Gwu is angry, as they say," he mumbled to himself. Small tremblors weren't too unusual in Atlantis, and anyway, Hulu was caught up in his work. The documents provided a fascinating look into the Ho'oule organization. Most Ho'oule income seemed not to come from theft of government storehouses or shipping, as he might have thought, but rather from the revenues of a network of somewhat shady but legitimate businesses: winehouses, moneychangers, message runners, even a quite profitable tattoo parlor.

The second rumble caught his attention, and didn't stop. After the shaking had gone on for several seconds, knocking over candles and juddering the solid stone walls, Hulu grabbed a torch from a sconce and headed out the door. There were shouts from other rooms. He wasn't sure how many tons of rock might be overhead, but he remembered how high the grating in the corridor had been that first night he'd spent in the Puku. He'd rather be on top of that rock than underneath it.

In the vestibule, Malu was already organizing his men for a flight from the prison. In flickering torchlight that struggled to provide light through the rising dust, Malu orchestrated order from confusion, sending attendants for documents and valuables, ordering burly porters to stack crates and trunks. One man came in hefting the bronze code-reading mechanism. Malu pointed to Hulu. "Give it to him."

"Me?" Hulu asked, taking the heavy apparatus. "Are you sure?"

Malu kissed him on the cheek and spoke into his ear. "You're the only one here I trust with the code reader, my friend. The others wouldn't appreciate its value. I know you won't abandon it unless your life is truly in danger."

"I'll do my best," Hulu said.

"I know you will." Malu gestured to a large man with a prominent hooked nose and dark, close-cropped hair that Hulu had seen attending Malu a number of times. The man carried a torch in one hand and bore a rough, heavily packed sack on a strap over his other shoulder. "Follow Kaneke here. You two should take the back way."

"Isn't the front gate closer?" Kaneke asked.

"Yes, but we can't trust the guards to have opened it up, rather than fleeing in panic. Back way's a better bet. The rest of us will be no more than a few minutes behind you. If it's safe when you get out, wait for us."

Kaneke set off into the tunnels of the Puku at a quick stride, Hulu following close behind and trying to keep track of Kaneke amid the dust and bits of rubble crumbling down around them.

FIFTEEN

Though the journey back to the shore should have been only half a day, weird currents slowed Kai's progress, sometimes sweeping him up and carrying him miles back before he could escape their stream. He swam nearly to nightfall. Many times he considered dropping the sack of mother ink as a hindrance, but each time something told him to hold on to it. *Might prove useful at some point*, he reasoned.

Everywhere along the way was the same—dull gray ocean floor stirred up by the earthquake, interspersed by rocky ridges covered with mud and debris. Even the earth's magnetic lines, which all kaimen could feel and which normally provided them an unerring sense of direction, were in flux, so he was not even exactly sure he was headed the right way, and at times became almost hopelessly lost. He was exhausted and hungry. But still he kept on. *What else is there to do?* he thought. *I won't reach home any quicker by giving up.*

Now, after so long without color, interest, or most importantly, food, he came over a final ridge and beheld spreading before him a coral basin full of greens and reds and purples, illuminated by the setting sun to the west, busy with life, sloping up to the tip of the mainland of Atlantis in the distance. His heartbeat quickened a bit seeing the beauty of the valley. It was still a trip of a week or more to the mangroves, of course, but for the first time, he felt he was truly on his way home.

He descended into the warm waters, slinking close to the ground, keeping among the seagrasses. He didn't have the energy to catch a real meal, but before long he found a colony of what his people called starve crabs, because you'd only eat them if you were starving. *Well, so I am,* he thought, and snatched one, crunching its shell between his teeth and sucking out the scanty meat inside. Not quite stomach-filling, but it would have to do.

Nearby he came across a protected hole where he slept fitfully, and when morning came, he woke and continued on his way north, following the shoreline. He had only traveled an hour or so when the water began to grow warmer. Not pleasantly warm, like the coral reef, but really, uncomfortably warm, and positively hot as he advanced.

Still, heat was better than cold after so many weeks in the mother ink fields and he soldiered on. He reached a place where the water ahead of him glowed faint orange. He floated to the surface for a gulp of air and for the vantage of height. Several miles ahead there was a huge underwater mountain he did not remember from his original journey, with reddish-orange liquid bubbling out of its top and creeping slowly down its sides, the heat undulating the water above so it all appeared blurred.

Kai swam onwards but it wasn't long until the temperature became unbearable and he couldn't continue. He would have to go around the strange mountain, and that meant a choice. Either he could swim out into the deep, or he could crawl up to the surface and go overland, through the territory of surface men. He did not relish an overland journey, but he remembered the other prisoners' story of the cruel pentapi. At least in the world of surface men he could possibly trade some of the mother ink they valued so highly. Overland it was, then. He gripped the sack and headed towards dry land.

Hulu and Kaneke emerged blinking from a hole on the craggy edge of Middle Island, the smooth waters of the Wai River flowing below them, the massive stone abutments of the Southern Road bridge towering over them. They took a minute to catch their breaths, having made their way through shuddering tunnels while carrying their loads. *Amazing*, Hulu thought. *A completely unguarded, ungated entrance to the Puku. No wonder the Ho'oule can get in and out at will.*

From overhead came the sound of bridge traffic much heavier than normal for this early in the day. The squeaky rolling wheels of laden carts, heavy footsteps, murmuring, weeping, shouts here and there. At one point coordinated stamping, and Hulu could see the tips of spears over the bridge railings. A company of Shabengee guardsmen, no doubt. They scrambled a bit up the slope to get a better view of the bridge traffic and the city.

It was still an hour or more before dawn but Hulu's heart almost stopped when he observed how bright the sky was, an orange glow reflecting against the low cloud cover and interspersed with black ribbons of smoke rising from several parts of the city. Fire, of course. Hulu slowly spun, counting areas of particular brightness that must be the center of conflagrations—busy Portside, the wealthy Cho district, the quiet neighborhoods along the Mountain Road, the dense slums of Bonetown with Mount Ipu silhouetted behind them, even the low-density Wool Quarter around the Temple of the Sheep. Neither rich nor poor had been spared.

What there was no sign of, not after a few minutes, not even after half an hour, was anyone else emerging from the opening. Hulu and Kaneke glanced at each other uneasily.

"I think we should go back in," Hulu said. "They might need our help. Relight your torch and we'll go."

"I disagree," Kaneke said. "If they're not out by now, either they went to the other entrance, or it's too late for them."

"But they could be caught in a tunnel collapse. We could help dig them out."

Kaneke shook his head. "If so, there's little we'll be able to do. Perhaps if we were a whole team of men.... No, we should be on the move. This is a lawless night and I do not believe it would be good for us to be caught here."

"So that's it?" Hulu said. "You're just abandoning Malu when he may be in need?"

Kaneke stiffened. "If it puts ourselves in danger for little reason, yes. The cause is bigger than one man."

"Very well," Hulu said. "I'll go back in. Give me the torch."

"Here, take this also." Kaneke dropped his sack to the ground with a clink. He untied the drawstring and pulled out a handful of bronze and silver coins. "You might need it."

Hulu pocketed the coins in a pocket inside his cape. "Malu entrusted you with the Ho'oule treasury, then."

"What I could carry of it, yes."

"And now you can live like a prince, I suppose," Hulu said.

"Even after spending these days with us, you still doubt us?" Kaneke regarded him coldly. "Should Malu be dead, this money will go towards rebuilding. Finding new recruits, funding new operations. This earthquake does not mean the end of the fight against Regent."

"Yes, of course," Hulu said, embarrassed at his crass assumption of the other man.

"If Malu is still alive, he will know how to find me. If not, I think it best if we don't meet again." Kaneke turned away and began climbing the slope towards the bridge.

"Good luck," Hulu called after him. Kaneke did not look back.

Lono woke up early, as the sky was only just beginning to gray. She'd fallen asleep instantly from sheer exhaustion the night before, after she, Tua, and Aku had arrived at the cabin deep in the halipi tree forest, fleeing the chaotic city in the aftermath of the earthquake. She wrapped her cape around her and carefully opened the cabin door so as not to wake the others. Outside, she set off on the footpath, hoping a walk would clear her mind.

She had hardly had time to consider the events of the past few days, to try to make some kind of sense out of them. First, Tua's killing of his contact at the winehouse, their quick flight from the area around the Temple of the Bees to avoid Regent's agents, sleeping rough in an alleyway in Bonetown. Then waking before dawn the next day to the earth's rumbling and shaking that had toppled buildings, cracked streets, and sent masses of panicked people streaming out of doors, many weeping for lost loved ones or praying out loud for mercy from Nema 'Gwu, the earth goddess.

At Tua's urging they had left the city immediately, joining throngs of people headed along the Southern Road. Throughout the first day the crowds had thinned as the people found shelter along the way, inns or farmhouses where the owners might let a few souls stay. By the end of the second day, they were the only travelers left on the road. Seems this cabin was a Ho'oule safehouse Tua knew, a place where wanted men in Atlantis could lie low for a few weeks far from the city.

Perhaps Tua himself had had need of it at some point? She still did not know whether she could trust him. "Explain to me again why you killed the man in the winehouse," she had said to him during their journey.

"Aye. I did promise you an explanation, didn't I?" Tua had responded. "It's easy when you think about it, *one*. When Iule didn't show, I knew something was wrong, because I've been passing him things for years—Ho'oule business, you know—and he was never late before. So Regent's got to him, I figured. And that's why I thought poor Keki was too blame. The wheels in my head was turning too fast."

Keki had clicked with a bit of irritation from where he'd landed ahead of them on the road.

"That's right, bird. Not your fault. See, then Iule does show up eventually, stinking drunk, and he lets slip this knowledge of who's chasing us and who's missing from the convent. And maybe that's the word on the street, like he says. Or maybe it's something he knows from dealing with the enemy. And where's he been all this time, anyway, I asks myself? Giving us up, that's where. He'll meet with us, get our guard down, and deliver us some place with no fuss for Regent. And when this suspicion comes to me, I try to see Iule's eyes to know if it be true, and he won't meet my eyes. He just looks away. So I know in that moment it's him, and I give him the knife. You see, *'one?'*"

"But why'd he want the cylinder, Tua?" Aku had asked. "What's this thing for?"

"That I don't know, boy. But it's important somehow. We got to find a way to pass it on."

"Shouldn't we stay in the city then?" Aku had said.

"No, too dangerous. No telling what places might be compromised by Regent, or collapsed by the quake. We come back later. After things calm down and Regent forget about us."

Lono replayed the events and the conversations in her mind, trying to judge the plausibility of Tua's statements, the strength of his arguments. He was open and clear about his reasoning, and she couldn't see where he was wrong. But something about it all seemed off. Maybe it was the way he'd killed an old friend on a mere suspicion.

She shook her head. Probably she simply wasn't used to the violent world Tua and Aku seemed so familiar with. She hoped she would never become accustomed to seeing a man get killed. At least now they were here, in this beautiful but remote place, under the pleasantly fragrant halipi trees, with their twisty, overspreading branches and long, whiplike leaves. It reminded her a bit of the grounds at the convent.

And what about the convent, and her friends and the Sisters? Were they safe? Had the towering observatory remained intact, its strong stone foundations bearing up to the forces of the earthquake? Or had the centuries-old walls cracked, the great telescope collapsed, perhaps some people she'd known her entire life buried under tons of rock, or among the crowds fleeing the city? What of Iwali, maybe still ill, unable to move herself? Her throat tightened as Lono imagined Iwali trapped in an air pocket in the rubble, still alive but in great pain, too weak even to shout out for help.

"*Caw!*" came a short blast from a branch overhead.

"Oh, Keki, there you are. You wanted to come on the walk with me too?"

The bird chattered at her.

"You're right. I'm dwelling too much in my own misery. *Feeding one's worst thoughts is a vain indulgence,* as the Prioress would say. Let's get back and see if the others are awake, shall we?"

Back at the cabin, Lono was surprised to find a neat pile of mistberries on the front stoop. She plucked one from the pile and popped the fruit into her mouth. It was perfectly ripe, firm and bursting with tangy-sweet juice when she bit down. Tua must have found them. She gathered the whole pile in her cape and brought them into the cabin, emptying them onto a table in the center of the room.

Aku and Tua sat up from their blankets when she came in. They rose and the boys stuffed themselves with huge mouthfuls. At the end, there had been plenty for all and even a few left over.

"I have to thank you, young Miss, for bringing us breakfast," Tua said, wiping his mouth on the sleeve of his shift.

"Oh, it was no problem," Lono said. "They were already on the front step. I just brought them in. I assumed you'd gotten them."

Tua had a strained expression on this face. "So you didn't gather these yourself?"

"No." Lono's stomach dropped. "And you didn't either?"

Aku spit his last mouthful to the floor. "It's Regent, isn't it? They're poisoned."

Tua put a hand on Aku's shoulders. "Calm yourself, boy. The berries are fine. It wasn't Regent."

"Who was it then?" Lono asked.

"The Tree Folk," Tua said.

"The who?" Aku asked.

"Oh, the Mehani!" Lono said. "We've learned all about them. They come out at night carrying their beautiful lights, but you can't watch too long lest you become entranced."

"True enough," Tua said. "And you must know why you don't accept a gift from them, too."

"Well, I don't think we got to that part," Lono said. *But I bet Iwali would know. If she's still alive.*

"Figures," Aku said. "All that learning but nothing useful."

"Shush, boy," Tua said. "The reason you don't accept it is because it ain't really a gift. It's a trade. And now we have to leave something out before nightfall. Something the Tree Folk will find of equal value."

"And what if we don't?" Aku asked.

"Then they'll take something from us of their choosing. And sometimes, their choice be a person."

SIXTEEN

Hulu sweated and gasped for breath as he carried the heavy bronze code reader through the streets and alleys of the city. The air was smoky and thick from the fires burning throughout the city, the streets full of people at this early hour, some on urgent errands, others simply wandering aimlessly. Perhaps their homes had been destroyed, or maybe they merely feared the aftershocks that often occurred in the hours and days following a quake.

Hulu himself was covered in dirt and grime from his earlier digging in the Puku. He hadn't made it more than fifty yards in the tunnel before his way had been blocked by a rockslide. He'd tossed aside stones and pawed through soil for an hour, but made no more dent in the earth than a child digging a hole for play. He'd finally had to give up when the torch had run low. *I must not lose hope, though*, he reflected. *Perhaps Malu managed to escape out the front entrance after all.*

The light was dim even now that the sun was rising, its rays filtered by haze from dust and smoke. Nobody paid him much mind, everybody else being concerned with their own urgent business. On one side street, a five-story building began to collapse on itself even as he passed by, a weakened side wall crumbling and the roof falling in. Men and women fled from the structure, one young lady holding an infant and screaming about her young son still left inside. Other neighbors ran back in to dig out the debris and try to find him. Hulu considered stopping to help, but what difference could he make? He'd already tried once to save someone once, back at the Puku, and found one man could do nothing. And besides, he had his own mission to complete: protect the code reader.

He had to admit some satisfaction when he reached the very center of the island, passing through the Grand Plaza, with its imposing statuary honoring the Shabengee and overlooked by the Temple of the Shark, the Shabengee headquarters. Back when the site had been a place for the worship of We Honua, the octopus, the delicate workmanship of the aquamarine tiles covering its great octagonal walls had been the pride of the city. But that was ten years gone, before Regent had converted it. It felt like an act of justice that today, two of those immense eight walls had fallen, bringing down a portion of the soaring dome they supported. Black-garbed Shabengee guardsmen swarmed, removing rubble in a confused fashion, appearing not like sharks at all, but like helpless ants after their anthill has been crushed by a giant foot.

Across the plaza from the temple, Hulu skirted the Kumu House, the massive and ancient kimunu tree, spreading across acres of land, and the seat of Atlantis's government. Finally, he reached the Scriptorium. Going in the front gate was out of the question, of course, but peering through the latticework built into the brick wall, Hulu was gratified to see somebody in the garden. A figure in the simple brown hooded robe of an under-scribe sat quietly on a bench, his head in his hands as if weeping.

"Over here," Hulu called in a loud whisper.

The figure glanced up and hurried over to the bars. "Master, is that really you?"

"Ah, Opio! It's so good to see you again. Is there much damage from the earthquake?"

Opio wiped his eyes. "Not to the physical structure. Plenty of spilled supplies, of course. A fallen candle caught a store of parchment on fire, and we had to put it out. And naturally with Captain Ino's men hindering rather than helping the whole while."

"Naturally," Hulu said.

"Still, all in all, I think we were lucky this morning." He gazed at Hulu with hopeful eyes. "But without you, Master, this place is hard to bear. Captain Ino took over the minute you left. His men misuse us and do nothing but make our work and lives a misery, beating us badly for the slightest infraction. Have you been released? I don't suppose you're here to take back your old position?"

"I'm afraid not. You could call me an escapee."

"Oh, I see." Opio's eyes grew large. "It must be dangerous for you to be hereabouts then. Captain Ino bragged you had already been executed, although most of the scribes didn't believe him."

Hulu chuckled grimly. "I bet he'd like to carry out the sentence personally, if he had the chance. Listen, Opio, can you do me a favor?"

"Anything, Master, only name it."

"I have here something very important." He held up the bronze mechanism. "Do you think there is someplace you could hide it where the Shabengee won't find it?"

"Yes, I think so," Opio said. "What is it?"

"I'll explain when I return for it. Oh, and one more thing. Is there any way to get me some Mother Ink? Any amount is fine."

Opio's face turned thoughtful. "Not from the main storeroom, of course. But I think there is likely a room where we have a cruse that hasn't been mixed yet. All our work came to a halt amid the confusion this morning, as you might imagine. Yes, I think it can be done. Shall you pass me your item over the top of the fence, and then I go look for the ink?"

"Very good."

With some effort Hulu passed the bronze mechanism to Opio, who carefully took it and was about to turn to go.

"Say, Opio," Hulu said. "What's that smell? Is something burning? I thought you said the scribes had put out the fire?"

"Oh, master," Opio said. "Let me put this away and bring you the ink. There are many fires about the city."

"No, this is nearby. I can even hear the crackling of flames. What's happening, Opio?"

Opio's face was stricken but he didn't respond.

"Tell me now, Opio. What are they doing to my Scriptorium?"

Opio turned his head away. "Captain Ino's men are burning the scrolls in the garden."

"All of them?" Hulu said, his voice disbelieving.

"Well, not the contracts and financial records. But the legends and histories. They're emptying the storerooms even as we speak."

"Are they now?" Hulu said numbly. The storerooms of the Scriptorium contained one of the greatest libraries in the city, with scrolls going back five centuries, many written in the hand of those who had witnessed the events they described. Hulu had spent countless hours simply wandering among the shelves, pulling down and reading unique ancient scrolls that had never been reproduced anywhere. "All the scrolls, you say?"

Opio's looked back at Hulu and his eyes filled with tears. "Yes, master, every one. I heard one guard say they're doing it all over the city."

For a moment, Hulu imagined himself leading a charge of scribes against the Shabengee, shoving them aside, rescuing the priceless scrolls. But he shook his head. *Put that foolishness out of your mind. They are heavily armed, and the scribes defenseless. It would be a hopeless bloodbath. There's nothing to be done here, nothing.* "I'll just wait here for the ink, then," Hulu said to Opio. "Be careful and don't let them see you."

Kai hid himself in the thorn scrub, observing the two fishermen on the beach below. A father and a son, he thought, tying their boat up at a small wooden dock. He had been headed north for two days and found overland travel slow-going. True, the sun was warm enough that he felt energetic, especially in the afternoons, and could trot along at a nice enough pace. But at least twice a day he had to find a body of water to slip into for an hour or so to moisten his cracking skin. And then, too, the food situation was tougher on land, where he was not as nimble as in the water. Only a cache of turtle eggs he'd dug out on the beach on the first day had kept him going thus far.

The boat below held the promise of two solutions to his problems, however. First, he just might be able to trade for a meal. Second, if the fishermen had successfully plied their trade this day, it meant the sea was back to its normal temperature here, and he could resume his journey in the water.

He pulled himself up on his hind legs and walked as the surface men do, approaching the two slowly and with his arms spread, to show his good will. He spoke a bit of the surface men's language, having dealt with traders in the village near his home lagoon.

"Goood daay," he intoned when he stepped onto the dock. He could tell he was in luck, for there was a stack of big, juicy, spiny mackerels in the boat, some still wiggling. His stomach growled at the sight.

One of the men, the younger one, looked up from his business with the ropes. His eyes widened and he shouted. "Hey, get out of here!"

"Haave iink," Kai said. He held the bag out to show his intention. "Iink for youuu. Waant fiissh."

Now the older man had scrambled onto the dock, holding a machete. "Get back!" He held the blade up. "I mean it! Scram!"

This wasn't going well at all. He wasn't sure the surface men even understood he was trying to communicate with them. "Noo haarm. Waant fiissh."

The older man advanced, now within striking range. "Beat it! Get the hell away!"

Kai stepped towards the water, but stopped on the edge of the dock, wavering. Should he try again to talk? The negotiations seemed to have broken down, but he was so hungry. The old man lifted the machete above his head, convincing Kai of his course. He launched himself off the edge and leapt into the boat, snapping a mackerel in his snout, and slipping over the side into the water where he glided smoothly into the water.

As he chewed, he gazed far out to sea. Somewhere out there, the Great Kai-man lived, and watched over all his children. Surely the Great Kai-man had watched him steal the fish. Yes, he had done what he could to trade fairly with the surface men, and they'd refused to even offer him basic courtesy. Yet stealing was against the Great Kai-man's law, no matter how badly the surface men had behaved.

The mackerel was fatty and juicy, the first good food Kai had eaten in weeks, but it may as well have been sand in his mouth.

Tua rifled through his satchel, pulling out tattoo needles, a couple scraps of parchment with sketches, keys, his flintbox, bits of yarn. He regarded the pile with a frown. "I don't think any of this will satisfy the Mehani. Maybe we can try the flintbox."

"Let's give 'em *this* stupid thing," Aku said, taking the bronze cylinder from around his neck. "It's been nothing but trouble since the moment I got it. And before, actually."

"'Tis a temptation," Tua said. "But why don't you hold onto that? I don't know exactly how we deliver that at the moment, but we will, and it was worth Ho'oule lives."

"I have something." Lono pulled a ring from her finger, a simple silver band. "I can give them this. It was a gift from my friend, Iwali. Would the tree folk find this worth the trade?"

Tua picked up the ring and inspected it. "They might at that, girl. Still, there is one more possibility, though it's not my place to give it away." He pulled out one final item from his satchel and held it out to Aku.

"A flute?" Aku said, taking it and inspecting the polished wooden instrument. "Did this belong to Godi?"

"Aye. He left it with me at the tattoo parlor the day before your last mission. I think he had a premonition he wouldn't make it."

Aku held the tip up to his lips and blew on it but nothing happened.

Tua laughed. "Let me show you, boy." He arranged Aku's hands so his fingers were positioned over the tone holes and placed the blowhole under his lip. "Now blow gently on it, with the air passing over the hole, not into it."

Aku did and a pure, sweet tone filled the cabin.

"Very good." Tua took one of Aku's forefingers and placed it atop the first tonehole. "Now press down firmly and blow again."

Aku did and another dulcet tone came out, this one a half step higher than the first.

"There you are. You're a natural already. As you should be, considering your father."

"I remember him playing, I think," Aku said. "When I was very little."

Tua raised his eyebrows. "You would have been very little indeed. Your father died ten years ago."

Aku's voice had taken on a vague tone, as if he was struggling to recall. "He was playing with Godi and some other men. A man with a lute, another with a tambourine. We were in a…fancy room, with tapestries and high windows looking out over the city."

"Aye, could be, could be. Your father and Godi used to play at Ha'lekui. Firm friends, they were."

"Ha'lekui? The royal residence?" Lono asked.

"Yes, indeed," Tua said. "Aku's father sometimes played with the royal troupe." Tua closed his eyes in thought. "Could've been late enough for you to remember, I suppose. Before Regent took over. One of Regent's first acts was to dissolve the troupe and send home all the court musicians, artists, jesters."

Tua sighed deeply. "Ah, things were wonderful then. Your father used to play for Queen Makani back when she was pregnant with the Prince. She loved to hear him. Seems his flute was the only thing calmed her so she could sleep. And after he was born, your father played for the infant Prince Ka'moe. Before the Purge and the Exile."

"Is this the same flute Godi played then?"

"It must be. I never knew him to get a new one. Aye, I do believe he would want it to belong to you now." Tua looked thoughtful. "I think your father would too."

Aku pressed all his fingers from each hand over the toneholes and blew. This time the note was high, almost piercing. He put his arms back down. "But we need it for the tree folk."

"You know what?" Lono said. "You keep the flute. I don't mind if the tree folk take the ring."

SEVENTEEN

Kai swam sinuously through the dangling stipes of the kelp forest, enjoying the alternate cool and warm of the dappled sunlight. It reminded him a bit of the mangroves of home, the close hominess of the vegetation providing plenty of hiding places for fish to dart in and out, so unlike the stark barren vistas of the mother ink fields.

Still, there was something odd about this place, and not simply because he wasn't familiar with the territory. Of course as a kai-man, he was used to other fish fleeing when they saw him, but there was something positively paranoid about the fish in these parts. Schools of tiny feeder fish seemed in a state of permanent frenzy. A passing leopard shark exhibited not its typical cool disinterest, but instead kept a wary eye on him, circling a few times to see what he was up to. In the distance he caught a glimpse of an otter family, but the parents quickly herded the younger ones away when they saw a stranger approaching.

As the day went on, the feeling began to infect Kai as well. It was almost as if something was watching him, something he could catch sight of out of the corner of his eye, but not quite view full on. He thought at one point he almost saw something like a rockfish, but with a weird protruding jaw and stitching along its side, but when he swiveled, it was gone. Another time he was certain an octopus was trailing him, its camouflage shifting imperfectly as it followed. A quick pivot, a glimpse of something with too many eyes and a hideously curved beak, and then it too had disappeared, with Kai doubting whether he'd really seen it in the first place.

Kai had hoped to be through the kelp forest before nightfall, but when darkness came he had not reached its edge. He did not relish spending a night in this haunted place, but at least he was able to find a small rocky area near the shore with a protected cove that seemed to be unoccupied. *Not another day here,* he thought. *In the morning, I'll take my chances with the surface men.*

After the heat of the day, the cabin interior was stiflingly hot. Lono and Aku found the cabin's roof a cool alternative, its slightly angled surface providing a pleasant place under the stars. Aku sat, haltingly playing notes on his flute, while Keki preened himself on a perch on the roof's high ridge. Lono took the relaxed cross-legged sitting position and started her meditations. She was supposed to do them daily, even twice daily if she could, but she hadn't done them at all since leaving the convent. Some disciple she was.

Ne Wa'e, be with me, she intoned. *Ne Wa'e, be with me. Be with me and help me be wise.*

"What are you doing over there, anyway?" Aku said.

Lono answered without opening her eyes. "I'm doing my meditation."

"What does that mean?"

"I concentrate on the goddess so her spirit can flow into me."

"Well, that sounds like a load of dung to me," Aku said.

Lono sighed. "I think you're getting better at that flute. You're not making as many of those weird squeaks as you did earlier."

"Yeah, thanks." Aku practiced pulling one finger from a hole and replacing it quickly again, creating a trill. He liked the effect so much he repeated it for a full minute. Lono found it so distracting she opened both her eyes and frowned. When Aku finally stopped, there was an almost shocking silence, then a rising crescendo of insect noises from the forest to take its place.

Giving up on her meditation, Lono scanned the night sky. "Hmm. There's Ne'i Lapa, the dolphin, down low, just above the trees over there." She pointed to a constellation. "A good sign for us. Ne'i Lapa guides and protects travelers."

Aku snorted. "Figures you'd believe all that rubbish."

"What rubbish? That our ancestors watch over us?"

"Yeah, all those stars way up there, they're so concerned about what we're doing."

Lono leaned back on her hands. She regarded Aku silently a few moments.

"What?" he said, bugging out his eyes at her.

"Why don't you like me, Aku? What have I ever done to you?"

He waved her away. "I like you fine."

"No, you don't. You're always contradicting everything I say. I've been nothing but nice to you. I saved you from that hole in the park. I've hiked with you and Tua halfway across the kingdom, and still you treat my opinions with contempt."

"Okay," Aku said. "You really want to know why I don't like you?"

"Yes, I do."

"Alright." Aku shifted uncomfortably. He didn't look at Lono, but he felt her stare on him. "Okay. Ever since I met you, you're like, 'Thank the ancestors for this' and 'Blessed be Ne'i Dumb Lady for that.' You're just like all those adherents coming to Bonetown, trying to get us to accept their Bee God or their Sheep God or whatever. 'Accept our god and find inner peace.' But not a single one of you ever gave any food to me or my brother when we didn't have any."

"But that wasn't—"

"How can I have any inner peace, when my belly's empty and growling, huh? All of you, up in your temples or your convents or whatever, getting fat on donations from all the hungry old ladies in my neighborhood who give their last coins to some stupid priest or priestess. And then when Kuana died, after Regent's men beat him like a dog for stealing a piece of fruit in the market so we'd have something to eat that night, and I stayed up all night with him puking his guts out until there wasn't no more left, where were you then? But sure, in the morning, you're there. 'Oh, we'll prepare his body for burial. We'll have so much respect.' But not one of you had the respect to be there when it was actually important and you could have saved him."

"Wow," Lono said. "I'm sorry about your brother. I didn't know." She hesitantly put a hand on his back, expecting him to push it away, but he didn't. "Kuana sounds like he was a good brother."

Aku drew in a ragged breath. "He was the best."

"You know all that that wasn't me, though," Lono said. "I've only tried to be your friend."

Aku grunted in response. Lono tried to rub his back, but this time he did reach out and remove her hand. A nervous silence continued between them for a long time.

Finally, Aku spoke. "You know, if you wanted to, I guess you could tell me more about the stars."

"Are you sure? It's not too stupid?"

"I didn't say that," Aku said. "But maybe I don't mind that much."

Hulu huddled in a collapsed building with his cape wrapped around him, listening to the yelling and sounds of violence outside. It was near midnight, and looters ran freely through the city, evading the heavily-armored platoons of Shabengee guardsmen roaming the streets and cracking skulls indiscriminately. Some fires had died out, but others still blazed uncontrollably, burning through whole blocks of centuries-old kimunu mansions. *At least the scribes should be safe behind their heavy walls*, Hulu thought. *All they have to worry about is being beaten if they look at a guard wrong.*

His hands shook as he rolled a leaf. He had no aromatic herb mixture, so a pinch of sawdust would have to do the trick. It'd been almost a full day now since the last time he'd smoked, and he'd put it off as long as he could. He dropped in the three crucial drops, carefully leaving one tiny droplet behind. The cruse Opio had provided had only enough in it for one session, so this would have to last him. What would happen the next day Hulu hated to think. He lifted the leaf, but stopped when he heard a sound outside the ruined building.

Feet stamped and stopped directly in front of the warped open doorframe. Hulu could make out the silhouettes of several figures. *How did they know I was here?* And then, a snatch of song from a guttural, slurred voice. "Old Lohelo was a happy whore." And three or four men's voices sang back in unison, "She had two men in her bed and another at the door." The voices laughed and the feet stamped some more and the silhouettes disappeared.

Hulu exhaled in relief. He lit the leaf and sucked in. The harsh sawdust smoke sent him into a fit of coughing before he was half through, but at least it was delivering the ink. He felt his muscles relax and the buzzing in his head fade. *Now for the moment of truth*, he thought.

He took out a piece of charcoal from a pocket on the inside of his cape, and carefully tipped the cruse so the last tiny drop fell onto it. He waited a moment to let the ink soak in and then on a flat place on a fallen stone he started to write.

Malu is a-l-i. But his hand jerked before he could finish. He tried to start again, but found there was no more ink and the charcoal simply wrote as he wanted, not guided by the ink truth.

What did it mean? Had his hand jerked because it contradicted reality and the ink wouldn't allow it? Or was it simply a muscle spasm, and without meaning at all? Had Malu had died in the Puku, crushed under tons of rock, or escaped out the other entrance? Or worst of all, perhaps he was still alive, but trapped in an air pocket, slowly suffocating in the dark. Maybe that's what the ink meant, letting him start the word without ending it.

Hulu had never felt so useless. He could not return to the Scriptorium, where the Shabengee were burning the ancient treasures and beating the scribes. His friend was quite possibly dead or in need, and he had no way to help him. And to top it all off, by the next night at this time, he would be in withdrawal and well on his way to becoming a contemptible quivering mass covered in his own sick.

He closed his eyes and hugged himself in the dark. "Master Makule," he whispered. "Give me wisdom. I've gone so badly astray. To be of aid to those I love, I need to change my ways. Lead me to where I can find some help, somehow."

...moonlight shone through the branches of the evenly spaced trees, their smooth gray-white trunks continuing into the distance in every direction, like columns holding up the roof in some vast temple. Hulu reached up and pulled down one of the branches, laden with broad white flowers, the petals arranged in a circle around a pale yellow center, like miniature moons. Moonplum trees.

Hulu strolled through the tranquil space, his bare feet sensitive with each step to the individual blades of grass against his heels and among his toes, his skin alert to the slight warm breeze that gently ruffled the leaves overhead. In the distance, a slight figure wandered too among the trees, and he quickened his pace just a bit to catch up. As he drew near, he saw it was the young woman, in a long barkcloth blouse, her dark hair spilling halfway down her back in glossy curls, and when she turned, she was eating a plum. She had not heard him approach.

He reached out and brushed a finger against her arm. She looked up with surprise but smiled when she saw him. She had taken a single bite from the plum and its red juice stained her lips. She held it out to him and he took a bite, the pulp at first providing a bit of crunch, but giving way to softness and releasing a deluge of intense sweet-sour juice. He put his arm around her waist to pull her to him and they shared the plum down to its stone, its aroma mixing headily with the clean fragrance of her hair.

When they had finished eating, they kissed, the tang of the fruit still in their mouths, their tongues sensitive from the citrus. He held her close with one arm, and with his other hand explored her body, and when one hand slipped under her blouse she leaned into him.

Their mouths broke apart, and he nibbled the lobe of her ear. "I seek you everywhere," he whispered. "But you are not there."

"I'm along the Southern Road, two days' journey," she whispered back. "Come and find me."

EIGHTEEN

Lono stretched and yanked back a bit of her barkcloth cape from Aku, who had been hogging it all night. They had fallen asleep on the roof and Aku had huddled against her for warmth, and at some point she had thought to spread the cloak over the both of them. Not the most restful night of sleep she'd ever had, but it had been fun to sleep under the stars. At one point she'd awakened and noticed Ne'i Maki, the monkey, spinning overhead. She'd almost thought she could actually see the five stars of his long tail curling around his palm tree in the sky. He must've been playing tricks.

That'd certainly explain her dream. *One of those dreams again.* She supposed they were harmless enough, though she could not quite dismiss the shame of giving herself so easily to a strange man again and again. And yet, he was not really so strange anymore, was he? Not after appearing to her so many nights. He was almost a friend now—her secret nighttime friend. *I must admit I do enjoy my time with him*, she thought with a little smile, feeling a blush come into her cheeks.

Below them, fog filled the forest as thick as spider webs among the trees. The insects had stopped their evening singing and the morning birds were not yet awake. Even Keki sat on his perch with his eyes closed. All was quiet. In the middle distance, the fog swirled in an odd way and almost seemed to glimmer. Lono sat up to see it better.

The glimmer slowly resolved itself into a distinct light, about the size and brightness of a candle, bobbing slowly through and around the trees. The light seemed to shift colors as it moved, from a light blue to a deep indigo to a purplish-red. Soon, another light joined it, following behind at first, then taking the lead, both lights dipping and rising together. Then a third and a fourth, their ever-shifting colors weaving among one another as they crossed the forest floor. Lono could not remember ever seeing anything so beautiful, and as she watched, it became an entire orchestra of lights, each playing its part in concert with the others.

Gradually she became aware that something was shaking. No, that wasn't right. *She* was shaking. Something had her shoulder and was shaking *her*. Something, or someone, and that person was talking to her, as well. Yelling at her, actually.

"Wake up, girlie!" Tua shouted. "Wake up!"

Lono's eyes snapped open and she found herself sitting on a table in the cabin, with Tua gripping her shoulders and Aku standing beside her. "What are you doing? What's wrong?"

"Oh, thank God," Tua said. "Didn't you know not to look at the lights?"

"We thought the Tree Folk got you for sure," Aku said.

"Oh..." Lono felt embarrassed. Of course she should've known better. "It's just, we were on the roof, and I was watching the fog, and it started glowing somehow, and I wanted to see what it was, and—"

"And they got you." Tua laughed. "They be tricky, alright. Almost thought you weren't coming back that time, *'one.'*"

"Well, where were you all night, anyway?" Lono asked, irritated at herself and ready to change the subject.

"Hunting." He nodded at a rabbit on the table next to her, a bit of red staining the fur around its throat. "Soon as I get that skinned I'll cook us up some breakfast stew."

It took him all night just to catch a rabbit? Still, Lono reflected, from his accent, she thought Tua might be from one of the Eastern Islands. Maybe they didn't have rabbits there. In any case, Lono had to admit she was hungry. She looked down at her hand, realizing it had something clutched in it. She spread out her fingers. A single velvety-white moonplum petal rested on her palm.

Gray-Patch cruised slowly from side to side in her aquarium, observing the wicked man prepare for his latest operation, pulling on long leather gloves and arranging his instruments, yelling at his two hooded, black-robed assistants to fetch this or bring that. This operation particularly interested and horrified her because it was a water operation, likely a preview of her own painful future. The man had an octopus in a wide glass tray on a table, the poor creature panicked but unable to thrash about due to the tiny bronze clamps around the edges fixing its eight arms in place. It was not a common octopus or even one of the red giants from the deep. It was a type she had never seen before. It had a large, deep blue body with pale white mottles, and though flipped on its back, she could see underneath its blue eyes, open and unblinking.

She reached out and mind-tapped it, feeling its terror. From its size she had expected an adult, but she had the horrible realization this octopus was still immature, little older than a hatchling. She sent it soothing waves of sympathy and serenity, the way she once had with her own children when they had become frightened over something in the night. The young octopus calmed, its tentacles relaxed. *Close your eyes*, the ray's emanations said. *I'm here with you, young one.*

She stayed with the baby octopus throughout the operation, doing her best to relieve and distract the creature's agony, taking for herself as much of the pain as she could. The man used his obsidian blade to slice the skin open, and inside the body cavity he found the ink sac and made a tiny incision, carefully squeezing the contents into a small pouch. From a clay jar, he lifted something Gray-Patch didn't recognize, something round and spiky, maybe an organ or organic nodule of some sort, harvested from what pitiful creature she could only speculate. He inserted it into the ink sac and carefully stitched the incision, and then the outer wound as well.

After the operation and an assistant had carried the baby

octopus away, she speculated as to its meaning. What did the man want with the ink? It couldn't be the mother ink he used in his operations, for that was a gift from We Honua in the middle of the world ocean. As so often, she could only guess at the wicked man's motives and wonder at the depth of his evil.

She closed her own eyes and concentrated. Her ability to reach with her mind had been growing lately, probably as a result of the ink the man dropped into her own aquarium every morning. The mother ink was life-giving and invigorating, though the wicked man perverted its proper use to enable his test subjects to survive his horrible surgeries. But her increasing power was a side effect he had no way to anticipate, as he didn't know about her abilities in the first place.

She pictured her friend, the black bird she had shared the lab with for weeks, whom she had seen the man operate on so many times, until the one fateful day when the bird had used his ink-augmented strength and intelligence to break his bonds, fly up and attack the man, rip his face to shreds with his beak and claws before fleeing the bloody scene. She took the picture in her mind and sought it out, questing, pushing. Yes, there he was, she had found him. She sent an inquisitive mind-tap, and the bird felt her and responded, creating images in his mind she could see, as they had practiced so often in the lab.

Friends, the bird said, and she saw what he saw, the girl and the young boy. *Allies. And more people, too. Have faith. I will bring them soon, and they will help us.*

It was the odd-looking bird Kai noticed at first, with lopsided wings and a bulging eye, hopping around ahead of him. Might be an easy meal. Each time he drew closer, the bird flew off a bit down the road, but still close enough to keep Kai's hopes alive. *Probably injured,* he thought. *It should tire soon enough.*

After a ways, the bird stopped by a heap in the road's muddy sidetrack, looking back as if to check that Kai was still following, and flew off to a nearby branch. Maybe the bird wasn't injured after all. *But why would it lead me here?* Kai observed the heap cautiously. It seemed to be a blanket of feathers, with something groaning and shivering underneath. Kai peered more closely. It appeared to be a surface man in distress, curled into a ball.

Kai's first thought was to ignore him. There'd been a humid rain all morning and he'd been making good progress without his usual need for a hydration break in a pond or stream. Plus, the rain seemed to keep the surface men in their buildings, which meant Kai could trot along the road itself without fear of awkward encounters.

It was that last point that bothered Kai, though. The rain, and this man was out in it. He knew the surface men did not enjoy the rain as kai-men did. Perhaps the man needed aid.

Doesn't matter, not your business, he thought. *The faster you go, the sooner you get home.*

He continued on his way, but the image of the man wouldn't leave his mind. Had he been assaulted and robbed by brigands, left behind to die? The surface men could be barbaric, he knew that from firsthand experience. Still, what was a surface man to him? They could take care of themselves. *Best to keep going.*

But now, there was that bird again, hopping around ahead of him and regarding him with that one eye. It reminded him of the childhood fable of the little bird who had aided the Great Kai-man when he had crawled onto land and found himself tangled in a surface man's net. He'd told the story to his own hatchlings, with its moral of helping even those different than you. Mere words to put little ones to sleep? Or a meaningful tale to raise your hatchlings into the type of mature kai-men you wanted them to be?

Damn it. Kai turned around and returned to the groaning heap.

"Neeed heelp?" he asked, approaching slowly and on all fours so as not to loom over the victim.

The moaning and trembling continued under what was truly a fine blanket of crow feathers. Perhaps the man hadn't heard him. Kai tried again, louder. "Yoouu neeed heelp?"

A pallid face peeked out, long dark locks of hair sticking wet against the man's cheeks. He blinked a couple times, but did not react with fear, as Kai had been anxious he might. "Great," the man said. "Now I'm having hallucinations."

Kai didn't fully understand his response. "Yoou huurt?"

The man reached out with a shaking hand and brushed it against Kai's snout. "Real enough. You're one of those kai-men, aren't you?"

"Yeess. I kai-man."

The man pushed himself up to a squat and pulled the blanket tight around him. "You're a long way from home."

"I goo hoome. Buut yoouu. Neeed heelp?"

"Yes, but nothing you can provide." The man smiled sadly. "I do appreciate your kindness."

So, the man didn't think he could help him. True, Kai wasn't a medicine man, and even if he were, kai-man magicks might not benefit surface men. But he had the ink, and the surface men found it valuable. Perhaps they could trade for the services of a medicine man of his own kind.

"Haave iink. Caan traade. Geet heelp."

The man cocked his head. "I'm sorry, what did you say you have?"

"Iink." Kai held out the burlap sack.

The man took it and opened it, and his eyes widened when he saw what was inside. He whistled low. "You know, I do believe you can help me, after all." He handed the bag back. Kai was surprised when the man took his claw in his hand. "I'm Hulu, by the way."

His name, he meant. Kai had known a few men in the village near his lagoon, but he had never been honored with a name exchange ceremony. The traders there treated the kai-men gruffly, at best. This man, Hulu, he treated him with courtesy. "Ii Kai. Ii haave… priide to knoow yoou."

"Kai." The man nodded. "You're headed home, are you? Perhaps we can assist each other."

NINETEEN

The lake was an easy walk from the cabin and Lono had taken to strolling there in the early mornings to bathe, carrying a lump of soap she had made from the fat drippings of the previous evening's meal and ashes from the fire. Around dawn was best, before Aku was awake. Tua was usually gone by then, off to hunt game or at least mushrooms for their breakfast. The second day had seen a repeat of the mistberry delivery, but she had known to ignore them, and it had not happened again. At the lake's edge, as she was about to remove her barkcloth cloak and blouse, she heard splashing from down the shoreline.

She had certainly not expected company, and edged down to see, smiling to hear Tua's voice with a snatch of song as she approached. From behind some cattails she peered through. He was waist deep in lake water, rubbing his torso with some soap he must have borrowed from her. *Fair enough*, she thought. *I made enough of it, and he does provide our food every day.*

Tua plunged his brown bald head into the water and lifted it out again, shaking the droplets off with a whole-body shiver. Lono admired his wide shoulders, heavily-muscled back, and peaked biceps. Still, what most interested her was the tattoo across his back: a great sea turtle, with green-brown interlocking scutes, brown-freckled flippers, and a broad, beaked head. As Tua moved about in the water, the turtle appeared to swim across his back, showing it was a true mother ink tattoo. Lono reflexively touched the telescope on her right arm, now fully healed but still slightly raised under the skin.

Of course, Tua was a tattoo artist, so it was hardly an astonishment he himself should be inked, and with quite a handsome piece of art, as well. But still, Lono was surprised at the subject matter, as the sea turtle's symbolic powers of protection, of nurturing and homelife, were unusual for a man, especially one as gruff as Tua.

Still, she reflected, perhaps it helped to explain his watching over her and Aku. And the more she thought about it, there did seem to be something gentle under that tough exterior. Yes, he had knifed a man to death in front of them with frightening suddenness, but hadn't it been in their defense, as he understood it? And his constant instinct seemed to be to get them out of danger, to bring them to safety, and now that they were in a place of shelter, to create almost a little family, with himself as protector. Maybe that sea turtle was the way to reconcile some of the aspects of Tua's character she had previously found puzzling and contradictory.

Sensing his bath was nearing its end, Lono turned to return to her own usual bathing spot and screamed. A huge crocodilian creature, as tall as a man and standing on its hind legs, approached from only a few steps away. Evidently it hadn't seen her until the scream. Its head snapped towards her in surprise and it bared a jaw full of fearsome teeth and growled, raising its claws menacingly.

Tua was at her side in an instant, brandishing a fallen branch in the direction of the reptile. "Stay back, creature! I'm a-warning you!"

The thing took a few faltering steps backwards, waving its claws and making an odd hissing growl. With a few swings of Tua's branch in its direction, it spun around, fell to all fours, and scurried off into the trees at a surprisingly high speed.

Tua put a hand on Lono's arm. "Are you okay, *'one*? Did he hurt you?"

"I'm fine," Lono said, putting a hand over her eyes. "Maybe you should get your clothes back on."

"Oh, of course." Tua shook the excess water from his body and grabbed his tunic from where it hung with his cloak on a bush. "I'm surprised to see you here. I picked this spot because I thought you bathed farther up."

"I heard you singing."

"Ah, you couldn't resist my alluring serenade. My singing always has that effect on the ladyfolk. It's a curse, really. You can uncover your eyes now, girlie."

Lono did and was relieved to see Tua fully clothed. "What was that thing?"

"One of the Kai-men, I believe. Usually pretty harmless. I guess we just surprised it."

"Do you think it's safe for me to go in the water?"

"Oh, I expect he won't be back for a while. And I'll stay here too, just in case." Tua smiled. "Don't worry, I won't take a peek. We should respect one another's privacy, don't you agree?"

Lono only blushed and stammered.

Tua waved his hand with a laugh. "Don't worry about it, girlie." He sat on a log and faced away. "Strange about that creature, though. They live in lagoons near the ocean, so far as I've ever heard. I've not known of any making their home in a lake."

Lono mused while she undressed. "Another strange thing. When it hissed at us, I could almost believe it was trying to say something."

"I noticed that too. What do you think he was trying to say?"

"I wouldn't place an oath on it," Lono said. "But it sounded a bit like…'I sorry.'"

The chicken sizzled over the campfire. Hulu leaned over and gave the spit a quarter-turn. *Almost ready now.* He had to admit there were definite advantages to traveling with a kai-man, so long as one didn't ask too many probing questions about where exactly the fattened chickens and ducks came from. Hopefully a couple missing birds here and there weren't too much of a loss for the local farmers.

Not too onerous a travel schedule, either. Kai seemed to require two long soaking sessions a day and even when they were on the move, though he could trot on all fours at quite a pace, Hulu encouraged him to go on two legs. It was a far slower way to go, but Hulu calculated it would draw less suspicion from onlookers, combined with the hooded cloak he'd bought for his new traveling companion at an inn. Not much he could do with the snout, but Hulu gave other travelers on the road a wide berth, so he was hopeful no one was getting a good look.

He heard behind him the swishing sound he'd already come to identify as a tail sliding over the ground. "Ah, there he is," Hulu said without turning. "How was your bath?"

"Baaad." Kai laid his body in an arc near the fire, letting the waves of heat warm his belly.

"Why is that? Water not too your liking?"

"Waater fiine. But twoo peeople. Wooman sscreeam."

"I'm sorry to hear that," Hulu said. "I suppose we'd best move on soon, then. Don't want any trouble with the locals."

"Yess. Moove on."

Hulu pulled out his knife and cut a leg off the roasting bird. The meat was juicy and steaming hot. "They didn't hurt you, did they?"

"Noo." Kai reflected a moment. "Myy faault."

"Not your fault," Hulu said around a mouthful of food. "People are just scared around here. They're not used to seeing someone who looks like you. They jump to conclusions."

Kai waved a claw, as if to dismiss Hulu's argument. "Myy faault. Ii noot hiide. Oonly thiink…"

"Only think what?"

"Wooman. Loook kinnd."

"Ah, you thought she would be more understanding. These farmer's wives, though, they think every stranger is after their livestock." *And maybe with some justification*, he thought, swallowing a large bite of chicken.

"Noot wiife. I thiinnk yooung. Dauughter."

Hulu stopped with the knife halfway to his mouth. "A young woman, you say? Was she pretty?"

"Doon't knoow."

"Did she have dark hair, hanging down in curls? Brown skin?"

"Yess?" Kai glanced over, noticing Hulu was more than usually interested in this person. "Sshe haave... sshe haave piicture onn aarm. Heere." He pointed at the crook of his right arm.

"A picture? A tattoo?" Hulu was on his feet now, pacing around the fire. "What was it a tattoo of?"

"Noot knoow woord. Glasss. Foor sseeing."

"A glass for seeing. A telescope." It had to be the woman from his dreams. Who else could fit the description? *Come and find me*, she'd said, and out of options, he'd come south to do so. He hadn't really expected to succeed. It was a big island after all. How long had he been on the southern road, stumbling in a withdrawal haze, before meeting Kai? Three days? Four? But maybe the gods were smiling on him and this was truly her.

"C'mon, Kai," Hulu said. "Let's go see this lake of yours."

PART FOUR

One day when the Great Kai-man had crawled onto land to bask in the good warm sun, he spotted a surface man, walking on his hind legs. He followed the peculiar creature, but the surface man saw he was being followed and was crafty. The surface man led the Great Kai-man into a trap he had set out, for surface men do not always hunt nobly, but they set out snares to capture prey unaware.

The Great Kai-man found himself caught in a net, and despite all his strength, he could not escape. In fact, the more he struggled, the more his limbs and tail became entangled in the surface man's snare. When he saw he had captured him, the surface man ran back to his village to fetch a spear to return and kill the Great Kai-man.

Now a little Lopi bird with a white-and-red breast and black wings was hopping around searching for a meal, and he happened to hop near the place where the Great Kai-man was tangled.

"Little Lopi bird, will you help me?" the Great Kai-man asked.

"But how can I approach you?" the little Lopi bird said. "For when I come close, you will snap me up in your jaws."

"I promise I will not snap you up in my jaws if you help me escape," the Great Kai-man said.

So the Lopi bird hopped around the net, cocking his head to work out the problem. He used his beak to pull a strand here, or to tuck a strand there, and in a few minutes he had freed the Great Kai-man of his bonds.

"I thank you for your service, little bird," the Great Kai-man said. "If you are ever in any trouble, you may call on me and I will come to your aid."

Now it happened that a few days later, the Great Kai-man was basking again in the good warm sun, when he heard his friend twittering a frightened song. He followed the song and found a serpent had corned the little Lopi bird and was preparing to strike. Wasting no time, the Great Kai-man thrust himself between the two just as the serpent attacked, and the serpent's fangs bounced harmlessly off the Great Kai-man's scutes.

"Go, serpent, and do not bother my friend again," the Great Kai-man said. And off the serpent went, nursing his bruised tooth.

So little ones, it is thus that the Great Kai-man met the wiliness of the surface men: with straightforward, honorable dealings and loyalty to his newfound friend. And it was thus that the little Lopi bird made his escape: by helping one in need of aid, no matter how different that one was from himself. Nor should you forget that even the mightiest among us may sometimes need the help of the littlest.

--from *Stories Told by the Kai-men*

TWENTY

Aku tested his different fingerings on the flute, trying to make the switch from one note to another as smooth as possible. He'd been playing nearly nonstop in all his free time for a few days now, at first learning to string together notes into simple melodies, and now producing more sophisticated lines. Strange, but somehow the instrument seemed to come naturally to him. He'd always had little snatches of tunes in his head—bits of a song he'd heard an old lady singing as she hung her laundry in Bonetown, perhaps, or a late-night drinking song from a table of carousers at a winehouse, or even just something that popped into his brain from who knows where. All that had been missing was a way to express those musical ideas.

He was so wrapped up in his music he didn't even notice the pair of figures approach through the trees and wait patiently behind the stump where he sat. He nearly leapt in surprise when he paused for a breath and heard a throat-clearing behind him. Even more surprised when he turned around angrily and found it wasn't Tua or Lono, but two strangers.

"Oh! I...you should really watch it, you know that? You shouldn't sneak up on somebody!"

"I'm sorry to disturb you," the one man said with a smile. "I hated to interrupt your playing. We heard it all through the woods and found it quite splendid."

"Well, I guess that's okay," Aku said. The man had long dark hair and looked like he might be important, with his elegant feathered cape. His companion was odd, wearing a cloak with the hood pulled up, though it couldn't conceal his long, thin snout. "You don't have to hide your monster. I've heard about him already."

"He's not really a monster," the man said. "His name is Kai. And my name is Hulu."

Aku shook Hulu's proffered hand and hesitantly did the same when Kai put out his claw, though he wasn't sure he liked the hard, smooth feeling of his skin. "So are you his keeper?"

"Not at all. I'm his friend." Hulu laughed. "Well, Kai, no more need for the hood, I suppose."

Kai drew the hood back with his claw. His head was similar to the heads of the alligators Aku sometimes saw in the mud along the river bank back in Atlantis, although he thought it was somewhat smaller in proportion to his body. Kai's eyes were different, too. Softer, maybe, and definitely more intelligent, watching him intently to see how he'd react. Aku pulled back a bit when Kai opened his mouth, but it turned out he knew how to talk as well. "Goood too meeet yoou."

"It's...it's good to meet you too."

"You said you already heard about Kai," Hulu said. "May I ask who told you about him?"

"It was Lono, when she got back from the lake this morning."

"Ah," Hulu said. "Your sister. And your father was there too, I think?"

"She's not my sister!" Aku said with disdain. Seeing the confusion on Hulu's face, he added, "Lono and Tua are just friends of mine."

"I see. Traveling companions. Like Kai and me."

"Yeah, like that, I guess," Aku said.

"We'd very much like to meet your friends," Hulu said. "I hope Lono's not still frightened after seeing Kai."

Aku regarded Hulu and Kai suspiciously. *Why do they want to meet them? Maybe I've said too much already.*

Sensing Aku's reticence, Hulu added, "If we could see them, it would give us a chance to apologize for Kai's disturbance of their bathing this morning."

"I think she's over it," Aku said, standing. With his fancy cape and exaggerated manners, Aku decided Hulu was like Lono—silly but harmless. Kai he was still trying to figure out. His claws and teeth were still menacing, but at least he didn't seem dangerous at the moment. "I guess you two can come to the cabin with me. They should be there."

"Lono, you feeling okay, *'one*?" Tua had noticed the girl acting strangely since the arrival of the two strangers. Her face was flushed, and she kept to a far corner of the cabin. At first he thought perhaps she still feared Kai after their morning encounter, though she had accepted his apology readily enough. But after a time he perceived it was the dark-haired one she repeatedly, and none too subtly, cast probing glances at.

"I'm fine, Tua," she said shortly.

Tua turned back to the new arrivals seated across the table from him, Hulu politely eating the last of the rabbit stew from a wooden bowl, Kai awkward in his chair, not sure where to put his tail. "I don't understand," Tua said. "If your Scriptorium be not damaged from the earthquake, why did you have to leave?"

"Ah. While I was…away, the Shabengee guardsmen I mentioned took advantage of the situation and seized the facility," Hulu said. "The captain of the guard would kill me on sight if I were to show up there again."

"So you're laying low until you can go back and lead the scribes in killing all the guards?" Aku said from where he sat, back to the fireplace.

Hulu chuckled. "I wish it were that easy, young man."

"Why isn't it?" Aku asked. "That's what I'd do."

"I don't understand why you let the guards in the Scriptorium in the first place," Lono said, speaking up for the first time in the conversation. "At the convent where I'm from, the Prioress made the guards stay outside in wooden shacks. They never even set foot in the convent."

"Ah, so you're a Sister at the Convent of the Ancestors?" Hulu asked, his eyes locking with hers. The corners of his lips rose slightly, as if he wanted to smile but didn't dare acknowledge his feelings in the present company.

"Not yet," Lono said in little more than a whisper.

Tua noted the exchanged glances and Hulu's barest hint of a smile, while Lono quickly turned away, her face redder than ever. There was something odd going on between these two. Was it possible they had met before? Or was it one of those cases of mutual attraction at first sight? He didn't care for this effete scribe himself, but he could see how someone like Lono might find his long hair rakish, his manners charming. As for why a grown man had interest in a girl on the cusp of womanhood like Lono, Tua knew all too well. He determined he would get the newcomers out of the house as quickly as possible.

At the fireplace, Aku broke the silent pause with a snort and giggling.

"Is something humorous, young sir?" Hulu asked.

"Let me get this straight. The girls at the convent just told the guards they had to stay out, while the boys at your script-place let them march right in. I thought you were the one in charge? Why didn't you kick them out too?"

"Well, they're armed for one thing. They say the quill is mightier than the spear, but that's not literally true, you know."

"So you're looking for weapons now, right?" Aku asked. "Then you'll go back and kill them all?"

"That's...an idea. I don't think it would work out that way. Scribes aren't usually eager for a fight."

"Why not?" Aku asked. "How many guards are there, anyway?"

Hulu stiffened a bit in his chair. "Eight guardsmen, plus the captain, all well-armed and trained for combat, and covered with shark tattoos to enhance their martial prowess."

"Yeah?" Aku said. "How many scribes are there?"

"We have eighty brothers," Hulu said.

"So eighty against nine. Sounds like an easy fight. Why don't you go back and beat them? You're not afraid of them, are you?"

"Enough, Aku," Tua interjected.

"But I was just—"

Tua rose from his chair. "You be keeping our guests from going on their way. They came to apologize for the misunderstanding this morning, not for an inquisition."

"Fine." Aku turned around to face the fire. For a moment, the top of his shift opened and something glinted.

"What's that around your neck, young man?" Hulu asked. He recognized Tua was trying to shuffle them out, but decided to try for just a bit more conversation, hoping to get Lono involved.

"Oh, this?" Aku pulled out the cylinder on its cord. "Just something I found."

Hulu exhaled forcefully through his nose. "May I take a look at that?"

"Sure." Aku took it off and tossed it to Hulu, who ran his fingers along the raised and depressed areas along its surface. It was definitely one of the coded message tubes like the ones he'd seen in the Puku.

"Just a trinket of the lad's," Tua said, taking the cylinder back from Hulu a little too quickly. "Nothing important."

Hulu blinked a couple times before responding. "Yes, you're right. Not too important."

"And I'm afraid we been detaining you during the best part of the day, sir. Said you was returning Kai here to his home, didn't you? We'd best be seeing you off, I think."

"Of course," Hulu said, rising. "Thank you for your hospitality, Tua. Perhaps we'll meet again, when it's safe for you to return to the city."

"Yes, could happen." Tua all but pushed the two visitors

through the door, anxious to break the parting gaze that had formed between Hulu and Lono. Not that it would ever be safe to return to the city with the children, and he certainly didn't intend for Lono to meet with this man ever again if he could help it.

"Wheen wee goo?" Kai asked, rolling closer to the campfire's warmth.

"We'll be back on our way early tomorrow morning, I promise," Hulu said. He put his chin in his hand. "Did something strike you as strange about those three? None of them related by blood, but living together as a little family?"

"Doon't knoowe." Who knew what was normal among surface men?

"And then, what Tua said, about finding the children trapped in the earthquake and rescuing them, their parents dead. You don't need to be smoking ink to see that story was made up. And the boy, in possession of that cylinder...."

The message cylinder. Tua had said it wasn't important, and the dance in Hulu's mind had faltered. Tua was lying, that was certain. But how much did he really know about the cylinder? And where had the boy found it? Even if it was just something he'd picked up somewhere, some shiny object discarded in a gutter, it was still at some point a message Regent's men had thought worth encoding. Possibly, it was no more than an out-of-date shipping manifest concerning some long-delivered cargo, or something along those lines. And yet, the one Malu had showed him had related to diverting mother ink. Maybe others did too?

The horrible lab from the shared dream with Malu came into Hulu's head. The place was an abomination to nature, and destroying it was Malu's dying goal. If the boy's cylinder could be a clue as to the lab's whereabouts, shouldn't he pursue it? And then, of course, there was the beautiful young woman, Lono. She'd been bashful at the cabin, but had clearly recognized him. Hadn't she said in the dream to come find her? Did she need rescuing?

All these images spun together in Hulu's head. It was as if there were some thread connecting them all, but he couldn't quite discern the stitching. He needed to get more information, ask more questions of Aku and especially Lono. And without that lying, self-appointed guardian of theirs around. It all pointed to another visit to the cabin.

TWENTY-ONE

Lono and Aku had made it a regular habit to sleep on the roof on nights it wasn't raining, escaping the cabin's heat and observing the stars, Keki watching over them from his perch. Nor had there been another visit by the Tree Folk, who apparently considered their business finished after taking Lono's ring the morning she'd fallen under their spell. Tua slept in the cabin, whether because he didn't mind the heat or because he considered sleeping on the roof undignified, Lono wasn't sure. He was gone most days hunting when they awoke.

On this night, Lono closed her eyes and went over the day's events yet again in her mind while Aku played his flute. Seeing Hulu, the man from her dreams, actually show up at the cabin had both frightened and thrilled her. Though, she *had* told him to come find her, hadn't she? Yet, to truly see, in real life, her mysterious man from the bird market, from her dormitory, from the moonplum orchard, the man who in her private nighttime reveries she had wanted to possess and be possessed by, in actual flesh and blood in front of her? She could not quite identify or understand the feelings she'd felt during his visit to the cabin, where he'd been fully as tall, his hair as long and dark, as she remembered. But he was different somehow, too, his manner more reserved. He had certainly noticed her, his eyes seeking hers eagerly, but he was not the same bold man who brushed aside all obstacles and social conventions to place his hands on her exactly where she wanted them.

"Psst! Are you up there?" A loud whisper came from below. "How do I get up?"

Aku walked to the side and peered down. "It's the scribe-man from earlier," he said to Lono. In a louder voice, he called down, "What do you want?"

"Shh, keep quiet! I want to come up and talk to you two."

Lono and Aku looked at each other. Lono felt another of those scared, excited shivers go through her. "Well, tell him how to get up," she said faintly.

"Around back there's a tree. You can climb up on the first couple branches and reach the corner of the roof from there."

In a couple minutes Hulu had scrambled up the backside of the roof and stood before them. Keki clicked a couple times and cooed at seeing him.

Hulu smiled awkwardly. "Hello, Aku. Good evening, Lono." He gave her a nod and she waved back. "Is this your crow?"

"It's Lono's," Aku said. "It follows her everywhere."

"Odd. I think I've seen it around myself."

Lono wanted to tell him, to explain all about the crow and how it'd adopted her, led her to Aku, watched over and protected them. Somehow, the only word that came out of her mouth was, "Keki."

"Pardon?" Hulu said.

"That's...that's the bird's name," she said.

"Ah. Keki. Do you mind if I sit here?"

Aku ignored the question and tapped his foot. "So what are you doing here, anyway?"

Hulu took a seat just below the roof's ridgeline. "I came to check up on you two. Are you doing well? Is Tua holding you under any duress?"

"Of course not," Aku said.

"Are you sure? Kai told me he was your father, but when I came here and found out he wasn't related to you at all, I became concerned about his intentions."

"He really is a friend," Lono said, finding her tongue. "I know he can come across as gruff. But he's been keeping us safe here."

"I'm glad to hear that." Hulu nodded and waited a beat before introducing the next topic. "The other thing I'm here about is that cylinder you have on your cord, Aku."

Aku eyed him suspiciously. "Why would you care about this?"

"Well, for one thing, I know the story about you simply finding it somewhere isn't true. I wonder if you would tell me where you really got it?"

"None of your business," Aku said.

"You're absolutely right." Hulu stroked his chin. "I shouldn't pry into your secrets. But I'm going to tell you a secret of my own. And maybe after you hear it, you'll understand why that's no mere trinket, as Tua called it."

Aku didn't say anything. Lono leaned forward, eager to hear anything about her mystery man's past.

"I knew a man, a very powerful man, who had a device that could read coded messages. And the way the device worked was that it spun cylinders just like the one you have around your neck in a mechanism and the words appeared on a panel. I have reason to believe your cylinder has a very important message on it."

"What happened to the man?" Aku asked.

"He died in the earthquake. And practically the last thing he did before dying was give me the device."

Aku looked skeptical. "Where is it now, then?"

"Hidden somewhere safe."

"What sort of important message do you think is encoded?" Lono asked. "And what would you do with the information?"

Hulu breathed deeply. "There's a place where one of Regent's agents performs experiments on birds, fish, and other animals. Horrible experiments. He twists them and makes them into things they shouldn't be."

"Things like whisper birds?" Aku said. The mention of Regent had shifted his tone from distrust to attentiveness.

"Exactly, like whisper birds. Other things too, all sorts of creatures warped in unholy ways. And I believe your cylinder may be a clue as to where that place is."

"*Caw!*" All on the roof turned their heads to Keki, who stretched his wings to show the stitching on his back, as if to demonstrate proof of Hulu's assertions.

"Keki! Is that what happened to you?" Lono reached over and stroked him behind the head.

"Will you give me the cylinder?" Hulu asked Aku. "Will you help me find out where that dreadful place is?"

"I…I don't know—"

"He'll give you nothing," came a deep voice from behind Hulu.

Hulu whirled and found Tua looming right behind him, knife in hand. Hulu took a step back, wondering how the large man had climbed onto the roof without making a noise.

"I'm going to count," Tua said. "And by the time I get to ten, if I still see you, I cut you open from throat to groin, and your reptile friend have to be finding his own way. You understand me?"

"You must have heard what I explained," Hulu said. "Don't you believe I'm telling the truth?"

"It's only because I believe you that you're not dead already. One." Tua raised the knife so the tip nearly touched Hulu's nose.

"I just want the cylinder. Then you'll never see me again."

"Two."

Hulu stepped to the edge of the roof. He gave a shrug and a half-smile to Lono.

"Three."

Hulu lowered himself and dropped to the ground. He retreated into the trees without another word.

Lono rolled in her blanket in the airless hot cabin. A trickle of sweat rolled down her forehead. Tua had insisted she and Aku sleep in the cabin after the incident, and she hadn't had a minute of sleep in the hours since then. Of course, her insomnia could also have been because of the roiling emotions and thoughts in her mind. She went over again and again Hulu's story of the lab, the very lab that had disfigured Keki, and his belief that Aku's cylinder might be a clue to its location. And Tua's reaction to him, not disputing the story at all, but threatening her beautiful mystery man with a knife.

What drove Tua, anyway? Why was stabbing his first solution to every problem? She knew his intentions must be good. He had the tattoo of the sea turtle, a true mother ink tattoo that could not help but reflect the nature of its bearer. Still, his idea of protection didn't match hers. She wondered if he really ever intended to let her leave the cabin and return to her home at the convent.

Her mystery man was traveling though, headed back to the city with his alligator friend. If she joined them, would she be safe? What if the alligator man got hungry? And... what if Hulu wanted to touch her, like in her dreams? What if *she* wanted Hulu to touch her like in her dreams?

Ne Wa'e, be with me. Lono calmed her breathing. She needed guidance. *Be with me and help me be wise. Be with me and help me discern the path I should take.*

She meditated for a long time but no answers came into her head, no visions of the proper course of action. Ne Wa'e's voice, or at least somebody's voice, had been clear enough in her head back at the convent when it could get her in trouble, lead her away from the comfortable path to Sisterhood she'd been preparing for all her life. *But of course now, when I really need help, the voice is nowhere to be heard.*

It sure didn't help her concentration that Aku was four feet away from her, tossing and talking in his sleep. She gazed at him in the faint moonlight for several moments. He wore only his loincloth, and had pitched off his blanket at some point. His body was skinny, ribs showing through the skin. The cylinder rested on his chest, rising and falling with his breathing.

Lono rose quietly and fetched a cooking knife, the sharp one

Tua used to debone rabbits. She knelt beside Aku and carefully took the cord that held the cylinder between her thumb and forefinger, rubbing the knife against it. It sliced through one strand, two strands.

"Don't," Aku murmured, rolling his head to one side. Lono froze. But Aku did not awaken, so she continued, cutting each strand of the cord until it broke free. She gently lifted the cylinder, letting the cord slide free through the eyehole.

Rising, she picked up her barkcloth cape and dropped the cylinder into an inner pocket before slipping it on. After a moment's consideration, she dropped the knife in the pocket as well.

At the door she surveyed the room. Aku, in the same position she had left him in. Tua, snoring in the corner. *Do I really dare go through with this?*

Yes, she did. She lifted the latch and opened the door slowly, not making a single sound, not even a creak, and once she was out, closing it with the same care, and treading lightly on the steps. It would do no good to leave if Tua woke up and caught her thirty seconds later.

Once she was a considerable distance from the cabin, she took a deep breath. She'd made it. The air outside was refreshingly cool and delicious in her lungs after the stuffy cabin. *Where to now, though?* Hulu and Kai must be encamped somewhere near the main road, she supposed, though that still left a lot of area to search.

A fluttering of wings and Keki landed in front of her, bobbing his head.

"Of course." Lono smiled. "Lead on, feathered friend."

TWENTY-TWO

The pond water was warm and muddy. It reminded Kai a bit of the lagoon waters of home, though there was something about fresh water that just never felt right to him. Yes, it moisturized his scutes like seawater, but he always came out of fresh water feeling clammy rather than refreshed, and his pores leaked water for the next hour, making the robe Hulu had given him damp and uncomfortable. Still, a good soak was a necessity after hours in the open air, when his skin started to itch all over.

He emerged from the water into the early morning light and trotted on all fours back to the clearing near the road where he'd left his friend and the young lady. She'd shown up in the middle of the night with that cylinder Hulu was so interested in and her funny bird companion. They'd broken camp immediately and been afoot since then. A-two-foot, that is. Kai was getting better on his hind legs, but he knew he was still slowing them down. It hadn't been a problem when it was just Hulu and him, but the young lady seemed to think speed was a matter of some urgency.

As he approached, he heard the two talking. He stopped in a thicket of foliage outside the clearing and listened. That was another thing he was getting better at, making out surface man speech. His sensitive nostrils detected a bit of combusted material and the earthy burnt odor of Hulu's smoking, that odd habit of his. *Is smoking frequent among the surface men?* Kai wondered. *Who would ever think to stick a leaf in your mouth and light a fire at one end of it?*

"What is that, anyway?" Lono asked.

"It's mother ink."

"It smells…weird. Why do you do that?"

"It helps me relax." Hulu let out a long exhalation, and Kai could picture the smoke ring puffing out from his lips and spreading through the air. "Normally I don't smoke it straight like this. But I don't have my regular herb mixture with me."

"Isn't mother ink really expensive? At the convent, the Prioress treats our store of it like it's a pot of gold."

"Unfortunately, yes. But you know, ink is the reason we've been able to, um, meet before."

Some sort of shifting sound. "What do you mean?" Lono said.

"That tattoo on your arm. When did you get it?"

"A couple weeks ago. Two days before the earthquake, actually."

"I suppose your order has some sort of elaborate ceremony when you receive it," Hulu said.

"Yes, we do," Lono said. "What does that matter?"

Another exhalation and Hulu's voice came out a bit hoarse, as it did after he'd been smoking. "The mother ink connects you to the All-Dream, the collective thoughts and feelings of every living thing. When you got that tattoo, the ink entered your body, and the training you've no doubt undergone taught you how to tap into its power in some way. But when you're asleep, that connection doesn't end. Without your waking mind in control, the ink takes you where it wants you to go. Shows you what it wants you to see. That we met in our dreams was no accident."

Lono's response was quieter and Kai had to concentrate to hear it. "I'm not sure I really understand what that means."

"I don't fully understand it myself."

Some sort of rustling noise and then Lono's voice, strained somehow. "I… I don't think that's a good idea."

"But we've kissed before," Hulu said.

"That was a dream. This is different."

Kai wasn't familiar with the mating rituals of surface men but it occurred to him he might be overhearing a private moment, albeit one that didn't sound like it was going entirely smoothly. Time to make his presence known. He rose up and walked into the clearing as if he'd just arrived. Hulu was sitting on a fallen log, while Lono sat a few feet away with her arms crossed. Kai thought her face seemed redder than normal.

"Goood moorning."

"Good morning, friend," Hulu said quickly. He stubbed out the last of his burning leaf on the ground. "Ready to go?"

"Yess... buut."

"What is it? Is there something wrong?"

"Wheen wee sleeep? Wheen wee eeat?"

"As for sleep, not until tonight, I'm afraid." Hulu rose and put on his cape. "Lono thinks Tua might come after us for the cylinder, and I for one have no desire to be gutted by the big fellow. As for eating, keep your eyes peeled for a farm, and you can work your magic with the chickens."

"Eyyes peeeled?"

Hulu clapped him on the shoulder with one hand and handed him his robe with the other. "Just an expression. Be alert, I mean. And put this robe on, for modesty's sake."

Modesty. It wasn't that the surface men were embarrassed about their naked bodies exactly, although to be sure, Kai found their scaleless skin odd-looking enough. It was just that they didn't like anyone to see them unclothed. *Yet another weird concept of the surface men I need to figure out.*

The washerwoman was wrinkled and brown, but she walked with perfect posture as she balanced a basket with a heavy load of clothes on her head. She came down the middle of the road, on the high, relatively smooth part between the rutted wagon tracks.

"Hail, good lady," Tua called as he and Aku approached. "How goes it this morning?"

"I'm still a'walking on my own two feet, long as Le'i Hipa please it," the woman answered without changing her pace, so as not to upset the basket.

Tua changed direction to walk with her, snapping his fingers to signal Aku to do the same. "Tell me, good lady. Have you seen three travelers on this road? A man, a young woman, and an *'ele* covered up?"

"Ay, I did. And a right peculiar fellow that old one was, too."

"With a nose like a snout, you mean?" asked Tua.

"Ay, that's the fellow. Young man had some very pretty manners though. Stopped and asked if I knew of a place where they might find stew and a crust of bread. Said he and his sister and grandfather been on the road all day without a bite to eat."

"Uh huh. How long ago was this?"

"Oh, let's see." The washerwoman rolled her eyes while she considered. "Sun was right about midday, I'd say."

"Thank you, good lady. And where did you advise them to eat?"

"Why, at Hoa's inn, up the road a piece. If you be hungry, they'll fill you up for half a bronzer."

"I see," Tua said. "You've been a great help. Take care, good woman. May Le'i Hipa watch over you."

He and Aku switched directions again. *Midday, so roughly a couple hours ago*, Tua thought. The thieves may have had a few hours head start, but that reptile of theirs slowed them down. If the three had stopped for lunch, they might be very close indeed. Of course, he and the boy would need to break for food too. Aku was a good traveler, mile after mile with no complaints. But he was just shy of twelve years old, after all, and Tua knew from his atypical silence he was tired. He decided they would find a seat at the inn, if only for a quarter hour and a bite of something. Anyway, they might get a more accurate read on how far behind they were from somebody at the inn.

Tua had passed the inn many times on previous trips, but never found the ramshackle place, carved out of a long-dead kimunu tree, to hold much promise of a decent meal. *I suppose today is the day we find out.*

Aku tugged on his sleeve. "Do you think they're here?"

"No, boy, they've probably passed on by now. But you never know."

"You won't hurt them, will you?"

"It's not my intention." Tua absent-mindedly tapped the hilt of his knife through the cloth of its hidden pocket. "But if the scribe be not willing to part with what don't belong to him, he may need a bit of convincing."

As Tua and Aku passed into the inn's interior, a crow stirred itself in a dead branch overlooking the entrance. Keki waited a minute to see if the two would come back out, and when they didn't, he flew off, headed north along the road.

The wicked man had moved the octopus into his lab permanently, occupying a tank across the room from Gray-Patch. Over the course of days and multiple surgeries, the young creature had grown from confused and scared to angry, and now terrifyingly and permanently enraged. Gray-Patch no longer tried to mind-tap comforting feelings and images to him, for she was frightened by the malevolent feelings she received in return. When the black-robed assistants brought their food and dropped it into their aquariums, the young octopus delighted in tormenting the poor fish or shrimp, slowly tearing their parts off and watching them wriggle in their suffering, leaving little trails of blood swirling in the water.

On days when he was not undergoing surgery, the assistants came in twice daily and harvested the ink from the octopus, stretching him on the table and holding down his thrashing arms, putting pressure at a certain place on its mantle until the ink oozed out. Gray-Patch noticed the ink was no longer black and thick, but brownish and runny. As ever, she could only speculate as to their purpose.

In the ocean, a bright young octopus uses its ingenuity not just to find food, but to provide itself entertainment. So too in the lab as well. That very morning in the first gray light of dawn, Gray-Patch had watched as the octopus pried the lid from its tank, squeezed himself through a crack she never would have suspected he could fit through, and made his way into the birdcage hanging adjacent. He had reached his arms through the bars, reaching the sleeping red bird, who had arrived only the day before, and leisurely choked the life out of the poor creature. When he was done, he cast a glance at Gray-Patch, as if to make sure she'd seen, and returned to his own home. Was that glance a message? Was she next?

Possibly even more terrifying, the wicked man had taken to observing Gray-Patch, taking notes and making drawings on a parchment sheet. This was his typical preparation for surgeries, although he seemed to be taking an unusual amount of time with hers. She suspected he had something special in mind, but she tried to think about it as little as possible. No matter how painful the ordeal, no matter how twisted his physical abuse, she determined her mind would not become like that of the evil octopus across the way.

She closed her eyes and sent a desperate message to the black bird. *I beg of you tell our friends to hurry. Tell them every moment counts and they should not tarry a moment on their journey here.*

TWENTY-THREE

Lono and Hulu sat across from each other with the campfire between them. The sun had fallen and an insect orchestra accompanied the crackling of the flames. Kai was off on one of his twice-daily submersions. Lono had come to like Kai and his gentle spirit, but the leisurely pace he required on the road frustrated her. Finally, she was on her way to return to the convent, to see if Iwali was in good health, to finish the ceremony and become a Sister, but it was taking forever. Keki had chattered at them all afternoon, flying ahead and urging them on. Lono took it as a message their pursuers were close behind and speed was of utmost importance to stay ahead of Tua.

What's Tua's concern with the cylinder anyway? she wondered. *If it only contains information about the location of some sort of laboratory or something, as Hulu says, what is that to him?* But it must be important to Tua somehow, because she'd seen him kill over it. *Maybe he has a better idea of what the cylinder is than he lets on.*

And what would they do if Tua did catch them? Hulu, her mystery man, was proving to be rather less bold than she'd assumed he would be, and his smoking the ink that morning had left him lethargic and apathetic for hours afterwards. She had a hard time imagining him taking on Tua in combat, if it came to that. She tapped her foot impatiently and scanned the surrounding trees. Tua could be approaching even as they bathed and dawdled. *Maybe I could talk him out of killing Hulu and taking the cylinder if he shows up? But what would I say?*

Hulu idly poked a stick into the fire. "What are you musing about so intently over there?"

She looked up, her concentration broken. "Nothing, really. You will help me return to the convent when we get back to the city?"

"Of course," Hulu said. "That was our agreement."

"And how will we get there?"

Hulu thought a moment. "I suppose we'll go around the Ring Road. And if, as you say, the path to the convent is being watched, we'll have to go through the foothills and approach from the back."

"But what if there are Shabengee guards on the Ring Road? What if Puhi hunters are after me for helping Aku? What about Regent's spies?" Her voice rose with anxiety as she spoke.

"Take a moment and calm yourself, Lono." Hulu's stoking toppled a leaning log that fell into the red-orange coals in the center, sending up a mass of sparks. "I think that Tua fellow has rubbed off on you. Nobody will be looking for us or expecting us, and we'll have you delivered where you belong in no time."

"And what will you do with the cylinder?"

"Take it to the decoding device and find out what it says, I suppose." Hulu took a breath as if to say something else, but he was interrupted by a loud Caw! from the woods.

"Keki!" Lono whispered, holding up her hand. She gazed into the night, letting her sight adjust to the darkness after the brightness of the fire.

"Do you see something?" Hulu whispered.

Lono took several steps away from the fire to where it was darker. She peered into the trees, straining to see. As she concentrated, her vision resolved and she could make out two figures standing on a knoll some distance away, a larger one and a smaller one. They didn't move, but seemed to be observing the campfire.

Silently, Lono edged back to Hulu and signaled him with her finger to follow. He grabbed the sack and followed her in the direction of the stream where Kai was bathing.

"Hold," Hulu whispered when they'd gone far enough that the fire no longer provided any illumination. "I can hardly see. How are you moving so fast?"

"I can see fine," she whispered back. She glanced at her arm. Her tattoo was glowing faintly. "Put your hand on my shoulder."

She led him among the trees, avoiding roots and outcropping rocks, reaching the rushing water in a few minutes. They walked along it, her eyes sweeping the water for a sign of a six-foot reptile. At a place where the stream spread into a pool she spotted Kai's outline.

"There he is," Lono said. "Should we wade in and get him?"

"No need to get wet." Hulu leaned over and picked up a pebble. "We have a system. Toss this in near him."

A small plop and Kai rose to the surface. "Iiss prooblem?"

"We have to go now, friend," Hulu said. "I think we have a long night ahead of us. Come on out and get your cloak on."

Tua squatted down at the campfire and inspected the area. A place with crushed leaves—one of them had been sitting there. Some chicken bones tossed into the flames. And of course, the fire itself, still going. They had abandoned their camp pretty recently. In fact, he almost could have sworn he'd seen a figure moving around when they'd first approached, but the distance had been too great to be sure.

"You ready for some nightwalking, Aku?" he asked.

"I guess so." Aku's voice was tired. "I don't get what we're doing, anyway."

"Why, we're tracking the scribe and getting Lono and taking back what he stole from us. You know that."

"Yeah, I know that. But why?" He kicked at a stick, and it landed in the fire with a little shower of flames. "He didn't kidnap

Lono, she went on her own. And when Godi and I stole that cylinder in the first place, it was to help us fight against Regent. But what we're doing now isn't hurting Regent."

"We are still fighting against Regent," Tua said. "But sometimes there's a time for confrontation, and sometimes you have to bide your time."

"Okay, we're biding our time," Aku said. "But the scribe seems like he knows what to do with the cylinder. Let's just let him have it."

"No!" Tua forced himself to speak calmly. The boy didn't know. "That cylinder can't enter the city."

"But why not?" Aku's voice had a whining edge. He knew he needed sleep. They both did. Still, they were so close.

"I can't explain right now. But I will. When the time is right. You have to trust me, Aku. We're going to catch up to the scribe soon, maybe even within the hour, and take back what's ours. And then you can sleep. In the morning I'll explain it all."

"You promise?"

"I promise," Tua said. "Now let's keep going, while the trail is fresh and that reptile be slowing them down."

The early morning sun was beginning to burn off the fog when Hulu, Lono, and Kai came across an abandoned farmhouse made of fieldstone, a tree growing through its roof, ivy and other shrubbery overtaking its walls. They had been afoot the whole night, Lono in the lead and Hulu following with his hand on her shoulder. With little risk of meeting someone in the dark, Kai had taken to all fours and trotted swiftly. Indeed, he was faster than the humans. They'd avoided the road but tried to stay roughly parallel to it. There had been no sound of anybody behind them since they'd fled.

"We have to stop, Lono," Hulu said. "We have to sleep, at

least a few hours. This place isn't visible from the road. We'll be fine."

"But Tua, he's—"

"He's human, just like us." Hulu glanced at Kai. "Well, some of us. Anyway, we just passed our second night without sleep. We're exhausted, and if Tua's been following us the whole time, he'll need sleep too. Especially if he has Aku with him."

Lono ran a hand through her hair. She blinked her eyes several times, seeming to have trouble keeping them open. "I guess it would be okay."

"I figure we're about half a day still from the city," Hulu said. "We can sleep this morning and finish the hike this afternoon, enter the city after dark. We'll have you back home by midnight this very day."

"Sleeep heere?" Kai asked.

"Yes, friend, time to sleep now." Hulu opened the farmhouse's wooden front door, sending mice scurrying. The thatch roof had partially tumbled in and any furniture there might once have been was long gone, but the place was otherwise serviceable. A broad wooden floor, a large hearth at the back, and four solid walls. Perfect for laying low for a few hours.

Hulu sat in a clean corner of the room and pull out a leaf and an ink globule from Kai's sack. Not the refined, liquid ink he was used to, but it worked just as well to stave off the withdrawal symptoms. It made for a rougher smoke, of course, but he could deal with that. If he was careful, there could be enough in the sack to last him a year. He glanced up and saw Lono staring at him.

"You disapprove of this," he said.

"Your hand's shaking so you can hardly hold the knife." Lono frowned. "You're sweaty and pale. That's only after one day. What will you do if you ever don't have access to it?"

"It's happened. And I intend to make sure it never happens again."

"Maybe you should try breaking the habit."

Hulu ignored her, pulling out his flintbox and leaning back

against the wall. He sparked the leaf until it lit and brought it to his lips, sucking in the ink-laced smoke. Instantly his trembling hands calmed, the soreness in his legs seemed to belong to somebody far away. He heard Lono's voice in the distance. *By Master Makule's beard, is she still talking?*

"...wouldn't you rather be free of it?" she was saying. "Not having to arrange your life around your next smoke?"

"We arrange our lives around our next meal," Hulu said. "Our next sleep. Getting dressed. Washing ourselves. How is this different?"

"It just is."

Hulu studied her hazily. Her hair, dark and curly. Her arms on her hips. The way her pretty mouth turned down at the corners when she was upset. So much like Alani. He felt a stab of guilt. The first time he'd truth-smoked had been a week after Alani had...left for good.

"You're right," Hulu said. "Someday I'll end this, Lono. But today is not that day."

...the sun shone but the air was cool beneath the wild-growing kirikiri trees, with their broad leaves and fragrant white nuts spreading their spicy perfume. Lono longed to stop here and sit, just for a moment. Her feet hurt and her legs ached from walking all day and night. She couldn't stop, though. She had to keep going. She had to get back to the convent and take care of Iwali.

"Lono!" called a man's voice from far away, but when she turned, Hulu was right behind her.

"Why did you wake me up?" she asked. "I'm so tired. I need to rest."

"I didn't," he said. "You're still asleep."

She blinked at him, then realized what he said was true. This was a dream. "Does that mean I can do anything I want?"

"Yes. It means we can do anything we want." Hulu reached for her, brushed his fingers across her arm.

The sensation irritated her. What she wanted was to tell Hulu exactly what she thought of him, to let all her anger out. "Don't touch me!"

He withdrew his arm in shock.

"You touched me in my dreams so many times! You're the reason I didn't get a proper message from the ancestors! You're the reason I had to leave the convent and abandon my friend and now I'll never be a Sister! And after that, when we meet in real life, you're nothing like I thought you were. You're not strong at all! All you do is smoke your stupid ink and it makes you weak and lazy!"

Hulu stood before her, fidgeting with the edge of his cape. He didn't raise his eyes to meet hers. "Real life isn't the same as a dream. There are consequences for what you do. It's not always safe."

"There are consequences in dreams, too!" she shouted, and shoved him as hard as she could. Hulu flew back and tripped over an exposed tree root, falling to the ground in slow motion. As he fell, his body dissolved into mist.

Lono began to run, hot tears running down her cheeks. Had she killed him? No matter, it'd been worth it. Nothing she'd done had ever felt so good as letting out that anger at the one who had been the most exciting thing to ever happen to her, only for it all to turn out a mistake. She ran without direction, her surroundings a blur. After she'd run for what felt like hours, her energy spent, she drew in a deep, ragged breath and slowed to a walk. She emerged in a glade, and at its far end was the back of her dormitory building at the convent.

She strode towards it. When she opened the door, the Prioress was waiting there in her owl-feather cape. She held out her hand. "Come with me, child."

Lono gave her hand to the prioress and accompanied her through the hallways. She felt like a little girl again with the Prioress tall and wise beside her. She knew where they were going. Up the familiar stairs. Down the familiar corridor, and to the familiar door: Iwali's room.

"Knock, Lono," the Prioress said.

Lono did so.

"Come in," came Iwali's voice.

Lono went in and found Iwali sitting on the floor, arranging the little wooden pieces to a game on a playing board. Lono looked back at the door and the Prioress nodded at her.

"Aren't you sick?" Lono asked. "Shouldn't you be in bed?"

"Not anymore," Iwali answered. "I was sick a long time, but I got better. I even heard my message from the ancestors while I recovered. I wish you could have been here for it."

"That's wonderful news! I wish I could have been here too." Lono sat on the floor next to her friend. "I'm sorry. There was something I had to do."

"I know," Iwali said. "Prioress told me about it. And you're not finished yet, are you?"

"No, I'm not," Lono admitted. "But I'm tired of that. I want to come back home and be with you. I should be here tonight."

"You will be here, soon enough. But not tonight. You must complete what you set out to do. Help your new friends."

"I'm not sure my friends are who I thought they were," Lono said. "I did something daring because I thought it was the right thing, but now I'm not sure the ones I'm with have the determination to see their task through to the end."

"Why not give your friends another chance?" Iwali said. *"Perhaps they just need your guidance to become who they ought to be."*

"But what if I'm wrong?" Lono said. *"What if I picked the wrong group? What if I did the wrong thing? It's all so confusing! It would all be so much easier if I just came back here."*

"You should trust your instincts," Iwali said. *"Anyway, you're the last person I'd have expected to give up so easily."*

"You're right. You're absolutely right." Lono put her hand on Iwali's. *"But before I return, I want to play this game with you."*

"We'll play the game once, and afterwards you can go back. Deal?"

"What if I lose the first time?" Lono asked.

Iwali smiled. *"Always the same, aren't you? We'll make it two out of three."*

TWENTY-FOUR

Aku's legs felt like boiled mutton, his feet like beaten dogs. It was an act of will each time he had to put one leg in front of the other. He and Tua had been tracking the others all night, eternally coming across a wet footprint or crushed leaves that showed Lono and her friends were only a quarter hour ahead of them. Now somehow Tua had lost the trail altogether, and no amount of his checking for prints in the mud or bent branches revealed which way they'd gone. It was a relief when the trees opened up to reveal a little tumbling-down farmhouse.

"Please, Tua. Can we stop here and sleep? Only an hour, I promise."

Tua set his jaw grimly. "They could be practically to the city by now."

"Why does it matter? Can't we catch up with them there just as well?"

"No. It be too late for all of us if they reach the city." Tua glanced at the mid-morning sun. "Still, they must have stopped to rest somewhere. That be why the trail's gone cold. We simply overtook them."

"So we can stop?"

"You go and have a nap, boy. I'm going to check around a bit more."

Aku was already at the door. He opened it eagerly but stopped at the threshold. Inside were three sleeping figures, the nearest covered with scales and lying prone, with a tail extended straight back across the wooden floor and ending in a little curlicue. Beyond slept Lono, on her back with a piece of wood as a pillow, her hair spread in curls, her eyes closed peacefully, and beside her, the scribe snoring away.

From the rafters came a fluttering sound. Aku looked up and spotted Keki, who stared back curiously. *What a strange bird, to be so dedicated to a girl,* Aku thought. For a moment, he had a pang of sorrow in his gut. He instinctively touched his flute tucked into his belt. Lono had said his playing was getting better. She had even seemed to enjoy it, on those nights on the roof. He wished he could go right in and play a soft song for her, and maybe in return she could rub his back a bit to help him sleep. He would lie down next to her and just close his eyes and drift off.

But it's not to be, he thought to himself. He remembered the earlier conversations with Tua, how he couldn't explain why they were seeking the cylinder, only that he'd tapped his knife and said the scribe might need convincing to part with it. *I'm sorry Tua. I just don't know if I can trust you. I really don't.*

Aku closed the door quietly and found Tua at the edge of the clearing, peering at a stand of shrubs.

"What's the matter, boy? Go get some sleep."

"The place is full of rats," Aku said. "I'll sleep somewhere else." He paused a bit. "It's dangerous if they reach the city, yeah?"

"All our lives be in danger then."

"But why? How'll Regent even know about the cylinder?"

"His spies be everywhere."

Aku still didn't quite understand by what means their lives would be threatened, but it didn't matter. Only that Tua believed it. "What are you looking at?"

"Their reptile been here. See how these harpflowers be trampled? The whole length here, like a tail been dragged across them. But I can't tell where his trail leads afterwards."

"It looks to me like their headed that way." Aku pointed into the woods, away from the farmhouse. "We'd better get going. We can't be far behind."

"Hmm." Tua examined the harpflowers a bit more before rising with a sigh. "Aye, you're most likely right. You're a brave lad, you know that?"

Aku smiled wanly. "Every second we waste they're getting farther ahead, right?"

Lono stretched and gazed up at the rafters, their empty framework forming a criss-cross pattern against the blue sky. It must be past midday or later. Kai made a funny sort of wheezing sound when he breathed on one side of her and Hulu snored on one side. *So Hulu's not dead, after all,* she thought.

She stood and stretched her sore calves. A bit of birdsong reminded her of a flute, and Lono thought of Aku. Was he angry at her for stealing the cylinder? How was he faring with Tua? And how close were they now? *No telling how long we've been asleep. They're probably not far behind at all.*

"Time to wake up, boys. We don't want to be late."

Kai was awake instantly and fumbling his way to his feet but Hulu only moaned. She squatted by him and shook his shoulder. "We have to get going. Reach the city around dusk, remember?"

"Of course, of course," Hulu mumbled. He sat up and rubbed his eyes. After a moment, something seemed to occur to him, and he gave her a questioning look.

He's wondering about the dream, Lono thought. *He probably thinks I hate him.* "By the way. When we get to the city, you don't have to take me to the convent."

Surprise crossed Hulu's face. "What do you mean? What about our agreement?"

"I want to continue on with you, to where you have the device hidden," Lono said. "Then to the lab. I want to help you destroy it. And even to deliver Kai to his lagoon. I've started this undertaking, and I want to see it through to the end."

"Are you sure? It could be dangerous, you know." Hulu gingerly pushed himself to his feet, as if every muscle in his body was tender. "No, I think it's best if I take you back to the convent."

"If it's dangerous, you'll need me there all the more!" Lono said. "I can see things, you know. Far away and in the dark. The power from my tattoo."

"That's true," Hulu said. "But I think—"

"And you're hardly in a condition half the day to do anything."

Hulu's eyebrows arched. "Now half a day is an exagger—"

"Listen. You need me there. You know I can help you."

Hulu didn't respond for a moment, then took his cape up and fastened it at his neck. "Well, then, if you're so determined, we'd better get moving."

TWENTY-FIVE

"Please, sir, spare a bronzer?" The pitiful stooped woman, clad in barkcloth rags, held a cup out to Kai as he passed by. He turned his head and she startled on seeing his face underneath his hood, wheeling back into the crowd. "You're...you're a monster!"

"C'mon, Grandfather," Hulu said, tugging at Kai's sleeve. Lono took his arm on the other side and they proceeded down the block, leaving the old woman stammering in horror. Nobody seemed to pay her or them any mind.

Of course Kai had heard about the great city of the surface men, just as he'd heard of the great city of the rays in the far ocean. He'd never seen either, though, and never thought he would. The reality of Atlantis was different from his imagination. For one thing, the sheer concentration of so many people in the street, crowds of them, even now at night, as they talked and walked, or beseeched passersby for food or alms, or hurried about on errands, was almost overwhelming. The never-ending busyness reminded him a bit of a reef, except there it was a profusion of species, living together in a harmonious dance. Here it was just surface men in their thousands. *How can they stand to live like this, crushed together so closely?*

As for the buildings, even Kai could see the terrible effects of the recent earthquake. Everywhere, what must have been mighty structures had been reduced to rubble, dusty piles of stone or wood, or mere burned out shells, still smoking even so many days after the catastrophe. Still, there were plenty of buildings left. Most impressive, Kai thought, were the homes and shops carved out of the huge kimunu trees, looming over the streets as he, Hulu, and Lono made their way along.

One advantage of the press of people was that nobody seemed to care about any of them, even if one of their party possessed an unusual, toothy snout sticking out of his hood. After passing through the giant arched gate at the city entrance, Hulu had quickly hustled them off the main road and into the relatively quieter side streets, keeping Kai sandwiched between him and Lono, but it didn't really seem to matter. Even the Shabengee guards, striding around in their black breeches and sharkskin capes, cudgels in hand as if they might have to use them at any time, paid no mind to them. Kai perceived a curious glance here or there, but except for the one beggarwoman, everybody was in such a hurry, so intent on their own affairs, they just didn't have time to worry about one oddity.

The darkness helped, though there was not as much of that as Kai would have liked. It was nearly a full moon on a clear, star-filled night, for one thing. For another, the intersections of streets were lit by lanterns suspended from poles, and torchlight spilled out of the windows and open doorways of stores and residences, at least the ones that were still intact. Even many passers-by carried their own lanterns or torches. The effect was of a sort of endless, murky evening, where night was not quite banished, but only able to creep in around the edges. Kai wondered if Atlanteans ever slept.

"Hoow faar?" he asked.

"I suppose we're halfway there," Hulu said. "We have to reach Middle Island at the very center of the city."

"And that's where your device for the cylinder is located?" Lono asked. "Do you have it hidden in some alleyway?"

"You'll see, you'll see," Hulu said.

Hulu and Lono continued to bicker about the device, but Kai's mind stuck on Hulu's description of their position in the city. *Only halfway to the center?* They'd entered the city an hour ago! Kai's mind boggled at the size of the metropolis. Still, one thing he'd started to notice was the proliferation of delicious smells. It seemed every block had some well-lit building with the mouth-watering aroma of roasting meat floating out. He still preferred his meals raw, but he he'd tried Hulu's cooked meat and had to admit the smoke and heat added something to the flavor. "Eeat sooon? Haave huunger."

Hulu halted. "You make a good point, friend. We've been on our feet for hours without a bite, haven't we? Let's see if we can find some low establishment where the patrons won't ask many questions."

It turned out there was just such an inn on the next block, and Hulu led them in to find a table. None of the three noticed the dark, winged shape observing them from a nearby rooftop. It fluttered off with a hiss as soon as they passed inside.

Tua became increasingly agitated and fearful as he wandered the streets of Atlantis with Aku, convinced that spies might be watching them everywhere they turned. *This whole undertaking has become a cursed fiasco*, he thought. He'd realized at some point on the road that they must've passed their quarry, and decided to linger about a mile outside the city gates hidden in heavy ground cover, waiting. The problem was that after two days with little sleep and near-constant walking, he and Aku had fallen asleep in the warmth and softness. By the time his eyes had snapped open it was well after sunset. The three they sought must have long since entered the city.

And now, here they were, in the one place they shouldn't be, the one place he had agreed he and Aku would never step foot in again. Free to go anywhere on the whole island, that was the deal with the Puhi, so long as neither he, Aku, and Lono, nor the cylinder, ever returned to the city. *Why didn't I take the cylinder, melt it down, and bury it deep in the ground?* Because he was still a member of the Ho'oule, that's why, and who knows, someday he still might have made contact with someone he could pass it on to.

Of course, none of this would've ever been a problem if that damned scribe hadn't come along with his long hair, his fancy cape, his weird reptile friend. Tua hated to think what that debauched conman had gotten up to with Lono. *Probably spent the whole journey trying to seduce her, and she only just over the threshold of womanhood.* He had to admit, Lono seemed a fairly sensible young woman. He just hoped she had sense enough to resist Hulu's oily advances. Tua gritted his teeth.

"Where are we going?" Aku asked with a tug on Tua's shift.

Tua stopped short and looked around. Without thinking, his feet had brought them to the familiar environs of Bonetown. But that's not where the scribe would go. *And I suppose I can rule out the fellow returning Lono to her convent, since he's no doubt keeping her for himself. Where then?*

The scribe had mentioned something about hiding a decoding device for the cylinder. Of course, Tua had little idea about the rich friends such a man as a master scribe might have, what with their palaces and dinner parties. He had no hope of tracking them down if such a place were their destination. But what if the scribe had hidden it in the one place he undoubtedly knew best, the Scriptorium? *It's a place to start the search, anyway.*

"Our destination be Middle Island, boy," he said.

"Are we going the right way?"

"Yes. Well, right down this street, then." He ducked into a lane and came out the other end headed the opposite direction. *Hopefully I can get the cylinder, convince Lono to come with us, and get the hell out of the city before daybreak and with no trouble.* But if force was needed, he wouldn't cry if he had to tangle with the scribe. Tua patted the place on his side where his knife was sheathed.

Hulu and Lono leaned against the large basalt bowl of the decorative pond while Kai floated submerged, hidden under a layer of watercress. They had scrambled over the walls into the Scriptorium's garden with little trouble, simply waiting for a moment when the street outside was empty of people. Hulu was surprised to find himself almost brought to tears to be in the garden again, among its beautiful arrangements of ahi grass and fire lilies, listening to the soothing burbling of its fountains, and bathed in the scent of lavender, ragmint, and sweetpearl weed from the herb beds. He'd planted many of the plants here himself, though it seemed he'd always been too busy to spend as much time here as he'd like.

"How long will we need to wait?" Lono asked.

"I'm not sure," Hulu said. "It's not unknown for a brother to take a late night turn in the garden, though. Especially with all the work we've had lately, we're often awake into the small hours. This is the perfect place to rest weary eyes."

"It reminds me of the convent," Lono said. "But I would never have expected a place so green in the city itself."

Hulu risked putting his hand on Lono's. He was pleasantly surprised when she grasped it back. The moonlight was so white and gentle it felt like cool rain. It felt almost like one of their dreams. Hulu hardly dared to breathe lest it disturb the moment. Slowly, carefully, he turned his head and observed the side of Lono's face, her large brown eyes, her fine bronze skin. She turned to him and they leaned towards each other, lips brushing.

The sound of padded footsteps came from behind a screen of pink-flowered ili-ili vines growing on a trellis. They pulled apart, sitting up straight. A brother in a brown-hooded robe strolled around the corner and spotted them.

"Oh, I'm sorry, I didn't mean to interrupt—"

"It's okay. Is that you, Opio?"

"Master!" In a second, Opio was in front of him, bowing.

Hulu rose and put a hand on his shoulder. "Please. There's no need for formality." He gestured at Lono. "Lono, I'd like to present Opio, one of the brothers. Opio, this is my…friend, Lono."

Opio offered his hand as he gave a wondering glance at the young woman. "Oh, so good to meet you, Miss Lono." A wave of concern passed over his face. "But you shouldn't be here, Master. Captain Ino knows you're on your way."

"He does?" Hulu asked. "How?"

"I'm not sure, but I overheard him and the guards talking about it earlier. And, I'm sorry, but I've let you down."

"Why would you say that?" Hulu asked.

Opio lowered his head in shame. "Your bronze device, Master. I hid it deep in an archive, among heaps of scrolls that hadn't been disturbed for years, but the Shabengee found it somehow. Only yesterday, in fact. Actually, the guards searched the whole Scriptorium. Ransacked the place. as if they knew what they were looking for."

"That's not your fault at all," Hulu said. "And still, maybe it's not too late. Perhaps we can—"

"*Caw!*" From somewhere in the garden came a mad fluttering of wings and a horrible hissing, followed by stamping footsteps.

"Keki!" Lono cried, springing to her feet.

Opio pulled Hulu and Lono along one of the paths, speaking in a low tone. "Please, Master, come this way. We have to get you and Miss Lono out of here before it's too late."

They rounded a corner and came face to face with Captain Ino, two guards at his side.

"I'ke Regent!" Captain Ino called. "Good to see you again, Master Scribe."

Hulu and Lono spun around, but two more guards blocked the path behind them.

"You were saying it's too late, Opio?" Captain Ino cast a disdainful glance at Hulu. "I know not how you survived this long, Master Scribe. You are most persistently annoying."

"You knew we were coming," Hulu said flatly.

"Indeed we did, Master Scribe."

Hulu swallowed. "And I suppose you plan on doing me the honor of executing me yourself?"

"A tempting thought. But yer fate is out of my hands." Captain Ino took a step forward so his face was only inches from Hulu's. "Regent has some questions for you, he does. Wants to know all about that device of yours, and what you planned to do with it. Two special agents are coming round in the morning to pick you up."

"Special agents?"

"Aye, special agents." Captain Ino glanced at his arm, where his hammerhead was shaking its head fiercely. "And their tattoos make mine look like a wee tender bunny rabbit. I hope you like eels, Master Scribe."

PART FIVE

Master Makule spent eight days with the gods on Anuane Island, studying the letters with Ne'i Peo during the day and supping with them around their fire at night. They treated him as an honored guest, giving him food to eat and wine with honey and herbs to drink. They gave him a cape of feathers, one from each type of bird on the earth, woven by Ne'i Lopi for Master Makule to wear.

And on the eighth day, after he had learned the letters and how to write them with a quill and how to mix the tints with the mother ink, so that only the truth could be written, Ne'i Lapa built a raft for Master Makule, and hitched it to four dolphins, to pull it to Atlantis.

"Remember what you have learned here, and record the deeds, great or shameful, of the kings and heroes of Atlantis," Ne'i Peo commanded Master Makule. "Record them so that your sons and daughters might remember their ancestors and their history and know what sort of nation they are."

Master Makule promised to do so, and he waded into the ocean and boarded the raft, and the four dolphins pulled him back to his home before the sun had reached its height. When he reached Atlantis, he did as he had promised, and recorded the deeds, great or shameful, of the mighty kings and heroes. Nor did he neglect to teach others the art of letters, and of writing, and of mixing the ink, so that the deeds of each generation, great or shameful, could be recorded in their turn.

--from the *Chronicle of the Scribes*

TWENTY-SIX

Tua and Aku had circled the Scriptorium compound twice from a discreet distance, but noticed nothing unusual. The glowering Shabengee guard at the front gate seemed uncharacteristically alert for the night shift, but perhaps things were still tense from the earthquake. There was no sign of Lono or Hulu. Tua was about ready to give up and try something else when Aku pointed something out.

"Tua, look at that man over there." A hooded figure huddled in a crevice of the building across the way, his long robe wrapped around his hunched body.

"An old beggar. So what?"

"A beggar with a snout?"

Tua studied the figure more closely in the dim light. Sure enough, he did have an unusually long and prominent nose. Rather toothy, too, now that he was paying attention. Maybe they'd come to the right place after all.

"Kai, is it?" Tua said as he approached.

The figure looked up and rose slightly as if to run, then apparently decided it didn't have time to get away and sat back down. The movement caused its hood to fall back, revealing crocodilian features. "Ooh! Goood niight!"

"Yes, it be a good evening," Tua said. "What are you doing out here? Shouldn't you be with your friends?"

Kai regarded him with those yellow eyes, probably trying to decide if he could be trusted. "Frieends goone Caaptured. Noot mee. Meen doon't fiind mee."

"You're that good at hiding, eh?"

"I goood at staay in waater. Poond in gaarden. Meen doon't loook."

An accidental stroke of good fortune, or was the creature a coward? Tua still couldn't get a read on him. "How long ago did the guards capture them?"

"Noot tooo loong. I thiink oone hoour."

"I see," Tua said. It was about what he'd imagined. That damn fool scribe had come in here with all the subtlety of a wild boar in rutting season, thinking he'd get his device without anybody noticing. It was surprising he'd made it all the way to Middle Island, and hadn't simply been dragged into a back alley on the way by some thug on Regent's payroll. "Are they still holding them inside?"

"I noot seee theemm leeave," Kai said. "I waatch heere."

Tua had to admit the reptile had picked a good spot, with the entrance to the Scriptorium in view, yet far enough and hidden enough not to seem like he was keeping an eye on things. Just another beggar trying to stay out of the elements. Maybe he was smarter than Tua had given him credit for. Tua wondered if those teeth of his would come in handy in a scrap, as well. He'd always heard the kai-men avoided conflict, but he bet they could be tough bastards if backed into a corner. Yes, maybe the reptile could help with the plan already beginning to form in his mind.

"Are we going to rescue them, Tua?" Aku asked.

"Have to, boy. Got to get that cylinder back, or the deal's broken and we're in for an ocean of trouble."

"What deal?"

Tua glanced at Aku, whose wide questioning eyes looked up at him trustingly. Sometimes the boy seemed so mature, even jaded, and other times he'd do or say something to remind Tua he was really little more than a child. "Don't you worry about that. We'll figure a way to get the cylinder, and Lono too."

"What about Hulu? If they were both captured, he needs rescuing too."

Tua sighed. "Yes, I suppose the scribe is part of the package."

But if he causes one bit of trouble, he gets left to his fate.

Lono and Hulu sat back to back in the otherwise unoccupied sleeping chamber of a novice scribe, bound to each other with a long length of hihi vine, and their hands tied with shorter lengths. A bit of moonlight came through the high window, and straw for bedding was strewn around them on the wooden floor. Even if they could untie themselves, the chamber's door had been bolted from the outside, a development Hulu had immediately noted. *Does Captain Ino use this chamber as a jail cell? How many brothers has he locked up that he needed to have a bolt specially installed?*

Pondering that opened the floodgates for a surge of fears and regrets. What had the Shabengee been doing to his scribes and his Scriptorium while Hulu was away? How had they been twisting the sacred and ancient art of truth writing, so vital to Atlantis? What false contracts or histories had they been concocting? And all because he hadn't been wise or strong or persistent enough to stop them, to save himself, to save anyone or anything for whom he loved or cared. Not his brother scribes, not Malu, and not Lono or even Kai, wherever he was now. *Master Makule would not be proud,* he reflected darkly. *Neither would Alani.*

"You breathing is ragged," Lono said.

"Well, I feel like we're under a lot of pressure here."

"You should take deep breaths," Lono said. "It will help calm you. Follow my words. Breathe in through your nose—good—now slowly, out through your mouth. Again, slowly in through your nose. And now out."

"You know what?" Hulu said. "That does help."

"I have been praying to Ne Wa'e. She will help us."

"What if she's busy?" Hulu asked.

"If Ne Wa'e has decided this is our time, then she will help us conquer our fear in our last moments."

"Hmm." Hulu's breathing sped up again, his breaths turning

short and shallow. "What would really help me conquer my fear is in that burlap bag we left by the pond downstairs. If it's still there."

Lono was silent for several moments. "Is that all you can think about? Your bag of ink? And the next time you can smoke it?"

"No, that's not all I can think about. That's the problem. Every single thing that's going wrong keeps circling around in my brain like a whirlpool."

"Your smoking doesn't help that," Lono said. "It only makes it worse. It saps your energy for dealing with your problems."

"You're wrong." Hulu shook his head. "That's why they call it truth smoking. It lets me see what the truth is. You don't know how many decisions the head of the Scriptorium has to make. Should I deal with this or work on that? Should I assign this to one brother or another, or put it off for something more important? When I smoke, I know what the right decisions are. The false ones break the dance."

"Break the dance?"

"You know what I mean. They don't feel right."

"So you don't use your own judgment when you make decisions, you just do whatever the ink tells you to do."

"No!" Hulu faltered. "Well, maybe. But you do the same thing! Didn't you tell me only a moment ago you prayed to Ne Wa'e to tell you what to do?"

"I don't pray to the goddess to make my decisions for me," Lono said, her tone indignant. "I pray for wisdom and strength, so I can make my own good decisions."

"Well, what if your decisions aren't the right ones?" Hulu asked.

"Have your decisions been the right ones?"

Hulu didn't answer.

"I thought you were so bold in our dreams," Lono said quietly. "The way you touched me without hesitation. Without worrying about whether it was the right thing or the wrong thing. It was what you wanted, and that made it the right thing. Now I know, you only do what the ink tells you."

Neither spoke for a long time after that. It was difficult to tell how much time passed. At some point, a scratching sound came from underneath the floor in the far corner of the room. A stone panel rose and the grinning face of a scribe came into view.

"Opio!" Hulu said. "How did you do that?"

Opio put his finger to his lips before lifting himself up. "Captain Ino uses this room as an isolation chamber," he whispered. "A way to punish brothers who've brought down his ire. He puts us in here for days with no food or water."

"So you found a way to provide for them," Hulu said. "Ingenious."

"It was Oleli who came up with the idea," Opio said. He pulled out the small knife the scribes carried to sharpen quills and went to work on their bonds. "There. Now to sneak you two out of here."

"Opio, do you think all the scribe brothers would follow my orders? Even if I asked them to do something dangerous?"

"We would follow you without hesitation, Master. Only give the word."

Hulu wavered. What he had in mind would put the lives of many brothers at risk. And that's even if his idea worked. How could he know if it would succeed, without smoking the ink? So many could die if this went badly. But he remembered what Aku had said back at the cabin. Eighty scribes against nine guards. The numbers were on their side.

He looked at Lono, who was rubbing her wrists to restore the blood circulation. She sensed his eyes on her and coolly returned his gaze. It seemed like a challenge: *If you're really the man from my dream, do it.*

Hulu set his jaw. "Opio, pass the word to every brother. Tell them to gather quickly in the Great Hall as soon as the first morning bell tolls. And to bring their knives. We're going to kick out the Shabengee."

"Okay, let's go over the plan," Tua said. The three stood around a barrel in an alleyway with a crude map of the Scriptorium grounds drawn in the dust on the barrelhead. "Aku, what be your part?"

Aku pointed at the garden door represented in the dust. "I sneak in through here like a mouse and scout out each level without a soul seeing me. You'll be waiting at the stairwell. When I find where they're holding Lono and Hulu, I come back to you."

"Right. And what be the sign of the place where they're holding them?"

"Probably a guard posted outside. And if there is a guard, I'll call out from one side to get his attention while you come up the other side and knock his brains out."

"Excellent. Kai, what be your part?"

Kai leaned over so his short arm could reach the barrel and pointed at the garden door. "Iii waait heere aand keeep oopen. Choomp guaard if neeed."

"Right. If things go well, me and Aku be coming out in a hurry with Lono and the scribe, and nobody else the wiser, so keep that door clear."

"Yeess."

Tua turned to Aku. "And then me and you hightail it out of town before anybody even knows the cylinder was here."

Aku looked troubled.

"What's wrong, boy?" Tua asked.

"Tua, what if Lono doesn't have the cylinder with her? What if the guards have already taken it when we get there?"

Tua tapped the barrelhead a couple times. "We'll figure that out when the time come. We have to rescue them before we can know." *And if that be the only thing that goes wrong tonight, it'll be a minor miracle.*

TWENTY-SEVEN

Captain Ino felt uneasy. There seemed to be a buzz in the air, a tense expectancy that some frayed knot was about to break. It was hours past midnight, and all should be quiet. Yet he sensed movement, heard the footsteps of scribes in their sleeping cells, even the low murmur of voices.

He supposed the brothers had learned of their master's return. Captain Ino had hoped Hulu's capture would remain a secret, at least until he could turn the man and his wench over to the Puhi in the morning without anybody else being the wiser. Probably Opio had spread the word. *I'll have that little fool flogged after this business with the Puhi is done*, he thought. *Ten lashes ought to teach him to keep his mouth shut.*

A quick turn through the halls couldn't hurt anything. At the least, the ring of his heavy boots on the stone floors would be a reminder to the scribes to settle down. He certainly wasn't getting any sleep, not this night. Perhaps what was bothering him most was Hulu appearing at all. Obviously, he had escaped the Puku during the earthquake. If the Master Scribe been smart, he would've fled the city and never come back. But to show up here again, after all these weeks? Captain Ino had written Hulu off as a simpering little grease addict, passive and weak, but his plan to sneak into the Scriptorium right under Ino's nose showed real balls. Stupid, but courageous. The exact opposite of Captain Ino's original assessment of the man.

And what of the report he'd received on the Puhis' first visit that Hulu would have allies with him? The wench they'd mentioned had clearly come along, but where was the great large bald man, described as a fierce fighter and not to be underestimated? The reptile? The boy thief? Perhaps the crew had a falling out. After all, those hardly seemed like boon companions for the bookish scribe. *Or perhaps they're still out in the city, waiting for Hulu to come back to them. Well, they can wait until they rot. Or maybe a little rough handling can shake some answers from the Master Scribe.*

Captain Ino gave a mighty push to a door at the end of one hallway, and it opened with such force the ever-lit torches flickered in the rush of air. One of the scribes, a slight fellow with wispy hair and a sickly complexion, froze halfway down the corridor.

"You there!" Captain Ino yelled. "What are you doing out of yer cell after curfew?"

"Please, sir." The man shook like a leaf as Captain Ino lumbered towards him. "I get indigestion."

"Indigestion? Shab's balls! What's your bedpan for, then?"

"It's just...I thought a bit of a walk might help. My stomach gets so upset, you see."

Captain Ino looked the scribe over as if he were the most preposterous thing he'd ever seen. "And what's that? In your hand?"

"My...my sharpening knife, sir."

"You needed your knife for a walk to aid yer digestion?"

"I must have grabbed it by habit."

Captain Ino hated the way the man shrank before him. Actually, he hated all the scrawny scribes and their smug, pale faces, their inane little in-jokes, their sneaking around and stealing ink and begging and cringing when caught. These weren't real men, not like his guards, good straightforward fellows who enjoyed a full measure of life, who could go a whole night of drinking, carousing, and whoring and come in at dawn for a day's duty.

He gave the worm a cuff on the ear he wouldn't soon forget, knocking him to the ground and sending the knife skidding across the floor. The man cried out with a pitiful "oof" and made no attempt to get up.

Captain Ino addressed the quivering mass with a growl. "Don't ever let me see you in these halls again before the morning bell, unless you fancy the taste of the lash." *Lesson taught*, he thought as he walked away. It would be just the thing for his mood if there were plenty of other scribes needing lessons before the night was through.

Hulu and Lono sat in simple wooden chairs in Opio's sleeping chamber. Opio had gone to rouse the brothers, leaving the two of them alone. Hulu suspected the Shabengee had an idea something was up, as he'd heard the boots of a guard pass by outside the door at least twice in the past half hour. His stomach churned and sweat rolled down his temples. He wasn't sure if it was anxiety from the coming revolt or because he was nearing the time for his normal ink dosage.

Lono sensed his nervousness and took his hand. "What are you thinking?" she asked.

"Just going over the plan in my mind. And the hundred ways it's sure to go wrong."

"Tell it to me," she said. "Let's figure it out together."

"All right. Opio's told all the brothers to be in the Great Hall at the morning bell. But we'll likely only have a couple minutes before the guards realize something's up. We'll need to swiftly divide everybody up into teams. Nine men per team, I think, one for each guard."

"Sounds sensible so far," Lono said. "How will you divide them?"

"First, I'll designate the team leaders. Myself, of course. Opio, Oleli, a few other brothers who can act decisively."

"What about me?"

"You?" Hulu said. "You'll be here, safe until I get back."

"I certainly will not," Lono said. "I came along to help, not to sit around waiting for you. If you don't have something for me to do, I'll find a job myself."

"I don't think you understand how dangerous this might be," Hulu said. "These guards will be armed. They might fight back. You could get hurt."

"All the more reason to put me on a team, rather then leave me alone. What if a guard comes across me here by myself? Better to be in a group."

"Well, you do have a point, but—"

"Great. And now that I'll be on a team, put me in charge of it."

"But…I…" Hulu *was* having trouble thinking of eight brothers who could run a team. The scribe's vocation attracted followers who valued an ordered life and quiet, careful reflection, not action or command. Lono certainly seemed more comfortable giving orders than most of his men.

"Well?" Lono asked. "Why not?"

Hulu sighed. "Fine. You'll head one of the teams. After that, I'll assign each leader a part of the Scriptorium to sweep, and each team leader will grab eight men. As soon as they do that, they'll fan out to your locations. Ideally, each team will encounter one guard, though of course it probably won't work out that way. If an area is clear, then they'll move on and see if some other group needs help."

"And what will we do if we do come across a guard?"

"Capture him, and bring him back to the Great Hall. Try not to hurt him. Hopefully, they'll surrender when they see they're outnumbered. But if it comes to a fight…"

"We'll do what we have to do to subdue them," Lono said.

"Right." Hulu narrowed his eyes at Lono. "But not you. Don't even think about it. Leave the fighting to the brothers."

Lono drew in a breath as if to argue even that point, but saw Hulu's jaw set and seemed to think better of it. "It sounds straightforward enough."

"It needs to be. We don't have time to practice anything more complicated." Hulu shook his head. "I just hope no brothers get hurt. And I don't know how I could forgive myself if any of them were to get killed."

"Don't think about that," Lono said. "Once the guards are captured, what then?"

"We'll tie them up in the Great Hall. I'll have to see how this plays out before I really know, but I suppose at that point I'll start negotiating with Captain Ino. After that, I'll get out the decoder and see what that cylinder around your neck has to say. And of course, we need to find out what happened to Kai. Hopefully he got away, but we might have to search for him in the city."

Lono gave his hand a squeeze. "I think your plan is great. I'm sure it'll work fine."

"I appreciate your confidence, but I don't share it." Hulu frowned. "My guess is, even as we speak, some confounding variable is at work."

Tua stepped silently behind the guard posted outside a room on the third floor. He held a flat round stone from a pool in the garden, and conked the guard on the back of the skull. The guard slid to the floor like a paper doll dropped from a child's hand.

Tua gestured to Aku at the end of the hall. Everything so far had gone according to Tua's plan. Well, more or less. The winding, criss-crossing passages had proved time-consuming for the boy to navigate, and they'd both had to avoid wandering scribes and guards. *Doesn't anybody here sleep at night?* Tua had thought. As a result, it'd taken them longer to find the room than they'd hoped, and it was nearing dawn. Still, here they were. If they could untie Lono and Hulu and bolt from the Scriptorium swift as an awi bird, they would be gone before anybody noticed.

"Is he dead?" Aku whispered, pointing at the guard.

"No, lad. Just dreaming."

Tua pulled back the bolt and unlatched the door. It slowly swung open. Tua and Aku peered in.

There was no one there.

"Damn the luck!" Tua muttered.

"Look, here on the floor," Aku said. He picked up the sliced hihi vines. "They were here. They must have escaped."

"Three days of tracking and we still can't catch them." Tua took a vine and inspected its end. Cut clean, as with a knife. "They can't have gone too far, though. They guard didn't know they were missing, so they must still have been in here recently."

"But where are they going now?" Aku asked. "Do they have the device with them?"

"Right," Tua said. "The device." *They wouldn't leave without the device, that's why they were here, right? But with the guards on the lookout, there's no way they could get it back. Unless…*

"What is it?" Aku pulled on Tua's sleeve. "What are you thinking?"

"That can't be right, can it?" Tua thought back on the events of the evening. So much activity, so many scribes sneaking around, and every one he'd seen had been holding a knife. And from behind closed doors, the low tones of urgent conversations. He could have sworn he'd even overheard voices saying Hulu's name. "Surely he's not really planning…"

From the bell tower at the top of the Scriptorium came a heavy *bong* that reverberated throughout the building.

Bong.

Bong.

Bong.

Bong.

Bong.

Six times. The morning bell calling the scribes to their day.

TWENTY-EIGHT

Lono led her eight scribes up the stairwell to the sixth floor of the tower, the very top of the Scriptorium, as they'd been assigned. She carried a quill-sharpening knife lent by a scribe who'd had an extra and a roll of twine normally used for tying rolled scrolls, but today to be used to bind any captured guards. Actually, she suspected Hulu had given her team the area he thought least likely to hold a guard, but just as well. The group she led seemed even scrawnier and more anemic than the average, judging from the brothers she'd seen gathered at the assembly. Still, they had a job to do—check and clear each room, while keeping on the lookout for the decoding device.

At the top, on the landing before the heavy door to the corridor, she turned to her troops. "Everybody ready?"

One scribe, leaning over with his hands on his knees, raised a hand. "Miss?" He breathed heavily. "Can we take a minute to catch our breaths?"

"Sure," Lono said. "That's a good idea. One minute."

A short fellow standing next to her tapped his foot repeatedly and rolled the hilt of his knife over and over between the palms of his hands.

"Are you nervous?" she asked him.

"A little, Miss. Not too much. Just ready to get going."

"What's your name?" she asked.

"Akahi, Miss."

"So Akahi, what's up on this level?" Lono asked. "Sleeping

chambers?"

"Not on the sixth floor," the man answered. "This is the toughest floor to reach, so it's mostly archives and storage, things we don't need to access too often. Oh, and the master's apartment, as well."

"I see," Lono said. Hulu's personal chambers. "A bit inconvenient for him, all the way up here, isn't it?"

"That's true, Miss, but more private as well. And you should see the view."

The view? It's Hulu's ink habit, she thought. *He would want as much privacy as possible.* She turned to the group. "Time to go. Everybody pair off, and take a room. When your room's clear, move to the next unoccupied one. If anybody needs help, yell and others will come running. When we have the whole floor checked, we'll regroup here and see if they need help on the fifth floor."

Lono pushed the door open and the scribes went to work. There were four pairs, plus her. She considered joining a pair but decided she didn't need a partner. They probably weren't going to encounter anybody, anyway.

The first rooms were empty except for shelves, probably once full of scrolls the guards had burned. *Priceless treasures, forever gone,* Lono reflected. But finally she checked a room that the guards must not have finished with yet. It was full of scrolls strewn about in heaps up to her knees, the shelves where they had been stored smashed and splintered. On a whim, she picked a scroll up and stood under a window so she could see it better in the dawn light. She untied the binding, spread the yellowed vellum out and started reading:

> *The people see the deeds of the wicked but do not condemn*
> *How rare is the man who treasures righteousness in his heart!*
> *Count yourself not among the crowds, do not follow them*
> *Put your trust in Ne'i Lopi and he will take your part.*

It seemed to be a collection of wisdom sayings dedicated to

Ne'i Lopi, the robin god, who watched over children and mothers, and prayed to by those wishing a blessing for new projects, especially concerning the house and family. *I wish I had time to read more.* She smiled and put the scroll back on the heap where she'd found it. This room seemed to be clear.

The layout of the sixth floor would have been a challenge to map, honeycombed as it was with passages and side halls. Still, they were making quick progress. She advanced past several more rooms where the other brothers were already searching and stopped in front of a room with a large, heavy wooden door. She pushed it open slowly.

The chamber inside was clean and sparsely furnished. A writing desk stood against the far wall under a window with closed shutters. Scrolls hung on the walls, and she recognized from the archaic words and phrases they must be an ancient from of Atlantean. She stopped in front of one particularly ancient and yellowed one. Even the alphabet on this one was different, recognizable letters mixed with unfamiliar ones. *Iwali would love to see those*, Lono thought. *I bet this is Hulu's apartment.*

In an adjoining chamber, the mattress on a bed had been slashed open and the contents of a wardrobe thrown on the floor. A single, rose-colored gown still hung on its hook. Lono took it in her hands, running her fingers over the finely-made silk. She held it up to her body. It seemed to be exactly her size. She brought the fabric to her face and breathed in, detecting a trace of fragrant op'ia oil. Her eyes narrowed. *Does Hulu have a wife? Or perhaps a mistress? He's never mentioned her. But if she's a secret, why would he assign my team to this floor?*

Before she could puzzle further over the matter, a shout came from somewhere outside the room. Lono hastily replaced the gown on the hook and rushed into the corridor.

Hulu took his team straight to the corridor on the second floor where the Shabengee guards had set up their barracks in the building. These were the Scriptorium's largest and finest rooms, with large windows overlooking the river that surrounded Middle Island, and had once been reserved for the senior scribes. Now they served as the guards' quarters, armory, and lounge.

He had put on his team the largest and most physically vigorous of the scribes, such as they were. Nevertheless, he hoped to catch the guards unprepared and avoid a real fight.

Luck was with them for they checked the armory first and encountered the guard retiring from the night watch, sitting on a stool in his loincloth having just shed his armor, scabbard, and weapons belt, which lay jumbled at his feet. He looked up with bewilderment at the scribes entering the room.

"What be the idea? You lot ain't allowed in here!"

"On your feet, Shabengee," Hulu said. "You're now a prisoner."

The man eyed the eight scribes brandishing knives in his direction and decided on surrender. He rose with his arms raised and hands open.

Hulu's hands shook as he unrolled a length of twine. How long had it been since his last dose of ink? He tried to recall. *Fairly early yesterday morning,* he thought. *Not quite a full day yet.* He'd hardly noticed the beginnings of the withdrawal pangs in all the excitement, but the cramps and queasiness were becoming too strong to ignore now.

"Twine?" the guard sneered. "Do I look like papyrus to you? I could break this in my sleep."

Hulu ignored the taunt. "Arms behind your back, if you please. That's right. Now, if you would be so good as to accompany my scribes down to the Great Hall."

"Captain Ino will have yer hide for this, you know," the guard said. Despite his bravado, Hulu could tell the man was rattled. His tattoo sharks stayed perfectly still on his skin.

"Ka'le, Maki, take him down," Hulu said briskly, choosing two scribes he knew to have good sense. "Seat him in a corner and keep an eye on him. Have your knives at the ready, but otherwise don't interact. Understood?"

"Aye, master," the scribes responded.

Hulu clapped his hands and the three left. One guard down, eight to go. He could only hope the rest of the uprising was going so smoothly.

Captain Ino paced impatiently by the door at the garden entrance. Seemed his expected guests were allergic to being seen coming in the main entrance—stealth and secrecy and all that. He could hear shouts and running footsteps from inside the Scriptorium, even occasional clangs of metal or thunks as of something falling to the ground. Following the unstill night, it's clear the scribes were attempting a coup, and he should be inside leading his men. But he had an agreement to meet his two special callers here at dawn, and if there was anybody in all Atlantis he did not want to keep waiting, it was Puhi hunters.

Anyway, their visit should be fast. He would simply take the Puhi up, hand over the odd bronze device to them, as well as the master scribe and his wench, and be in their good graces for doing them the favor. Then he could join his men for the mop up of the rebellious monks, ferreting out who the leaders were and meting out appropriate punishments. He grinned inwardly at the punishment part. *Mr. Lash will be getting quite a workout before the mid-morning bell, I warrant.*

He stopped for a moment in front of a decorative rock sculpture where water trickled through thick mosses and stony outcroppings before dripping into a broad, shallow basin at the bottom. Such a typical scribe-ish piece of useless art, undoubtedly meant to inspire quiet contemplation or some such nonsense. Captain Ino made a note to himself to have the garden torn out and replaced with an exercise yard. This rock sculpture would be the first thing to go. Might be a good spot for some fencing dummies.

He took a few steps back to the door. A crash of broken glass came from somewhere inside. He gritted his teeth. *Where are they, anyway? You'd think mysterious unstoppable assassins might know something about punctuality.*

A splash of water behind him. *Ah, that must be them.* Captain Ino spun around, readying his greeting for the Puhi. A few simple words of honor, he thought. Busy men didn't have time for flowery phrases. Should he hold out his hand for a shake? Maybe not. At their first meeting they had simply given him meaningful nods. They didn't seem like the types who liked rubbing the flesh.

Captain Ino blinked, his mind struggling to interpret what he was seeing. Instead of two hooded figures approaching, there was a dripping, man-sized crocodile emerging from the basin of the sculpture. It rose up on its back legs, its gray-green scutes glistening in the rays of the rising sun, its claws extended, its mouth opened slightly to show lines of long, curved teeth.

So, the Puhi report was correct and the master scribe's reptile ally accompanied him after all. The creature didn't move, just stood there dripping and growling. After a few moments, Captain Ino realized the beast was actually trying to speak.

"Iff ssuurrender, Ii noot haarm."

"Surrender?" Captain Ino put his hand on the hilt of his sword and laughed. "You know, brute, I prefer sharkskin boots. But I think a pair made of alligator skin would cover my feet just as well."

TWENTY-NINE

Lono flew down the corridor toward the room where the shout had come from. There were scribes crowded around the door, and shouts and groans and the scrape of metal emerged from within.

"Is everything okay? What's going on?" She pushed her way through the scribes, who seemed to be vying to get a good view. She wasn't sure exactly what she expected to find—perhaps a cornered guard, refusing to give up, or even one of her men taken hostage. What she saw was even worse.

One of the scribes held a guard from behind, clutching his arms. The guard was in full uniform but his bronze helmet had been ripped off and tossed into the scattered scrolls. His face was a mess of blood and bruises.

Another scribe, Akahi, the short one she'd spoken to earlier, stood before the guard, one hand balled in a fist and the other clenching his knife. As Lono pressed into the room he brought the knife hilt down hard on the guard's temple with a sickening thump. The guard moaned and his eyes wandered in their sockets, his pupils dilated.

"Who spilled the ink now, you stinking cur?" Akahi shouted. "Who spilled it now?"

The guard's watering eyes fluttered and closed, and he slumped against the scribe who held him.

"Oh, don't you dare pass out on me, you bastard." He raised his fist as if to strike the unconscious man. "We're not done here, not by the curly tail of a kiki pig."

"Stop it!" Lono yelled, inserting herself between the guard and Akahi. "What are you doing?"

Akahi took a step back and stared up at her with red-hot eyes. "Retribution, Miss."

"This is not what we agreed to do," Lono said. "This is not what Master Hulu ordered."

"I'm only giving back to them what they've given to us, day after day after day." Akahi spoke through gritted teeth.

"And so when the tables are turned, you're no better than they are, is that what you're saying?"

Akahi breathed hard through flared nostrils. "You don't know what these swine did to us."

"You're right, I don't know," Lono said. "But I do know that all my life, I've heard about the honor of the Order of the Scribes. I can hardly believe this would be conduct becoming of Master Makule's Oath. Would it?"

It grew quiet as a prayer room. She regarded the faces of the gathered scribes. To a man, they turned their heads away, refusing to meet her gaze. Inwardly, she gave a quick word of thanks to Iwali, who had forced her to study the lore and customs of the various civic organizations of Atlantis. What had seemed the most boring of lessons at the time may have just saved a life. That bit about Master Makule had really struck a nerve. *Guess these scribes take their five-hundred-year-old Oath seriously... when they remember it.*

"How many rooms are left to check on this level?" Lono asked.

"Just a few, Miss," one of the scribes said.

"Good." She pointed at a pair of scribes by the door. "You two, take this guard, attend to his wounds, and watch him in the corridor until we're all ready. Akahi, you and your partner come with me. The rest of you, finish the search."

Lono strode from the room. She was gratified to hear that the scribes were scrambling to follow her orders behind her.

Kai studied the surface man standing before him with his bronze sword drawn. The man's hammerhead shark tattoos seemed to swim along the curves of his sizable biceps, their heads sweeping from side to side as if on the hunt. His eyes were bright and his mouth had a slight upward cast at the corners. His sweat odor was strong but had no hint of fear in it.

Kai was no expert in surface men expressions, but he believed this man was eager for a tussle. Overall, he found his entire demeanor suggestive of arrogance and disdain for his surroundings. Though Kai was a peaceful kai-man, it was clear he would need to fight in this situation. *No time to waste, then,* Kai thought. *Tua and Aku could be coming through that door any minute and I need to clear their way.*

Kai lunged at the man, pushing off with his tail to give his attack extra speed, coming in low to avoid the sword and get his claws between the protective copper strips hanging from the man's belt and the greaves protecting his legs. The force of the lunge pushed the man back several paces. Kai felt the sword come down on his back and bounced painfully off his scutes, but it did not pierce him. He found soft flesh on the man's thigh and dug his claw in, raking upward and producing a welling of blood. The man grunted with pain but with his other leg, he got a knee in to Kai's chest that knocked him to the ground. Kai rolled out of range of another sword blow and swept behind him with his tail, hoping to catch the man's feet. No luck.

Kai tried to push himself back up onto his hind legs, but the surface man tackled him from behind and knocked him back to the ground. No matter, wrestling was to Kai's advantage. The man was on Kai's back and had gotten his hands around Kai's snout, pulling it back painfully. Kai rolled himself repeatedly until they reached the basin beneath the rock sculpture, where he rammed the surface man against the stone edges until his grip slackened. Kai gave a great shake and the man tumbled off him to the ground.

Kai swiveled, hoping to get a claw in or perhaps clamp his jaw around a limb if the surface man was stunned. Instead he found the surface men already in a crouch, and grinning.

"You're faster'n you look, reptile, I'll give you that," the surface man said. "But this fight's over."

"Yoouu ssuurrender?" Kai asked.

"Ha!" the surface man said. "I think not."

Kai felt a tap on his back. He slowly turned his head. Behind him stood two hooded surface men holding long obsidian daggers so black they seemed to suck in the dawn light.

Hulu bade a pair of his men to escort the second Shabengee they'd come across to the Great Hall and resumed the search with the remainder of his team. They had found the bronze mechanism in Captain Ino's quarters, so that was a relief. Still, Hulu had thought he might catch three or four guards still lying abed, perhaps even the Captain himself. His relative lack of success meant the other teams would have more work to do. He hoped Lono fared well up on the sixth floor. *I sent her team to what's likely to be the quietest spot. Maybe she's even inspected my former apartment, whatever it looks like now.*

A withdrawal cramp started to build in his calf, shooting up through his hamstring and into his lower back. It came quickly, before he had time to grab onto anything, an agonizing stiffness that sent him flailing to the floor. He crashed into a row of shields that spun off in every direction.

"Master, is everything alright?" came a voice, but a flashing in Hulu's eyes kept him from seeing who had said it. When he tried to respond his throat didn't make any words, only a sort of "hnnn" sound.

"He just fell, I don't know why," the voice told somebody who must have come into the room. Footsteps and murmurs, but the pain was too intense for Hulu to concentrate. Finally the cramp crested and control of his muscles returned. He pushed himself onto his knees.

He felt hands on his arms, helping him to his feet. "Can you stand, master? How do you feel?"

"I'll be okay in a second." Hulu blinked his eyes to clear his vision. Two of the young under-scribes supported him, another two stood behind them with worried faces. He shook them off. "Don't worry about me. Have we searched every one of the rooms?"

"Yes, master," one of the scribes said.

Hulu wished he could remember their names. He'd always prided himself on addressing each scribe by his name, a recognition of brotherhood. His brain simply couldn't handle that task at the moment. Hopefully it'd come to him soon. "Alright, since we're all done here, let's get back down to the Great Hall and see if any other teams are reporting back."

Hulu gestured towards the door and the scribes filed out ahead of him. He took a deep breath. He'd have to get his regular ink dosage soon or the next attack would be even worse.

THIRTY

Tua and Aku ran down the hall leading to the garden door. They'd had to evade bands of crazed roving scribes with knives in their hands and violence in their eyes, and at one point had passed a fleeing, blood-soaked Shabengee guard in the stairwell. His tattoos had been cut right out of his arms.

Hopefully the reptile done his job and kept that exit clear, thought Tua. He flung open the door and he and Aku dashed out, only to come to an immediate halt. A Shabengee guard and a Puhi hunter held Kai pinned against an outcropping on a rock sculpture, while a second Puhi stood in front of him with his maka. The Puhi had shed their customary cloaks and were clad in only their loincloths, eel tattoos slithering across their torsos, up and down their legs, spiraling around their arms. The one holding Kai displayed silvery pike conger eels with long, narrow snouts and daggered teeth, the other pulsed with moray eels, yellow with thick brown speckles and wicked spiked teeth their jaws could barely contain.

They'd already cut Kai once, a long thin line of blood red against his soft white underbelly. The three men grinned in anticipation of what was coming next. The door slammed shut behind Tua and Aku. All turned to look at the newcomers. The one in front of Kai slowly turned around, his morays slithering in a frenzy.

Aku pulled on Tua's sleeve. "That one holding Kai, he's the one who hunted me in the park."

"Aye," Tua said softly. "They be known to me as well."

Water trickled down the rock sculpture and several whisper birds hissed as they circled overhead. Nobody moved for several seconds.

"Tua," Moray called out in a rasping voice. "You've broken our deal. Did you think we wouldn't find out you and the boy'd returned to the city?"

"Shut up!" Aku yelled back. "Tua would never make a deal with you!"

"Shush now." Tua put a hand on Aku's shoulder to calm him. "We'll discuss that later."

"I'm glad they broke it." Conger spat. "Me and the boy got unfinished business."

"Just let us finish dealing with this reptile," Moray called out. "We'll get to you next. Don't bother running. Or do. You know how my brother and I love a good chase." He inhaled deeply. "And we won't have any trouble tracking you. I can smell the panic in your sweat from here."

Hulu stood on a circular stone dais set in the center of the Great Hall and assessed the situation, while struggling to keep his withdrawal symptoms in check. He'd addressed the scribes countless times from this spot, but never in a situation like this. Eight of the ten teams had reported back so far, and five guards sat at various spots around the Hall, hands and feet bound with scroll twine. A sixth guard was in the infirmary, his tattoos dug of his arms by knifepoint, the mother ink sharks still wiggling. The team leader swore the injured guard had put up a fierce struggle, but Hulu had his doubts. He'd have to look into it later.

No sign yet of Captain Ino himself, though, nor of Lono's team, two of his three main worries. At least his own team had found the bronze decoding mechanism in Captain Ino's personal quarters, and it rested now on a nearby table, where scribes stood around regarding it like exotic booty captured by a conquering army.

There was a feeling of exultation in the air, in the voices and gestures of the scribes who talked excitedly among themselves. Hulu couldn't share it. His eyes kept returning to the double doors at the bottom of the stairwell at the far end of the hall. He felt relief when the doors opened and the next team arrived. *Thank We Honua, here's Lono at last.*

Lono led her eight men and a battered-looking Shabengee through the crowd of scribes. She stopped before the dais, her face serious and beautiful. Hulu observed how the scribes deferred to her. Even as a woman and as young as she was, there was something in her bearing that demanded respect.

"Looks like you faced some resistance," Hulu said, nodding at the guard, whose bloodied face already puffed blue and black from the blows he'd received.

"Not actually." Lono waited for the crowd to hush and clearly chose her next words carefully, knowing all were listening. "My team was overeager in our capture. But the men remembered their oaths to Master Makule before things got out of hand."

"I see," Hulu said, making a mental note to ask her later for more details. He could kiss her for reminding the assembled of their oaths. Still, he heard muttering among some of the scribes, thought he could even pick out a phrase here and there—"serves him right," or "Shabengee got what he deserved." It was an ugly sentiment, this sense that the scribes were in control now and the guards in their power, and he'd have to watch to make sure it didn't flare up.

A cramp built in Hulu's lower abdomen. *Not here, not now.* He closed his eyes and held in his breath to concentrate on the effort to push it down. Instantly Lono was by his side.

"Are you all right?" she asked in a low tone. "How long until you need to smoke?"

"Soon, soon." Hulu straightened himself. He'd succeeded in staving it off, at least for a short while. "Hopefully the final team will be here momentarily with Captain Ino and we can settle things quickly."

Should I go look for them? Hulu wondered. *Or send somebody else to assist them? What if they've cornered Captain Ino, and he's putting up a fight? For that matter, what if Captain Ino has fled? Who will I negotiate with then? What if someone on the missing team has died? And for the gods' sake, whatever happened to Kai?*

Despite all the scenarios he'd had gone over, all the possibilities of things going wrong he'd rolled over in his head for the past hours, Hulu would never have guessed at what happened next. The door from the corridor to the garden slammed open, and the boy from the cabin dashed in shouting, "Help! We need help!"

Lono's eyes widened in surprise. "Aku! What are you doing here?"

Tua was fast with his dagger, but the Puhi were unbelievably quick. He was using every trick he'd learned in years of street fighting and bar brawling in Bonetown, but the Puhi countered every thrust and slash, almost as if they sensed his intentions even before he initiated an attack. And the Shabengee Captain was a danger, too, not as fast as the Puhi hunters of course, and injured with a nasty bleeding wound on his upper leg, but nonetheless using his bulk and strength to hem Tua and Kai in so they couldn't back away or take advantage of the space in the garden.

The reptile, though, this fight would've been over at the beginning if not for him, Tua thought. Kai's powerful tail prevented their opponents from approaching or lashed at their feet to keep them off balance, his armored skin bounced blows away, and his claws could slash or dig deep. Tua found himself grateful for Kai's skills and was sorry for ever thinking he might be a coward. Yes, the reptile was a worthy fighting companion. Still, the outcome of this fight was clear if they didn't get help soon.

The Puhi were already learning Kai's tactics and dealing with them effectively. Moray hopped over of Kai's sweeping tail and lunged at Tua, his maka knife catching Tua's belly as Tua sidestepped him. The wound was superficial but Tua cringed at the unnatural cold that spread from it. *Keep your head in the game, Tua. Don't let that distract you.*

The force of Moray's lunge carried him past Tua and Tua spun, ramming a fist into Moray's back with a strike that sent the Puhi crashing through a wooden planter of herbs in an explosion of soil and fragrant leaves. Instantly Tua was on him, hands clutching for his throat, but Moray somehow managed to spin out of his grasp, slippery as the eels slithering across his body, leaving Tua on his knees grabbing at air.

Now it was Tua in a vulnerable position, still on the ground with splintered wood from the planter around him, with Moray already back on his feet in front of him and Conger leaping on Tua from behind. Conger wrapped his legs around Tua's midsection. Tua bucked and roared but couldn't throw him off. Out of the corner of his eye, Tua saw Conger raise his right arm over his head, ready to bring down his maka in a killing blow. Could Kai help? No, Tua spotted him grappling with the Shabengee yards away. Tua knew this was it.

From out of nowhere, a fluttering of wings, a blur of black feathers, and a loud *caw!* Conger's legs went slack and dropped off Tua's back. Tua leaped to his feet and spun. Conger was slashing the air with his maka, his face full of blood. Keki had already flown out of range, an eyeball in his beak with a ganglion of nerves dangling from it like streamers.

"Get that damn bird!" Conger shouted. "I can't see!"

Moray sprang in the air higher than Tua would have thought a man could leap, snatching Keki in mid-flight. On Moray's return to the ground, Tua sidekicked him in the stomach, and Moray sprawled across the gravel, releasing Keki as he fell.

Meanwhile, only a few yards away, Kai was on his back with the Shabengee on top of him, avoiding blows to his sensitive belly area by twisting to the left and right as the guard threw punch after punch. He snapped his jaws at the guard's arms but couldn't quite angle his head far enough to reach. The guard shifted his weight, trying to get his knee onto Kai's throat to hold his head down, and Kai took advantage of the Shabengee's change in position to toss the guard off him and into a broad bed of ferns under a trellised arbor. Kai sprang into the bed after him.

Some sort of watering system released cooling mists from above them, and Kai felt himself refreshed from the spray. It'd been way too long since he'd had a soak and the droplets seeped into his scutes as he wrestled, making his tight, scratchy skin feel pliable again, bringing him strength. The wetness only handicapped the Shabengee, however, who found the reptile suddenly too slick to grip, too fast to counter. Soon, Kai was firmly in control, winding his tail around the guard's body and rolling the through the mud until his prey was stunned and immobile.

No, not prey, Kai reminded himself. *Surface man.* He stopped himself and checked the guard's signs. He was still breathing. Good. Subduing him was one thing, but killing him would be an offense to the Great Kai-man. He rose from the muddy fern bed and dragged the Shabengee out.

Hulu, Lono, Aku, and a couple scribes Hulu had charged to accompany them, stood agog at the scene outside the garden door. The fight was already over, but its ferocity could be clearly seen from the smashed flowers and sculptures and planter boxes, the mud covering everything, and worst of all, the Puhi hunter on his knees moaning, blood dripping from an empty eye socket, while another Puhi lay crumpled next to him, his head at an unnatural angle and blood gushing from a huge gash across his neck. Above them both stood Tua, breathing heavily, sweat glistening on his torso, knife at the ready in case the new-created cyclops should get any ideas.

From a shaded bower, Kai emerged, pulling a limp, mud-drenched body behind him. It took Hulu several moments to realize the body was Captain Ino's, and then only from the pattern of his armor. Kai dropped the body next to the Puhi hunters and with his other claw, wiped mud from his eyes. A weird, choked *caw* came from somewhere above them all.

"Keki!" Lono cried out, running to a decorative lantern post atop which the crow was perched. "Are you okay? What are you doing up there? And, in the name of Ne Wa'e, what do you have in your mouth?"

The crow hopped to face his friend and leaned over. A long red stalk hung from its beak and at the end of it, an eyeball seemed to peer at the proceedings.

THIRTY-ONE

The bronze mechanism sat on a writing desk they had pulled to the window for better light from the early morning sun. Hulu and Lono stood around it expectantly. Aku sat on a desk nearby. Finally, Opio came in with Tua and Kai, freshly cleaned of mud, sweat, and blood, though Tua's face was still a puffy mess of bruises and contusions.

Nevertheless, Tua seemed energetic, upbeat even. He spotted the machine and stepped right up to it. "So this is that coding device what all the trouble's been about, eh?" He ran his fingers around a few of the gears, over the panel of miniature wheels covered with letters.

"This is it." Hulu gave a slight bow to Aku. "Shall we see what's on that cylinder of yours, young sir?"

Aku pulled the cord from around his neck and handed it to Hulu, who cut the cord and slipped the cylinder off. After a moment's consideration, Hulu handed the cylinder back to Aku. "You know, you should really be the one do this. Come over and slide the cylinder over this spindle."

Aku rose and carefully placed the cylinder where Hulu pointed, sliding it over the upward pointing spindle. Hulu lowered the spindle into a gap in the machine, where it clicked into place. He turned a handle on the side of the mechanism, and the cylinder rotated. As it did, gears and rods began to whir, turning and pumping, and the wheels on the panel spun around, rotating until the letters imprinted on them assembled into syllables and words.

The handle clicked to a stop. "That's all of it," Hulu said.

The six leaned in and studied the read-out. Finally, Tua said what they were all thinking. "But it don't mean anything. It's just gibberish."

Aku spat. "I can't believe it! That's the message Godi and Mohelo died for? A bunch of random words? Some of them aren't even real letters!"

Opio looked thoughtful. "Maybe it's some sort of code. Perhaps we can break it, we'll have the real message."

"A code of a code, Opio? Why would Regent go to all that trouble? These cylinders are meant to be read by somebody after all, not endlessly translated." Hulu's shoulders slumped. "I had thought it would be a clue to the vision. A way to find the lab, the ray..."

Hulu suddenly bent over, his face contorted. Instantly, Lono was by his side. "Are you okay?"

He forced himself back up. "I'm fine. Don't worry about." He took a final glance at the bronze machine. "Well, I suppose this was a dead end. No matter, we have business in the Great Hall, and then we must see about getting Kai and Lono back where they belong."

The scribe Ka'le, who had trained in the medical arts, took the compress infused with healing pala oil and knelt by the bed where the hurt Shabengee lay. He pressed the compress gently against the open wound on the guard's arm. The guard's eyelids fluttered and he moaned and drew back.

"Be still now," Ka'le said. "This will prevent infection. Get you back on your feet in no time." He took a bandage with his other hand and wrapped it around the compress, tying it off at the end. "Now wait a few moments, and I'll be back for the other arm."

Ka'le rose, but the guard reached out and grabbed the sleeve of his barkcloth tunic. "Tell me something, scribe."

"Yes, what is it?"

"My sharks are gone?" the guard asked. "Cut out?"

"I'm afraid so," Ka'le said.

"Then don't bother healing me," the guard said, letting go of Ka'le's sleeve and settling back with a pained exhalation. "Just let me die."

"So without your tattoos, you're giving up?"

The guard spoke with his eyes closed. "Haven't you ever heard our pledge? *Our sharks are pride and honor, source of strength and spur to glory.* Without them, I'm nothing, only a common man. Life without them is worthless. Let me go peacefully."

"Mm-hmm," Ka'le said. "Unfortunately for you, your wounds are not life-threatening. My medicine will prevent the eating sores, though. So unless you want to be alive but armless, I suggest you accept my assistance."

The guard groaned but spoke no further. Ka'le turned to the other bed in the infirmary to check on his second patient, the Puhi hunter with the missing eye. Now that was a more serious case, one Ka'le was not at all sure he could treat. Even aside from the missing eye, the Puhi's injuries were extensive. It was good he had passed out, for the pain would be nearly unbearable. It could be he would never awaken.

Ka'le blinked, disbelieving. The bed was empty, aside from the blood-soaked blanket the Puhi had been lying on. He crouched, checking to see if the Puhi had somehow rolled off the side and underneath. No sign of the man.

A slight shift in the air behind him and Ka'le swiveled. The door had opened and Ka'le caught just a flash of something silvery in the corridor. He rushed to the door and glanced to the left and right, but nobody was there. But later, when he thought back on it, he would swear the silver something he had seen had been a conger eel on skin, its wicked mouth grinning with frighteningly sharp teeth.

Opio spoke in a low tone into his master's ear. "We've gone over the whole compound. The eighth Shabengee is nowhere to be found."

"Thank you, Opio," Hulu said. *Odd. Maybe the man fled. I can certainly understand how one of his men might take advantage of the chaos to leave the good Captain's service.* Hulu scrutinized Captain Ino, who sat across from him at the table, a sort of negotiating forum hastily arranged on the dais in the Great Hall. Even cleaned up and wearing a fresh uniform, the Captain hardly looked better than he had a couple hours before. His face was puffy, his eyes blackened and lips swollen.

In the front row of seats, Tua looked little better than the Captain, though both men sat erect and proud, unwilling to acknowledge their pain to onlookers. Lono, Aku, and Kai also had front row seats, Kai drawing many curious glances from scribes and guards alike. Keki perched on one of the several hanging bronze chandeliers, overlooking the forum. The Shabengee guards were seated among the scribes with their hands bound, the twine from earlier replaced with tough hihi vines cut in the garden. At Captain Ino's request, they were not gagged, and so far they had followed his orders not to speak out of turn.

The only ones missing were the Shabengee with his tattoos cut out, the Puhi hunter with the missing eye, and a scribe assigned to treat them in the infirmary. Tua had wanted to kill the injured Puhi on the spot, but Hulu had flatly forbidden it. The Puhi killed in the course of the fight was one thing, but cold-blooded murder something else entirely. Actually, Hulu was relieved and a bit surprised that the only fatality was the other Puhi. The uprising had gone incredibly well, if not exactly to plan.

The last scribes were taking their seats as the mid-morning bell struck nine times. Hulu cleared his throat and glanced around the hall at the expectant faces, all eyes on him and the Captain. He took a deep breath to steady himself. The large cup of wine he'd drunk a half hour before was helping to stave off the ink urgings a bit. He hoped it would last through the entirety of the proceedings.

"Captain Ino," Hulu began. "I hereby declare the Order of the Scribes and this Scriptorium to be free and self-governing, under the terms of our charter issued by King Atlas in the tenth year of his reign and renewed by every succeeding sovereign."

Captain Ino chuckled. "And I hereby declare that every one of you in here allowing this joke of a trial to go on will be whipped like you never been before, once Regent's rightful authority is restored. I'ke Regent!"

"I'ke Regent," Hulu said. "And this is not a trial, Captain. As we discussed before, and as you agreed at the time, these are negotiations. Am I to assume your position is that my authority is illegitimate? Who then do you propose should lead the negotiations for the Order?"

Captain Ino slammed the table with his fist. "Damn right yer illegitmate."

Hulu stiffened. "I was the assistant to old Master Mokelo when he died, and on his deathbed he appointed me his successor, as confirmed afterwards by a unanimous vote of—"

"Yer a whelp who made a mess of things," Captain Ino said. "You can stuff yer unanimous vote in a stinkchuck's bolthole. Regent's Council sent me here because this place was running through mother ink like bathwater, and I get here to find scribes putting in half a day's work and with nobody watching 'em, nobody accounting for supplies, and Master Hulu passed out all the day long up in his tower room doing only Ne'i Shabengee knows what. Except, we do know what, don't we, Master Hulu? I wonder if the brothers knew what was happening to all their ink when they voted for you? That you was smoking away the very lifeblood of your precious little quill society?"

There were angry murmurs through the crowd of scribes, even shouts of "unfair!" Hulu felt his face redden with anger. He was angry at the Captain's speech, angry at the guards who'd invaded his realm, but if he was honest, angry with himself because Captain Ino did have a point. It was his own behavior that had given Regent an opening to make the Shabengee intervention possible. A cramp started to build in his lower abdomen.

It struck Hulu as so obvious now—why had the Prioress at Lono's convent so confidently forbidden her Shabengee guards from entering the convent, while he had meekly accepted their presence at the Scriptorium, acceded to their demands for quarters, given in to Captain Ino's usurping his power and contradicting his orders at every level? Because the Prioress knew with certainty that she was in the right and had the complete confidence of her charges, while Hulu was beset with doubts, knowing that his truth-smoking and his inexperience prevented him from leading his brothers as he should have. How many times had he cursed the Captain, the Shabengee, Regent, and anybody else he could imagine, when all along the problem had been him? The cramp had spread to his back. He closed his eyes and forced the contraction down.

Hulu became aware that the Great Hall had grown silent again and all were waiting for his reply. He pushed his chair back and rose, staring Captain Ino directly in the eyes. "I do not deny that the charges of truth-smoking were true. Nevertheless, I am the valid authority and representative of this institution, which has chosen its own leaders for five hundred years, and proved this morning that it wishes this tradition of independence to continue. When I organized the uprising against your seizure of power here, Captain, not a single brother scribe refused to follow me. Not a single one! Their actions have spoken, and power has returned to its rightful owner. Now, shall we negotiate in good faith, or shall I take advantage of my superior position and simply name my terms?"

A scattering of applause and cheers started up in the crowd, quickly growing into a full-throated chorus of approval for Hulu's speech. He sensed his control over the brothers, how at this moment he could command them to do anything and they would obey—even tear the bound guards to pieces if he ordered it. He raised an open palm for silence, and the crowd quieted.

"What say you, Captain Ino?" Hulu asked. "Negotiations in good faith?"

"Aye," Captain Ino said. "Let's get this foolishness over with."

"Do you want one of these jayfruit tarts, Tua?" Aku asked, holding out the round, brown-baked pie sprinkled white with sugar. "It's really, really good."

Tua smiled at the boy. "No, you eat it. One of the scribes gave it to you, did he?"

"Opio did. Said it's a specialty of the house. And later, he said he'd show me some fingerings on my flute."

Opio again, Tua thought. *He seems to be everywhere and think of everything needed for this place to run.* He glanced through the door. Knots of scribes spoke excitedly outside during the break from negotiations, discussing some point of importance, or recounting events of the already-legendary uprising to mates who had served in a different area of the compound. The storage chamber where he and Aku sat on a spare table was stacked with stone dishware, bronze utensils, wooden serving bowls, and everything the compound needed to serve thrice-daily communal meals to eighty brothers.

"Tua, did you really make a deal with the Puhi hunters?" Aku asked.

Tua swallowed. "Aye, lad. 'Tis true."

"Tua, how could you!"

"It was for your own sake, though you may not believe it."

Aku shook his head. "I don't understand."

Tua looked away. "You saw the aftermath of what happened at the tattoo parlor. When the Puhi hunters got there, nobody was prepared. Defenseless we was, weaponless, artists and customers, old men mostly. There was three Puhis, running through the place, killing everything they saw. People was yelling and screaming, running out of doors and jumping out windows." He balled a hand into a fist. "But I fought back. Figured I couldn't take all three on at once, but I could take out at least one. I managed to catch the one with the pike congers. I had a knife to his throat, ready to cut it. But the other two offered me an arrangement. Said a boy had escaped them, they knew he'd come find me sooner or later. It had to be you. The Puhi said if I let the one go, and left the city with you and that cylinder of yours, they'd let you live."

"That stupid cylinder." Aku's brow wrinkled. "You shouldn't have done it, Tua! You should've killed him when you had the chance."

"Aye, maybe I should've. But without that agreement, they would've come after you and never stopped tracking you. Flayed you alive and laugh to do it. Guess you embarrassed them by getting away how you did, and you being a kid." He tousled Aku's hair. "For me, it wasn't no choice at all."

"So that's why we had to leave the city. It wasn't the earthquake like you told us."

"No," Tua said. "And when you showed up with Lono, that complicated things. What's more, I still had the meeting arranged the next day with Iule, near the Temple of the Bees."

"That was the day you almost killed Keki."

"And good thing I didn't," Tua said. "Lono never would've trusted me. But I was crazy, trying to figure out who betrayed us to Regent, who caused the deaths of Godi, of Mohelo, of all the others."

Aku nodded. "So when you figured out it was Iule, that's why you knifed him."

"I didn't want to kill him in front of you kids, but that's how it worked out," Tua said. "I suspected from the beginning he might be the one, take the cylinder and turn it over to Regent, but I had to see his face to be sure."

Aku licked a finger, covered with the sweet tart residue. "It's because of my father, isn't it?"

"What do you mean?" Tua said.

"That's why you want to protect me."

"Oh, me and your Dad and Godi was mates going way back, since I first arrived in Atlantis from the Eastern Isles, not much more than your age. Your dad and Godi made good with their jobs in the royal troupe. I stayed behind in Bonetown, watched over the neighborhood. But when Regent came to power and the order went out to dissolve the troupes during the first Purge, they had to come back. We three was practically the first to join the Ho'oule. Oh, your father and Godi hated Regent like anything."

"And that's when my dad died?" Aku asked.

"We can only assume he died. He got carried off to the Puku, and never heard from again. Me and Godi, we swore we'd look out for the two boys he left behind, one not much more'n a toddler."

"And that was me and Kuana." Aku frowned. "We were hungry a lot though."

"Yeah, well." Tua rubbed his thumbs together a moment. "Times was tough for everyone, wasn't they? We'd get jobs for Kuana when we could, and you after he was gone. Find a room for you to stay in so you wouldn't have to sleep in the streets at night. Some said you and Kuana was too young to be doing Ho'oule work, but what choice did we have? Anyway, it worked fine. Until it didn't."

"Yeah." Aku didn't speak for several moments. "I wish I had some more of those tarts."

"I'll get them," Tua said. "I need to stretch my legs anyway."

Aku brought his flute to his lips and blew out a little tune. Tua was halfway down the corridor when the music stopped abruptly. He glanced back at the half-closed door. Something inside hit the ground and rattled. Tua stepped back and opened the door, an uneasy feeling in his breast. Aku wasn't there, but his flute rolled around the ground where it'd fallen.

"Aku, you playing games with me?" Tua called.

The window shutter banged against the outside of the wall.

Tua dashed to the window and looked out. In the courtyard, a Puhi in his loincloth ran with an easy lope, carrying a limp form under his arm. It was Aku.

Tua's guts went cold at the sight. He couldn't even conceive what twisted torment the Puhi had in mind for Aku. He looked down. It was a sheer drop of at least three man-lengths to the cobbled stones below. The Puhi was already almost to the gate. No time to waste. Tua pushed a chair against the wall and stuck one foot out the window, then the other, dangling by his hands. He took a breath and let himself drop. When he hit, he felt something twist in his left ankle. He didn't stop to inspect it, sprinting to the gate and ignoring the dull pain in his leg. With a caw, Keki flew from the eave of the scriptorium and winged after him.

THIRTY-TWO

Hulu jotted a few notes on a scroll, preparing his argument for when the negotiations resumed. Captain Ino sat across the table from him with his fingers steepled.

Hulu glanced up irritatedly. "Would you mind not staring at me?"

"Do it make you nervous, Master Scribe?"

Hulu was about to respond when Opio came running in. "Master, look what I found!" he cried as he approached the table.

Lono hurried over from her seat. "What's wrong? What's happened?"

"I found this in the pantry, on the floor." Opio handed Aku's flute over.

Hulu took it. "What, where are Tua and Aku?"

"No sign of them," Opio responded.

"Tua and Aku are gone." Hulu thought a moment. "Did it look like there'd been a struggle?"

"Not so far as I could see," Opio said.

"That is strange." Hulu's face fell. "I guess after the message, they didn't see any point in sticking around."

"They can't have left on their own," Lono said. "Aku would never leave his flute behind."

Hulu closed his eyes. The cramp was building again. *No time for this. Push it down, no matter how much it hurts.* He forced his eyes open. Captain Ino had a slight smile on his face, obviously aware of and enjoying his discomfort. *Don't give him the satisfaction.*

"Should I send somebody to look for your missing friends, Master?" Opio asked.

"Don't bother," Hulu said. "We have no idea where they've gone. Wherever it is they're headed, Tua is surely capable of handling it. They'll return when they can. Our job is to finish the negotiations here."

"Let me go!" Aku twisted and beat with his fists, but the Puhi held him firmly under his arm as he ran, like a sack of flour.

Conger laughed and the eels slithering around under his skin grinned. "Keep fightin', boy. I love it when prey fights back."

The Puhi's left eyesocket was crusted over and his body was covered in abrasions and bruises, but his strength sure seemed fully recovered. Aku sensed the futility of his effort and calmed himself, instead keeping track of their route.

They were already on the bridge leading away from Middle Island and towards Portside. Merchants and workers out on their early morning commutes gave them questioning glances, but nobody dared intervene. Once over the bridge, the Puhi left the main road and navigated his way through Portside's alleys and backways, past the rope factories and cooperies, the low-rent winehouses and cheap tattoo parlors. Few fine buildings housed in kimunu trees here—these were tumble-down structures the residents had built of whatever leftover lumber they could scrounge from the nearby shipyards. It was a part of the city Aku had rarely visited, but it reminded him a lot of Bonetown.

"Where are you taking me?" Aku asked finally.

"You're special, boy," Conger said. "Prey that's proved especially elusive. Prey that's earned the right."

"I don't have the cylinder anymore. I can't give you anything."

"Don't matter," Conger said, taking a set of stone steps into a public courtyard with two upward bounds. "Job's over, but like I said, you're prey. Puhi always get their prey in the end."

"What's that mean, I earned the right?"

"A real honor. You're going to see something special, something reserved only for the bravest and slipperiest little fishes."

Aku could've sworn one of the eel tattoos actually opened its mouth and tried to catch him in its teeth. He wiggled around, trying to avoid it.

"Ah, ah. Stop squirming, boy. If you make it too hard, I'll have to knock you unconscious. And I'd hate for you to miss a minute of this."

"Why don't you just go ahead and kill me?"

"No can do. Papa Eel likes his food alive." Conger's maniacal laugh rang through the small street they passed through.

"Who's Papa Eel?"

"You'll see when we get to the temple. Don't want to spoil it."

"What's the—"

"Enough chitchat," Conger said, squeezing Aku harder under his arm. "Just enjoy the ride."

Lono observed Hulu as he sat at the table, carefully inscribing characters onto a parchment with a long swan quill as he personally wrote out the agreement he and Captain Ino had struck. Opio attended to his right, ready to deliver messages or conduct whatever little errands Hulu might require. Kai had headed to the garden to soak in a fountain and only a few scribes remained in the Great Hall, watching over the Shabengee guards. Hulu had sent the rest off to begin the clean up.

A scribe came in carrying a burlap sack and carried it to Hulu. Lono recognized it as Hulu's stash of mother ink.

"Master, we found this in the garden." The scribe held the bag out to him but Hulu did not take it.

"Ah, good, I was wondering where that went to," Hulu said. "Opio, would you take that down to the vault? On the ledger, you can mark it as a gift to the Scriptorium."

Opio took the bag and glanced in, his eyes widening in surprise. "Are you sure, master?"

Hulu raised a finger. "Opio, before you go, how much ink would you say is in there?"

"Well, it still needs to be refined—"

"Of course," Hulu said. "Offhand, just an estimate."

"Perhaps a hundred drams, I should think. It would be about six months' worth."

"Six months. Very good. Thank you, Opio. You may go now."

Hulu mused, and Lono knew what he was thinking: he was calculating if this gift to the Scriptorium would balance out all the ink he had smoked over the years. After several minutes, he nodded to himself with satisfaction and returned to his task, finishing his writing at the bottom of the parchment with a flourish just as Opio returned.

Hulu pushed his chair back and rose to his feet, only to sway and nearly tumble off the dais. Instantly, Opio and Lono were on either side of him, holding him up until he regained his balance. Hulu's face was pale and sweat ran down from his temples. Lono noticed the hand that had so steadily written out the document only moments before now trembled violently.

"Two things, Opio," Hulu said in a strained voice.

"Name them, Master."

"Take this parchment to Captain Ino's personal chamber and get his signature. As soon as he signs it, have the Shabengee guards released from their bindings."

"Master?" Opio hesitated a moment. "Is that a good idea?"

"Don't worry, Opio," Hulu said. "Captain Ino is many unpleasant things, but dishonorable is not among them. He will keep to what is written here. But before you do that, something else."

"Yes, Master?"

"Help me up to the chamber the Shabengee were using as an isolation cell, and bolt me in. Unbolt the door three days from now, and not before, no matter what noises you hear from within. Do you understand?"

"Perfectly, Master. But what if—"

"Not even then," Hulu said. "You are to be in charge of the Scriptorium while I'm indisposed. In the meantime, would you send a messenger to the Convent of the Ancestors? Tell them we have one of their acolytes here, but there are spies along the road and we aren't sure if it's safe to get her back. Ask how they think we should proceed."

"What? No!" Lono said. She stared at Hulu, and he met her gaze. The muscles in his face were tense with the effort of controlling his pain, but his blue eyes were calm and determined. Those were the eyes of the man she had met in her dreams, the bold man who had known exactly what he wanted and did not hesitate to take it.

"What do you mean, no?" Hulu said. "Don't you wish to go back to the convent?"

"Well, yes," Lono said. "I mean, not yet. What will you be doing in that room for three days?"

"I will be freeing myself of a burden I should have rid myself of long ago," Hulu said. "And I'm not entirely sure I'll live through the effort."

"You will," Lono said. "I know you will. But what will you do when you come out?"

"When I come out, I suppose I will travel to the Black Marsh with Kai." He glanced almost shyly at Lono. "Will you come with us then?"

"When you come out, I will follow you anywhere," Lono said.

...Hulu found himself wandering through a vast palace, each succeeding room he happened through more richly decorated than the last with thick carpets, ebonywood furnishings, brocaded curtains studded with jewels, and statuary and paintings depicting heroic Atlantean figures and their legendary deeds.

In a huge hall, he felt his footsteps guided toward a spiraling bronze staircase rising in the middle. He began to climb, passing the level of the hall's ceiling and entering a tower with windows spaced along the ascent. Outside the windows yellow and orange clouds floated past, light and shadow playing across their misty surfaces as they moved. Hulu climbed he knew not how many hundreds of stairs, the clouds becoming thicker as he went.

Finally he came to a room at the top of the staircase, a round chamber, not too large, but made entirely of glass. The swirling clouds outside diffused the light, so a sort of gentle glow seemed to come from everywhere. A large bed with soft white sheets stood to one side, and on its edge sat a woman.

At first Hulu had to turn his face away because her clothing was so bright, but after his eyes adjusted he studied her and realized it wasn't the clothing that was bright, but that she was actually clad in something like starlight. Her beautiful round face he knew, of course, the long dark curls and creamy brown skin, the deep chocolate eyes, bright with the pleasure of seeing him.

"Alani," he said. He strode towards her and she reached out her hand for him to take. He leaned over and gave her a light kiss on those full lips. "It's been so long since we've seen each other."

"The mother ink hasn't been leading you to me," she said. "It's had other ideas for you."

Hulu felt himself embarrassed and unable to explain where his ink dreams had taken him. He stammered something but Alani squeezed his hand.

"The ink has led you to another," she said with a smile. "I know. I have *already seen her. She's lovely."*

"She should be," Hulu said. "She looks so much like you."

"What else?" Alani said. "Tell me about her."

"She has your same passion for life, Alani. And she has a good heart. But she's different too. Impetuous. Willful even."

"I have watched her since before you know," Alani said. "Impetuous? Perhaps, at times. But Lono is strong in a way I never was, and courageous as well. Most important, she wants what's best for you."

"About that." Hulu sat on the bed beside Alani. "This is probably the last time we'll meet. Even now, the ink is leaving my body and I go through the withdrawal pains, and it's my intention to never truth-smoke again."

"It is right that it should be so," Alani said. "I have been selfish to let you continue doing it. I will help lessen your pain as best I can from here. I shall miss your visits, Hulu, but you must pursue your own life. As time unfolds, we will be re-united."

"But you'll be here waiting!" Hulu frowned. "All alone up here, for years without anything to do."

Alani laughed, and in a way Hulu could not explain, there was starlight in her mirth. "Oh, Hulu. You don't understand how it works here. For you the time will be long, but for me it will be short. Nor am I alone here at all. This place is full of souls, though you cannot see them. Old friends and new, and those who were already our friends even before we were born. But you will learn about all that when you return. Now our time grows short, for I sense that the ink has something else to show you. Let us spend our remaining moments in a more joyous pursuit."

She stood before him and lifted her starlight dress, tossing it into the air where it dissolved into thousands of floating points of silver light. She playfully pushed him back onto the soft sheets and climbed on top of him, kissing him from his navel up to his lips.

"If it's to be our last time together for a while, let's make it count," she whispered in his ear.

PART SIX

Young octopus is gaining weight rapidly with infusion of three drops of mother ink daily. Milking of brown ink daily up to half a cup. His production continues to increase in line with bodily growth, and within six months he should be producing enough to replace our current source. I only hope the old girl lives long enough to prevent a gap. The last thing I need is Regent's Council sending a representative to investigate why production has dropped off. Some Shabengee sticking his nose in where he doesn't understand a thing would cause no end of nuisance.

Positive results from the field on the brown ink continue to come in. It seems after so many faulty batches I have perfected the formula. Apparently, the scribes grumble at copying our new histories, but they do their jobs. They are rewriting history without even knowing it.

Still considering the ray. Such a strange and mysterious creature. She certainly seems intelligent, and reports from our allies in the waters are that the rays have societies and villages of sorts and even, in some distant sea, a city. But how do they communicate? Perhaps by pheromones emitted in the water, though my water sampling has revealed no unusual byproducts. Saving an operation until I can learn more about her. Until then observation, and requests for more information from the pentapi.

--from the *Diary of Imi Au'o*

THIRTY-THREE

The missing Shabengee returned about noon, entering the front door of the Scriptorium in a formal way and accompanied by a messenger from Regent's Council. The messenger wore the cape of sleek gray awi bird feathers indicating his profession and carried a rolled parchment. He insisted that both the head of the Scriptorium and the captain of the Shabengee contingent should be present.

"I'm sorry, Master Hulu is indisposed and not to be disturbed," Opio explained in the Great Hall, where he and the other scribes sat at table. "I am heading the Scriptorium in his place."

"Very well," the messenger said. "Have the Captain brought then, if you please."

"Of course," Opio said, signaling one of the scribes to go and fetch him. While, they waited, Opio observed the missing guard, who he felt carried a rather smug expression. "And how was it you weren't here to serve with your brothers this morning?" he asked him.

"When things went crazy here, Captain Ino sent me off to the council." The mudshark on his arm bobbed up and down. "Said I was his insurance policy."

Opio barely had time to consider what that meant when Captain Ino showed up with another guard in tow. Captain Ino too had a smirk on his face suggesting he thought the day would go his way yet.

The missing guard gave a salute and the captain acknowledged him with a nod. "Pray, read your missive out, good messenger," he said. "Say it loud, so all present may hear."

The messenger broke the wax seal on the parchment and unfurled it. He pumped his right fist to his ear. "I'ke Regent!"

"I'ke Regent," came the response of the gathered, Captain Ino's voice conspicuously louder than anyone else's.

"An order from Regent's Council, in the seventh month of the tenth year of His lawful reign," the messenger began. "The man known as Hulu Scribemaster, head of the Scriptorium and lately imprisoned on various charges, shall be relieved of his duty as Master of the Order of the Scribes forthwith."

The messenger paused and glanced up. A grinning Captain Ino lifted his hand in a gesture of encouragement. "Yes, yes, go on with yer reading."

"In light of the recent escape of so many prisoners from Regent's custody during the recent disaster that befell the city, and the destruction of custodial facilities for detaining said prisoners, all pending charges against Hulu Scribemaster shall be suspended until the next new moon, provided he repay the Order any debts he may have accumulated owing to the charge against him of grand theft.

"It is the wish of the Council that the Order of the Scribes shall choose a new master according to their traditional customs, and said new master shall judge when Hulu Scribemaster's debts have been discharged."

"Ah, well, it could be worse." Captain Ino's expression betrayed his disappointment. He turned to go. "Still, good to see Regent's justice prevail."

The messenger cleared his throat. "Part the second!" he cried, and Captain Ino spun back around.

"As there is an urgent need for Shabengee guards to keep the peace due to the aforementioned disaster, six of the contingent of eight guards serving at the Scriptorium of the Order of the Scribes shall depart forthwith, and report to the Temple of the Shabengee for reassignment."

Captain Ino paled.

"The responsibilities of investigating malfeasance, securing the

Order's supplies, and keeping order among the scribes shall pass from the Shabengee guards to the Order's newly-chosen master, and the remaining guards shall report directly to the new master.

"Furthermore, Captain Ino shall be relieved of his duties as captain and report to the Shabengee temple for immediate re-assignment."

Captain Ino's face had turned positively stormy.

"Finally, within the fortnight, the council shall appoint a bursar to review the accounts of the Order of the Scribes. The Order shall accord him its full cooperation and access to any records or areas of the Scriptorium he sees as necessary to carry out his duties.

"In the name of Regent, this order is hereby proclaimed and entered into force. I'ke Regent!"

"I'ke Regent!" came the response from all present, though for once, Captain Ino's voice was not loudest among them.

Tua rushed through the city after Keki, who managed to keep ahead of him but still in sight, flying from building to building. Tua shoved through the late-morning shoppers, stepped sharply to avoid the crowds of beggars approaching him with palms raised upwards. When there was open space in a street or a plaza, he ran as fast as his hobbled ankle allowed. *Whatever I thought about that bird previously, I take it all back,* he thought. Without Keki, the chase would've been over long before. As it was, the Puhi hunter and Aku were out of Tua's sight, and only Keki's high vantage kept them within reach.

As he passed through streets and alleyways, Tua's mind kept going over the events of the past few weeks—especially the way the whisper birds, bearded vultures, and giant centipedes kept showing up, the way the Puhi hunters always seemed to have a good idea where he and his charges were. *I wonder,* he thought, *if their spies be watching us the whole time?*

The chase took Keki and Tua over one of the bridges

connecting Middle Island to the mainland and through the increasingly fashionable neighborhoods towards the northeast. Vast mansions in ancient kimunu trees replaced stone buildings, servants carrying baskets replaced hawkers pushing carts. Eventually, Keki flew into Cho Park, once an extensive spread of beautiful gardens and fountains around the royal residence of Ha'lekui, but over the past decade overgrown with saplings and thick underbrush. The chase slowed here, as Tua pushed his way through thorny vines and dangling branches.

Still, Keki kept flying, and Tua followed as best he could. *Just hold tight, Aku,* Tua thought.

Lono stood in front of the wardrobe in Hulu's apartment in, holding the rose-colored dress with the trace op'ia fragrance. She had waited outside the bolted door where Hulu was working through his addiction for hours, listening to the horrible howls from inside the cell, audible even through the thick kirikiri wood of the door. Despite her exhaustion, she had remained awake and sitting in the hallway, praying constantly to Ne Wa'e for Hulu's well-being, for an easing of his suffering. But after noon had come silence, and that was perhaps even worse. Many times Lono had felt herself tempted to pull the bolt back and throw open the door to check if Hulu still lived. But each time she had resisted. He had to go through the process without interruption.

Finally, she'd had to flee, find someplace quiet and lonely. She'd wandered in and out of various storerooms and corridors, but eventually ended up here. Maybe it was a way to feel connected to Hulu without torturing herself with his withdrawal symptoms.

The sound of footsteps approached from behind her, and Lono whirled around. "Oh, Opio, it's only you."

"Only me, nobody important," Opio said.

"That's not how I meant it," Lono said.

Opio smiled and nodded at the dress. "That belonged to Alani, you know."

"Who was Alani?" Her voice came out sharper than she expected.

"His late wife."

"Oh!" A feeling of relief swept through Lono's chest, and then a stab of shame at being happy over someone's death. "How...how did she die?"

"Illness," Opio said. "She was healthy and beautiful one day, and terribly sick the next. Nobody could help her. She was dead by nightfall."

"How long ago did that happen?" Lono asked.

"Oh, about two years," Opio gently took the dress from Lono's hands and hung it back in the wardrobe. "It was then that the master started smoking the ink. We all knew it here, of course. But nobody said anything. Maybe we should have."

Opio put a hand on Lono's shoulder and let her to the front room. She glanced at the wall, noticed the scrolls hanging from the wall. She stopped and stared at the ancient, yellowed one, with its strange script.

"Opio, look at that!"

He glanced at where she indicated. "Old scrolls. One of the interests of the master. That one's from the second dynasty, I believe."

"No, look at the letters," Lono said.

"Yes, odd aren't they? Old Atlantean used a different alphabet than we do."

"Opio, aren't they the same letters from the code on the cylinder?" Lono asked.

Opio peered closely. "Why, yes I believe you're right." He blinked twice. "Then maybe that gibberish message wasn't garbled at all. Maybe..." He grabbed Lono's hand. "Quick, let's go down and check."

They flew down all five flights of stairs to the storage room, Opio brushing past scribes stopping to ask him about various points of administration. "Later, we'll talk later!" he called back as and Lono rushed by.

The bronze mechanism was on the writing desk under the window where they'd left it. Opio looked over the message spelled out on the dials, still as unintelligible as ever. "Maybe the master can read it, if he knows it's Old Atlantean." He mused. "Though he's not to be disturbed. Still, some of the older scribes have studied such things. We could get them in here, see if they can make sense of it."

Lono was inspecting the machine, touching the various gears, pulling at the rods. With some effort, she tilted the machine onto its side to see the bottom.

"Be careful with it," Opio said.

"Look, what's that?" Lono asked. There was a slot underneath with a knob in it. At one end of the slot, the letter "A" was embedded in the bronze. At the other end was one of the unfamiliar characters from Old Atlantean.

"Do you think this is it?" Lono asked. "Maybe this is a way to switch between the alphabets."

"Yes, that's possible." Opio spoke rapidly with excitement. "Slide that knob and see what happens."

Lono slid the knob from its position at the unfamiliar character over to the proper Atlantean "A." It moved smoothly, as if meant for this purpose. She lowered the machine back onto its base. "The message hasn't changed."

"You have to turn the handle," Opio said.

"Oh, of course." Lono turned it, and as she did, the letters began flipping, forming into words, becoming coherent. When the mechanism clicked, the letters had created a message:

deliver to lab – Coast Road – past Owls – one league – side path – sign of skull – Twist Tree – must receive by – Feast of Nihea

"I think they're directions," Opio said.

"We have to let Hulu know," Lono said.

"But the master said he wasn't to be—"

"I know what he said! But he didn't know about this when he said that." Lono already had her hands under one end of the machine. "Come on, Opio, help me carry this. We have to show this to Hulu right now."

THIRTY-FOUR

Gray-Patch cruised half-sleeping in her tank, the only illumination the filtered sunlight shining through the skylight at the top of the room, but she snapped to full awareness when she perceived a human. Surely not the wicked man, come in for some insidious purpose? He usually conducted his operations at night. No, the wicked man had no hair on the top of his head, and this figure had long locks. Moreover, the figure had the blurred edges and ethereal appearance of a dream-form. Ah, it was the crow's friend, the gentle young man whose dream-form had visited once before.

Gray-Patch concentrated and sent out a querying mind-tap to the man, hoping to establish a connection. *Friend?*

He responded right away, as if expecting her. *Friend,* the man's mental state read. There was a vagueness in his responses, to be expected from one not practiced in mind-tap communication, but his meaning was clear enough.

Come to help? Gray-Patch asked.

Wish could. Don't know way. You know.

Gray-Patch couldn't help feeling a bit of disappointment at that answer. *Sorry. Don't know.*

Something stirred across the way. The baby octopus had sensed the conversation and was waking up. His blue eyes opened and tracked the dream-form intruding in their space. He propelled himself up and squeezed himself out of his tank through a tiny crack near the top. He scuttled down the side of the tank and across the floor. Gray-Patch couldn't help smiling. The baby didn't understand this wasn't a real visitor he could touch.

Must find way, Gray-Patch mind-tapped to the man. *Keep searching.*

I will, the man answered. *Will try.*

The octopus had reached the man and was vainly flailing his arms, which passed through the dream-form without hindrance. Gray-Patch could feel waves of hate emanate from the baby. The man glanced down.

What is?

An experiment, Gray-Patch answered. *A sample of the evil done here.*

The man bent down and Gray-Patch could sense he was opening his mind to the octopus.

No! she cried, but it was too late. The baby octopus had already grabbed the connection and sent a painful, angry blast of mental energy through. The man had no defenses, no way even to know what was about to happen. Gray-Patch inserted her own mind in between and took the brunt of the mental attack.

The pain coursed through her, psychic shock waves inflaming every nerve ending. Before she passed out, she saw the man's dream-form flicker and disappear.

The Puhi temple appeared to be little more than a pile of huge glass-like stones, black and polished, rising into the sky in the deepest part of the wilderness along Cho Lake, not far from the crumbled ruins of the buildings that made up the old royal residence. It took Tua several moments to realize that what appeared merely a jumble was actually an arrangement, a careful interlocking of obsidian blocks in a sort of spiral, rising up like the end of a giant conch shell emerging from the soil. Tua had visited nearly every part of the city at one time or another, but he'd never seen this before, nor even known it was here. Despite the gap in the trees, it seemed darker here than in the surrounding pines, as if the stones themselves were sucking in the sunlight, leaving everything cast in hazy shadow.

Tua saw no sign of Aku. But this was where Keki had led him before flying off on business of his own, and the Temple made perfect sense as a destination for the Puhi hunter and Aku. Tua's gut urged him to rush the place, charge one of those dark holes that led to the building's interior, shove aside or stab anyone in his way until he found the boy. But good sense overruled his initial impulse. If the Puhi hadn't killed Aku back at the Scriptorium, he was keeping him alive for a reason, and a rash attack wouldn't help keep him in that state, or himself either. *Stick to your plan,* Tua thought. *Observe and get a feel for the situation. Maybe wait for nightfall, slink in and scope things out, and spirit the boy out with none of the Puhi the wiser.*

Tua found a tree near the footpath and climbed to a branch high enough to see all who approached while keeping hidden in a thicket of leaves. A bead of sweat trickled down his face in the humid air, but he didn't brush it off. The more he moved, the more likely he would be noticed. And though to the inattentive the place seemed deserted, that was illusory, for he noticed the numerous openings and crevices embedded in the obsidian, visible only after studying the structure a bit. Not doors, exactly, but more like...bolt holes. Hiding places. Just the spot for an eel to lie in wait for unsuspecting prey to pass by on the trail below.

He didn't think the Puhi had detected him, but had little confidence in that judgment. He'd approached by wading up one of the black streams flowing from the temple, an upsetting decision, as it'd permanently stained his leather boots with whatever polluted water sprang from that stinking pile of rocks. He'd also picked his current position partly because it was downwind of the temple, to evade the Puhis' enhanced sense of smell. *Still, better not to assume the advantage of surprise.*

Over the course of the afternoon, a number of people entered or left the temple—tattooed Puhi hunters in loincloths, female priests in hooded black robes, even a couple normal-looking merchant types pulling carts—and so far as he could tell, no one had sensed his presence. Tua also counted at least three whisper birds fluttering about, settling awkwardly in surrounding trees with hisses. He could stay as still and silent as he wanted, move as carefully as humanly possible, but in a situation like this there was simply no way to guarantee he wouldn't be seen.

A mosquito landed on Tua's forearm and he twitched, trying to get it to fly away. The bug inserted its proboscis into Tua's skin. Tua blew on it, but dared not brush it and the mosquito continued drinking, its abdomen bulging with warm blood. Finally, it flew away, heavy and sated.

At least it wasn't a spy, Tua thought. But it occurred to him he didn't know that for sure. The area buzzed with flies, bees, little white butterflies, all flittering about the blooms on wildflowers growing from the marshy soil or rising into the air and darting to and fro. None of them had the abnormal size or odd wounds that were signs of Regent's tampering, but Tua could hardly check every insect to be sure. What about that squirrel on the far side of the road? What made those ripples on the surface of the black stream? The longer Tua sat, the more it seemed the eyes of enemies were watching from every direction.

Lono, Opio, and Kai stood outside the bolted door, Lono holding a steaming cup of pala tea, Kai bearing the bronze mechanism. The bell had just rung the third hour and there was no sound from within. The howls from earlier were almost better than the silence. Opio's hand took the bolt and hesitated a moment. Lono knew he feared what he would find. It was a fear she shared.

Opio drew the bolt and let the door swing slowly inward. A horrible stench wafted out, a mix of excrement and vomit and something even viler Lono's nose could not identify. She forced her revulsion down and followed Opio in. Hulu sat in a corner, wearing only his loincloth, his arms and legs covered with bloody scratches. He looked up at them with clear eyes.

"Master, are you all right?" Opio asked.

"Mostly," Hulu answered in a small, hoarse voice. "It will be several days before the symptoms have completely passed, but I do believe the worst is over." He nodded at Lono. "Is that tea for me?"

She bent over and offered it to him, and he took it with steady hands. With the first sip, he closed his eyes, savoring the soothing liquid.

"Thank you," he said. His voice was already stronger. "I'm sorry you three have to see me like this, but I'm glad you came." He nodded at Opio. "You are early, despite my explicit instructions. You would only do so if you had important news for me."

"Master, we discovered something with the coding mechanism."

Hulu perked up immediately. "What is it? Show me now."

Kai set the machine on the ground and Hulu leaned over to read the new words on the panel. "A different message? How did you find it?"

"We found a knob on the bottom," Opio said. "You can slide it to change the alphabet."

Hulu read the words carefully. Speaking more to himself than them, he began murmuring. "Yes, that makes sense. I should have realized earlier." He looked back up at them. "I think this is not really a coding machine, it's a translation machine. I wouldn't wonder if that's actually what it's meant for, an aid to some clever scholar deciphering ancient works into modern language."

Opio brightened. "Yes. We could use such a machine here, in fact."

"But what about the directions?" Lono asked.

"Why, they tell the way to find Imi Au'o," Hulu said. "The one who creates the whisper birds and his other twisted servants. The one I have to find and stop."

"It says the Coast Road, past the Temple of the Owls." Opio said. "That would be in the Black Marsh, wouldn't it?"

"Yes, I believe it would be," Hulu said.

"But it's reputed to be very dangerous there, once you get past the temple," Opio said.

"Dangerous?" Hulu said. "Why Opio, all I have to do is journey to the center of the Black Swamp and defeat Imi Au'o and his army of misshapen animals. Easy as stealing a paapaa bird."

"Foor mee, iss closse to hoome," Kai said.

Hulu drank down the last of the pala tea and closed his eyes a moment, as if in thought, then opened them and spoke. "Well, there's no time to waste then." He held his hand out and Opio pulled him to his feet. Hulu wavered unsteadily for a moment before catching himself.

"Master, there's something else," Opio said. "A representative from the Council came while you were indisposed."

"Oh? Am I to be re-arrested?"

"No, for now. I think they're too preoccupied to bother. If you repay the Scriptorium for the lost ink, they'll suspend the charges until the next new moon."

"Gives me some breathing room, at least," Hulu said. "Did he say anything else?"

Opio gulped. "Well, you've also been…relieved of your duties. Permanently, I mean."

"It's as I suspected. And just as well, I suppose. You'll make a much better Master of the Scribes than I did."

"Me, Master?" Opio said.

"Of course. Or did the Council appoint someone from outside?"

"No," Opio said. "We're to choose a new Master according to our traditions."

"Then I'll recommend you to the Order, and I'm sure the vote will support you. Let's proceed down now, and you can call the brothers together. We don't have much time to lose, for I need to leave as soon as possible. Kai, I can accompany you as far as the turn off from the Coast Road."

"No, I coome witth. Heelp in fight."

Hulu put a hand on Kai's shoulder. "This is not your fight."

"Iss my fiight," Kai said. "Alwaayss help friendss."

"Thank you, my friend. That means a lot to me." Hulu brushed his eye, as if wiping a tear. "We'll depart directly after I make my speech, and should be able to arrive at our destination by dark, if Opio will be so good as to assemble the things we'll need for our mission."

"What will you need?" Opio asked.

"The turpentine we mix to thin the ink. How much do we have?"

"Quite a bit," Opio said. "A new delivery arrived a few days ago."

"Perfect," Hulu said. "Fill three sacks with it. But first, would you bring water and a scrub brush so I can clean this room?"

"Master, no. I'll assign one of the first-year scribes and—"

Hulu held up his hand. "Thank you, Opio. But this is something I must do to recover. I would not have another do it. If you want to help me, have a brush, a cake of soap, and a basin of warm water brought up immediately. Understood?"

"Yes, Master." Opio gave a slight bow and left.

"And what of you, Lono?" Hulu said. "I really should try to dissuade you from coming with me, if that is your intention."

"Of course that's my intention." She gaped at him, as if in disbelief he would even suggest she should't come along.

Hulu gave her a tight-lipped smile. "I see by your stare you're horrified at my appearance."

"You're wrong." Lono looked him up and down. She approved of this new, energetic, take-charge Hulu. His hair might have been sweaty and mussed, his body pale and covered with self-inflicted wounds, but no matter, *this* was the confident man she had seen in her dream so many nights. "Right now, I think you're the most handsome you've ever been."

THIRTY-FIVE

Kai knew he was the one slowing the group down. If he could walk naturally, on all four legs, he could set the pace at a quick trot, but the need to be upright, not to mention the constricting hooded robe he had to wear, meant they could only advance with painful slowness.

"Yoouu twwoo, leeave mee," he ventured at one point to Hulu and Lono. "Ii tooo sloow."

"It's not a problem," Hulu said. "Besides, we need a third person to help carry supplies."

By which, Hulu meant the burlap sacks the three carried, with their vile turpentine scent. "Yoou goo ahead. Ii caattch uup."

Hulu shook his head. "We stick together. We may need your sharp senses and teeth more than you think."

They continued walking. Even now, at the supper hour, they had only reached the outskirts of Atlantis along the Coast Road, where the buildings thinned and greenery crept into the landscape. The northern reaches of the city were far different from the cultivated, well-drained farms and orchards of the southern approach. Here the vegetation was wilder, lush ferns and sedges growing from the boggy ground among tall pine trees, and on occasion there appeared a gray-trunked cypress tree, with their knobby, spreading roots and the beard-like moss tendrils hanging from their branches. Kai's heart sped a bit to see them, for when they reached a place where the cypresses grew thick right out of the tea-colored water, it would mean he was close to home.

At the very end of the city, the last ramshackle houses petered out and the air turned cool and moist under the thick pines. They began to hear gentle, melancholy harp and flute tones drifting to them from somewhere, their interweaving melodies almost hypnotic. Searching for the source of the sounds, Lono glanced to the left, to the right, and finally looked straight up and gasped.

High above them, a network of netted catwalks spread in the canopy, with tiny figures walking along them between the trunks of the pines. "The Temple of the Owls," Lono breathed in. "I've read about it, and always wondered if it could be true."

"It's amazing, isn't it?" Hulu said. "How do you think they get up there?"

Far above, little heads poked over the edge and peered back at them. Almost at a signal, the melodies shifted keys and took a brighter tone, as if to welcome the visitors.

"Oh, I wish we could stop and visit," Lono said. "Wouldn't you love to be up there, so far above the earth?"

Kai didn't think that would be appealing at all, actually. Kai-men were versatile, able to live in the sea or on land, but the sky was decidedly not their element. The three passed over a series of simple wooden bridges, the planks under their feet decorated with painted motifs of different species of owl. Underneath trickled little brooks with clear burbling water. Now *that* was tempting—a nice soak in the pure, running water for an hour or so. No time, though, they had to keep moving.

There was a sudden whoosh from somewhere above. *Whisper bird?* Kai thought, crouching and baring his fangs. From behind them, a deep voice rang out and the three whirled around.

"Put away your teeth, good Kai, for you are welcome here." A man with weathered brown skin, a long hooked nose, and short-cropped black hair stood behind them. He wore a cape not unlike Hulu's, but made of red and white spotted owl feathers, and broader, as if it could be spread like wings. "In the name of Ne'i Peo, greetings to you, good Kai, and also to honored Lono and friend Hulu."

"How do you know our names?" Lono asked.

"We know much that is uncommon at the Temple of the

Owls," the man said. "For we fly by night and see what others do not, and our flights often cross over the boundaries of this world. Yes, we have watched you often in the All-Dream, Lono."

"Well, I haven't seen you," she said.

"Ah, but you could have," the man said. "Have you not dreamed of birds in cages, or moonplum orchards under the moon? Do you not think owls might have observed you in such settings, along with friend Hulu?"

Lono reddened at that remark, and Kai struggled to understand her emotional state. A reddened face generally meant anger, but Kai didn't think that fit here. Was it perhaps shame, or embarrassment? Such strange creatures, these surface men.

"If you know that much about us, perhaps you know where we're going now," Hulu said.

"Indeed, we have an idea. And we would like to help you, as well. But please, let me make my introduction. I'm He'u, the head priest here." He held out his hand and each shook it in turn. "Won't you please come up and join us for an evening meal?"

"We really should be—"

"Yes!" Lono cut Hulu off. "We'd love to!"

"Very good, then. We won't delay you long, friend Hulu." He'u let out a high-pitched hoot and a few moments later a sort of net cage lowered on a rope from somewhere high above. Kai had been afraid of something like this. "Just step in and we'll be above in no time."

The four of them stepped into the cage and took hold of the fibrous bars. Lono chattered excitedly next to him concerning the view or some such but Kai could hardly pay attention. He closed his eyes and tried to ignore the lurching in his stomach as the cage lifted slowly upwards into the trees.

There were a dozen prisoners besides Aku. Their open-air bamboo-barred cage sat on a ledge overlooking a huge black underground lake. Yellow jets of flame flared from the tops of stone pillars jutting from the lake. Below the cage, on a little archipelago of bamboo platforms floating on the water, sinewy eel temple priestesses clad only in loincloths and with patterns painted on their faces played metallophones and hanging gongs of various sizes with mallets. Their wild, unkempt hair swung as they struck out hypnotic beats and melodies. Others moved to the music, swaying and shaking and leaping high in the air in a complicated, coordinated dance. Tattoos of transparent eel larvae glided under their skin. Sometimes one or two would take a break, squatting by the edge of the water and smoking herbs in rolled leaves, the aromatic smoke from their spicy mixture drifting up to the ledge.

The other prisoners hung back in the shadows, some whispering prayers to themselves in their final hours, others staring dully, lost in their own thoughts. Aku took no notice of them, making himself busy testing each bamboo bar, pulling back and forth to check if it was loose, or pressing a shoulder between bars to see if his body could fit. He took a quick look at the guard, a brawny Puhi with zebra-striped eels swimming on his skin, currently snoring lightly as he leaned back against the bars near the door.

Aku wasn't quite sure what he would do if he did manage to squeeze through—Conger had carried him through a dizzying labyrinth of barely-lit passages, the moistly glistening black rock of one tunnel hardly distinguishable from the next. It could take hours to find the right passages out. Still, better to be searching for a way to escape than be stuck here.

Presently, one of the other prisoners rose and came forward into the light, a lean older man with a gray-flecked beard and a dark blue kihei shawl. He spoke in a soft voice. "You know there's no way out, don't you? We've only a little while until their ceremony."

Aku turned back to his work. "Plenty of time to break out of here, then."

The man reached out and rubbed Aku's upper back. Aku stiffened.

"I'm afraid there's really no hope," the man said, his fingers kneading Aku's skin. "It will be easier for you if you accept that. But we can still enjoy the time we have left to us."

Aku took a step away and the man took a step forward.

"Such a pretty face you have." The man smiled at him. "Has anybody ever told you what a sweet boy you are?" He continued advancing, backing Aku into a corner.

"Stay away from me." Aku put a hand in the pocket of his shift where he'd hidden the knife he'd already pickpocketed from the guard. He hoped he didn't have to use it. *Even if it makes this guy back off, it's going to be awkward explaining to the guard why I'm holding his weapon.*

The man reached out and tried to touch Aku's face, but Aku knocked his hand away with his free hand. The man laughed. "Oh, you dear, spirited lad."

He reached out to grab Aku when a figure leapt from the shadows, a tall man with a hooked nose and dark, close-cropped hair, shoving the older man against the bars.

"The boy said to stay away," the tall man growled. "I suggest you do what he asked."

"I didn't know," the old man muttered. He shook himself off and made a little bow. "So, so sorry. You should have said something if you wanted him for yourself." He scuttled away into the rear of the cell.

Aku's eyes were wide with recognition. "Hey, I know you. I've seen you at the tattoo parlor. You know Tua, don't you?"

"Tua is an honored friend of mine," the man said. "I'm Kaneke." He held out his hand and Aku shook it. "And I believe your name is Aku, is it not?"

"How did you know that?"

"I should have introduced myself earlier, but I wasn't sure it was you." Kaneke inspected the boy. "You're older and taller than when last I saw you. You don't realize it, but I know a great deal about you. But tell me, is Tua still alive?"

"He was as of this morning," Aku said.

"I knew it," Kaneke said. "I knew they couldn't put the tough bastard down." He took a seat and leaned back against the bars, patting the ground next to him for Aku to follow suit. "I don't know how much of a future we have, but I think we have a great deal of the past we can catch each other up on."

Reaching the owl temple dining room required crossing a long netting of taut hihi vines knotted together to create a walkway. Lono was delighted at the feeling of being in the sky, only the handguides between her and total freedom. She let Hulu and He'u go ahead while she looked over the side, the features of the surface world like a doll's house a hundred feet below. It reminded her of the afternoons spent with Iwali on the roof of the dormitory, observing the distant city through a telescope.

A moan came from somewhere behind her and there was Kai, no more than a quarter of the way along, clutching one of the handguides with both claws and looking distinctly green. Well, greener than usual. Lono walked back a bit. "Are you feeling okay?"

"Tooo hiigh. Noot foor kai-men."

"Here, take my hand," Lono said. "It's not that far to the end. Can you put your weight in the middle? It's easier if you're not leaning to one side. There you are. See, that's not bad, is it?" Slowly, with Lono coaxing him each step, Kai made it to the other side.

The walkway ended at a broad wooden platform built around a pine trunk, shaded with a roof thatched from pine straw. Men and women occupied a dozen or so tables, a few wearing owl-feather capes like He'u's, drinking steaming liquid from tiny, delicate cups. A harpist sat at the edge, plucking out a minor-key melody that reminded Lono of a song she couldn't quite place, perhaps something she'd heard as a small child. The conversation quieted a bit when the four of them entered but soon picked up again.

He'u seated them at an empty table, pulling out chairs for them, thoughtfully directing Kai to the one closest to the trunk. He signaled to an attendant, murmured a few things into the ear of the young man, and took the final seat himself.

"Honored Lono, how have you enjoyed your journey?" He'u asked her. "I believe the past weeks have taken you far from home?"

"Enjoy is a strange word for you to use," Lono said. She thought back over all the things that had happened to her and places she'd gone—starting with the message she'd received during the ceremony that she was still pretty sure was *not* from the ancestors, all the sites around the city with Tua and Aku, the trip south to the cabin and north again to the city, the scribes' revolt, all the dangers and hardships and discomforts. And on reflecting, she realized He'u was right. It was the most fun she'd ever had. The only thing that could have made it better would have been if Iwali had been there to share it with her.

An attendant interrupted her reverie, bearing food on a large tray held at shoulder-level and distributing plates and cups. For Lono and Hulu, herb salads with a light glaze. For Kai, a pile of pink round dumplings, or so Lono thought until He'u spoke. "Shaved mice, good Kai. I took the liberty of ordering yours raw. Is it to your liking?"

Kai popped one in his mouth. "Perrfeect."

Lono shuddered and turned to her own meal. She tested a few pale green leaves and found the sweetish dressing brought out the subtle flavors of the tender, slightly bitter plants beautifully. She took a sip from her cup and the dark ruby liquid turned out to be a hot, fruit-infused tea, deliciously tangy. She studied the cup itself, which seemed to be formed from tiny bones, perhaps from a mouse, fused together, as was the tableware.

"Is the food to everybody's taste?" He'u asked, himself receiving only a cup with tea. Seeing only nods and assurances of the supper's excellence, he tapped his fingers on the table. "In that case, I'm afraid we must speak now of a grimmer topic. I assume the three of you are on your way to Imi Au'o's workshop?"

"Yes, that is our destination," Hulu said. "What can you tell us about it?"

"Not too much, I'm afraid," He'u said. "We've known of it since Imi Au'o moved in, of course. It's located in a fine old kimunu tree where the royal family kept a summer residence until the Exile. You know how hot it can get in the city, and it's so much cooler out here in the shade. The owls used to be good friends with Queen Kamani and her entourage, and the King's hunting parties found good sport in the Black Marsh. Lovely gardens they kept there, sadly overgrown in the past decade."

Hulu's tone was a bit impatient. "But when did Imi Au'o move in?"

He'u took a sip of tea and considered. "Oh, it's been about three years now. Yes, three summers ago. And not long after that, the creatures started appearing. The whisper birds you know about in the city, of course, but here we see other things, as well. Birds, insects, all manner of creeping things, grown to a huge size and all…angry. Vicious. Only a few at first, but in ever greater numbers as time has gone on, until the forest has come to be dominated by the malignant creatures. We are hard-pressed here now."

"But," Lono said. "If you knew what Imi Au'o was doing all this time, why didn't you intervene?"

"Honored Lono, you must remember your convent's teachings. Surely you've learned that the Temple of Ne'i Peo is pacifist, our priests and followers sworn to never engage in aggressive conduct?"

Iwali would've remembered, Lono thought. "You could have asked for help, requested aid to fight this evil so close to your temple."

"Who could we have asked?" He'u said. "The city guard of Atlantis, run by the Shabengee, who are in Regent's pocket? Or should we have asked your own order? Would your Sisters have marched into Imi Au'o's domain with weapons drawn?"

"I suppose not," Lono said.

"We did the best thing we could. We prayed to Ne'i Peo in the All-Dream that he would send us deliverers." He'u smiled and spread his arms. "And here you are."

Lono was silent. He'u's words reminded her that she had often chafed at the deliberate pace of life in the convent, often felt constricted by the endless scrolls and study and prohibitions on leaving the grounds or exploring. Now here she was, taking direct action where her sisters would still be discussing the problem. *Maybe a sister's life is not really for me, despite what I've always thought.*

"You said you were hard-pressed," Hulu said. "What do these creatures do?"

"What don't they do?" He'u said. "Every night our owl friends find their hunting territory more restricted. And when they meet one of the nasties, a fight is sure to ensue. Our priests treat many a case every day now. Deep wounds, broken wings, gouged eyes. Truly malicious injuries. And that's if the owls make it back." He'u shook his head. "We've lost many of our friends."

"That's so sad," Lono said, her thoughts turning to Keki. She was glad he wasn't nearby. *Although come to think of it, where is he?*

Hulu dropped his fork on his plate with a clink. "So they'll know we're coming."

"Oh, yes. They likely know already," He'u said. "That's where we come in. If you're willing, we can help you."

"We're hardly in a position to refuse aid," Hulu said. "What do you have in mind?"

"Continue on your journey," He'u said. "When you leave here, an owl will join you to ensure you don't lose your way. You should reach the sign of the skull in an hour or so, right around nightfall. That's the time when the owls are at their best, when they can most assist you in fighting off the resistance you will undoubtedly encounter." He smiled at Lono. "Our priests may be pacifist, but our feathered allies are decidedly not."

"Won't it be dangerous for them, though?" Lono asked.

"Yes, but it will be far more dangerous for the three of you," He'u said. "You'll not reach the tree unmolested, but we'll do our best to ease your passage. At that point, you'll be on your own."

THIRTY-SIX

In the twilight, Tua waited for a moment when no one was around to climb down from the tree. He quietly slunk among the obsidian juttings until he reached a crevice he had seen someone exit from earlier that day, but that otherwise seemed little used. The entrance was low and he had to duck a bit, but once inside it opened up into a long tunnel, lit only by a single flickering torch ensconced about halfway down.

He advanced silently, alert for any movement, ears straining for the slightest sound, but he heard nothing but the ever-so-slight swish of his leather boots on the smooth obsidian floor. The tunnel ended at a T-intersection, each way as dimly lit and empty as the tunnel behind him. He picked the left passage for no particular reason and followed its long curve and gentle downward grade. Now he could make out distant sounds—the strike of metal on rock, a distressed cry that ended in a choke, a woman's mocking laugh.

He hesitated at one point, feeling eyes on him. He slowly slid his hand to the hidden pocket in his tunic that held his knife. But when he turned, nobody was behind him. Could there be viewholes in the walls? Possibly, though a quick glance didn't reveal anything. He continued on his way, reaching a short set of stairs leading down to still another T-intersection. This time he picked right, as his cheek felt a hint of a cool breeze from that direction.

Where be all the people? Tua thought. He must have seen a couple dozen visitors go in or out throughout the day, and temples generally were busy with activity, both religious and the everyday necessities of life. *Where are they? For that matter, why all this space if it be unoccupied?* He had the unsettling feeling he was missing something, some concealed place that would be obvious if only he knew where to look.

The breeze grew stronger and he hurried his step. He could see at the far end of the passage a brighter light shining in. *Finally, I'm getting somewhere.* He followed it as quickly as he could without making a sound. There was no noise at the end so he simply walked through the opening.

"Shab's balls!" he muttered, finding himself standing outside under moonlight, back amidst the obsidian jumble. He had crossed straight through the temple. From somewhere deep inside came the faint echo of the woman's mocking laughter.

The Coast Road narrowed to little more than a misty path as Hulu, Lono, and Kai followed the great owl whom He'u had assigned as their guide, his wingspan nearly as wide as a man's spread arms, his coat speckled with gray, black, and red, and with little tufts of feathers on his head that looked almost like horns. The owl led them along the winding way, turning his head all the way around from time to time to make sure they hadn't fallen behind, taking them through waterlogged fields interspersed with fern-choked islands and broad-trunked cypress trees.

It was nearly nightfall and drizzling when they reached a spot where a rounded basalt stone formation protruded from a brown pool. It was as tall as a man and had hollows carved out around head level to look like eye sockets, an open grinning mouth, and nasal cavities.

"I would say we've found the sign of the skull, don't you think?" Hulu said.

"Who would make those eyes like that?" Lono asked. "It seems to be staring at you."

"Iss waarning fromm Great Kai-man," Kai said. "Telll myy

peeople, noo goo faarther, iss woorld of suurface menn passt heere."

"Oh!" Lono said. "Here I was assuming it was a sign for people coming from the city. But as you say, it could just as easily be a message for travelers from the other direction instead."

The owl hooted, impatient for them to keep moving. "Give us a few minutes," Hulu called to it. "We've been on our feet for more than an hour. We need to rest." The nightbird gave a hoot in assent and fluttered off into the trees.

Hulu and Lono seated themselves on flat gray rocks and Kai shed his cloak and slipped into the brown pool, only his eyes protruding above. None spoke, perhaps tired from their long hike, or possibly due to the unsettling feeling that the skull-shaped stone was watching them.

As the sun passed below the horizon, Lono kept catching movements out of the corner of her eye, but finding nothing there when she turned her head. It seemed to her that they were surrounded by places an enemy could hide—dark, leafy undergrowth, rocky outcroppings, murky puddlings. Nor was it merely her imagination to think they might be under observation, for she knew Imi Au'o's spies might well be tracking them.

An odd cracking came from somewhere in the trees. She grabbed Hulu's arm. "I think we should go now," she whispered to him.

"Our owl's not back yet. We'll go as soon as he returns."

"But don't you feel like we're not the only ones here?" she asked.

"Give me another minute," Hulu said. "I'm dealing with a nausea wave. Anyway, you're just spooked by the skull."

"Maybe you're right." Lono tried to calm her mind. It had probably been her imagination. No, there *was* something moving, an undulating in the mud by a tuft of sedge. She peered at the mud, trying to make out what it could be. Slowly a huge armored beetle pushed its way out of the soil, fully as large as a man's fist, a single horn growing from its head and pincered mandibles opening and closing.

Lono's grip on Hulu's arm tightened. "Do you see that?" she whispered, pointing.

"I don't see anything," Hulu said. "It's too dark."

Lono's arm itched at the telescope on her elbow, but she hardly dared move to scratch it. Another beetle emerged from a rotting pile of fallen leaves, still another pushed its way out from under a pebble. In fact, everywhere she turned beetles were appearing. Dozens, maybe hundreds, as if the ground itself were boiling, and out of each bubble popped out a huge beetle.

"What's that clicking sound?" Hulu asked.

"It's their pincers, snapping closed," Lono said. She stood and stepped onto the rock where they'd been seated, pulling Hulu up with her.

"What pincers? What are they?"

Kai rose from his pool, dripping not only water but beetles rolling off his scales. One had latched onto one of his scutes and was trying to dig into him. He knocked it aside with a flick of his tail and a growl. "Whaat theese?"

"They're beetles," Lono said. "Huge, disgusting beetles." She kicked one away that had crawled almost to them, and it emitted a high-pitched whine. "And they're everywhere!"

"I can't see them," Hulu said. "How many are there?"

"You don't even want to know. I don't think we can wait for our owl any longer, Hulu."

"How do we know where the side path is, though?" Panic was beginning to creep into his voice as the clicking grew nearer.

"Can't you see it?" Lono said, craning her neck. "It's on the far side of the rock formation, where that gap in those trees is."

"It's so dark out, I can barely make out that there even are trees," Hulu said. "You'll have to lead the way."

Lono took his hand. "Ooh! I don't want to run through them."

"Fine, we'll just stay and let them crawl over us," Hulu said. "I'm sure they're friendly."

Ne Wa'e, be with us! Lono repeated to herself three times. "Get ready, Kai, we're going!" She took a deep breath and gave Hulu's hand a squeeze. He squeezed back. "Now!"

They jumped from the rock together and took off around the pool, Kai following with his cloak draped over one arm. The beetles were so thick that Lono had to high-step, at times finding no place to put her feet but right on top of the writhing insects, crushing them under her shoes with a series of damp crunches. "Eee! This is vile!"

Hulu's foot sank in a muddy sinkhole and several beetles hopped onto his leg. "Nebas' curses!" He yanked his leg out with a slurping sound and shook it violently as he ran, sending beetles buzzing through the air. "They're taking chunks out of me!"

They dashed into the gap in the trees and down the path, Kai loping after them. Finally, they reached a place where Lono couldn't see any more movement on the ground. Hulu dropped her hand and put his hands on his knees, recovering his breath.

"So…there…aren't any more now?" Hulu asked between breaths, daubing one finger at the oozing welts on his leg where the beetles had latched on.

Lono looked at him and screamed. The biggest beetle she had seen yet, fully two hand-spans across, had found purchase on his cape, and its pincers were slowly closing on the back of his neck.

A snap, and the tip of Kai's tail knocked the beetle from its perch and against a nearby tree trunk, where it hit with a wet thud.

"Goot iit," Kai said with a toothy grin.

THIRTY-SEVEN

The priestesses on their bamboo archipelago had been joined by Puhi warriors, more than fifty of them, who had appeared on the edge of the underground lake and dived in the water, emerging a few minutes later dripping on the little artificial islands. The priestesses shared their smoked herbs with them and increased the tempo of their music. The assembly took on the feel of a party, with clusters of barely-clad warriors and priestesses talking and laughing, or sitting on the edge dangling their feet in the water. *All they need is some entertainment,* Aku thought as he watched from where he sat next to Kaneke. *And I bet I know what that will be.*

Just when the party was getting raucous, the gong music stopped and the priestesses and warriors fell silent, as if upon some unseen signal. A priestess stepped to the edge of the center-most platform, tall, dark-skinned, and slender. She pulled a flute to her lips and began to play, the clear tones penetrating to every cranny of the cavern, the melodies fluid and exotic. Aku stared, transfixed, his eyes on her fingers as they danced along the wooden tube. *I've got to remember some of those fingerings.* She played with her eyes closed, swaying a bit, and then lifting one foot to rest on the knee of her other leg, like a flamingo.

As she played, the water on the surface of the lake rippled, at first just in a few places, but soon all over. "Look at all those fish coming to the surface," Aku said to Kaneke.

"Look closer," Kaneke said. "Those aren't fish."

Aku peered, and found Kaneke was right. They were eels, thousands of them. Most were gray, but there were others too, green and yellow and red ones, speckled and striped, twisting and writhing at the water's surface as if hypnotized by the flute.

The prisoners jumped when the door to their cage opened with a bang. The Puhi guard with the zebra-striped eels stepped in and growled. "I need one of you. No volunteers, eh? All right, I'll take you in the back, trying to hide." He pointed at the older bearded man who had accosted Aku earlier.

The bearded man whimpered and tried to shrink away, but a heavily-muscled young man with scars on his cheeks and a crooked nose shoved him forward, and he fell to the feet of the Puhi. The warrior grabbed him by the hair and yanked him up.

"Why me?" the bearded man sniveled. He pointed at Aku. "What about him? Why not the boy?"

"'Cause hes' a brave one, not even shivering." The warrior gave the old man a shake, as if he were a little girl's doll. "Papa Eel hungers only for the bravest. The boy goes later. A coward like you goes first, to feed the babies."

The Puhi dragged the shaking man to the edge of the water. A sort of raft waited on the edge, a square frame of bamboo with a hollow center. The warrior grabbed the man's hand and forced it into a bronze manacle affixed to the corner of the frame, clicking it closed. He followed suit with the man's other hands and feet, so that the man was spread in an X across the empty place in the middle of the raft.

"What's your name?" Kaneke asked the crook-nosed young man who'd pushed the victim forward.

"Okoa. And it didn't sit well with me what the bearded one tried with the boy. If you hadn't stepped in, I would have."

Kaneke nodded. "I appreciate that."

The young man folded his powerful arms across this chest. "I've got no love for these eel-worshipers. But I can't say they're not giving that one what he deserves."

The Puhi lifted the raft and gave it a shove into the lake, where it slowly drifted across while the shackled man sobbed and begged for someone to help him. The priestess's flute song shifted to a higher key and sped up, and the other warriors and priestesses began to chant in unison, their eel tattoos gliding and twisting around their bodies in bloodlust. Aku listened but couldn't make out the words of the chant. It didn't sound like Atlantean, but felt like something old, even older than Atlantis itself, from a wild, free time before the gods had showed men how to live in cities.

The bearded man struggled in the raft, pulling and shaking the bonds with his arms and legs, trying to break loose. The water began to boil around him, and little snouts poked up. The man screamed, and within seconds his whole body was covered in squirming eels, eating their fill as the water turned red.

As horrible as it was, Aku found one thing strangely concordant. *His screams match the rhythm of the music perfectly.*

Hulu followed Lono's lead, keeping one hand on her shoulder in the near-complete darkness, unable to make out more than the most general shapes. Despite the urgency, they walked slowly and carefully, for the way was hard-going. The path was little more than a ribbon of solid ground winding among marshier areas, and Hulu frequently stumbled over protruding roots. One relief was that Kai easily kept up with them, now that there was no need for him to proceed on his hind legs. Kai's vision, too, seemed as acute as Lono's in the low-light conditions, perhaps because he was accustomed to the murkiness of his mangrove home.

All around them, they heard sounds of battle in the trees. Owls hooted and screeched, unseen creatures hissed and spat, wings fluttered frantically. The noise came from every direction, but if the hissing got too close, a flurry of hoots would follow, and the hissing would be driven back. As promised, the three remained unmolested.

"I hope our guide is okay," Lono said. "Do you think he was hurt? Or just couldn't find us after he fled?"

"I'm afraid he's probably gotten caught up in the fighting," Hulu said. "But there's no way to tell. Perhaps we can find out in the morning."

After a long while of walking, Hulu began to worry they had missed their landmark. "Do things look different? Any sign of a twist tree?"

"I don't think so," Lono said. "Although that's a strange term. What does a twist tree mean, anyway?"

"I suppose it's the way it's growing," Hulu said. "I should stop worrying. It will be recognizable enough, I expect. The directions on the cylinder were likely meant for someone who had never been here before."

They'd hardly taken a step further when multiple shapes flew at them with hissing so high-pitched it was almost a whistle. Lono shrieked and in an instant, Hulu was in front of her with his knife out, guarding her with his body and stabbing blindly in the direction the hisses came from. He hit something solid and felt hot liquid on his arm, but whether it was his own blood or he'd made a lucky hit he couldn't be sure.

A chorus of hoots closed in, and the hissing was driven back as quickly as it had started. There was even a distinctive caw in the mix. "Keki?" Lono said to herself.

Behind them, Kai was up on two feet and snapping his jaws. A hissing abruptly ended in a crunch, followed by a gulp. Feathers drifted down from his mouth. "Goood snaack."

Then Lono let out a little "Oh!"

"What is it?" Hulu asked.

"The twist tree. It's right here!"

"What does it look like?" Hulu asked.

"It's a huge kimunu tree. I've never seen one this tall, but the branches and trunks all wind around each other, spiraling upward. It must have taken centuries to grow like this."

The competing hissing and hooting grew closer again.

"Can you see an entrance?" Hulu asked.

"Yes, straight ahead," Lono said.

"Then we'd better go in while our owl friends are providing us the chance."

THIRTY-EIGHT

The wicked man donned his tunic of red and green spiders and climbed the ladder through the skylight to the top of the tree, as he did every night. Gray-Patch could see only glimpses of him through the square of the skylight as he strode around above, but she knew what he was doing. He was commanding his creatures, all the birds and other poor souls he had twisted and corrupted and who now attended to his will. His orchestration seemed far more intense than usual this evening, his face contorted with effort and sweat running down his temples.

Gray-Patch mind-tapped her friend, the black bird. She sensed he was close and their connection was so strong she could hear through his ears. It sounded like a brawl, with squawks and cries and hissing. *What is happening?* she asked.

A great battle, came the black bird's answer. *I join the animals of the forest. Tonight we are fighting back.*

Gray-Patch's heart sped up. Dare she hope that help was coming, at last? *Why tonight?*

The friends are near and the end is close. I will concentrate, so you can see through my eyes.

Slowly an image resolved in Gray-Patch's mind, three figures walking, seen from above, as from a branch in a tree. She recognized the long-haired man, whose dream-form she had seen twice now. With him was a smaller figure, also with long hair, but more delicate features. A female of the species, Gray-Patch decided. The final figure was surprising—a kai-man, his kind well-known to her as neighbors in the lagoons. Rather plodding animals, but loyal as allies and tenacious as enemies. Of course she knew they could go onto dry land, but she had never heard of one spending much time there, much less befriending humans. Were these three capable of taking on the wicked man?

Perhaps. And she could help them, of course. Best of all, she recognized their location: they were at the very front door of the tree.

Tua bided his time, waiting for someone to show up. He'd tried twice more to enter the temple, only to find each time that after a quick journey through dim tunnels he ended up back outside again. He was outwardly calm, but churning inside. Each minute that passed reduced the chances that Aku might live, or lengthened the time he might be subjected to Gods only knew what sort of maltreatment.

When finally a woman came up the moonlit path, it was all Tua could do not to leap out and grab her and demand she show him how to get in. But drawing attention was not the right way. Instead, he pushed down his urgency and waited for her to pass, then followed silently at a discreet distance.

The woman had a short robe and long, lustrous black hair to her waist, and she bore a basket, green tips of herbs or vegetables poking out of its top. She stepped with a sure stride, the toned, compact muscles in her legs suggesting she was a dancer or an athlete. She picked one of the crevices in the temple exterior without hesitating. Tua waited outside about half a minute and ducked in after her.

He had almost missed his chance. Upon entering, he spotted her about a third of the way down the corridor, when she immediately disappeared, slipping off to the right. Was it his imagination, or had she glanced his way with a grin as she departed? Impossible to tell in the dim light. No matter, he made his way to the spot as quickly as was consistent with silence.

A quick scan of the wall revealed nothing but a mostly smooth obsidian surface, albeit with numerous grooves and uneven places. Perhaps there was a hidden panel that could be pushed in? Tua chose a likely looking place and pressed his hands against the wall, surprised when he fell right through and reeled down a set of steps. He had a brief impression of a well-lit space with a table in the center, covered in heaps of leaves and stems and with three women standing around it, before stumbling on the last step and falling hard on his back.

It took several moments for his head to clear, and when it did the three women were squatting around him. One was the woman he'd followed, her face quite pretty, with dark, almond-shaped eyes and a mocking half-smile. The other women's faces were harder to read, for they were painted in swirling patterns of red, black, and white. None of them seemed surprised that he had just landed on the floor.

"Mmm, Keola, look at the puppy you brought home," one of the painted ladies said, her green eyes flashing. "He's delicious. I love him."

"Me too," the other painted lady crooned, rubbing her fingers along Tua's bicep. "He's a big pup, isn't he? I wish we had time to play." She smiled, and her teeth were filed to points.

Tua reached for the hidden pocket with his knife, but Keola was faster, and had somehow produced a Puhi maka and put it to his throat before he could pull his blade out. "Ah, ah, ah," she said, shaking her head. "You're such a naughty boy."

"And we do like naughty boys," the green-eyed lady said.

"We surely do," Keola said. "But unfortunately, we need this one to take part in the ceremony."

"What part would I have in a ceremony?" Tua asked.

Keola tittered. "The main course."

Hulu, Lono, and Kai entered the twist tree through the gnarled, arched branches that formed its foyer, emerging into a large chamber with multiple stairwells and corridors leading off of it. It was similar, though not identical, to the place Hulu had visited twice in the All-Dream: the first time with Malu, the second that very morning, one of the final dreams as the ink had left his body during the throes of withdrawal. Somehow in the dreams, the proportions had been distorted, the colors saturated, the locations of doorways switched from one wall to another.

It all seemed dingier, smaller, less *real* in actual life. Still, Hulu felt confident he had a rough idea of the floorplan, and chose a stairway up to a torch-lit chamber crowded with cages. At first, things were uncannily silent, the birds and small mammals moving to the rears of their enclosures and eyeing the figures warily. But now that they saw they were newcomers, they let forth with a deafening chorus of squawks, whistles, screeches, and cage rattling.

"Are they happy to see us or angry?" Lono yelled at Hulu to be heard over the racket.

"I'm not sure!" Hulu shouted back. "Could be both."

Lono glanced into a cage of frightened awi birds shrinking away from them. "Shouldn't we be setting them free?"

Hulu shook his head. "They may be under the control of Imi Au'o. I don't think we should free them until he's been defeated."

Lono winced away from the grasping paws reaching through the bars of some snarling creature they passed. "You could be right about that."

The next room they entered was roomier and quieter, with neat glass-covered wooden tubs around its edges, though the place stank of reptile. Bulbous eyes appeared through ferns under the steamy glass, and a lumpily misshapen toad glistened on a branch before hopping off and splashing into a little pool of water when they neared his tub.

"I don't suppose they're cousins of yours?" Hulu asked Kai.

"Veery faar coussins." Kai grinned. "Wee havve oover foor dinnerr."

Footsteps sounded from the open portals around the chamber, and three black robed assistants to Imi Au'o stepped in, hoods covering their heads and hiding their faces. Each held a wooden staff.

"You there, intruders," one assistant said, a bit taller than the others. "You disrupt our master's important work here this night. Leave now or face the consequences."

Hulu ducked his head, trying but failing to see under the man's hood. "We have business with your master. You may take us to him now."

In response, the taller assistant swung his staff at Hulu, who leapt back, anticipating the reaction. Hulu was no expert in such matters, but he thought the blow weak and poorly coordinated. *These black-robed fellows are no trained warriors,* he thought. *Just lackeys more used to dealing with frightened animals.*

"We can handle them," he said to Kai and Lono. "I'll take the taller one. Kai, you take the bulky one. Lono, you take the short one."

The three assistants, seeing they were to meet resistance, let their robes drop to the ground. Lono cried out in shock.

Their skin was covered with long, keloid scars, some still raw and oozing. Animal parts grew from them in unnatural places. The tall one facing Hulu had furry ears on his shoulders, feathers on his forearms, and a row of scutes like Kai's down his back. The stouter one facing Kai, had a furry, ape-like paw hanging from his side as a third arm and silvery fish scales on his limbs. Lono's opponent had several extra blinking eyes inserted in a pattern across his abdomen and gills embedded in his throat, and not one, but two tails emerging from his coccyx, one bushy and one straight, with tuffs of mismatched fur growing randomly around his body.

I hope I haven't made a mistake here, Hulu thought as the three deformed assistants advanced.

THIRTY-NINE

"Look Kaneke, something's happening," Aku said.

The drums had quieted after the eels had fed, and now a raft came in from a dark tunnel on the far side of the lake, poled by a priestess. Two other priestesses also stood on the raft, between them a man on his knees, his hands bound behind his back. As the raft floated into the circle of torchlight near the archipelago, the man's features became visible.

"Tua!" Aku stood and shouted through the bamboo bars. "Tua, I'm here! It's me, Aku! And Kaneke's here too!"

"Quiet in there!" the zebra-striped Puhi snarled from his post outside the door.

Tua glanced up and gave a quick nod to the cage. He appeared perfectly cool and calm, as if there was no place he would rather be than in the heart of the Temple of the Eels, about to be sacrificed in a blood ritual.

On one of the islands, a bruised and scratched-up warrior pushed his way to the edge and yelled out to the raft. "That one is mine."

The music stopped and the cavern was silent except for the lapping of water. The lead priestess on the raft, with waist-length dark hair and a red-and-black checkerboard pattern on her face, called back. "This one invaded our sacred halls. By the Law of the Bold he is meant for Papa Eel. What right have you to him?"

"That one took something that belongs to me." The warrior pointed to his empty left eyesocket, still encrusted with blood around its edges, and the conger eels on his body went into a frenzy. "By the Law of Unfinished Combat, he belongs to me. Papa Eel can have him when I'm done."

Tua laughed. "Unfinished combat? I'd say I finished it just fine, boy. But if you want another go, I'm ready for you."

"You only won because of your damned bird." Conger spat in the water. "Take me by yourself and we'll see what happens."

"A bird! A bird!" Tua's guffaws echoed from the cavern's walls. "You all think you're fierce Puhi warriors, and one of you lost a fight because of a little birdie! I'll take you all on!"

"Enough!" the dark-haired priestess cried. "There will a combat. A point for either a fall or blood drawn. Three points makes the winner. The loser has the honor of swimming with Papa Eel."

She signaled to Tua to rise and cut his bonds with her maka. He was too far away to tell for sure, but Aku thought the priestess looked at Tua with something like admiration.

The fight in the tub room went well at first. Hulu took on the taller assistant with the shoulder ears and feathered arms. He blocked the assistant's staff blows with crossed arms and grabbed a feathered elbow, swinging the assistant around and sent him tumbling into one of the tubs, crashing through the glass cover. The assistant's head landed in a batch of ferns, and several toads, grown to an unnaturally large size, hopped over and squeezed their eyes, squirting steamy, milky liquid into his face. Shoulder Ears screamed and clutched his hands where the jets of fluid burned his skin.

Kai made even quicker work of the stouter assistant with the ape arm. He easily ducked Ape Arm's swinging staff and swept him to the floor with his tail, leaping on top of him and snapping his jaws close to the man's face. He took care not to actually bite the fellow, of course, but the assistant blubbered in fear, slapping his three hands ineffectually against Kai's armored back.

Meanwhile, Lono advanced towards the assistant with the extra eyes and the two tails, whose balance seemed worsened rather than improved by his extra features. She aimed several quick kicks at his body, simple foot thrusts to exercise the abdominals and legs from the Convent's daily regimen of exercises. Her opponent cringed away, seemingly confused by the multiple visual inputs his brain was receiving, or perhaps just overly sensitive that his delicate abdominal eyes might be hurt. Emboldened by this success, she followed up with a flurry of punches.

But Two-tails managed to wrap his long, straight tail around one of Lono's ankles and yanked, sending her thudding painfully to the floor. Before she could recover herself, he pressed his open palm to her exposed neck and she gave a little shout. Two-tails stepped back to observe. Lono tried to push herself up but fell back to the ground, her eyes staring but her limbs frozen.

Ape Arm also had slipped a hand onto Kai's soft underbelly and pressed with his palm. Within moments, Kai, too, seemed to experience a loss of control of his muscles, and the still-sniffling Ape Arm rolled the heavy reptilian off of him.

Only Hulu remained in the fight. Shoulder Ears had recovered from the toad spray, though patches of his face still steamed. He and his two companions surrounded Hulu, who fended them off with thrusts from a staff he'd picked up from the floor. The three assistants each raised one of their hands, showing that each palm had a raised red area with a small, beak-like proboscis.

Hulu gave a final thrust and attempted to dash out from the circle but a furry ape arm grabbed him in a strong grip, and Shoulder Ears pressed his palm to Hulu's neck. The proboscis punctured the skin and Hulu felt something cold enter his blood and spread through his body in moments. He collapsed to the floor.

"Each of you grab one," Shoulder Ears said. "We'll take them to the master now."

Ape Arm answered with a growl and Two-tails with a meow.

Tua and Conger circled each other on a floating platform no wider than two men placed head to foot, both stripped to their loincloths. Conger had his maka out, black and honed to a wicked edge, Tua, holding his trusty knife. Tua's sea turtle swam calmly across his back, while Conger's eels slithered over and around one another, reflecting the actual eels rippling the surface in the water around them.

Both were experienced knife fighters, keeping light on their toes and shifting their weight from foot to foot as they orbited each other, Conger thrusting often to test Tua's nerve, Tua drawing back and waiting for the right moment.

Three bloods? Tua thought. *One could be enough if it severs a tendon in a knife hand.* He sensed the eyes of nearly everybody present on them, including the guard of the prisoners, standing fascinated at the water's edge. And, out of the corner of his eye, he spotted Aku, otherwise unnoticed, picking the lock of the cage above the distracted guard.

At that moment, Conger lunged at Tua but was a bit off-center, perhaps not judging depth well with only one eye. Tua easily sidestepped, grabbing the Puhi's forward arm and yanking, trying to knock him off balance, while Conger's back arm flailed against Tua's body. But Conger caught himself and spun, and both faced each other once again.

"First blood," the priestess yelled.

First blood? But I didn't strike him. Tua glanced at his own abdomen, where blood welled in a long line from his pectoral muscle to his hip. *How did he do that?*

Conger grinned. "Not expecting that, was you boy?"

It was then Tua realized Conger held something in the palm of his back hand, probably a small razor. *Did I really expect this fight would be fair?*

FORTY

The assistants dragged the limp Lono and her companions up ladders and stairwells, through torch-lit chambers full of overgrown and damaged birds and centipedes and lizards and fish and other animals as well, all in their cages and tanks. Lono could not move but she could hear the cacophonies of caws, roars, and whines, and smell the stink of poorly-cleaned enclosures and animal fear. Ever onward they wended their way to the top of the tree. *Not the way we intended to reach Imi Au'o*, she thought. Finally, they climbed a ladder and passed through a trapdoor into a large room with two huge aquariums spanning either end. The assistants dropped them on the floor in the center of the room and left.

Lono found she had the power to lift her head a bit, just enough to survey the room. One aquarium held a huge dark blue octopus with white mottles, fully as large as a man, the other a ray, light gray with a dark patch around one eye, sweeping from one side of her tank to the other. A silver table was pushed to one side of the room, next to a rack of bronze and obsidian scalpels, calipers, and other instruments. Shelves full of reagents in bottles, parchments covered with scribbled notes, and jars of dissected animals in preserving liquid lined the walls. Overhead, the wispy top branches of the tree were visible through a skylight, with the starry sky beyond that.

This must be the operating room. Lono shuddered at the sight of the surgical instruments, but quickly turned her attention back to the octopus and the ray. The octopus seemed to glare at them hatefully, but the ray's eyes were sympathetic. In fact, Lono could almost imagine the ray was trying to ask her something, or maybe it was an invitation…. She felt something warm inside her brain, a gentle probing, almost a tickle. It was an odd feeling, but not unpleasant. *Is that the ray doing that?*

It is the ray, answered Hulu's voice. *Let her complete the connection.*

Lono was so surprised at hearing Hulu in her head she jumped, albeit an internal jump, as her muscles didn't respond. She turned her head to Hulu and he nodded at her.

Lono closed her eyes and let the mental probing continue. It expanded, spreading warmth until her whole mind seemed to buzz. Somehow she could feel the presence of Hulu, determined but scared, and there was a warm mothering presence as well. *That must be the ray.* She heard Kai grunt next to her, and then he too was in her head, protective but yearning. The connection grew stronger, and soon they could not only feel each other's general presences, but actually see and hear inside each other's minds.

It was disorienting at first, sharing each other's thoughts, being able to see what another creature was picturing, hear what they were thinking, even feel what they were feeling. Kai had in mind his mate Kaipo and his hatchlings, longing to see them and sick for his home lagoon, but full of fierce loyalty to his new friends.

Hulu's mind was contradictory and busy, full of drive and ambition to fulfill his promise to Malu to destroy this evil place, but equally full of worry that he might not be capable of seeing it through. Images and feelings bubbled that he had been a failure as head of the scribes and would fail again here, and soon they would all be dead and it would be his fault for leading them poorly. Yet, there was hope too, for victory somehow, and after, for a future with Lono, her pretty face smiling at him, her fingers slowly unbuttoning her blouse… *Hulu!* Lono thought. The fingers stopped unbuttoning, his thoughts tinged pink. Finally, underneath all that, there was a residual craving for the ink, nibbling at the edges of his consciousness, a sucking need to feel that sweet smoke in his lungs and nerves.

Even Keki's thoughts showed up in the mix, but this connection was weaker, little more than vague visuals of his current frantic flight in the forest, searching for enemy birds to harass, and fear that he himself was being targeted.

Strangely, Lono could see her own thoughts too, as the others were seeing them. It was like examining her own brain from the outside. Memories of her best friend Iwali, of the Prioress, of the dorm rooms and gardens and girls at the convent. Recollections of her recent journeys with Tua and Aku and all the places she'd been. Concern for Aku, worry for her own situation, and fear for the safety of their group. All this interspersed with images of Hulu—Hulu with his shirt off, Hulu with his long hair wet from a shower, Hulu handsome as he took command, Hulu reaching with his strong hands and pulling her to him. *Who needs to watch their thoughts now?* came Hulu's voice. She felt embarrassed and tried to pull those last images back, but couldn't. If she shared something, she shared everything.

Behind all this was the ray's presence, binding them all together. A gentle tickling in her head, in all their heads. It was the ray, probing to see what sort of people they were, and reassuring them that she found them good and noble souls.

What is your name? Lono asked her.

The ray answered, not in Atlantean, yet still in a way that Lono could understand. *I am Gray-Patch. It makes me happy that you have come.* And with that introduction, she shared her own memories of the freedom of the ocean, gliding through the water with a feeling of flying. But too, there was an underlying anxiety for how the evening would turn out, and what it meant if the wicked man wasn't stopped. Finally, a deep warmth, a sad, loving, mothering feeling of one who had lost her own mate and pups, and was adopting those in the room as her new family.

And then the connection dissolved, her consciousness returned to her own mind, with a final warning from Gray-Patch in their heads: *The wicked man comes. Look above you.*

Lono could turn her head fully now, and even lift her shoulders off the ground a bit. A tall man let himself down from the skylight, dangling for a moment from the skylight's edge before landing on the floor. He was tall and impossibly scrawny, as if his body had been stretched out, and his face was criss-crossed with scars. He wore a fine barkcloth tunic decorated with red and green spiders. *Imi Au'o*, Lono thought.

"Ah, there you are," Imi Au'o sang out in a high, jovial tone. "Hello! Hello! I see you've met my pets." He frowned when they didn't answer. "Nothing to say? The paralyzing agent is not long-lasting. You should have your voices back, or will in a few moments. Then we can talk, yes, yes? We have much to discuss, I think."

Aku noticed that Kaneke had positioned his body so that he blocked the view from the people below of Aku picking the lock to the cage. *Not that it's really necessary*, Aku thought. All eyes were on the fight between Tua and Conger. A collective gasp from the crowd—Puhi priestesses and warriors, the guard below them, even the other prisoners standing against the bars—pulled Aku's attention from his task. Conger was on the ground, his second fall. The score was now two to two. Two falls against Conger versus two bloods against Tua, who sported nasty slashes on his abdomen and right thigh.

Aku returned his mind to the bronze lock mechanism. The first problem was that he couldn't really see his work, as the lock was on the outside of the cage and he had to reach through the bars. The second was that the maka he'd lifted from the guard's tunic was meant for fighting, not lockpicking, and its tip was barely smaller than the slot for the key. There would be no finessing the tumblers on this one. His best hope was to simply jam it in and hope he could break something loose. Two times he forced the blade in, three times, nothing. But on the fourth time, the tip hit something that fell inside the mechanism with a tiny metallic clink. Aku gently pressed the handle on the outside of the barred door and found that it opened easily. He pushed the door slightly ajar and tapped Kaneke on the shoulder, indicating what he'd done.

Kaneke nodded.

Another collective gasp, followed by an uproar of shouts and hisses. It seemed Tua had caught Conger on his forearm, the eels swimming furiously around the bloody gash. Third point. The dark-haired priestess poled her raft over and stepped onto the combatants' platform. She raised her arm for quiet.

"The visitor has won the combat and his freedom," she shouted, gesturing at Tua. A few angry shouts from the warriors, but she silenced them with an imperious glance. She pointed at Conger, who clutched his wounded forearm. "And the loser will feed Papa Eel."

A priestess on one of the islands hit a huge gong with a mallet, and the reverberations echoed throughout the space. A pair of priestesses at one end of the cavern began to turn a great wheel connected to a chain leading into the water. As they turned, they chain wound and a heavy grate slowly lifted.

Tua stepped forward, standing next to the dark-haired priestess. Even in the cool air, sweat ran from his face, and blood trickled across his chest and belly and down his right leg. The sea turtle glowed on his back. "Puhi!" he called. "I know you owe me more nothing more than my release. But I request a favor from you."

More shouts and cursing from the warriors, but the priestess held up her hand. "What is your favor?"

"I am not the only one here in bondage. Let me name one present that I wish to take with me."

"No," Kaneke said under his breath, and Aku understood why. Tua thought he was doing good by asking for the release of a prisoner, just when the door was open and they could all escape. Already, eyes drifted to the cage, eager to see which condemned man Tua might choose.

"Papa Eel is powerful," the priestess said. "And it is the pleasure of the powerful to bestow mercy. Your request is granted. You have but to name the one."

"And I may name anyone to take with me when I go?" Tua asked. "This is no deceit? You and your people will keep to your word?"

"Do not question our honor!" the priestess said. "I vow it, and my vow will not be broken. Only say the name."

"Then I name…" Tua hesitated, and all was quiet except the clanking of the chain as the priestesses continued to turn the wheel. "I name you, Keola."

It was impossible to see if the priestess blushed under her paint, but her lips parted slightly in surprise. There was a moment of shock, and then a frenzy of shouts and hisses from the warriors and priestesses. Aku and Kaneke looked at each other, and understood. Whether it was his intention or not, Tua had diverted attention away from the prisoners. Aku pushed the door open and quietly exited, Kanake behind him, the other eleven prisoners noticing and following suit.

It was perhaps a hundred paces along the ledge to the tunnel that had brought him to the cavern, and Aku was nearly there when a yell came from the lake. "The prisoners, they're escaping!" Aku surveyed the situation with a quick glance. The guard had turned around and now realized his mistake, but he was just one man. Anybody else would have to pole a raft over, which would take several minutes. They were nearly home free.

On the bamboo platform in the lake, Tua looked up and nodded at Aku with a slight smile on his face. From behind him, Conger charged and grabbed Tua by the waist, knocking him off balance. They both tumbled into the water. On the far side of the cavern, the priestesses had drawn the grate completely open and the water rippled as a long, massive form entered, its gold and brown spotted skin visible below the shimmering surface. Papa Eel was out and in search of prey.

FORTY-ONE

"So, so!" Imi Au'o said to the three prisoners in his sing-song tone. "The three of you have caused quite a bit of trouble this evening. But I'm willing to overlook that, in the interest of hospitality. After all, I don't get many visitors here. Let's sup together, and afterwards you can be on your way. What do you say?"

Hulu was able to push himself onto his elbows and regarded the tall man in the spidery robe. He found Imi Au'o's rapid patter and unexpectedly cheery manner discombobulating. *What's he up to?* he wondered. Hulu strained to open his jaw and work his tongue. When he spoke, the words came out slurred. "I'm sorry. We can't just leave."

Imi Au'o tapped the tips of his fingers together, so long and bony they almost seemed to be twigs from a kulu tree. "So. So. I was afraid of this. Hulu, is it? We haven't been formally introduced, you see." He paused, as if waiting for an answer.

"Yes, Hulu's my name."

"Thought so, thought so. We're both men of learning, aren't we? You, the master of the scribes, I, the master of breeding for Regent. So, so, I'm sure you'll understand when I say that you're far too late for whatever it is you intended to do here. I'll explain it all over supper and we'll have a good laugh. I'm a bit peckish, you see. Shall we descend to the dining room? No, of course not, you can't move yet, but we'll make do, make do."

Imi clapped his hands and after a minute the head assistant poked his head up the ladder from below, the extra ears on his shoulders just visible.

"Anahua," Imi Au'o said. "Bring chairs and a table, bread and wine, and goblets. How many goblets? Three or four?" He looked imploringly at Hulu. "Your reptilian friend, does he drink wine?"

"No," Hulu said from the floor.

"No wine then, just as well."

"No." Hulu's voice came out stronger, encouraging him to continue. "I mean, we won't be eating with you. Not tonight or ever."

"You turn down my hospitality then?"

"We would never share a table with someone like you," Lono said. She had rolled onto her side and Kai's tail twitched.

Imi Au'o's face darkened but Anahua blurted out before Imi could speak, "The prisoners brought sacks, Master."

Imi nodded. "Yes, yes, bring them up then. But never mind about the table and chairs." Anahua descended the ladder and Imi turned to Hulu and Lono. His eyes flashed but then calmed and he folded his hands, squatting to be closer to his guests.

"I understand," Imi said. "I do, I do. You believe I'm doing something wrong here. You see these animals, these creatures I've improved and all you perceive is the ugliness. The scars, the pain. All worthwhile, I assure you. Even the worst things can be ennobled if the end is glorious. I learn how to use the ink and the scalpel better every day."

"You're twisting them, not improving them," Lono said. "There was nothing wrong with them in the first place."

"You're wrong, you're wrong! You'll see. Ah, here they are." Anahua had returned, along with the other two assistants, bearing the sacks that Hulu, Lono, and Kai had brought from the scriptorium. Imi took a sack and loosened the rope tie at the top, pulled a rag from the sack and held it to his nose. "Turpentine. So the plan was to burn us out, was it?"

Hulu did not respond, but worked his tingling hand into his pocket, searching for his quill-sharpening knife. Feeling was returning to his legs, as well, although he couldn't yet feel his feet. He noticed Lono and Kai were sitting up, and attentive.

"No matter, no matter," Imi went on, dropping the sack to the ground. "I'll demonstrate what I mean. Kikima, come here."

Kikima turned out to be the assistant with the extra eyes in his abdomen, the gills in his throat, and the two tails. He stood only in his loincloth, his abdominal eyes blinking now and then.

Imi Au'o spoke as if lecturing a class of students. "Kikima here was afflicted in his boyhood with a fever. Left him nearly blind and trouble breathing, you see, you see? His family abandoned him, but Regent brought him to me and I took him in, made him better." He pointed a frighteningly long finger at Kikima's gills and eyes. "Now, now? He breathes fine, his sight is adequate. He can make out forms, colors, correctly count the fingers I hold up on a hand. Is it not true, Kikima?"

"Can you see out of those eyes, Kikima?" Hulu asked.

The fellow made a sound as if to speak but all that emitted from his throat was a coarse, assenting growl.

"He says yes," Imi translated. "Do you understand now? Is it not glorious? Is it not a most noble miracle? This new world Regent makes?" Imi began pacing and gesticulating. "These operations, old King Pono prohibited them, you know. Sent me into exile, he did, he did. I lived here in the swamps, continued in secret as best I could. But when Regent came to power, after some years, he found me. Recognized my genius, gave me this place for my laboratory, provided these assistants, all the specimens. And most importantly of all, a steady supply of the precious ink, of course, of course."

"So now you do Regent's bidding," Hulu said. "Build him an army of spies."

"His bidding? No, you don't understand yet. How can I explain?" Imi stopped pacing and turned to Hulu, spread his arms, so thin veins twisted around them like cords. "Regent wears the mantle of greatness. Not like fat old Pono, sitting dissipating around his palaces listening to his musicians tootling on flutes all the day. Not Regent. Regent has a plan, a grand vision. He's showed me the new world he's building."

"A hell on earth," Hulu said.

Imi shook his head. "No, no! Why can't I get through to you?

It's to be a true paradise on earth. And best of all, the part I'm to play. I'm to use the ink to heal, to create. He's showed me how it will be." Imi pointed to his assistants. "See? See? Eyes for the blind! Ears for the deaf! Arms and legs for the lame! A world of miracles and ease. But we must start over to get there. New people, new animals, new history, new society. None of the frailties and pains of the old world."

He had bent down so his face was almost level with Hulu's, Lono's, and Kai's. His brown eyes were wide and manic, his breathing whistled through his nose.

"You'll join me, won't you? One such as you? A man of letters? We could do so much together, you and I." Hulu was drawing breath to speak but Imi lifted a finger. "I know you have no place at the scriptorium now, Hulu, nor beauteous Lono at the convent. Why not join me here? Join me in the grand plan? Even your reptilian friend could stay, if he likes, or return to his people peaceably. We'll work together. If I'm doing something wrong, you'll teach me better, we'll learn the proper way together, yes, yes?"

Imi, still only inches away, gazed at Hulu with pleading in his eyes. He appeared vulnerable—lonely and desperate for friendship. *Maybe he's not truly evil*, Hulu thought. *I do believe he is trying to do good and is only misguided. And his work here is remarkable. Maybe with a friend, a partner, this really could be a place of miracles. Is it possible?*

"And of course, of course, all the ink you need for your, let's say, little habit," Imi went on. "You need never worry about going without again. Yes, yes, that's known to us too."

Hulu's eyes narrowed.

Tua barely had time to draw a breath before he and Conger splashed into the water. It was cool and felt good against Tua's wounds. The lake was murky and he couldn't see more than ten feet in any direction. The bottom certainly wasn't visible. The gloom seemed almost alive, undulating in and out, and Tua realized that was from the mass of eels swimming just at the edge of the darkness, their bodies constantly shifting and swarming.

Conger's arms were still around his waist and he was kicking, propelling them both deeper. *Puhi made a mistake now*, Tua thought, feeling the warmth of the sea turtle awakening on his back. Vigor flowed into his limbs and his lungs felt full. *This be my place of strength.*

They both left little wispy clouds of blood and eels of every description followed the trails. Tua spun himself out of Conger's grip and around to face him. One of Conger's hands held his maka and Tua grabbed his wrist before he could thrust with it. With his other hand, Tua grabbed Conger's upper arm, twisting the Puhi's body to fend off an eel that came too close.

Conger jabbed back with his elbow and broke Tua's hold on him. His bladed arm arced through the water and Tua danced back to avoid it. As the Puhi's body swung by him, Tua drove his fist into Conger's abdomen, and bubbles burst out through his nose and mouth, floating up to the surface. Conger glanced up and Tua knew he wanted to get a breath. *Don't give him a second to recover.*

With a powerful scissor kick, Tua closed in on Conger and locked one arm around his chest, preventing him from swimming up. With the other he held Conger's knife arm. The Puhi struggled against him, but his movements were weakening.

Hundreds of pairs of round, unblinking black-pupiled eyes watched the two men fight, waiting to see how it played out before moving in. And then, the eels all disappeared at once. From behind Conger, Tua watched the snout of a huge gold and brown moray slowly emerge from the murk, its body so long its tail wasn't even visible. Its mouth opened to reveal double rows of inward-facing crystalline fangs, each fully as long as Tua's forearm. Tua released his grip on Conger and flicked his head at the eel. Conger glanced back and froze.

FORTY-TWO

Kai had listened to the ongoing dialogue between Imi Au'o and Hulu. The tall man spoke quickly and Kai hadn't gotten every word, but he'd caught the overall meaning well enough. He'd made Hulu an offer to join him. And to Kai's amazement, Hulu seemed to be considering it. *Or maybe he's only buying time for us to recover,* Kai thought. He tensed and relaxed the muscles in his body. The paralysis had nearly dissipated and everything responded normally. If there was a need for sudden action, he felt fairly sure he could act. *Stay alert and be ready to help your friends.*

He took a quick inventory of the room. He, Lono, and Hulu, still on the floor. Imi Au'o before them, arms spread beseechingly. The three deformed assistants, standing behind and looking a bit bored. The ray, swimming from side to side in her aquarium. And in the corner, the huge dark blue octopus, impossibly squeezing its body out through a tiny opening at the top of its enclosure. It was almost all the way through, its wet body glistening in the open air, only a pair of tentacles still to draw out like long threads. Kai had an intuition that the creature meant no good to anybody else in the room. Somehow, hate and contempt seemed to emanate from its blue eyes. Kai wondered if his companions had noticed it escaping. *Imi and his assistants certainly have not.*

Ah, Hulu was about to respond to Imi's offer. Hulu glanced at Kai, at Lono. Lono had an unusual expression on her face, but Kai couldn't quite read what it was. "I admit your proposal is tempting, Imi," Hulu said. "But I've seen too much of Regent's work to ally myself with him in any way. And I don't believe what you do here is redeemable."

"You refuse me? Interesting." Imi studied Hulu curiously, but somehow disinterestedly, as if a madman had just explained a fascinating delusion. "Why? Do you think you can still win? Don't you realize you're too late, too late?"

Kai sensed Imi was about to launch another monologue. *This one loves to hear himself talk even more than most surface men.* The octopus had freed itself completely now and was slowly, silently inching its way down the outside of the aquarium, careful not to attract any attention to itself.

"A demonstration, yes?" Imi was yammering. "We can do it right now, easily. You'll see, you'll see. Remember the legend of Princess Nihea's abduction by the giants? And what a great beauty she was supposed to have been, rather like our lovely Lono here."

"Go on with the story," Hulu said.

"You know it, yes, yes? What happened after she was kidnapped? Tell me what happened."

The octopus had reached the floor and made its way around the back wall, hiding itself behind the silver operating table and the rack of tools. *Am I truly the only one who sees it?* Kai thought. He glanced at Hulu but couldn't tell. *Or is he purposely stalling?*

Hulu sighed, as if Imi's story were one he'd heard a hundred times. "King Hree'u led a band of a hundred men into the mountains. And there they met King Ukua, the giant king, while he bathed. And Ukua was forty hands tall and killed them all with his bare hands."

"Yes! Yes!" Imi Au'o squealed gleefully. "But one lived and slew the giant king! Who was it? Who was it?"

"It was Ha—" Hulu stopped himself after the first syllable. His brows narrowed in consternation.

"Who slew the giant king?" Imi Au'o cried. "Who slew? Who slew?"

"It was... Prince..."

"So? So? The story has changed, hasn't it?" Imi cried. "You're too late, much too late. We've already succeeded in changing history, Regent and I! Come now, you've already lost. Now, at last, will you join?"

The octopus stretched its long tentacles across the floor, their tips wiggling with anticipation. They had almost reached the assistants.

"The brown ink," Hulu was saying. "Having the scribes write all those sham histories. Burning the old scrolls after the earthquake. That's why you're making the brown ink." Hulu became angry. "But why? Why change the story?"

Imi Au'o pulled himself up to his full height, proud of his part in the work. "Yes, the brown ink. The mother ink can only write truth. But we're making our own truth, our own history, you see! Not the accidental one that really happened. A new one, a better one, a deliberate one. Soon, soon, there will be no Regent. There will only be King, and he and his allies will have been in charge since the beginning."

"No," Hulu said. "It's not possible."

The tentacles were reaching for the legs of the assistants, another stretched towards Imi himself. In the shadow of the operating table, the octopus's blue eyes burned with fury.

"It is, it is!" Imi continued. "You've already seen it. The story of Princess Nihea, and a thousand others too. All changed, all improved! The way they always should have been!"

"You're depraved," Hulu said. "I thought for a minute you might not be evil. But I was wrong. Everything here must be destroyed."

"So it's to be thus." Imi Au'o's face fell. "Unfortunately, my dear Hulu, you're in no shape to do the destroying. Such a shame, such a shame. Anahua, give them another dose of paralyzing agent. And then prepare the operating table. I have a lot of work to do this evening. We'll start with the kai-man." Imi spun around.

At that moment, the octopus's tentacles closed around the legs of Imi and the assistants and pulled them off their feet, dragging them towards the silver table. The hapless assistants emitted animal screams. Hulu and Lono leaped up, and Kai realized they had also seen the octopus all along.

Kai's muscles tensed but he paused before acting. *Who is the enemy? Should we leave Imi and the assistants to the octopus? If we don't run, surely we're to be next.*

Tentacles thrashed the assistants violently against the table and floor, breaking bones with horrible cracks and snaps. Another wrapped around Imi's neck and choked the life from him. Kai stared, appalled at the horror. Still, it was no more than they deserved, wasn't it?

No, the Great Kai-man would not approve of leaving anyone to a horrible fate, even an enemy, if I can help them. Kai launched himself at the nearest tentacle holding an assistant and bit down.

At first, the huge moray seemed to move in slow motion, leisurely gliding out of the blackness. Its gold and brown speckled scales rippled, its eyes not yellow like the other eels, but pale blue, with round black irises coolly surveying the situation. Then, quick as thought, the moray struck and snapped at Conger, its huge jaws tearing a chunk out of his ribcage.

The maka blade fell from Conger's hand and went spinning down. Tua dove after it, the mass of smaller eels parting to let him pass. When he came back up, Conger was thrashing aimlessly as foamy blood and spongy bits of lung drifted away from the gaping hole in his side. The moray swallowed the morsel it had ripped out and snapped another chunk, this one from Conger's thigh. Gradually, Conger's body stopped moving and floated in a red watery haze. The smaller eels watched but did not dare move in on Papa Eel's meal.

Now the giant eel noticed Tua. It placidly circled him, taking its time to assess the man. Tua regarded the moray in return. His lungs screamed for him to breathe in air, his instincts cried for him to swim away from this monstrous predator as fast as he could, but Tua forced himself to remain calm. *Let Papa make the first move.*

Slowly the huge eel retreated and then curved around to face Tua. The hundreds of smaller eels surrounding them seemed to vibrate with anticipation. For a moment, the two remained still, staring at each other, daring the other to go first. Then Papa Eel charged.

Tua twisted away from the eel's snapping jaw and plunged the maka into the unblinking pale blue eye. The obsidian blade was as sharp as reputed and Tua drove his arm in and didn't stop, feeling the knife punch through bone and into soft tissue beyond, and he jacked his arm up, trying to scramble whatever passed for a brain inside this vile creature.

Papa Eel began convulsing and Tua withdrew his arm, leaving the maka in the brainpan. He swam away at speed, not wanting to get caught up in the eel's death throes, and broke the surface of the lake, sucking in huge breaths of sweet air.

Gray-Patch swam frantically from side to side in her aquarium, observing the battle in the operating room between Hulu, Lono, and Kai on the one side and the octopus on the other. The octopus had dragged Imi and his three assistants under the operating table and was alternately choking or pulling them to its mouth to peck at them with its chitinous beak, while fighting off his assailants with the other. Gray-Patch helped as she could, mind-tapping the octopus with false images and impressions of blinding sun, tidal waves, or shark bites at inopportune moments, distracting him and throwing off his timing.

Still, the fight was not going well. Kai was ferocious, taking on the tentacles with his teeth and tail, currently trying to pull one of the assistants away from the octopus's grip. But Hulu was no warrior, possessing only a small knife for scribe work, which he used to stab ineffectually at a tentacle wrapped around his leg. And Lono, athletic as she was, and having the foresight to have grabbed an obsidian scalpel from the rack of surgical instruments at the beginning of the melee, still found herself overmatched by a whipping tentacle, backed against a wall.

Something was needed, something to turn the battle around. Gray-Patch had an idea—the torches on the wall, that strange invention of the men they called *fire*. She knew it provided light, but also a dangerous heat, for Imi Au'o was exceedingly careful in dealing with it, and the animals avoided it altogether. She mind-tapped an image of a torch in his hand to Hulu, who was the closest to her.

Ah yes, of course, Hulu thought back, and though Gray-Patch didn't recognize the words, the general feeling was comprehensible enough. Hulu plunged his sharpening knife into a sucker on the tentacle and it swiftly withdrew. He dashed to the nearest sconce and pulled out the torch, thrusting it toward the tentacle trailing after him. The tip of the tentacle passed through the flame and snapped back, singed. The octopus shrieked. Hulu advanced now, sweeping the torch low at the tentacle until it retreated under the table.

Hulu grabbed a second torch and turned to help Lono, who was holding her own against her own tentacle, if just barely, due to Gray-Patch's frequent mind-taps. Lono stabbed at it with the scalpel, the tentacle leaking blue blood from several places she had successfully slashed it. Hulu pushed the tentacle back with the flames of the torches and handed one to Lono.

Meanwhile, Kai had successfully extricated the assistant with the extra ape arm and the scaly limbs. The poor creature had been slammed against a metal table leg repeatedly and, once freed, stumbled on all fours across the room, headed towards the ladder.

"Kai, take a torch!" Hulu yelled, and tossed it to Kai, who was yanked suddenly back by a tentacle and missed the catch. The torch careened off Kai's back and rolled towards the three sacks of turpentine.

Gray-Patch didn't quite understand how or why it happened. She only saw that the sacks caught aflame at the mere touch of the torch's lit end, and within moments had exploded into roaring conflagrations. But it worked, the tentacles dropping their victims and the octopus squeezing his way back towards the safety of his aquarium. The two assistants still under the table remained limp, unconscious or dead from their struggle.

Imi Au'o, however, was already on his feet and at the portal to the lower level, where he slammed the heavy trapdoor shut.

"Open that door!" Hulu shouted at him.

Through the minds of her friends, Gray-Patch could hear what Imi Au'o said, and again, though she didn't quite comprehend the words, his intention was clear enough.

"Afraid not, afraid not," he said. Kai approached him with bared teeth. Imi held up a large flask with a red liquid in it and pulled out the stopper. The liquid steamed when air touched it. "Stay back. See what I'm holding? A very potent acid. Quite enough to dissolve flesh and bone, should anyone get too close."

"Why?" Hulu said, coughing on the black smoke filling the room "Let's all get out while we can."

"Not going, not going. Not us. My life's work is here. Not worth living if it's gone. And if I'm to go up in flames, you're all going with me."

Hulu stepped towards Imi Au'o, who tipped the flask a bit and let a few drops fall to the floor. They sizzled where they landed, leaving deep holes etched in the wooden floor. "Not a ruse, not a ruse. Stay back, I tell you."

Gray-Patch saw that her three allies would die before long. She knew what she had to do. She closed her eyes and prepared her mind.

FORTY-THREE

Tua emerged dripping from the lake water. The sea turtle on his back only faintly glowed now, his triceps bulging as he pushed himself up onto the bamboo platform. The whole place was in a tumult, with some Puhi warriors and priestesses wailing and beating themselves at the sight of the lifeless body of Papa Eel bobbing on the water's surface, while others screamed instructions or recriminations at comrades who paid no attention. On the ledge with the cage, Kaneke and a couple others had overpowered the guard and the prisoners were fleeing. One group of Puhi had enough presence of mind to pole a raft over to the ledge, roaring ineffectually at the fleeing prisoners to stop.

Keola stood stunned, her almond-shaped eyes wide as she took in the scene, her mouth slightly open in her red-and-black checkerboarded face.

"Ready to depart, priestess?" Tua asked.

She blinked at him a couple times, then her eyes narrowed. "You. You did all this."

"That I did." Tua grinned. "And I believe I'm taking you with me. Or don't you remember your vow?"

"I remember," she said. And softer, "And will you still have me?"

Tua looker her up and down—her lithe dancer's form, her full breasts under her waist-length raven hair, the expression on her round face wavering adorably between hate for the meddler who was upending her world, and something akin to wonder at the bold, powerful man who had created such chaos. He held out his hand and she took it. "I will still have you."

Keola set her jaw. "Then come with me, and we will leave this place."

The operating room had quickly turned into an inferno, the rags soaked in turpentine inside the sacks burning hot enough to ignite the shelves of reagents and parchments and preserved animal dissections lining the walls. Whatever liquid was in the preservation jars proved explosive, the jars bursting in sprays of glass shards when the heat grew fierce enough. The heat was so intense it was hard for Hulu to breathe, and Imi Au'o still blocked the trapdoor with his flask of acid.

But Hulu felt a rush of air from somewhere above. He glanced up and spied the skylight, still open from where Imi Au'o had descended earlier. *Too high to jump for it,* he thought. *But perhaps we can help each other reach it. We'll have to move fast.*

"Kai! Do what I do!" Hulu called. He meshed his fingers together and held his hands low, and Kai followed suit. "Lono, step into our hands! We can get out above!"

When Lono had put a foot in each of their joined hands they lifted her up. Her fingers had reached the edge and she was pulling herself up. Hulu dared believe this might work.

There was a fluttering from somewhere above the skylight. Hulu peered around Lono's body, trying to see, his eyes watering from the smoke. *Is it a...bearded vulture?* It seemed to be pecking at Lono's hand.

Lone screamed and drew one hand back, falling from the skylight and tumbling down into Hulu's arms. Her hand was covered in blood, her middle finger missing from the first joint.

Imi Au'o screeched with laughter. "You see, you see! We're all dying together! Nothing you can do!"

"Kai, your robe!" Hulu shouted.

In an instant, Kai understood and had his robe off, using his teeth to tear off a strip of cloth. Hulu took it and wrapped it around the stub of Lono's finger to stanch the bleeding.

So the skylight's out of the question, Hulu reflected. The air was so hot breathing was painful and Hulu could feel the exposed skin on the back of his neck and legs searing. *Imi Au'o's right. We're all going to roast alive in a few minutes.*

Without warning, Imi Au'o dropped the flask and the acid steamed where it spilled. His eyes rolled back in their sockets. "Out, out!" he shouted. "Get out of my head!" He dropped to his knees, clutching his hands to his skull and emitting an anguished wail.

Hulu didn't understand what was wrong, but wasted no time in taking advantage of it. He grabbed the handle of the trapdoor and heaved it open. The air from below was blessedly cool.

"Lono, you go down first!"

She didn't move, only staring at Gray-Patch's tank. At first Hulu thought she might be in shock from blood loss, but then he noticed. The ray's eyes were closed and her whole body quivered. Her muscles jerked once, and Imi Au'o let out a final scream and crumpled to the floor. Simultaneously, Gray-Patch's body relaxed and floated to the top of her tank.

"She's dead," Lono breathed. "The beautiful ray is dead."

"Lono," Hulu said, grabbing her and pulling her to the trapdoor. "She sacrificed herself for us. Let's make use of it."

FORTY-FOUR

Aku and Kaneke led the prisoners through one black tunnel after another, but whichever way they chose simply led to another tunnel that looked like the first. For all Aku knew, they'd traversed the same corridors multiple times. And now, sounds of pursuit echoed around them. Aku had figured they would have plenty of time to reach the outside before the Puhi warriors reached the shore of the underground lake, but he had no idea if they were any closer to escape than when they'd started.

They came to a T-intersection, the same as a dozen others they'd already encountered. "Well, left or right?" Kaneke said.

"Left looks like it veers upward more," Aku said. "So maybe that way?"

"We've already gone that way twice!" came a voice from behind them. Others began to complain. "You're leading us in circles!" "Why did we leave if we were only going to be trapped out here?" "At least there was honor in being sacrificed to the eels!"

"Enough!" Kaneke roared. "We go to the left. Anyone with a different opinion can go their own way."

Nobody broke off from the group, and the tunnel wound in a gradually rising spiral. *Maybe we are making progress*, Aku thought. *We haven't seen one like this before.*

The tunnel came to an end at a short staircase, at the top of which was a small landing and a wooden door with an arched top and intricate carvings. Aku climbed the stairs and turned the bronze handle. The door didn't open. It was locked.

He turned around. Eleven sets of eyes looked up at him

expectantly. "I'll have to pick it," he said. "It could take a couple minutes."

More grumbling and complaining that came to a stop when a harsh voice called from behind them. "Here they are!"

The prisoners spun. Two Puhi warriors in their loincloths stood with makas drawn, eels swimming furiously under their skin.

"Aku, you get that door open. I'll take care of this," Kaneke said in a low tone. To the warriors, he called, "Puhi, there are five of us for each of you. We were brought here because only the bravest sacrifices are good enough for Papa Eel. Are you sure you want this fight?"

The Puhi warriors grinned. "Let there be blood drawn here tonight," one said.

Kaneke stepped forward. He pointed at the heavily-muscled young man with the crooked nose he'd spoken with earlier. "Okoa. You've been in some street fights, no?"

"A few." The young man cracked his knuckles. "I suppose one more wouldn't hurt. And if I die killin' Puhi, all the better."

Hulu and Lono waited at the bottom of the ladder for Kai, who pulled the trapdoor shut behind him and descended awkwardly on his stubby kai-man legs. The crackle and roar of the fire could be heard even through the floorboards. The birds in this room had smelled the smoke and were squawking in panic. It wouldn't be long until the whole place was in flames.

Lono swooned a bit but caught herself. In an instant, Hulu was holding her, steadying her on her feet. A bit of red was already soaking through the strip of cloth she held against her hand.

"Keep pressing on that," Hulu said. "We need to get you back to the owl temple and have them look at your wound."

She shook her head. "We have to free all the animals before the fire spreads. I feel fine."

Hulu studied her wan and sweaty face. "You don't look fine."

"Ii taake her," Kai said, stepping off the ladder. "Daark oout. Wee see, yoou not. Yoou freee creeatures, coome in moorning."

"I don't know," Hulu said. Kai's argument made sense, but he hated to leave Lono in her condition.

"Kai's right. Plus, he can protect me better if those things in the forest are still there," Lono said. "You'd only be a hindrance, slowing us down. You can follow after at dawn."

Hulu considered it. He had visions of the whisper birds and bearded vultures swooping down on them from the trees, but what was the alternative? Lono was right, he would slow them down. And the longer they waited, the more blood Lono would lose. There was no perfect option, but on balance, Lono was right. "All right. You two go. And be careful."

"We will be," Lono said.

"Kai, help her on the stairs going down. And let her lean on you while you walk. And keep pressure on your hand!"

"Stop worrying!" Lono said. "And start opening cages!"

He watched them until they'd disappeared down the stairwell and turned to the nearest enclosure. An abnormally large crow, unkempt and with several long stitched wounds, fluttered against the bars. A whisper bird in the making, but not yet. It reminded him of Keki. He pulled the heavy bronze bolt on the latch and tugged the door open.

"Go, you're free now!"

The bird waited until Hulu had moved on to the next cage before cautiously poking its head out. Once it realized it wasn't a trick, it flapped its wings and hovered a bit, spotted the exit, and dived down. *One down*, Hulu thought. *Hundreds to go.*

Keola strode briskly through the corridors, pointedly not looking back at Tua, who followed at a more languid pace. When she got too far ahead of him, he called out, "What's the hurry, priestess? I'd almost think you didn't want to be seen with me."

"Don't call me priestess," Keola said without turning her head or changing her speed in the slightest.

"Why not? Isn't that what you are?"

"Not after today, I'm not."

Tua jogged a little to catch up and walk next to her. "Why? They going to kick you out of your club over what happened back there?"

"Yes, in fact. By enabling and falling for your trickery, they'll hold me responsible for what happened to Papa Eel."

"That weren't your fault," Tua said. "I'll take the blame."

"The Puhi are not forgiving," Keola said. "Nor will they make fine distinctions in who caused which outcome."

"No matter," Tua said. "If Papa Eel be dead, what power do the Puhi have? And anyway, I'm here to protect you."

"That is not as comforting a thought as you seem to think." Keola dared a sidelong glare at Tua. "So. Am I to be your houseslave or your bedslave?"

Tua laughed. "No slave at all. And you know what? If my company be so odious to you, as soon as you get me out of here and I meet my companions, you're free to go."

"As if I have anywhere else to go to," Keola said through gritted teeth. They reached the end of the corridor and a wooden door with an arched top.

"I have some friends that could help you find—"

"Quiet now, if you're able." Keola put a hand on one of the many carvings in the door's surface. She closed her eyes and ran her fingers along a depiction of an eel chasing an octopus.

"Is it locked?" Tua said. "Why don't we just open the handle?"

"Shh," Keola said. After a moment, she added, "Doors can go different places."

"I certainly hope this door can go outside," Tua said.

"It can." Keola pressed a panel and opened her eyes. "But I think you'll be more interested to see something else first."

While Aku worked on the locked door, Kaneke and Okoa held off the Puhi warriors, circling their Puhi adversaries. The other prisoners shouted as a distraction or waved their hands and jumped as if to attack, trying to throw the Puhi off-balance. Still, the Puhis' maka blades were fearsome, and no one ventured within slashing range. Still, it was only a matter of time until one of the blades connected fatally.

Aku tinkered with the lock as fast as he could. He had the same problem here he'd had with the one in the cage, having only the unwieldy maka he'd lifted from the guard to probe with. No finesse work was possible, he simply had to force it in at different angles and hope he hit something that released the tumblers, or broke the mechanism altogether.

Finally, Aku heard something in the lock click. He tested the bronze handle and found he could swing the door inward. "Hey, I've got—" His voice faltered when he saw Tua and the dark-haired priestess on the other side.

"Aku!" Tua said.

"Tua!" Aku embraced his friend. "You made it! I was afraid you'd been eaten alive!"

"That old sea worm?" Tua said. "They'll have to find something tougher than that if they want to kill me."

The priestess rolled her eyes and stepped onto the landing. "Warriors!" she called out. "Stand down! These prisoners are free to go."

Without taking his eyes from Kaneke and Okoa, one of the Puhi spat. "We don't take orders from you no more, betrayer. After we take care of these ones, you're next." He lunged at Kaneke, who sidestepped and danced back.

Tua took his place by the priestess's side. "If not out of respect for her, then maybe out of fear for me." He raised a hand holding a maka. "This be the blade that killed Papa Eel. I warrant it ain't done tasting blood this night, if you don't turn and flee this very moment."

The Puhis looked up and saw Tua, hair still dripping from the lake, the fresh knife wound raw across his muscular torso, the ex-priestess servile at his side. Something in his bearing, in his expression, in his eyes, spoke of arrogance, of the confidence that he had killed Papa Eel and he could kill a couple of his servants with no trouble, and that he might even enjoy doing it. The warriors glanced at each other, and ran.

FORTY-FIVE

Hulu found one of the net cages already lowered and waiting for him as he approached the Temple of the Owls in the early morning. He stepped in it and attempted to brush the soot from his long hair as he slowly rose in the air. His whole body was covered with ash, and his cape and tunic stank of smoke, but he had taken no time to clean himself up. He had spent as long as he could liberating the animals from the kimunu tree, wetting a strip of cloth and holding it over his nose and mouth to breathe when the smoke had thickened. The birds had mostly flown out on their own, but small woodland mammals, amphibians, even insects he'd carried in a small pot he'd found and released them out the front door. He'd finally had to abandon the effort when the blaze simply became too intense to return inside the building. Stumbling outside, he'd found the sun dawning and departed without a break, feeling guilty over all the creatures he'd left behind.

He'u met him at the top, far above the forest floor, and helped him step from the netting. "Good morning, friend Hulu."

"Good morning, He'u." Hulu had to stop, as the very effort of talking caused a coughing fit from the smoke. Finally, he choked out, "Did Lono and Kai make it here?"

"They arrived when it was still dark," He'u said, ushering Hulu along a series of vine bridges. He raised his hand when Hulu drew breath to speak again. "Rest your lungs. I will put your mind at ease immediately about honored Lono. She will recover nicely, though I'm afraid she will never learn to play the harp with us."

They came to one of the thatched roof huts built around the

trunk of a pine. The place was bustling with attendants caring for dozens of owls, squirrels, and other forest creatures with bloody lacerations, gouged eyes, and torn wings. Among the casualties, Hulu spotted Lono, sleeping in a hammock under an owl-feather blanket, her damaged hand resting on her chest and wrapped in a large white bandage. Next to her Kai sat in a netted chair, where a young woman dabbed with a steaming hot poultice at the puncture wounds where bearded vultures had pierced his hide as he'd escorted Lono along the path.

Even Keki, on a high perch overlooking the hammock, suffered a nurse to clean and dress a gash across his back. The bird cooed on seeing him, and Hulu couldn't help smiling at the loyalty of their winged friend.

"Have a seat, if you please." He'u indicated an empty netted chair for Hulu. "Are you hurt in any way?"

"I'm fine," Hulu rasped, taking his seat. "Don't worry about me. You have your hands busy here."

"We are busy enough," He'u answered. "But for the one who has freed us from the scourge of Imi Au'o, we will make time." He clapped his hands and an attendant appeared. "Bring a soft cloth and a basin of warm water infused with op'ia oil for our guest to clean himself. And a cup of pala tea."

The attendant nodded and was off. "I have to thank you for your hospitality," Hulu said.

"Nonsense," He'u said. "It's the least we can do. I believe word has spread throughout the forest that you have killed Imi Au'o."

"Well, it wasn't actually me," Hulu said. "But he is dead, I saw him drop with my own eyes."

"Yes, good Kai here told us that much, although he does not have the words to explain how it happened. No matter, perhaps later today we will have time for you to tell us the story in more detail. For now, know that whatever hold Imi Au'o had on his servants is broken, and they are fleeing by wing or leg, as each is suited, along with the ones you freed."

"Where do you think they'll go?" Hulu asked.

"Back to where they came from, I suppose," He'u said. "Though I fear their own kind may not recognize them when they return. They have been changed and will find it difficult to fit in. But we shall see. Let us leave the future to itself and busy ourselves with today."

"I am sure you have much to do, and I cause you to tarry," Hulu said.

"You are right, friend Hulu. Let me leave you to your companions, and if you are all feeling up to it later, perhaps we can dine together." He'u made a little bow and went on his way.

Outside the Temple of the Eels, the rising sun sent fierce yellow rays beaming through the trees, burning away the morning mist, the obsidian darkness of the temple somehow not sucking in the light around it as it had the day before. In the sky, hundreds of whisper birds, huge bearded vultures, and other over-sized and twisted birds flew about aimlessly, as if not sure of what to do with themselves.

The prisoners lingered briefly, Okoa and a few others thanking Tua for what he'd done, the rest simply departing without a word, one by one, down the path back to the city. After a few minutes, only Kaneke, Aku, Tua, and Keola were left.

"Are we going back to Bonetown now, Tua?" Aku asked.

"I think first we might stop off at the Convent of the Ancestors," Tua said.

"Oh!" Aku smiled shyly. "And Lono will be there? And Keki?"

"I have a feeling we will find our friends there." Tua turned to Kaneke. "Speaking of friends, here's a rogue I thought never to see again."

Kaneke took one of Tua's hands, put his other arm around his neck and kissed him on both cheeks. "It's been a long time, Tua. And such a strange place to meet again."

"Indeed, strange be the word." Tua looked Kaneke up and

down. "And you look well. But I hear Malu has passed. Is it so? Who will lead the Ho'oule now?"

"He has passed," Kaneke said. "But let us speak of that on the road, and other things too. I wish to hear how you and Aku came to be in this place."

"Will you come with us then?" Tua said. "We go to the Convent of the Ancestors, and I have reason to believe they will receive us with hospitality."

"The convent?" Kaneke's eyebrows rose. "Your life has taken surprising turns indeed if you're welcome there. I will accompany you, if only to see if you speak truly. But please, let us depart. I do not care to linger here. The Eels may re-group sooner than we think, and they will thirst for revenge."

"Aye," Tua said. "Only one more thing." He cast a curious eye and a half-smile on Keola, who stood awkwardly a few steps away, staring into the trees. "And what of you, Keola? Will you accompany us?"

"Whatever you wish."

"No, not whatever I wish," Tua said. "You be no slave of mine. You are free to go. You can make your own way, whatever that might be."

"But what do you wish, mighty Tua?" Keola asked, turning to him. "Do you win me with trickery and force, take me from my home since I first became a woman, only to release me like an unwanted dog that's never lived in the wild? Do you not care to gaze upon me again?"

"I would gaze upon you," Tua said. He held out his hand. "Come with us then, but let it be from your own desire, chosen freely."

Keola wavered a moment before taking his hand. "I will go with you. But I will need time to learn how to practice this...free choosing you speak of."

Tua pulled her to him. "You will have your whole life to practice."

Keola ran a finger along Tua's arm and lowered her eyes coyly. "Are you so certain you do not need a bedslave, though? Perhaps I need be free only part of the time."

"Gross," Aku said. "Can we get moving?"

Lono gulped and knocked on the wooden door. Even now, she still felt a bit of fear from being called to the office of Prioress Wa'e, an echo of all the times growing up when she'd had to report here following the uncovering of some bit of mischief. Lono had always dared too much, going farther into the woods surrounding the convent than allowed, poking into forbidden rooms, even once making a pet of a hopmouse and hiding it under her cot in a little box. That last had worked fine until the mouse had escaped in the middle of the night and hopped its way around the dormitory, popping onto pillows and blankets and creating an outbreak of screaming girls. Lono grinned guiltily. *Poor hopmouse. Took hours to capture it again.*

"Come in!"

Lono pushed the door open a crack. "You wanted to see me, Prioress?"

"Yes, please come in, Lono. Have a seat there, if you like."

Lono sat in the wicker chair, her head lowered and her hands folded across her lap expectantly. A mele bird sang in a tree outside the open window.

Prioress Wa'e smiled. "You're not in trouble, you know. You can relax."

"Yes, ma'am."

"How's your finger doing?"

"It feels much better, thank you."

"No infection?"

"Not at all." Lono held out her hand with the bandaged nub of the middle finger. "My friend Kai assured me it wouldn't be long until it grew back, but somehow I don't think it will."

The prioress chuckled. "We surface men are not nearly as advanced as the kai-men, in some ways." She re-arranged a scroll on her desk. "He sounds remarkable. I hope to meet him."

"I hope so too," Lono said. "I asked him to come with us at the Owl Temple, but he wanted to get back to his family as soon as he could. Maybe he'll come visit someday."

"Or you could visit him," the prioress said.

"In the lagoon? How would I breathe?"

"There are ways," the prioress said. "Tell me, have you had a chance to spend some time with Iwali since you've gotten back?"

"A little," Lono said. "I've been occupied with Tua's sickness, and entertaining Aku, and Keola is here too."

"And Hulu."

"And Hulu." Lono's face reddened just a touch, and she quickly moved on. "But there's something different between Iwali and me now. And I'm afraid that even when things calm down again…"

"Afraid that what?" the prioress asked.

"Afraid that…" Lono shifted in her chair. "That Iwali and I simply may not have as much in common as before. I've seen so much in the past weeks, learned so many new things, met so many new people. I've tried to talk to her about it all, and she listens politely, but I'm not sure she really understands. And plus, she's a Sister, now, and has all her new duties."

"Yes, she's quite busy."

"And after all, I won't have a chance to be a Sister for another year. I'll still be in the dormitory and attending classes. And won't it be awkward if I'm in a class and Iwali is the one teaching it?"

Prioress Wa'e raised her eyebrows quite high. "Why don't you think you'll be a Sister for another year?"

Lono's face fell. "Because I ran out from the Ceremony of Sky. And Ne Wa'e won't return in the southeastern sky until next summer."

"It's not the Ceremony of Sky that makes one a Sister," the prioress said. "If you'll recall, Iwali was ill and not in attendance at the ceremony, either. It's the years of study and meditation and exercise that makes one a Sister, mastering one's mind and body and will."

"Yes, but she's heard a message from the ancestors since then. I didn't hear a message from the ancestors. All I heard was that stupid voice—" She hesitated, not having spoken of that before.

"Go on," the prioress said. "What happened at the Ceremony that made you leave?"

"I heard a voice telling me to go out the front gate and look for a sign. And when I did, that's when I saw Keki. Err, the crow that helped us so much."

"Who do you think sent you that message, Lono?"

Lono shook her head. "I have no idea."

"It was me." Prioress Wa'e rose and sat on a chair next to Lono. "I'm the one who sent the message to you, and I'm the one who called Keki to be waiting in the cherry tree that morning."

"You sent the messages in my mind?"

Prioress Wa'e nodded. Lono looked at her, noting the tattoos visible from under her owl feather cape, remembering at the Ceremony of Fire when she had seen her nude body, covered from neck to ankles with the living tattoos of the constellations. It struck her, if a single tattoo of a telescope could let her see in the dark, if a single tattoo of an eel or a turtle could provide such varied abilities to their owners, how much power then must the prioress have, with dozens of them?

Yes, it all makes sense, Lono thought. *If the prioress spoke to me with only her mind—perhaps that was an ability granted by the constellation of Ne'i Fafa, the ray. And calling Keki—maybe that was from Ne'i Lopi, the robin, or Ne'i Peo, the owl. And those are only a few of the tattoos the prioress has. What more is she capable of?*

"You seem suddenly lost in thought," the prioress said.

"I just... why did you send the messages?" Lono asked. "Why to me?"

"Well," the prioress began. "Let's start with the second question. Your spirit is restless here, Lono. You were not made for long hours of quiet study and meditation. With the help of Iwali and your own drive to succeed, you performed surpassingly well at everything we asked of you, but except for the athletics, none of it really suited you. You always craved something more adventurous.

Do you not think so?"

Lono could not help but nod.

"So when the convent was asked for help in a matter that might require bravery, boldness, even some danger and physical hardship, I knew who the right person was. Not Iwali, not any of the other girls. You, Lono, were the right person."

"But who asked the convent for help? And how did you know where Keki would lead me?"

"I didn't know where he would lead you. Your path is for you and the ancestors to decide, and I cannot tell what will happen. As for who asked us for help, that's a little more difficult to explain." The prioress sighed and looked out the window for a moment. "You know of the All-Dream, I think? The dream that's more than a dream?"

She knows of the dreams. So she knows about Hulu and me, too, Lono thought. *Of course she does.* "Yes, I do."

"It's a place linked to the mother ink, a space of infinite creativity and exploration. It's where We Honua creates the history of the world, dreaming everything that has ever happened and ever will. Our waking world is but an imperfect reflection of the All-Dream. But the All-Dream is threatened."

"Who would threaten the All-Dream?" Lono asked. "Who would be so foolish? And why would they do it?"

"There is one who seeks to change history and reality to suit his own ends. He has been gathering power and manipulating events for a long time. And one day he will need to be stopped."

"Is it Regent?" Lono said.

"Regent." Prioress Wa'e smiled grimly at the word. "Regent is both more and less than you think.

"But back to our story, and your place in it. There are those of us who protect the ink and the All-Dream, and we have been on the defensive for the past ten years. But we determined that one particular servant of the one I mentioned was going too far, becoming too much of a threat. And that servant was Imi Au'o."

"Oh!" Lono said. "Yes, I met him."

"We consulted in the All-Dream, and asked the ancestors for

guidance. Was it time to gather an army against this man? Perhaps send a team of great warriors to confront him? And the ancestors' answer was surprising. No army, no warriors. Instead, they sent us a vision of three who could be brought together. One was a girl on the cusp of womanhood."

"And that was me?"

The prioress gave Lono's hand a squeeze.

"And who were the others?" Lono asked.

"A young man, fallen from grace and troubled by grief."

"That must have been Hulu," Lono said. "And the third?"

"A boy, carrying a great secret to which even he did not know the answer."

"Aku!" Lono said. "And the secret was his cylinder."

"Perhaps," the prioress said. She looked away, as if considering whether to say more. "But yes, the third was Aku. So when Keki appeared outside our gate, saying he had been sent to fetch help, I knew it was time, and I knew who to send. The rest was up to the three of you. To find each other, and discern your undertaking, and see it through to success or failure."

Lono was silent a few moments. "But what of everyone else?" she said finally. "Kai and Tua and Keola and Opio and Kaneke? And all the others who helped us and played a part? Weren't they in the vision?"

"No, you three were the critical links. But as for all the others you've met along the way, I think we can say that We Honua's dreams are good. Don't you agree?"

EPILOGUE

Hulu spotted Lono across the convent's garden, sitting on a bench under a halipi tree, apparently lost in thought. He quietly strode over, approaching from behind.

"I've always liked the way these trees smell, don't you?" Hulu asked.

"Oh!" Lono glanced up in surprise and smiled. "Yes. This has always been one of my favorite places to think."

"Did you hear?" Hulu sat beside her. "Tua's fever has broken at last. He was awake and lucid for a short while, and now sleeps calmly."

"That's great news. Aku and Keola must be relieved."

"They are. You know, I suppose it was Sister Mana's pala oil that fought off the infection, but I'm not sure he would have recovered from his wounds so quickly had Keola not stayed by his side the whole time."

"I know, Lono said. "Who would have thought she would be such a dedicated nurse?" She took Hulu's hand and they sat silently for a few minutes. A pair of maka birds hopped about on the grass beyond the shade of the tree, searching for worms.

"You know I can't stay here much longer," Hulu said finally. "I'm still a wanted man. It's past the new moon, and I haven't turned myself in. Nor do I intend to. I endanger the convent the longer I remain."

"I know," Lono said. "That's what I'm thinking about. Well, part of it. Where do you think you'll go?"

"To the south, maybe," Hulu said. "Moku Harbor or one of

the villages near there. I'll find work on a boat or in the orchards. Or maybe I could find a business in need of someone who can keep the accounts. I may have to move from time to time. I'm a bit of an outlaw, you know."

"Yes, a big, bad outlaw," Lono said. "That describes you perfectly. Always headed straight into danger."

"And handy with a knife, as well," Hulu said, grinning.

"Sure, if you're sharpening the nub of a quill." They both laughed. Lono turned to look at his face. "It does sound like an adventure though."

"I like the way you think of it."

"I had a talk with the prioress today," Lono said. "We discussed my plans, and what sort of person I really am."

"Oh, and what did you decide?"

"Well, we didn't really decide anything firmly. But I do wonder if the convent is the right place for me."

"What do you mean?" Hulu asked. "You were raised here. Everything you know is here."

"That's true," Lono said. "But the prioress pointed out that's never been enough for me. Even if I didn't realize it at the time, or at least couldn't put it into words, I've always felt stifled here. I need more than this quiet life. I need to see things, experience the world."

"I can see that in you," Hulu said.

"And one more thing the prioress mentioned," Lono said.

"What's that?"

"I can never be a Sister here, and also…be with a man. I have to make a choice."

Hulu's eyes locked with Lono's. "And do you know which you will choose?"

"I do." She leaned forward and their lips met, their mouths opened and joined. She put a hand on the back of his head and he wrapped an arm around her, pulling her close.

In one of the twisty branches at the top of the halipi tree, Keki stirred himself and flew off in the direction of the window of the prioress's office to let her know what he had seen. He thought she would be pleased at the news.

I'd like to thank all the people who helped me in the writing and production of this book: Denice Jobe, Shea Megale, Steve Moriarty, and the members of the Writers of Chantilly, who did much to improve this book with their comments and suggestions!

I hope you enjoyed reading *Mother Ink!* Because Amazon reviews are one of the main drivers of book sales for indie authors, please consider leaving a brief but honest review on this book's Amazon page.

Sign up for my mailing list and receive ***Orphan Stone***, the free prequel to the Last Days of Atlantis trilogy! subscribepage.io/s8d7d6

Look for *Sister Honey*,
the start of a brand new trilogy
in the Atlantis series,
coming in Fall 2024!

Made in the USA
Middletown, DE
15 May 2024